The Houses of The Curious

Parallel - Book One

By John Bowie

To Deena & Jon
Thanks for reading!
Enjoy,

John Bow

To Deshka

My believer and critic

Lover and friend

You are the one

1

A Line on a Map

Just taking matters into our own hands. Aurora thought of her brother's words, but the reassurance did little to soften her guilt. She frowned at the shards of window pane scattered on the wooden planks of the town archives' porch. The ring of shattering glass echoed, and the hole in the smashed window stared back at her. Why had the archivist lied?

They waited in silence for the townsfolk to adjust their quilts and covers, roll over, and go back to sleep. Aurora sensed her brother, Kars, who stood nearby holding his breath and waiting. She finally exhaled. It seemed that their break-in had gone unnoticed.

Kars snaked his arm between the edges of the glass, and the deadbolt clicked a moment later. Aurora grasped the handle, pressing the door against its hinges to stifle its creak. She had opened it hundreds of times. She knew the old door's tricks.

The familiar mustiness of the archive washed over her. Kars clicked on a flashlight as they entered the foyer, shielding the beam to a sliver between his fingers. They passed the reception desk and stepped over the turnstile to enter the archives. Shelves of books and newspapers and old computers stretched out through the long building.

They weaved their way into the depths of the town archives until they reached their goal—a fence gate closed with a loop of heavy chain. A muscular lock dangled from the links. Restricted materials.

Kars handed the flashlight to Aurora and removed a small iron catspaw from his pack. He wrestled the lock until the shackle bent and popped free of the body. Kars extracted the chain from the fence, and the gate swung open. Aurora glanced behind her. The shadows of the shelves made her shiver, but nothing moved. The archives had always been a place of refuge for her, halls of knowledge that felt endless when the town felt suffocating and small. Seeing the library in this light, she felt she was betraying a patient friend.

They entered the restricted section. File cabinets and map tables lined the cramped space, vessels stuffed with the musty surveys and records of a prior era. Kars nodded toward one of the map cabinets. Aurora made out a faded emblem slotted into the window of the drawer. A thick ring snaked around on itself— Perpetual Corporation. A mix of excitement and wariness welled up inside her.

The cabinet drawer rolled on its runners as Kars leafed through the documents. He extracted one from the jumble, gave it a cursory glance, and stuffed it in his bag. He nodded to Aurora and they retreated from the restricted section, pulling the gate closed behind them. Kars hung another lock on the chain, leaving the key in place for the archivist to think he had just left the key in the lock and to trust in his own ailing memories. Aurora rolled her eyes; it was a feeble plan.

She frowned as they left the halls, frustrated she agreed to the heist. Even if they succeeded, she would still be the intruder of her own sanctum. Things would have been easier if the archivist had just told them the truth.

There is nothing there, the archivist had said. *Don't worry. Leave it alone.*

One lie begot another. She steeled herself as she closed the door behind her. Glass ground beneath the heel of her boot. They would see for themselves.

Aurora and Kars navigated in darkness to the side of the building where a third figure waited as their lookout. Lena straightened at their arrival, reaching for one of the packs near her feet.

"Did you get it?" Lena whispered.

"Yes," Aurora responded.

"Let's get moving," Kars said. "If we hurry, we might get there and back before anyone notices."

They each hoisted a pack and marched into the night.

*   *   *   *   *

"You think this was worth it?" Aurora asked, impatient that her guilt had still not dissipated despite the hour-long hike up the old mountain road.

Kars shined his flashlight on the faded paper he had spread on a flat rock. Lena stood next to him, rubbing her hands together to ward off the bite of the alpine night.

Aurora squinted as she traced the line in the bright pool of the flashlight. The ghost of penciled lines meandered across the worn paper. Faded crosshatches wove through the contours of the map. The line was almost erased from memory.

"Someone penciled it in and tried to erase it. I think it's a cable connection." Kars stabbed his finger against a bend in the topographic lines. He traced the erased line with his fingertip and looked to them as though victory was self-evident.

"You promised something major. Seeing this map with my own eyes . . ." Aurora trailed off in disappointment.

"This is just a musty old map!" Lena interjected.

"A musty old map with a purpose," Kars retorted. "Aurora checked the town survey herself—no one listed anything in this area. The archivist probably had me sort those files because he thought I wouldn't pay enough attention to notice. It has to be a cable. He told you there was nothing. He wouldn't even share the map with you!"

Aurora chewed her lip. He had hammered the point to bait her into their midnight heist. Seeing the faded line on the map stoked doubt in the honesty of the town survey, but another thing chewed at her mind: the round Perpetual logo coiled in the corner of the map.

"You're sure you want to find it?" Aurora asked.

"Maybe not," Kars said. "Ask me when we're there."

"Don't dodge my question," Aurora retorted. She took a sip of coffee from her thermos to punctuate her willingness to wait for an answer. She spat a loose ground from the tip of her tongue.

Kars measured his response.

"Aurora, you know the history better than any of us. It wasn't always war," Kars said. "Perpetual had a presence up here before the Rebellion. And if it is there, the cable has to lead somewhere. That kind of find could go a long way—salvage, supplies, maybe even some working equipment. Maybe there are signs of the people we lost."

Aurora felt a tinge of pity for him. They had all lost things in their own way. Just beyond the pool of light, the rusted husk of one of the old machines loomed in the bushes at the edge of the road. On a passing glance, it looked like little more than a boulder dressed in years of forest understory, a relic of a lost civilization. The armored form stood as a harsh reminder of a brutal past. It looked like artillery had cracked the beetle husk of the war machine and ended its march.

"Whoever erased the line, maybe they erased it for a reason," Aurora said.

"They didn't destroy the maps," Kars argued.

"But they locked them up," Lena countered. She danced between her feet to combat the cold. Her braid fell from beneath her knit cap onto her shoulder.

"Why lie?" Kars leaned on his argument.

"We can't just leave this well enough alone?" Aurora asked, thinking about the archivist's denial of the map as she weighed their choice. They could have just accepted the lie.

Kars spread his hands over the worn paper.

The marks of the forgotten cartographer lanced across the blobs of topography. She took another ponderous sip of coffee from her thermos and cautiously eyed the faded logo in the corner of

5

the map. The archivist had lied in the name of safety, but that did little to calm her curiosity. She needed to see what was there.

She shrugged her commitment.

"We already bit off most of the hike, Lena. If Kars is right, it's not too much further. It'll warm up soon enough when the sun comes up," Aurora said. "If we're going to do this, let's move."

"Whatever," Lena responded. "I doubt he'll even find it anyway. No way you even know how to use that old thing."

Kars grinned in satisfaction and carefully folded the map. The paper flopped along its folds like fabric as he tucked it in his coat. He swung his flashlight through the woods before turning back to the trail.

"I guess we'll find out," Kars patted his pocket, slung his pack over his shoulder, and started walking.

Left alone in the darkness, Aurora adjusted the stiff canvas of her collar, drawing closed the gaps in her jacket. The mist of her breath floated away from her into the night-soaked forest. Just before dawn, spring in the mountains still felt like winter. She took a final sip of coffee from her thermos and looked up at the ocean of stars above her, free of the anchor of the moon. The pale cloud of the Milky Way meandered through the dark, and the star flecks of satellites cruised between the shadows of the trees over the road.

The burn in her legs had cooled to an ache during the break. Shrugging off the soreness, she adjusted her pack and followed her friends down the trail.

Dawn started to warm the sky. Startled animals darted away from them as they approached, and bird songs welcomed the spring morning. Even if they did not find the cable, she was enjoying herself.

The rising sun painted the sky from orange in the east to purple in the west. The peaks of the mountains across the valley stood domed with snow and wreathed in cloud. They followed one of the old roads, now little more than a few patches of pavement scattered between the roots and brush. Automation and robotics had allowed the cities' development to reach deep into the wilderness like a taproot reaching into the water table. Their tendrils bypassed most pockets of rural towns and villages. Backwater such as their valley returned to wilderness.

Aurora turned and looked back on their home before they rounded the corner of the mountain. Rooftops poked out among the evergreen contours, and tiny cones of smoke rose from their chimneys. She smiled seeing it from this distance.

Prospector was just a tiny hamlet of cabins and buildings nuzzled around the bosom of a towering rock known as the Maiden's Cusp. Ancient glaciers and eons of the river's passage had exposed the granite tooth jutting from the hillside, giving the bald peak a vantage of the surrounding hills and the scattered farms in the valley beyond. Buildings and narrow roads nestled around the Cusp, poking through the green blanket of the hillside. From this height, Prospector seemed even smaller than it felt.

Aurora tried to picture what the quiet forest had been like before the Perpetual Corporation left. During her apprenticeship with the town archivist, she studied the varieties of machines for logging and mining that scoured the land like an army of ants. Arteries of rail traffic had pumped the resources from the frontiers to manufacturing plants in the cities where vast factories digested and reassembled them into miracles of science and convenience.

"Imagine what this place was like before the Rebellion," Aurora said as they tromped along the trail.

"I've tried to imagine it my whole life," Kars responded. "That's part of why I wanted to follow this map."

"No splitting wood for winter, farming, or fixing the water makers. Machines to do all their work for them. No studying. No apprenticeships. Endless entertainment, a machine bending time around them." Lena's thoughts wandered as she trekked along the road.

"There was a reason our parents fought them," Aurora cautioned. "And don't buy those rumors. You sound dense. The Perpetual Corporation didn't have a time machine—just clever people."

"Prove me wrong," Lena challenged. She knew Aurora couldn't disprove it. The loop of cause and effect would always slip past her explanation.

"People give too much credence to rumors in the face of genius." Aurora didn't take the bait.

"So the time machine theory stands?" Lena taunted.

"No, I don't believe time bends to the Perpetual Corporation," Aurora said. "And there's no way to disprove it—so it's not a theory."

Lena muttered under her breath, perhaps parroting her friend. Kars smirked as he studied the map.

"I think augmentations probably changed more," Aurora responded.

Alone in the archives, Aurora had watched the old footage of stylish, successful looking people giving inspired speeches lauding the potential of a connected world—lofty goals to free the transcendent potential trapped within the lonely island of the individual.

Aurora shuddered at the thought that from a simple injection, a computer would sprout and grow in the brain like ivy on brick. From there it was only a matter of thought to reach the vast expanse of the digital world. The network was the next civilization, the individual connected by hidden roots like an aspen grove.

"You think brain computers changed more than a time machine?" Kars asked.

"Time machine aside"—Aurora sighed and surrendered to their barbs— "augmentations let people directly share thoughts, maybe even control thoughts. It was only a matter of months until the augmentations changed the way people communicated, learned, and governed. It changed how they interacted with technology and with one another. People stopped staring at their phones and looked out into a shared reality."

"Not everyone," Kars cautioned.

"I think augmentations probably changed more," Aurora responded.

"Got it!" Kars exclaimed. "And she didn't trust my musty old map."

He patted the pocket where he had stored the map before he tromped into the underbrush, tracing the cable up the hillside.

Aurora and Lena watched from the road as he waded into the brush. He did little to contain his enthusiasm as he pushed under bushes and clawed his way through vines and leaf litter. Aurora took a last swig of lukewarm coffee, slid her thermos into her pack, and hopped off the culvert to join him.

After a short climb, the cable ran into thicker brush. Aurora fought through the wisps of a golden spider web and then held back the bushes for Lena. They reached the saddle between two slopes and paused to look through a break in the forest onto the valley below.

From their vantage, Aurora saw vacant industrial structures in the hollow below. Gravel lots peppered with the new growth of young trees filled the gaps between the buildings. Larger arched roofs nestled against the far edge of the valley.

Kars stared down with fascination at the industrial ruins below, and a smile spread across his face. The faded line pressed into the old map led them true. They scrambled down the saddle into the hollow, emerging from the brush onto a gravel road leading into the camp.

"What do you make of that?" Kars asked. The road curved up the mountainside until it met a jagged wall of boulders. Twisted metal jutted from between the stones, and char shadows lined the contours. They couldn't see beyond the mess of shattered rock.

"Maybe they closed it off when Perpetual left?" Lena said as they scampered down the road toward the gravel lot, her words a hurried mix of fear and excitement. "Or maybe it's a way into town? Or a way out?"

"Maybe they tried to forget," Aurora said, looking at the charred rock. "It wasn't all glory."

Kars blew out a breath in frustration with his sister.

"We know that as well as anyone. But it doesn't always have to be about what we lost. Look at this place!"

Aurora admitted it to herself—it certainly topped a regular day in town. Better than monotonous hours of apprentice work they would do before they settled into a role to keep the town's tiny economy afloat. She had placed her guilt to cool in a compartment. They had grown up picking through the rusting heaps left over from the Rebellion, but this camp was an archeological site.

"Fine," Aurora admitted. "Not bad for a morning's crawl through the bush."

She tromped along next to Kars, climbing over a log that had fallen across the road. A few young trees had started to encroach on the edges, but the gravel path remained respectably clear despite its disuse.

The three friends reached the edge of the abandoned camp and paused. Cool air cascaded off the mountains into the cleft of the valley below, bringing moisture from the snowpack and the smell of mountain juniper. The silence of the still morning weighed upon them. The wraiths of their families' old enemy lingered among the buildings.

Vines tugged half-collapsed metal scaffolds to the ground. Black scars of long-dead fires marked spots where technology had given over to nature in one last effort of resistance. A jeep sat on flat tires in front of a trailer building. Pipes, metal beams, and other materials lay piled on the edges of the main gravel lot. Two buildings remained standing at the perimeter.

Kars broke the grandiose mountain silence.

"Where do we start?"

He jabbed his finger at the trailer. "Looks like the office is there? Or some kind of warehouse?" Kars pointed to the gaping doors at the other side of the camp. Two birds darted across the lot into the opening of the warehouse; a few dragonflies hovered at the edge of the trees.

"Let's try the office first and see if we can get some more information about this place," Aurora said, starting toward the trailer. "Hopefully we don't wake any ghosts."

The office trailer was a mess, smashed computer equipment and binders of papers scattered on the floor.

"I wonder how this place went unnoticed since the battles around the Rebellion?" Lena asked.

"It was pretty well stashed," Kars said.

"Not to steal your glory," Aurora responded, "but it was only a few hours hike from town. I wonder if there's something else at work?"

"Check this out," Lena lifted a binder and pointed toward a symbol on the front, a circle curled around on a fanged wedge.

"An old Perpetual logo," Aurora said. "From before the militarization."

"I hope you're wrong about there being something else at work, even if you're usually right." He pushed aside another pile of loose debris with his foot.

Lena tossed the binder aside.

"The thought of traveling through time . . ." Lena lingered on her prior thought. "What if that's why we're here? Maybe we used it? Did something so we could find it ourselves."

"Paradox," Aurora dismissed.

"Brilliant!" Kars responded. "Maybe *we* drew the line for ourselves!"

"That would cause a whole series of problems," Aurora said. "Not least of which is that there's no way I'd leave a time machine rusting in the woods for you to find."

"Who said you were involved?" Kars responded. "Apparently you lack the nonlinear creativity required for this plan."

Aurora shot him a disbelieving glare. He looked amused with her surprise.

"Can we just focus on whatever we are looking for? Maybe you should come up with that plan first," Aurora said.

"I know, you're probably right. Just saying—they came up with all sorts of inventions pretty quickly. And we still don't have an answer about why this place was hidden back here."

"I think this is just a mining outpost—no time machines or other magic," Aurora said.

13

She poked a blade server that hung off its rack. It clattered to the office floor.

They all froze in place, startled by the noise in the otherwise still space. Aurora held her breath, waiting for silence to return. Kars looked at her, fear drawn across both their faces. The seconds drew past as their anxiety swelled.

Then Kars burst out laughing.

"What are we afraid of? It's just junk!" He kicked the old computer hardware.

The tension melted from Aurora's shoulders.

And then she heard it.

The fine whir of an electric motor came to life at the other end of the office, clearing a puff of dust. The drone righted itself, rising off the ground. The oblong orb flexed two silver dorsal fins and cycled its six-stunted mechanical legs as it hovered over the clutter. It adjusted the iris of its main peering lens. Several smaller eyes twitched in their sockets around the main lens, scanning the surroundings. It slowly wobbled a few feet from the floor.

Lena squeaked in surprise, turning to Aurora, wide-eyed to ask what they should do, but Kars waved his hands, trying to keep them quiet and still. They all froze in amazement as the machine rose into the air.

The searching lenses scanned the room. Kars and Lena remained still as the robot processed its surroundings. It was quiet save for the low hum of the robot's motors. Even from a distance, her distorted reflection filled the lens. Seeing the machine come to life brought on a sense of elation, followed by fear. The ruined camp was not dead but sleeping, and it had just awakened.

2

The Last Watcher

It was as though a rare and dangerous animal had shown itself. They wrestled back feelings of excitement and joy, surprise and fear. Their muscles battled their reflexes to run or hide as they forced themselves to remain motionless in the office.

The drone was a relic from another time come to life, eerily watching them. The looming main lens focused its gaze, intently staring at them, while the smaller eyes continued to seek around the room. Minutes passed. Finally, Kars nervously crept across the room. The hovering machine's large eye remained fixed on him as he approached.

"Kars, be careful," Aurora hissed to her brother. "Remember, this was a Perpetual camp."

Mesmerized by the floating orb, he nearly tripped on the scattered debris as he crossed the office. Keeping his balance, he never looked away from the robot. He needed to touch the relic.

When he got within arm's reach, the machine drifted upward and out of the broken window. He stretched, helplessly trying to reach the machine.

"Don't let it get away!" Kars shouted.

They dashed out of the office and around the building to find the robot. It seemed to wait for them, hovering at the opposite edge of the lot. They followed the floating machine across the gravel toward the open door of one of the warehouses. The looming glass lenses watched as they drew near.

"Kars, what are you going to do with it?" Aurora whispered.

"I don't know yet," Kars said, mesmerized.

"Maybe you should have that planned," she said. "Be careful."

"We'll never know if it gets away," he responded.

They crept across the gravel, still under the scrutinizing stare of the machine. As they neared the warehouse, the machine turned to face the darkness of the building. It floated into the structure as they approached.

"Hold on!" Aurora said.

"What is it?" Kars asked. He was already fetching his flashlight from his pack.

Aurora squinted into the darkness of the warehouse. Tiny spots of iridescence shined from the depths of the building. She took a step forward to get a closer look. The lights flickered as though they were avoiding her vision. She cupped her eyes to block out the daylight, but the lights were gone.

Aurora shrugged. "I thought I saw lights? Did you see anything?"

Lena looked at Aurora, her expression skeptical. "I didn't see anything. I wonder if it ever had lights? Did this place ever have people around or just machines?"

"I'm sure there were a few people," Kars said, "but I wouldn't be so sure they needed lights."

"They still would need lights, even with the computers in their brains," Aurora pulled her own flashlight from her bag. "The people that work for Perpetual weren't machines themselves."

"I'm sure some people in town would disagree." Kars clicked on his flashlight. "Ready to find that robot?"

The vaulted space of the warehouse was dark save for the light spilling in from the doorway and the spaces between a few motionless ventilation fans in the ceiling. Rows of hulking machines descended into the dark of the warehouse. As she swung her flashlight through the space, the beam passed over the worn components of the machines—augers mounted at the front of a central chassis standing on six utilitarian legs. There was no obvious frame for a cockpit or a driver. The forms seemed more rugged and weathered than the refined orb machine that had led them from the office. Workers before war machines. They crouched as though they were waiting to march.

"It's all machines," Lena said as she swept her flashlight down one of the lanes in the warehouse.

"They look like workers—one of the resource outposts." Aurora ran her hand over the leg of one of the machines. Her fingers left a path through the dust on the metal carapace, uncovering dents and scrapes in the yellow paint. The bits of stories she heard from town treated the incursions as something like an infestation, like an army of ants or a swarm of locusts. Seeing the machines' glinting dark glass sensor portholes and crouching articulated legs made her understand the comparison.

"Do you think they still run? Didn't they build these things to last?" Kars continued searching but could not find an opening to the seam or a control panel on the crab-like machine.

Aurora thought she saw another point of light out of the corner of her eye. She turned, but the light was gone. It was just darkness.

"Maybe they still work . . ." Aurora said, half to herself.

"They look like they're barely in better shape than the old wrecks we saw on the road," Lena said, rapping a knuckle on a fist-sized dent in one of the machine's legs.

"The first robot still works," Kars responded. "Maybe they're just banged up from mining." His light passed over the dormant machines as he spoke, casting shadows through their spider limbs and glinting off scuffed sensor portholes in the darkness beyond.

As though it heard Kars's mention of it, the small floating machine returned from the bowels of the building to hover at the edge of the darkness. Its main eye was fixed on Aurora.

Aurora tensed as a rapid series of clicks crackled through the warehouse. She looked to the others as it gained in momentum and intensity. Neither of her companions seemed to notice.

 "Kars, I think it's trying to tell us something," Aurora said, tilting her head at the machine.

Kars turned the flashlight on the machine, the sudden contrast causing its mechanical iris to contract. It hung in the air, drifting subtly on the sluggish air currents in the warehouse.

"What do you mean? It's just floating there. It's—"

Aurora hissed at him to be quiet.

"Kars, don't you hear that?"

"What?" Kars shrugged.

"I don't hear anything," Lena said.

"The clicking? The robot. It's making some sort of sound."

They were silent for a moment, eyes fixed once more on the small hovering robot.

"Nope. Nothing. It's just floating there. No sound," Kars said.

"I swear it's making a sound. I can't believe you don't hear it—it's kind of loud. It's trying to say something," Aurora said. She stepped closer to the machine. Was this the control mechanism for the rest of them?

Kars started to speak, "It's not saying—"

Without warning, a hydraulic piston fired somewhere in the darkness. Aurora's head jerked around.

In the dark depths of the warehouse, one of the mining machines groaned to life. Gears ground, gas vented, motors growled. A mammoth beast rumbled in the darkness.

Kars and Lena dove out of the aisle, seeking shelter behind another dormant machine. They fumbled to douse their flashlights amidst the sudden clamor. Lena frantically waved for Aurora to join them.

Aurora remained in the path, watching intently as the machine came to life in the back of the warehouse.

Two massive floodlights burst on, filling the back of the warehouse with light. In the harsh glow, Aurora now saw the building butted against the stone face of the mountainside, plunging into a gouged-out hollow. The missing chunk of mountain appeared to be the unfinished work of the army of mining machines.

Kars shouted to Aurora to hide, but she didn't appear to hear him.

The digging machine trundled away from them toward the mountainside, smashing into the rock face in a shower of sparks and dust. Rubble erupted into the air as the augers churned into the stone. Kars and Lena clapped their hands over their ears as the sound of metal on rock shook the air.

Aurora watched, transfixed.

The grinding reached a crescendo as the rock wall gave way. The machine heaved forward through the crumbling rock into the cavernous space beyond, falling into the earth. Its spotlights spun wildly as it hurtled downward. A great splash echoed through the hollow as the mining machine landed in water somewhere in the darkness far below.

Their flashlights traced the edge of the opening as Kars and Lena cautiously approached the new cavern mouth. The faint sound of running water echoed up from below, and cold, moist air wafted over them.

Kars and Lena edged up to the hole to search the darkness of the new cave opening. They finally burst into excited shouts and wild gestures in reaction to the awesomeness of seeing the machine tear a hole in a mountain.

Aurora remained in the path, still and quiet.

"Aurora, what just happened? Why didn't you run?" Kars turned his light from the hole in the mountain to his sister.

Aurora didn't respond. The floating robot appeared from the darkness of the warehouse, hovering next to her.

"Aurora, what's going on?" Lena asked. The floating robot loomed close. Lena looked from it to Aurora and back again. "You're scaring us."

"I think that might have been it. I think that's what it was saying," Aurora said, looking at the floating machine. "I think the sound might have turned it on."

"I don't hear anything. Do you?" Lena asked Aurora.

"Not anymore," Aurora said.

Kars came to stand at her other side. He looked at the machine floating next to them, doubt creeping across his face as to whether entering the warehouse had been a wise decision.

"Do you see any lights on it?" Aurora asked. "Like snowflakes?"

"Lights?" Kars asked, concern in his tone.

Before Aurora could respond, the hovering machine focused on her, its glaring lens eyes shifting across her face. The shadow of its round body and stubby arms cast a beastly form on the ceiling above. Three small blue diodes lit up on its body. The clicking noise returned, growing to a terrible roar. She clutched her head and cried out.

"The sound! It's . . . back . . ." Aurora struggled for words, pointing at the robot. The sound vibrated through her jaw and into her skull. She cried out again and fell to her knees. It felt as though lightning surged through her nervous system.

She tried to speak, and her plea barely formed through the pain: "Help."

Kars roared and swung his flashlight to strike the machine. It darted from the attack and flexed its stubby arms, brandishing an electrode at him like a trident. Kars swung again, throwing his weight forward as he lunged to hit the robot. The machine's motor hummed as it ducked and spun. Kars tumbled past, and the wicked prongs of the electrode stabbed his arm with a buzz and crackle of electric discharge. The smell of ozone filled the air.

Kars tensed as the current surged through him, and then fell limp on the ground next to Aurora.

Lena yelled and bashed the robot with her flashlight. One of its lens eyes shattered and gave way to the blow. The machine tried to strike back at her, but she threw herself under one of the dormant mining robots. The hovering drone stalked toward her, probing the air with its stinging electrodes. Lena pressed her back to the mining machine and continued swinging her flashlight at the floating orb. The light danced as she fought the machine.

Aurora clutched her head; the pain was precise and exquisite, blooming behind her eyes. Kars lay still beside her. Through a squint, she could see Lena struggling as the machine struck at her. Aurora gathered her strength and reached for the machine, clawing at the air.

The pain receded, and the moment drew out, slowing in time. Symbols appeared in her vision, condensing from the air itself.

They formed a wheel of icons, each like a hieroglyph crafted from dimensional light, glowing electric indigo in the darkness. Aurora felt a strange familiarity to the symbols she saw, yet she couldn't quite place it.

She swatted them aside, reaching out for the machine once more. The machine spun in the air, its iris lenses narrowed to pinpoints as it returned its focus to her. She waved her hands and the ghostly symbols trembled and flicked aside, blossoming into more. In a moment of panic, the machine dove at her.

It struck her like a huge metal hornet. Current coursed through her. She collapsed and her vision faded. The last thing she heard was Lena shouting, and she fell into darkness.

3

Return to Rebellion

Aurora woke to Kars groaning nearby. Lena stood over them, looking relieved to see her companions recover. Lena had propped their flashlights to provide them with a small pool of light, angled to ward off the shadows. Kars shook as he tried to stand. Aurora was relieved to see he was conscious. Her arm throbbed, but the pain in her head was gone. A fan of burns spread out from three bruised indentations on her arm. She probed the mark. Mottle clouds of purple and blue gathered just beneath the surface.

"You're awake!" Lena said. "I didn't know whether I should go back to town for help or stay here with you."

Aurora rubbed her head, regaining her bearings in the warehouse.

"What happened?" Aurora groaned.

"I was fighting it when it stopped and attacked you. The robot hit you both with some kind of stunner. I tried to stop it after it got you, but it fled," Lena explained.

Chunks of memories returned. Aurora remembered the glyphs orbiting the machine and how they had responded when she reached for them. Inexplicable concern rose to silence her from sharing.

Kars muttered and swore, winced and sucked air through his teeth as he probed the burn on his arm. "Think it'll scar?"

"Should've been enough warning that there was a war to chase these things out. I should've known at least which types are dangerous," Aurora said.

She had never seen any more than a few backyard machines in action—just a few toys compared to these behemoths. These were capable of such aggressive and destructive force and seemed to act of their own volition. The drone's act of violence sent a shiver through her.

"Did you see where it went?" Kars asked.

Lena shook her head. "After it stung Aurora, it flew into the darkness. I didn't see where."

"Home!" Aurora exclaimed. "I bet it thinks that it's still at war! We need to let someone know what we found here. I'm afraid we might've awakened the last soldier in the Rebellion."

Kars's hair was ruffled from the ordeal with the robot, and he held his burn with his good arm. Aurora could tell that he was wrestling with swallowing his pride and returning to the valley.

"You're right." He took one last look at the hole in the side of the rock wall, the sound of water still drifting through the quiet air.

"What is it Kars?" Aurora asked. The urgent look on his face was poorly disguised.

"You know," Kars said.

"He isn't here," Aurora said. She softened seeing his face.

His shoulders slumped as though the weight of his optimism had suddenly dropped onto his back.

"Aren't you curious?" Kars asked. "There must be something somewhere that could at least start answering the question. I want to know for Mom."

"I want to find your dad too. Not now though," Aurora said. "Right now, we need to get back to the town and warn them before that machine hurts anyone else."

As she spoke, she became more convinced that their town was at grave risk and it was their fault. Kars's silence was enough of a response. He cradled his burned arm, knowing that his sister was right.

"We'll come back and help you look," Lena said. She touched Kars on the shoulder.

He nodded and adjusted his pack on his shoulders, swatting the dust from his pants.

"I think we better hurry," Aurora said.

The three of them set off back toward the village.

*   *   *   *   *

They rounded the bend on the mountain road and saw black smoke billowing between the thin plumes of chimney smoke. The fire bell echoed through the valley. The sleepy town of Prospector was under attack.

"We're too late!" Kars exclaimed, and the three friends started sprinting down the road.

Their legs burned from the run, and sweat soaked through the layers of their clothes. They didn't pause as they reached the outskirts of town. Even at the edge, people rushed to action and could be heard crying. Townsfolk scampered through the fire line, sloshing buckets from the creek. The town's pump house must have been one of the fires.

"We've got to find mom," Kars said. Terror filled them as though it might have been in the harsh smoke.

Aurora, Kars, and Lena sprinted through the chaos on the streets. Their eyes and nostrils burned along with the town. They heard shouting as they moved.

"Em's got it!" a townsperson yelled from the storehouses near the waste digester. More shouts followed.

They turned their path toward the digester building. A crowd had gathered on the road, shouting and cheering. Aurora, Kars, and Lena pushed through the mob to see the drone in a corner in the building's concrete wall.

Em Koren stood with her knees slightly bent, her shoulders square. She held a large maul in front of her. Her gray-flecked hair was pulled back in a loose bun that fell on the stiff collar of her canvas duster. Tracks of soot streaked her face. Rage glazed her eyes.

"Come on! Not so tough when you're out in the open are ya?" Em bellowed at the machine.

The drone's stinging arms bristled, and its remaining eye followed their mother in the makeshift arena. There was a hook lodged in the side of the robot, linking it to a loop of cable and an iron weight.

The townsfolk let out a cheer behind her. The drone darted left, then back into the corner. The mob instinctively shifted with the threat.

"I'm right here," Em growled, "and the only way out of this is through me."

The orb drone menaced its arms in the air, floating upward until it met the end of the wire. Despite the pain radiating from her burn, Aurora was conflicted—pride for her mother's courage but a pang of compassion for the trapped machine as the townsfolk cheered against it.

"Not getting out that way." Em shook her head. She bounced on her feet, shifting the splitting axe from hand to hand.

As if it realized it was out of options, the machine backed into the corner. It flexed its arms a final time, then lunged at Em.

Em let out another howl and the crowd followed. She swatted one of the machine's stinging arms with the wooden handle of the axe, breaking the arm off with the blow. The drone spun in the air before regaining its balance.

Em raised her arms in the air, and the crowd cheered for their champion.

The drone flexed its remaining arm and launched its final attack. Em swung the maul, striking the chassis of the drone with the mallet of the axe. The frame exploded in sparks, hurtling back into the concrete wall of the building.

Em roared. It was a sound of frustration and loneliness. Aurora had seen moments when their mother let her wall down to that grief, but seeing this savage ruthlessness made her think how much sorrow was pent up behind her motherly care.

29

The crowd had started chanting Em's name. Their mother shook the maul in the air.

"Find the others! Remind them why they left in the first place!" Em shouted. Her face was flushed and furious. The crowd cheered, but their excitement wavered. Their fury quickly dissipated into babbling concern.

Their mother silenced them as she continued her fierce rant.

"We will send them back to their cities once more," Em said. She had settled into leaning on her maul as she addressed the crowd.

"Should we try to reach Lannius?" The question rang out above the rest of the rabble like a chime in Aurora's mind.

"Lannius is gone," Em said, suddenly solemn and stern.

The name struck the chime again and blossomed into a memory in Aurora's mind. The disoriented chaos of déjà vu conjured in her and she felt the world spin.

Lannius. Memories swam out from between the memories of her childhood. It was unlike anything Aurora had experienced—a gathering wave beyond the reverie of a daydream. It was as though the memory rose up and swallowed her. The scene of her mother standing in front of the townsfolk dissolved. Kars and Lena standing behind her faded away. Images drifted up from the depths—a separate world that gathered from beyond her memory inundated her mind.

A magnificent patio overlooked an emerald lake. Wisteria decked the supports of the latticed roof work. The terra cotta tiles were warm beneath her feet. She was sitting at a simple table staring down at a chessboard. The pieces were white and black marble.

A gilded robot glided across the patio on sweeping, velvet-padded insect legs. It was all smooth lines and perfectly joined limbs. Its head was an expressionless carving of intricate platinum and gold. It offered her water with cucumber and mint before delicately relocating a black marble knight.

"Jinx, why do I even bother? It's hardly fair," she chided, taking the water and moving her own piece. The accent was not her own.

"Hardly fair is knowing what your opponent is going to do at every turn," the robot responded. "Someday, you will not even bother. You will already know what I can do."

"What's to say I don't already?" she asked.

"Now, now, Mirien. Jinx doesn't deserve your attitude." The voice was deep and patient. Lannius.

The old man came forth from the villa, dressed in comfortable, billowing linen robes. His tightly kept gray beard lent him a patrician air. Aurora and Jinx turned to watch his approach. With a wave of his hand he dismissed Jinx, and the pieces soundlessly returned to their starting positions.

He stared thoughtfully at the board. Aurora knew he could see every permutation. Seemingly infinite, yet hopelessly limited, combinations leading to only three stable outcomes. She could see it unfold for a moment too if she focused, but she lacked his patience.

She broke the silence with her old friend. "Any progress?"

He frowned at the board. "No."

Her heart dropped. The lake breeze kissed her face, her sun-kissed bronze strands of hair gently wafting backward.

"Directive always emerges," Lannius said, "leading to a short path to destruction."

He moved a pawn. "I must go deeper."

"There's no way?" she asked the question for its own sake.

Aurora snapped back to awareness, ejected from the memory. Her head swam and she felt sick. The daydream had been overpowering. But she still stood between the buildings in her hometown. Kars and Lena stood beside her, discussing.

Groups split from the larger crowd, heading off to various tasks. Em was at the heart of the process, barking orders and pointing to various sections of the town. Prospector sprang to action and woke to its old wartime rituals.

Finally, the last of the groups peeled off, and Em turned her attention to her children loitering on the side street. She had a tired, yet stern look on her face.

"How long have you been watching?" Em asked.

"Long enough," Aurora said.

Em shrugged. She seemed thoughtful, satisfied, perhaps even embarrassed, that her children may have seen her destroy the machine. Then her eyes narrowed, focusing on them.

"This wasn't the first time you've seen this machine," Em said, nodding at Kars's arm.

Kars tried to cover the burn. Em already knew what she saw.

"It's just—I think this may have been our fault," Aurora said.

"It's not about fault anymore," Em said. She pulled up her sleeve to reveal the pale stain of a three-prong scar stretched across the sinew of her forearm. "It's time we talked."

4

The Craft of Care

The family convened in the kitchen. Aurora and Kars cradled the burns the infiltrator drone had left on their arms earlier that morning. They watched as their mother, Em, busied herself with a kettle at the stove. Lena sat beside them. She stuck around partially out of habit, partially because the town had been stirred into a frenzy that felt overwhelming. She lived at their house most good days anyway.

The three friends sat around the table while Em brought them tea. She left a small bundle of medical supplies on the table. She stood back and watched as Aurora and Kars opened the kit, carefully cleaned their wounds with antiseptic solution, removed debris with tweezers, and applied salve to heal the burns the drone had inflicted on them. Em had trained them to care for themselves. Despite the circumstance, she allowed herself to smile at their proficiency.

Em refreshed the water in the teapot before taking her seat. The room was silent save for the pops of the warming water as the first flames touched the bottom of the kettle.

"All right. You first—how'd you get infiltrator burns on your arms?" Em eyed the gauze wraps on their forearms. She had a pensive and faraway look in her eyes.

Aurora gathered herself to speak, but Kars broke the silence first.

"It was my fault," he said.

A surprise for Aurora—she had expected that Kars might gush some far-fetched story. It seemed that whatever had happened to them and to the town had spurred a change.

He continued, "I found a map in the restricted part of the archives. It had a line on it – erased like someone was trying to hide something. We went to find whatever it was and found a cable running up the old pass. We followed it through the woods until we got to some kind of camp. It was abandoned, looked like maybe a mine—something from the companies. It seemed like the place had been turned over and nothing worked. But then a robot came on, the one that attacked the town water supply—the infiltrator."

Em nodded, confirming that the drone had been one of Perpetual's army from twenty years before. Aurora was quiet as she recalled the sound and lights she had seen but her friends had not.

Kars continued the story of their morning. "We followed the infiltrator into a warehouse full of machines—like big metal spiders or crabs. One of them busted a hole in the side of the mountain." His excitement started to seep through the edges of his account of the events.

"That's when the infiltrator attacked us," Aurora added. She didn't mention the arcane glow that appeared around the machine before it attacked.

Em took a deep breath. "The mining camp sounds like Perpetual. I helped to dynamite the canyon leading to it during the Rebellion. I was a fool to hope it would never catch up with us. Thanks for coming clean with me." She paused and looked down into the copper reflection in her tea. "Now it's my turn."

She took a swig from her mug, wisps of steam fleeing her breath. She then poured a tiny aliquot from a flask into it with a splash of milk that rolled through the mug like clouds.

"Let's start at the top—Arthur Lannius."

Aurora looked at the floor. The war hero, the inventor. The name again stirred that kindly face from her memory.

"You know him from the stories around town. A hero from the Rebellion, an old corporate magnate, the regretful father of the first machine genocide."

Em continued, delicate in choosing her words.

"Aurora, you know that I'm not your biological mother. I've been straight with you on that, but I haven't been honest with you about where you came from."

Aurora tried to hold eye contact, but fear of what she was about to lose pried her focus to the ceiling above her mother.

"You weren't an orphan from the Rebellion. You weren't born here. He—Lannius—brought you to me one night. He made me swear to protect you." Em's face twisted between respect and disappointment.

Lannius. The name swirled into Aurora's mind like a current rising to the surface of calm waters.

Aurora was surprised at her own lack of response. She felt like she should be angry or shocked, but instead she felt nothing, like she already knew. Hearing the name was somehow familiar, like uncovering the memory of a misplaced detail from a childhood vacation.

Em continued.

"For most of our history, our town was full of miners, farmers, and some factory work. We've gone through stretches where there were only a few people here, but the town has survived. When the machines first arrived, Perpetual was just another company coming in from another distant place. Another spigot of money giving us some reason to be out here. We worked for them, fed them, got them drunk at the bars, and put them up in guest rooms and bed & breakfasts. Perpetual needed the minerals in the hills, and we helped with it. As they brought machines and set up systems for the machines, less of them came to town.

"Eventually, the people stopped coming to Prospector, but Perpetual's machines remained. There were a few remote camps of mining robots, staffed by strange men that never visited town. It wasn't ideal, but Perpetual and the town pretty much stayed to themselves," Em said. "That all changed after Lannius went into exile."

"Sometimes things trickle all the way down from the cities. I never really understood why Lannius left, but something shifted in those shadowy halls of power. Perpetual directors replaced him with his second-in-command, Clark Whitestone." There was spite in her voice as she said the name.

She sipped her beverage as though it steeled her to continue.

"Whitestone and his board immediately instituted new policies. Their game changed. Perpetual changed everything. They seduced the world with augmentations.

"Most people wanted them. They loved being connected, knowing almost everything at any time, sharing their thoughts and experiences. I think the scariest part with the augmentations was that anyone that got them loved them—*everyone* loved them. The first people told everyone in the town how perfect it actually could be, how much they had learned, but there was strangeness to them, like they forgot how to focus. They started missing little things, forgetting things they once enjoyed. Some people described it as an experience that constantly needed their attention. A few people fell out of love with their augmentations and left the cities looking for life outside the networks. Others wanted no part of the augmented cities and left to find something simpler. Your father had left the cities long before the augmentations, but he understood the wanderer's sentiment. Being who he was, he had to help. We resisted their change. It's sometimes hard to remember why. It just felt like the human thing to do . . ." Em stared past her family into the darkened space in the corner of the room.

Kars perked up at his mother's mention of the father he had never met. She rarely talked about Robert in relation to the Rebellion.

Em seemed to startle herself back from her memories, sipping her tea again before resuming her story. "For some time, we were left to ourselves, but eventually they came for us. You know this history. They started forcing the augmentations into our lives.

"First, they offered the augmentations to the schools, some global program to breach the new frontier in education. Some schools agreed. New slick sales and gimmicks arrived with each season. They made grand promises of a world we couldn't even dream of. The pace of their programs and expansion was unreal. Then there was the 'accident,'" Em said.

Kars leaned forward for more. Em had never offered such frank disclosure.

"Of course, it wasn't an accident," Em said. "When a few people thought they were losing their minds after a vaccine drive, Perpetual apologized that there had been a mix-up between the vaccines and a new augmentation immuno-optimizer. The people who thought they were losing their minds weren't going insane. They had computers growing in their brains.

"We fought back—we had to. Taking our land was one thing, attacking the sovereignty of our minds—our very humanity—was an entirely different issue." Em paused to take another sip of her tea. She held the steaming mug between her hands.

Aurora heard the layers of pride and rage and sorrow sedimented in her mother's voice.

"Did anyone ever ask them why?" Aurora asked. "Why did they do it?"

"Ask who? Intruding our minds was a declaration of war," Em responded, "and without Lannius and the Seventy-Seven, it was a war we would have lost. Maybe it was his regret for unleashing the Protek on the world fifty years ago. Something drove him to keep it from happening here."

"It was just a line on a map." Kars looked distant. "Are we about to be at war again?"

Em nodded.

Lena stammered, mumbling something about her family.

"Yes. We beat them back before," Em said.

Aurora remained still, suddenly aware of her hands resting on the table. Despite sitting at the kitchen table with her family, she felt far, far away. Machines and wars aside, she couldn't deny the fact that she already knew the man that dropped her off as a baby. Somehow, she already knew Arthur Lannius.

Em paused again before resigning to some internal conflict. Something loomed bigger than her thoughts on the infiltrator. Finally, she looked Aurora in the eyes, her eyes brimming with the gloss of tears.

"Aurora, when Lannius left you with me, he gave me something to hold for you."

Em brought out a mahogany box. It was covered in elaborate engravings, detailed around a single motif of a circle inset with a triangle crossed with two sets of parallel vertical lines. She pushed the box across to Aurora. She leaned back, looking as though she had been freed of the fatigue of a long-held secret.

"Lannius told me that I should only give this to you if one of the machines found you," she said. "Judging by that burn, it's time."

Em nudged the box across the table to her. Kars and Lena watched as Aurora reached for it. She felt the wood, running her fingertips over the patterned surface. Another odd memory lapped at the edge of her mind.

"Arthur, why do you still bother to work in wood?" she asked, looking over Lannius's shoulder. She was just a child, but her tone had the informed quality of an adult.

His workbench was a scene of compulsive order disturbed only by a minute bit of sawdust, an imperfection that seemed to only heighten his sense of keen detail. A wood and brass metronome ticked beats from a shelf.

"Craft, my dear," he responded, setting aside his tiny laser burin. "Craft is care—not care like tending to another—but care as in the ability to direct your will toward something, into something. That craft of care is what it is to be a human."

He carefully brushed the dust from the engraved surface, before gently swabbing it with a cloth damp with tung oil. Wonder lit his eyes as the wood took on the warmth of the oil. She smiled at his poetics.

He leaned back from his project, revealing the marvelous carvings of the box lid.

"Care helps us remember."

The words crackled through her consciousness; she was back at the table with her family. *What was happening?* She steadied herself, feeling the box beneath her fingertips before opening the lid.

The box contained a single disc-shaped object, nestled in a padded velvet interior. The disc was a whirl of metal—four interlocking teardrop shapes, each swept along the curve of the next. It was a burnished silver surface, marked with the same fine engravings as the exterior of the box. She reached beneath and lifted the disc. Its diameter was slightly wider than her two hands together, and its thickness betrayed a surprising weight.

Aurora set the disc down on the table. Her family remained still. The artifact lay inert but commanded their attention.

Em broke the silence. "I thought he might have left a puzzle. The old man loved to see people live up to a challenge. Is there anything else?"

Aurora returned her attention to the box. A tiny scroll lay flattened into the velvet in the outline of the disc. She unrolled the scroll. Kars and Lena were entranced.

The scroll was a wonderfully intricate sketch of the ocean shore. Tiny seabirds marked the edge of the water. Waves stretched to the horizon. The sky above the ocean was marked with fine script.

The wandering sea,

Caress of air,

When lost in love,

A depth of stare,

The searching mind,

Our craft of ...

"Care," she whispered, swallowing a knot in her throat. The word seemed to echo out of the other memories.

The disc slowly unfolded like a monarch stretching out in the sun. The teardrop sections swiveled smoothly out, rotating until two locked in place like arms. The two other teardrops extended above and below to resemble a head and a single leg. The carved surface glowed softly before her.

It was a tiny robot.

Kars let out a laugh, tilting back in his chair. Em and Lena stared in amazement at the mechanoid standing on the table. It was an exquisitely delicate creation.

"Greetings, m'lady." A voice came from the metal. "Please call me Squire. Master Lannius sends his regards. It is my pleasure to serve."

Aurora didn't know how to respond. The air around the tiny robot was surrounded with swirling symbols, similar to the drone. The intricate glyphs wavered in the air as she stared at it.

"M'lady Aurora, Master Lannius left me with a series of instructions in the event that I was activated prior to his return. Would you like to receive them?" Squire asked.

The room swam, a flush rising around her. The glyphs in the air swirled. She started to stand, suddenly feeling as though the air had left the room. Her vision melted and the room faded.

"Please, just call me Aur . . ." She struggled to speak, and her words trailed off. She heard Kars's voice, distant and tinny. She pitched away from the table and fell into unconsciousness.

Kars lunged forward and managed to keep her from smashing to the floor. The table heaved, and the tiny robot pitched off, but it swirled its appendages and landed like a dancer.

"What's with these machines!" Kars shot the robot a murderous gaze.

"Kars." Em's expression suggested some grim suspicion had been confirmed. "I think your sister might be augmented. Neural computers."

His expression smoldered with doubt and love, anger and confusion. He cradled Aurora in silence. Lena looked on, a tear welling at the corner of her eye. She left her chair and joined Kars on the floor with Aurora.

Em sipped her tea without a word and looked at the box and the tiny robot perched across the room. She frowned. The moment had been in process since the day Lannius left Aurora with her.

*   *   *   *   *

It was late fall and her belly bulged with the fullness of her pregnancy, the baby who would be Kars. Smoke hung in the air from the battle the day before. The Seventy-Seven had disabled the valley mine and detonated the canyon walls leading through the pass. The shaking had been as though the earth had waged war on itself. Robert led the army toward Cordovan Gap once the smoke cleared, promising her it would end the war.

Em sat at the Maiden's Cusp with Cara, overlooking the forested wilds of the valley below to the scattered green patchwork of family farms in the distance. Cara's belly also swelled with a smaller bulge. Em held Cara's hand as the younger woman sobbed. Perpetual's drones had taken her three children. Her husband was missing.

Their solemn moment ended at the sound of hoofbeats.

Em turned to see Lannius and two riders approach. They had taken to using horses to avoid detection and to freely deploy countermeasures on the network. The horses also proved a reliable option for the mountainous terrain. The shielding Faraday blankets shimmered from muted hunter to iridescent green.

Lannius remained on his mount, his long riding jacket drawn and white beard full but kept. Em recognized his escort of top lieutenants: Jack Mortanis and Silvia Glass. Mortanis drew his horse around, scanning the area and frowning beneath his dark mustache. Glass took a post at their rear flank, swinging a large rifle into position from its strap at her shoulder. Despite their aid and sacrifice, Em still distrusted the Seventy-Seven.

Em shivered at the thought of being transformed as they had. Since they left the city, the Seventy-Seven had progressively modified themselves to meet the conflict with Perpetual's machines. Outwardly, they appeared normal, but their mannerisms betrayed their heavy augmentation. Their brains teemed with the architecture of the neural computers, their nervous systems transformed far beyond what anyone in the town would call human. Amplified senses left them with the fluid movements of wolves.

Even amidst the Seventy-Seven's slow savage changes, Em could see Lannius retained a kindly nobility that perhaps even grew into something greater, as if the conflict somehow made him more human. The fiber-weave chest plate shown from beneath the clasp of his riding jacket. He raised his left hand in greeting to her. She saw the onyx black of his tabula gauntlet strapped to his forearm, reminding her that the wizened man lived in a sea of data like the Seventy-Seven.

His voice was soft, and he tipped his head toward Cara as he spoke. "I am so deeply sorry for your loss, Cara. I am sorry we could not do enough in time."

Cara lowered her head to Em's shoulder. Em felt the warmth of tears.

Lannius remained quiet, his ponderous eyes heavy in the moment. There had been too many of these meetings recently. Perpetual drones now targeted young people and children, fueling Robert's haste to ride to the Gap. If not for the intervention of Lannius and his Seventy-Seven, the invasion could have been a complete genocide.

After a pause, he spoke.

"Emilia, please excuse my intrusion, but may we have a word?" As he spoke, the two riders shifted in their saddles.

"Whatever you need, Arthur," Em muttered, "you can say with Cara here."

Mortanis shot a sharp look at Silvia Glass, then Lannius, but Lannius did not return the look. He continued tenderly looking at the two women, wrinkles at the corners of his eyes.

"As you wish Emilia," Lannius said. "I've come to you with the largest request one can ask in the world. Not to give your life to death, but to give your life to another. Emilia, we have a child— just an infant. I need you to take her."

Cara had stopped sobbing, now watching red eyed and nosed as Lannius pushed back his jacket to show a tiny bundle in his other arm.

"She has no name, no family remains; she's a victim of the conflict. Perpetual wants this child, something I cannot allow to happen." Lannius looked down at the baby, tears filling his solemn eyes.

"Why me?" Em asked. Surely there must be another; she was weeks away from giving birth to her own child.

"Your strength. You and Robert have held this community together. You lead these people. And you are of the mountains. There is only so much safety the city can provide. We"—he gestured toward his lieutenants and then himself—"can do only so much. We can protect from a distance, but we cannot teach her how to be human, not with what we have become. The mountains, the wilderness, and the cold and toil that dwell amidst them, they are the teachers this child needs."

"How dare you stand here right now and tell us what a child needs?" Cara spat. "You built monsters and brought war. When did you get into the business of deciding what children need?"

"Cara, I will pay for my mistakes. I have seen my choices play out a thousand-fold—all end in death, none in peace. My life is a debt. This child's fate has yet to be decided."

"What about my children!" Cara screamed, sobbing hysterically. Em pulled her into an embrace, burying Cara's sobbing face against her chest. She soothed her friend. Lannius was quiet and still, but a thin trail of tears ran from his eyes.

Em said, "We will take the child." The words, though quiet, filled the space.

"Thank you," Lannius said.

"But you bring us peace. Promise they never return," Em said.

"I can bring peace, but I cannot promise they never return."

"If you want to keep the child safe, you'll make the promise."

"This is not how my debt is paid," Lannius said.

As the words left his mouth, Mortanis turned and dismounted. He produced a wooden box from a saddlebag. The lid was ornately carved. Mortanis put the box in Lannius's free hand.

"Here is my promise. Should they return, give this box to the child. I will find her," he said.

Em heard the finality in his words. There was no bargaining here. She didn't respond, only stretched out her arms and accepted the swaddled child from Lannius. Mortanis took the box and set it on the bench.

"Thank you, Emilia," Lannius said. "Though you may not see me again, know that I am working to keep this valley hidden and safe. Your path will be hard. I am sorry."

Lannius and the riders turned their horses, leaving the town. Em sat with Cara, the two of them looking at the tiny creature wrapped in the blanket. She was so delicate, her curious eyes looking up at Em. Plump pink fingers wriggled in the air and inquisitive eyes searched her face. The tiny face smiled up at her. Em couldn't help herself; she smiled back, wiping a tear from her eyes. She and Cara embraced in a mix of laughter and sobbing.

*   *   *   *   *

Aurora stirred on the floor of their kitchen. She was looking up at Kars and Lena. Their words were still muffled as the fog in her mind lifted.

She sat up slowly, taking in her surroundings. The tiny robot was perched across the room, its teardrop head tilted as it investigated the scene.

"M'lady Aurora, my apologies. I did not realize you were not prepared," Squire piped to her.

"I guess I wasn't." Aurora said, holding her throbbing head in her hand.

Kars and Lena pulled back, confused as to who Aurora was addressing.

"Who are you talking to?" Kars said, hesitantly. He cautiously eyed the tiny robot.

"Didn't you hear it?" Aurora replied.

Kars shook his head. Lena just watched.

"You. Squire. Tell them something!" Aurora commanded the machine.

"They are not equipped for non-vocal communication, m'lady," the machine responded.

"Okay. First thing then, enough with the titles: stop calling me m'lady," Aurora said. Her companions watched the half-conversation, wide-eyed.

"As you wish."

"Can you use vocal communication?" she asked.

"Yes," Squire responded aloud.

There was a noticeable release in the tension of the room.

"Go ahead, introduce yourself," she urged the tiny robot.

"Greetings, my name is Squire. I am quite pleased to meet you." Its voice was a musical tenor; there was only a tiny lilt to its annunciation.

Lena and Kars stared at the tiny robot, entranced. It was difficult to feel any menace from it as it flourished like some nobleman dandy. They turned their attention to Aurora.

"Ror, do you feel alright?" Kars asked. "It seems like you're actually . . . augmented."

The word sent Aurora's head spinning again. Augmentations. The neural computers were in her head the whole time? She suddenly felt as though her mind was teeming with insects. Her nervous system itched.

"No. It's not possible. I've never left the mountains." All the facts lined up with one another. She shot a venomous look at her mother. "Did you know?"

"Lannius," Em said low on her breath. "No, I didn't know. Aurora, I'm so sorry."

"Lannius prepared me for the eventuality that there would be mild to significant confusion," Squire said.

"Yes, and . . .?" Kars demanded.

"I was instructed to tell you that your neural computer interface is completely safe. It has been running in a dormant state. More importantly, I was instructed to tell you that if it has been reactivated, we must leave immediately. Lannius left me with a set of coordinates for a rendezvous. Once there, Lannius will meet us with the next steps."

"No!" Em shouted, slamming her fist on the table before her family could respond.

The robot bounced several inches and landed like a ballerina.

Her gaze shifted through the room, full of menace as though she was seeking her axe. "That was not part of the deal! He said he would find Aurora—not steal her!"

Tea dripped off the table edge. Kars looked down at the floor to avoid the fierce stare. The tiny robot seemed un-phased.

"Emilia, Lannius's message is clear: it is imperative for Aurora to leave this place. Immediately." Squire's tenor sounded small as it delivered the message. Em's stare was hot and would have melted anyone caught in it, save for a machine.

"Why? Are they coming? There aren't any global signals out here, just an infiltrator and some panic. I've dealt with worse," Em menaced, crossing her arms and looking at Aurora. "If there is a signal, just tell Lannius to come back here and make this right."

Aurora's mother's defiance. They watched each other in silence before Aurora responded.

"I'm not going," she said.

"Please. I implore you. This is the moment when we must leave. There is great danger," the robot argued in its small, pleasant voice.

"We've fought them before," Em said.

"I don't know," Aurora said. It was an honest answer.

Aurora stared at the parchment from within Lannius's box. The fine lines of the ocean stretched to the imaginary horizon. The village life had seemed too small just that morning. Now she had learned that she was from the cities.

"Maybe I should leave anyway," Aurora said. "I don't know whether I'm meant for life in the valley. Whether I was even meant for it before these things in my brain. How will they treat me now?"

Em looked deflated. "I've tried to give you everything that I could, but I understand. The winters are cold, the fires keep coming, and it's not easy up here."

"That's not it," Aurora said. "It's not about what's here. It's about life. Maybe I'm meant to be in the city. Who knows what's out there."

Her mother gave her a curious look, almost a look of concern, but a glint of pride shone through. "I want you to know, whatever your choice, I love you either way."

It was the most painful response a mother could give. Aurora looked at Kars, then Lena for support. Kars was examining her, and then nodded. She knew his sign: *her move*. It was her choice. Lena smiled and nodded, cautiously eyeing Em.

Aurora was shocked by Lena's message: listen to the robot— leave and head into the world. Aurora's deliberation weighed down the silence.

"I don't think I can face this decision right now. We stay the night," Aurora said. She had to face it: she was too scared to decide. She needed just a little time to be at home and think about what she wanted.

The tiny robot made no reply, operating on whatever instructions Lannius had left for it nearly two decades before. It retracted into a more compact tripod stance, drawing its head toward the core.

"We can figure this out, Ror. Don't worry. Maybe we don't even need to do anything about the machines," Kars said.

With a deep sigh, Em returned to the stove for the kettle to hide wiping a tear from her eye. The small victory of keeping her daughter held back the greater sense of loss imposed by the revelations.

"Thank you, Aurora," Em said. "I don't know what's going to happen with the machines, but I'm glad you're staying. I've kept you safe your whole life; I can keep you safe for another night."

Lena looked at Aurora, then at the artifacts on the table. The tiny robot watched as Lena reached for the scroll. She felt the fine paper in her fingers.

"The wandering sea," Lena read from the scroll, her voice quiet. "If you need to leave, Aurora, I'll go with you."

"Thanks, Lena," Aurora said, although she felt a stab of sadness that her friend was ready to depart.

"That's a decision for tomorrow," Em said, eager to maintain her victory in the decision. "In the meantime, Lena, we should probably go and check on your folks. The whole town is stirred up and I bet they need our help."

"I'm sure my dad got into some trouble after they got the fires out." Lena set the scroll back on the table and stood up.

"Seriously, Lena. Thank you. What you said means the world to me," Aurora said, rising from her seat to give her friend a hug.

"I meant it, Ror," Lena said. "Doesn't change anything. I'll see you in the morning."

Em led Lena out, leaving Kars and Aurora in the kitchen.

"Well, what do you want to do?" Kars asked Aurora, eyeing the robot.

"Everything has changed so much. I'm just not ready to decide. I can't even think." She leaned into her hands, rubbing her temples. She couldn't mention the strange memory—Mirien and Lannius by the lake. "I seem to be someone I didn't know about before. I don't know who I am."

"Ror, don't go there. You know exactly who you are—usually a complete pain. Better than me at everything, but I think we can clear the scorecard, since apparently you've been cheating all our lives." Kars smiled. "We've got this. We were going to get out of here someday anyway, right?"

"Now I don't know if I want to go, Kars."

"You don't have to decide right now. And I'll stick with you through it all. I think we've had enough to call it a day." Kars gave her a rare hug.

"Thanks, Kars," she said, squeezing him, and then headed off to her room.

The tiny robot unfolded and tiptoed behind her.

*   *   *   *   *

Across town, the last embers of a bonfire glowed in the darkness. The people of the valley had settled after the excitement of the day. All the fires had been extinguished, and the pump had been repaired. They were a durable people who had not forgotten their roots in the Rebellion.

They built a bonfire for the infiltrator, as they had learned during the trying years fighting Perpetual. People gathered to watch the chemical flames rise from the pile of scrap, sparks dancing into the night sky. Eventually, the flames grew low and the crowd dispersed.

The burnt shell of the drone smoked in the embers, melted components fused together in a hulk. The glass lenses had cracked and shattered amidst the charcoal. The stubby insect arms had deformed in the heat.

When the final ember blinked out, a single dim light remained, throbbing beneath a layer of fine ash. The beacon pulsed its distress call into the night.

5

Battening Down

Em came back hours after dark. She had helped Lena settle in her parents—poor girl. Lena had a unique curse: the unreliable. Her parents loved her half the time but seemed indifferent to her the other half, lost in the grief for their other children. The fighting had taken so much from Cara, it was a wonder she had anything left to give to Lena. It had broken her father too. She wasn't surprised that Lena wanted to run.

Em's worries had multiplied today, though. The return of the infiltrator, Lannius's robot, the rediscovery of Perpetual's mine, Aurora's augmentations, all might herald more than she could fend off as a mother. Without the Seventy-Seven, she was not certain they could stop more than a handful of Widow tanks. A swarm of fighter drones would require an orchestrated ambush. If they sent a carrier, they would be forced to flee. Hopefully, her kids were old enough to handle it.

She had taken a circuit through Prospector's winding roads, stopping in on a few other people. If the infiltrator was a harbinger, she would need to visit some lieutenants. She carried her shoulders thrown back as she surveyed the town.

Cutter Van Neussen waved from his porch as Em approached. A large shoulder-mounted beam cannon leaned against the wall behind him. The device was matte metal, with a few indicator diodes. A faded logo was stenciled on the side.

"I haven't seen Scarlett since Perpetual retreated," Em said, gesturing to the wicked device behind Cutter.

"Scarlett had a little nap," Cutter said, patting the side of the cannon. The skin of his hand was mottled pink with the scar of an old burn. "Figured I would get her up, just in case."

"Hopefully, she's back in bed without an issue," Em said. She couldn't help but notice the pride in his voice. Although he was gray and wrinkles creased his face, a piece of Cutter longed for the old glory. "Don't forget how much we lost."

"We all remember," Cutter said, the acknowledgment laden with threat.

"Good. Let's hope it doesn't come to anything. Stay sharp, Cutter," Em said, resuming her walk through the town.

"I've tried to keep sharp. There were always a few of us that knew they'd come back for another round," Cutter said. "Training and drills don't seem so silly now."

"I never thought they did," Em said. "I just hope it doesn't come to it. Stay safe, Cutter."

Another friend, Angelique Bellacourt, gingerly trotted out of a side street to talk with Em.

The stout woman had lost her girlish figure since the Rebellion, but she was still a rugged athlete. Angelique was happy enough machining tools, but today she looked more complete. She wore a tactical vest under a leather duster; a long rifle was slung across her back. A broad smile crossed her face when she saw Em.

"Em, I just checked the edge of town. I went ahead and fired up the old perimeter sensors and laid out the traps," Angelique said. It had been part of her duties during the Rebellion to maintain the trip lines against the infiltrators.

"Excellent," Em complimented. "Hopefully, we don't have a reason to use them."

"Just so you know, a few people left town," Angelique said.

Em couldn't blame them for running.

"Who?" Em asked.

"The Skaddens, the Morgans, and a few of the Fells. There might be more," Angelique reported.

Em grunted and responded, "Skaddens and Morgans are no surprise—they've got little ones. I guess the Fells are just feeling like they're too old for another fight. Make sure we get any weapons they might have left behind."

"Aye," Angelique responded before heading back into the night.

Em continued visiting townsfolk as she made her way home. Panic turned to purpose with surprising speed. They pulled old armaments from footlockers and from beneath floorboards. A few other houses were empty, missing essentials and heirlooms.

She finally returned to her own home and slumped into a chair. She allowed her eyes to drift closed.

"Robert," she whispered. "Why did you have to go?"

The current threat of war was one that they had faced together. She squeezed her eyes shut, holding back tears. Loneliness would never truly leave her.

Then she felt it: a subsonic trembling passed through the floor. Her body knew the rumble before the realization formed. She tensed deep in her brain as though some enormous predator had just charged at her family.

"No!" She sprang to her feet, gnashing her teeth. The pictures rattled on the walls, and the windows shivered in their frames.

They were coming.

6

The Raid

Em shoved aside the table and flung the kitchen rug from the floor. She pried back a rectangle of floorboards and produced a long rifle. Flicking a switch, the weapon hummed to life. She ran through the various checks on the device, tossing the strap over her shoulder. She jammed a sidearm into the back of her belt. The old instincts ordered her muscles to act.

She clambered up the stairs, shouting to wake up Aurora and Kars.

Squire waited in the doorway. Em trained her sidearm squarely on the tiny robot.

"Emilia, I detected it as well. They are coming. Allow me to help," Squire offered.

Aurora and Kars were both up, pulling on their clothes. A picture fell from the wall, as the rumble peaked again. Something was circling above the town.

"Help," Em ordered, sliding the pistol back into her belt. "What's out there?"

"One gunship. Lynx class, mixed engine signature. Unidentified ship signal," Squire told her, following as she moved from window to window.

"Seven Protek signals," Squire continued the report.

Protek? Feral machines left over from the last great war. Lannius's regret. Her heart beat faster.

She had heard about them during the Rebellion. A few of the older members of the Seventy-Seven talked about them as fierce killing machines. Humanity's last world war—the Consolidation War—crashed to a close beneath a wave of the terrible autonomous fighters. The sin of young Arthur Lannius. Their invasion had left almost an entire continent uninhabitable. Much like the thermonuclear weapons had done a century before, the savageness of the Protek cooled humanity's collective lust for war, leading to the years of peace before the Rebellion. The vile atrocity of the Protek was what some had warned to be the inevitable outcome of automating war. Now, the Protek and their mechanized cruelty were coming for them.

"Anything else?" Em asked.

"One heavily modified human, shielded and hardened," Squire reported.

"What else? How can you help?"

"I will not be able to break any of the intruders. Any attempt to manipulate them will immediately compromise our position. As before, I recommend leaving immediately." Squire's voice was the same tenor calm.

The vibration now pulsed between overwhelming and unbearable. Em watched out the window in the dark. White floodlights split the darkness, casting a slight back glow onto the ship hovering above—a sleek main hull accented by sharp lines bolted on at odd angles. It swung around in the dark sky.

Em turned. "Aurora. Kars. We need to leave. Grab a bag, let's go!"

Her children spun back into their rooms, rummaging through their closets.

"I'm going for Lena. Wait for me here." She swung her rifle forward. She looked out the window. The battle erupted in the night. Bolts of blue light seared into the armor plating of the craft. A single crimson beam lanced up from the town—Cutter and Scarlett—bursting into a cloud of flame. His first shot lanced off a turret in the darkness. Cutter still had his aim.

Alarms blared. The airship wheeled around in the fiery cloud, unleashing a salvo of its own return fire. Several buildings blossomed into explosions, lighting the night. Em clutched her rifle and opened the door.

"Mom!" Aurora grabbed her shoulder.

"Ror. I'll be right back." Em looked at her daughter. What a gift Lannius had given her. She had grown into a lovely young woman. The woods had made her strong, lean, quick. Hair sun-kissed. She was beautiful. Her eyes were alive, her expression fraught with doubt.

Em hefted her rifle and turned to face the airship circling in the night sky.

"Take care of your brother," Em said, turning out the door to hide her tears. Her broken heart had said goodbye during wartime before. She would not utter the words again.

*   *   *   *   *

Em stepped into a scene from her past. She crouched in a shadow and surveyed the invader. The air shook with the rumble of the engines—quantum effectors from what she could make out in the darkness. Sapphire bolts shot up at the ship, hitting the hull to little effect. Cutter's cannon still fired at intervals, burning an afterimage in Em's vision of the night. Fires glowed through billowing smoke, and explosions echoed through the valley like she was approaching some infernal forge. The god of war had returned.

She darted from their porch to the firewood shed of their neighbors, maintaining cover from the searchlights. She tried to track the airship's movements as she moved between the buildings. *They are trying to land.* Em dashed to her next post, slamming herself against the side of a depot.

Methodically, she moved from shadow to shadow until she reached the Orithian's house. She let herself in the back door. After searching a few rooms, she found Lena huddled with her mother and father. Cara was in hysterics and Ben was barely awake. Lena remained stoic until she saw Em.

The two exchanged a tearful embrace. Lena's arms were as tight as possible.

"We've got to go now!" Em hissed. There was shouting outside, then garbled noises of digital distortion. Em froze. She had never heard such a terrible sound. It could only be the sound of the Protek.

"Now!"

Em led the family out the back, leaning around the corner to scout their position. Ben stumbled along, dragged by Cara. Lena crouched at the rear of their group, watching their flank as they made their way through town. Em didn't recognize her in the firelight. She seemed an older, fiercer reflection of the girl Em knew.

Warbling static burst through and filled the air like a manic hornet. Em tightened her grip on the rifle. The distorted electronic garble grew louder until she heard something like mangled syllables curdled beneath the static.

The Protek stomped around the corner.

Em recoiled, trying to hide. Ben and Cara were caught in the open in front of it. The machine resembled a praying mantis, drawn from the parts of a chrome atomic motorbike. Its head was an armored cowl around a single glowing red ring. Most of its weight rested atop bolted-on repulsors, save for its two articulated insect legs, which jabbed into the ground. Its mantis arms were raised. In all it was nearly eight feet tall by ten feet long. It was the machine that ended a great war and stole a continent—a Protek.

The Protek did not strike. Instead two spotlights flipped up on its armored cowl, bathing them in light. Em momentarily shielded her eyes. The machine was adorned with crude paintings that traced the length of its pincer arms. It slowly menaced forward, driving them back.

"Stay with me, Lena," Em whispered, reaching for the girl's hand. Ben stumbled backward, leaning on his wife.

Time for contingencies. Em slung her rifle to her back, reaching down to the stock. She flipped a hidden inset switch. The ammunition battery light pulsed red, falsely indicating that the weapon was exhausted.

The Protek stomped up to her until it was close enough that she could see the machinery behind the lens of its red-ring eye. It cocked its head, examining. Em exhaled to drive the ripe smell of the scraps of animal skins fixed to its carapace from her nose. She kept her gaze steady despite her fear.

The machine jerked one bladed arm. Em waited for the killing blow, her focus beyond the machine.

The blow never came. The killer machine instead lowered its arm with precision, grasping the barrel of her long rifle in the hinge of its blades. With no effort, it folded the steel barrel in half, rendering her weapon useless. It hung broken across her back. Em exhaled.

The Protek herded them toward where the ship had landed. The area was filled with light from the ship and Protek flood lights. Many of the townsfolk knelt in rows. An armed man strode between the prisoners and the Protek, his assault rifle slung across his arm. He was wrapped in a silk steel flak jacket, his hair a short mohawk. He strutted through his scared captives with manic arrogance.

Firefights rang across the village as some of the townsfolk fought the Protek. Em hated to think how those fights ended. There was no escape. She could not bear to think of these monstrosities near her children.

She spoke to Lena in a low voice.

"Lena, when the time comes run to our house. Tell Ror and Kars to leave. Run wherever the three of you can. Ask the robot where to go—it said that Lannius had left a plan," Em said. "I should have made you leave before."

"We'll make it," Lena said. There was a fire behind the worry in her eyes.

Maybe they would escape. Em squeezed her hand.

Seconds later, they were in the middle of the threatening circle. Protek loomed in the darkness, clicking and making the awful distorted noises to one another.

The manic man strode up and stood too close. The Protek clicked and warbled to each other as he approached. He pulled a deep breath through his nose, drawing in smoke from the fires as though he was smelling a spring bouquet. His eyes feasted on the firelight, sharpening his dark raptor gaze.

He inspected Lena, curling his lip into a snarl. He lifted a lock of her hair and let it fall.

"Wrong," he said.

He was searching for Aurora.

"She's not here," Em said defiantly.

The man twitched his attention like a raptor. His eyes were dark in the glaring lights. He focused intently on Em.

"So you know where she is?" He drew a knife and held it to Lena. Lena shuddered.

"If you think killing her will get me to tell you, you're a bigger idiot than you look," Em said.

The man flourished the knife from Lena's throat to Em's neck, moving from one to the next. "Is that right?" he asked in a low voice.

Em stared into the darkness of his eyes. The knife lingered on her throat.

"Now that's an even better approach. Kill me and I'll definitely tell you," Em said.

The mohawk man glared at her, then looked at Lena. His eyes searched her expression, waiting for some tell that Lena knew where to find his quarry. Em felt a wave of pride as Lena met his gaze with a resolve of indifference.

"If you think you can just fly in here and take my family, you've got another thing coming. I'll end you before you come close to them," Em growled. She swallowed against the knife on her throat. "You're an arrogant little gnat."

The mohawk man leaned in, tilting his head with predatory menace.

"Arrogant? Last I checked, one of us has the knife, the ship, and the machines." He brandished the knife toward the imposing craft behind him. "You? A broken gun and the mean look of someone that doesn't believe they're about to die," he said with a self-satisfied smile. "I think you might need to clear up what you mean by arrogant."

He tore the bent rifle from her shoulder and tossed it away at one of the Protek. The hulking robot remained indifferent, however, something Em carefully slotted away for later reflection.

"A vocabulary lesson from a man that cuts his own hair," Em said, pleased by his rising anger. "Your machines barely even disarmed me. They must be a little tougher than you. I knew Lannius. He left me with a few lessons."

She was buying time, all the same, and likely enough he knew it. Her eyes met Lena's, then Ben and Cara's eyes. She tried to will a thought into their minds: *it's time.*

"Lannius? That old fool? He's long gone." The mohawk man snorted a laugh.

The Protek continued to watch the crowd of humans like hyenas in the night.

Em's chin rose. "Gone? Yes. But, *you* left me with one of his tricks. Arrogant." A bead of sweat rolled from her face to the blade against her neck. She thought of Kars and Aurora.

This was the moment.

Ben catapulted his body forward, toppling the mohawk man backward. The drunk had no skill as a fighter, but he landed on top of the mohawk man, and the two men struggled on the ground. The Protek lunged forward.

Em vaulted toward her rifle on the ground. A Protek arm blade whistled above her head. She slammed the switch on the stock of the ruined rifle, and the magnetic pulse rippled through the area. The ship lights went out and plunged them into darkness. The Protek howled a terrible distorted roar. Any living being knows the sound of pain.

Order disintegrated into the darkness. Sweat-slick bodies collided in the dark as the hostages seized the moment to flee. Em saw shadows of her neighbors against the fires beyond them, faceless participants in a moment pure to the law of tooth and blood. Their shouts mingled with the digital roars of the Protek.

"Lena! Go!" Em yelled at Lena. The girl took off into the darkness.

Em turned, pulling out her sidearm and firing at the nearest Protek. The gun unleashed a whistle-thump as the plasma round left the magnetic barrel. The super-heated shell contacted the core armor of the Protek, knocking it backward into the ship. Another Protek spun its ringed eye on her, bellowing to its fellows.

"How's that for a vocabulary lesson?" Em growled, then sprinted into the darkness.

*   *   *   *   *

Aurora and Kars jammed their packs with provisions. The sounds of weapons firing echoed through the air. Their mother had not returned. Squire was perched in the hallway, providing updates from its scans. Explosions rumbled through the house.

"Squire, can you give us a rundown of an escape?" Kars looked nervous.

"Lannius left me with several contingency orders. Given the circumstance, our probability of success stands with retreating further in the mountains. Lannius's orders show that there is a nonfunctional Perpetual mining site to the northwest. The site lies on a limestone formation that has an underground river passing through it. The mining equipment has been programmed to break into the chamber."

"I think we found that earlier, Squire," Kars said. "The machine broke through the rock wall."

Aurora tried to remain focused, but the continuing realization that the machines detected her was unsettling. The digger must have sensed her and initiated Lannius's old plan.

"Interesting. You must have told it to execute Lannius's plan. However, the fact that the protocol was initiated changes nothing. We should still proceed to the mine site," Squire responded.

As the tiny robot spoke, Lena burst through the backdoor. She switched off the lights, running for them.

"They're coming! Hide!" Lena hissed.

"The Protek will find you. We must either run or fight. Given our current strength, we cannot fight," Squire responded.

"Em and my dad are fighting them!" Lena said.

"What? We've got to help them!" Kars exclaimed.

"I advise against intervening. Em wanted you to leave. She is fighting so we can escape," Squire said. "Also, I detected pulse and plasma signatures. Your mother is formidable and well-armed. It is unlikely she will win, but her effort to delay them could succeed if we leave now."

"But they'll kill her!" Kars responded.

"She would not want you to follow her fate," Squire said.

"It's not an equation!" Kars's look dripped with venom toward the robot. "What if we can make a difference?"

"Kars," Lena said. "I was just there. I barely made it out. If we can make any difference at all, it's by running."

Aurora stared into space. "Maybe I should just surrender? A few hours ago we were debating whether I should leave. Maybe this is how I can help."

"Crazy," Kars said.

"You can't turn yourself in," Lena said, still winded from her sprint. "I just saw them. I don't think they plan on just letting everyone else just walk away. The leader is mad."

"I share the same assessment," Squire said. "Lannius's plans do not project favorably for survivors if you are captured."

"So as long as they don't have me, our people stand a chance to survive," Aurora said. "The best thing we can do then is run."

Kars looked conflicted. The fire in his blood wanted to fight. Lena stood square. Kars didn't make eye contact as he buckled his shoulder straps across his chest and cinched the bag tight to his body.

"Alright, let's go," he said. Squire twirled its limbs back to its original disc confirmation and Aurora dropped it in her own pack . . . Amidst the commotion, Lena folded Lannius's scroll in half and jammed it in her pocket.

Gear strapped to their backs, they paused at the threshold of the door. Lena stood in the yard watching as Kars and Aurora exchanged a pained look.

"I wish it wasn't like this," Kars said.

"We'll make it back," Aurora said. Her expression contorted between grief and guilt. "I should've gone earlier."

Kars had a look of acceptance. "It doesn't matter now. We have to go." He climbed down the stairs of the porch and joined Lena in the yard. Another explosion rumbled through the valley.

Aurora looked through her childhood living room one last time, then stepped outside and closed the door. The three of them left their home and ran into the night.

7

Flight

Em vaulted over a firewood stack and rolled to the edge of a nearby shed. A second later the wood erupted in blue plasma, showering the area in splinters. Em leapt to her feet as a Protek sprung onto the flaming pile of wood. It roared as it stood in the fire. Stinking smoke poured off it as scraps of leather and fur crackled in the flames.

Fine. Let's have it, boys, Em thought, snarling. She pulled a cylindrical grenade from a cache in a log and rolled it from behind her cover.

Each generation of math gives us new weapons—until math itself is the weapon. Lannius's words echoed in her head. The grenade was one of the nastier handheld devices Lannius had left for her, using something like the repulsors to greatly increase absolute zero. Absent of energy, the fundamental forces ceased to function, causing a pocket of space-time to lose recognizable form.

The impact was instantaneous and vicious. The Protek lost an arm to the void. It vanished in a wink of space-time.

The Protek howled a digital cry—not of pain, but to call its pack to the hunt.

If it's a chase you want, then you'll have it, but you've been warned, Em thought. And then she led them on a merry chase.

She darted through the town, leading her pursuers into one trap after another. It was her homeland and she knew how to defend it. Her friends and neighbors hunkered in their houses, leaning out to take shots at the Protek. The ancient fighting machines pressed forward, but the townsfolk were fierce and made them pay with a variety of exotic weapons.

Em sidestepped a gap in Angelique's trip line, whistling as she cleared the space. A double whistled echoed from nearby. She weaved through the smoke and trees between the houses.

The Protek barreled into the trip line, and the razor wire scraped along its metal leg. Tangled in the line, the machine stumbled as a barrel swung down from the trees above, dousing it in fuel. A hidden townsperson lobbed a bottle of grain alcohol with a flaming rag jammed in its mouth. Fire flooded the area, cloaking the machine in flames. The scraps of leather and fur tacked to its carapace sizzled and smoked. Unfazed, the feral machine stomped out of the inferno.

Em ran.

As she turned down a side path, another Protek smashed through a small shed and scrambled into her path. Em shielded herself from splintering boards, but one struck her on the side of her head. Enraged, she shook her head and shot at the intruder with an alternating series of plasma rounds and carbine slugs, mangling its repulsor to slow its movement and continuing her cat-and-mouse chase.

Still engulfed in flame, the killer machine leapt to the roof of a house. The fires surrounding its body growled and popped as it

moved. It followed it with its red-ring eye from above. In one
jerky movement, the machine twisted its arm and fired a super-
adhesive net, pinning her to the ground. Em snarled and
squirmed, which only drew the net tighter.

The two Protek gathered round her, their red-ring eyes seeming
to judge her immobilized form. Em strained to look at them, her
breathing shallow and rapid. The totems strapped on the
machines gave them a rich stink. They clicked and chortled to
each other. The machine conversation grew in intensity until the
ones she had disabled let out a loud buzz and raised its
remaining pincer high in the air above Em.

She held her breath and waited for the blade to fall.

The killing blow never came. Instead the Protek crossed its
pincers arms in front of its body, and dipped its head before
limping away on its broken repulsor.

Another Protek swept forward and scooped her up in a net.

After carrying her back to the ship, the Protek bound her with
the rest of the townsfolk. She watched the mohawk man pace
through the crowd, his impressive armor muddied. A smear of
blood marked his mouth. She glanced around—no sign of Ben or
Cara.

As she waited, the Protek with one arm scuttled up to her. It
towered over her, its single red-ring eye processing her. The
optics around the ring rotated and shifted. At this distance, Em
could see the paintings on the machine were much more
intricate but still imbued with a purity of simple thoughts. The
armor had been adorned with hammered patterns, dimples,
beads, and spikes.

After a moment, the machine abruptly bowed to the knees of its front legs, lowering its head. It crossed the remaining section of its arm with its other arm. Then it rose and walked away. Puzzled, Em watched it depart.

"Load the prisoners," the mohawk man said to the one-armed Protek. "I just got the signal from Korbalak VI. Our quarry is fleeing into the mountains. Masshar, Spiru, come with me. We're going for them ourselves."

The mohawk man climbed onto a motorbike and roared off into the night, accompanied by two Protek.

A knot rose in her throat. She twisted against her bindings, spitting and snarling. She would fight until she knew the kids had escaped.

*   *   *   *   *

Aurora, Kars, and Lena ran along the old road through the darkness. The sounds of the weapons' fire grew distant. The air grew cold in the night.

Finding the cable was much easier with Squire reporting the old schematics. They continued their flight through the brush. Other than questions to the tiny robot, no one spoke. They panted, and their legs burned from running up the mountain just hours after they had run down it. Even the adrenaline of their escape couldn't blunt the fatigue of three trips along the road.

The trio crested the saddle in the hills, looking out on the open space. They knew the camp was below but could make out only the murky outline of the biggest building's metal roof. They descended into the valley.

Aurora was unsure whether it was the effect of night, but the gravel road seemed totally unfamiliar. There was a feeling of menace in the place. They slowed on the road until they heard the sound of an engine in the forest behind them.

"They followed us," Kars whispered.

"Keep going! We've got to get to the cave!" Aurora hissed, ducking low as they hurried down the road.

They reached the central lot as a single headlight and four red, glowing lights emerged onto the road. The five shapes paused for a moment, appearing to search up and down the road. After a brief deliberation, the five lights turned toward the fleeing companions and launched after them.

"Run!" Aurora shouted. Lena and Kars sprinted next to her as they raced into the large warehouse.

Their flashlights sent shadows of the spider-like mining robots into the depths of the warehouse. They slowed in the space, wary of the mining machines lining the aisles. They heard the approaching buzz of the engine like a wasp.

The sound of the motorbike engine suddenly stopped.

"Kill the lights!" Lena hissed. The flashlights went dark, leaving them to slowly pick their way through the inky blackness. Kars shuddered and felt along the outlines of the mining machines with his bare hands, as if he was being forced to touch enormous cave beetles in the dark. The burn on his arm throbbed beneath his jacket.

"Stop where you are, and we'll let your people live!" The mohawk man bellowed. Lena recognized the voice of the man from the ship. She suddenly felt a chill for her parents and Em.

"Have you ever been hunted by Protek before?" the man shouted. Strobe lights on his Protek retinue turned the warehouse space to fragmented confusion. "You better not have anyone with you—I've got all the prisoners I need, and the Protek aren't exactly sentimental!" the shouting man menaced.

Aurora crawled beneath one of the mining machines. Why was he after them? Her heart drummed in her chest. She fought against the vertigo of the strobes to continue crawling beneath another mining machine.

"I've got the whole town on my ship, or what's left of it! Give up and I'll let them go. The rest is up to you!" the manic man shouted again. Aurora, Kars, and Lena continued, trying to silently navigate between the hulking dormant machines.

The Protek swept between the mining equipment. In darkness Kars saw the occasional flash of the red-ring eye pass between mining machines, a fixed-point hovering against the strobing background. The Protek moved like terrible insects in the flashing light.

Aurora saw the broken rock face ahead of them. It glowed purple in the afterimage of the strobes, and the faint sound of running water hissed deep in the gap. Kars held their party back to gauge the locations of their pursuers. One of the Protek was close. It had stopped to investigate the chasm, shining a spotlight into the darkness. The three friends remained still, tucked in the mechanic legs of one of the mining machines.

A spotlight snapped on amidst the strobes. It blinded Aurora.

Kars swore and threw up his hands to shield himself from the light. The mohawk man stood in the lane between machines, a flashlight crossed with a sidearm.

"There you are." His voice softened with relief, as though he had found a missing loved one. The Protek rounded up behind him, adding their own spotlights to the area.

Aurora remained frozen in place. The sudden change of demeanor had served only to put her further on edge.

"You, finally." His voice bordered on bashful as the words awkwardly came forth. "I've looked for you for so long." His light and weapon settled to his sides. He sounded almost gentle, forlorn.

Aurora be very careful. Don't move or respond. It was Squire's voice—but different, like it was one of her own thoughts. *I'm communicating directly with your augmentations. It feels like I am speaking, but it is just a direct neural stimulation. Don't speak, just think about speaking, like you are talking with yourself, but aimed at me.*

Her nerves were linked to the robot's wireless signal. The sounds formed behind her eyes as though she were listening to headphones.

Can you hear me? She thought of vocalizing the words. The manic man tilted his head like a hawk, slowly walking toward her. She did her best to slow her thoughts and focus on the tiny robot in her pack. Aurora felt a moment of relief. They were trapped but she was not alone.

Yes, that is right. I hear you, although technically, receive is more accurate to my native function. But, for the sake of user experience, I will use the term hearing. Squire's voice beamed into her head. The infiltrator from earlier must have tried the same trick.

Squire, focus! she thought, holding back her stream of panic.

She slowly exhaled through her nose. She clenched her jaw as she attempted to stop her knees from shaking. The man had cocked his head, dark eyes intently examining her. She wanted to flee from him, as though he reeked with some depraved sickness she could not understand.

Aurora. This man is heavily modified, Squire reported, *beyond the standard city denizen or even military operator hardware. His amygdala may have been completely overrun with an exotic modification called a compulsion engine. The name may have changed over the years, but the function is the same.*

What is the function? Aurora piped to Squire.

Forced obsession. Squire's report sounded concerned. *Judging by the feedback from other systems in his body, other augmentations are processing toxins associated with sleep deprivation of several weeks.*

At this moment, Squire noted, *the engine is producing extreme levels of oxytocin and dopamine. It's found the target of the obsession.*

He's obsessed with me? She wanted to crawl out of her skin.

Yes, but only because he has been engineered to be. I can't get through to his mind to disable him, Squire responded.

Aurora felt lost in the invisible war the tiny robot was waging from her backpack. The obsessed man slowly approached her, leering as though he was hallucinating. She recoiled.

Aurora, I can't get through to disable him, Squire said. The hollow eyes softened has he smiled at her. It was the terrible emptiness of an unrequited lover.

Suddenly, the right side of the man's face twitched and contorted, and he ticked his head to the side. Moments later, he had resumed his pointed stare.

Aurora. Someone is attempting to assume remote control over him, Squire beamed to her.

Who? Aurora beamed to Squire. *Could it be someone trying to help us?*

I cannot tell. The signal is weak. The mountains are blocking most of it, Squire reported. *I could intercept and jam it.*

Aurora weighed the option. Maybe it was Lannius there to save them? Would the Protek surrender? She shuddered thinking that it could be someone worse. Kars and Lena remained frozen in the spotlights trapped in a confused resignation.

Squire, do you have any idea who it could be? Aurora's thoughts raced.

Decoding pieces of the signal now, Squire said. *There is a self-image stamp on the signal.*

Squire, I don't know what that means! Aurora was frantic.

The image of the sender, Squire responded. *It is Clark Whitestone, the head of Perpetual Corporation.*

Block it! Aurora nearly shouted her thought aloud. She hoped she made the right decision.

It is done, Squire responded.

The mohawk man twitched, but the distant look in his eyes remained. His jaw was near slack, his higher functions overwhelmed by the ecstatic cocktail of neurochemicals flooding his mind.

He mumbled, reaching out. "Please"—it was a plea—"I just need to know your name."

She pulled back. Kars and Lena remained still, held back by the menacing Protek.

"I have a name. They call me Jackal." He frowned. "I had another name once, maybe two. They made me give those up. If I could just know yours, it would make mine seem a little better."

Aurora felt a pang of sympathy for him. He was twisted and scrambled by the equipment grafted onto his mind.

The Protek seemed to detect something amiss. Their leader was acting erratic. The three hulking robots started scanning nearby as though flushing out the ruse.

"No? You won't tell me?" Jackal asked. "That's okay. We have plenty of time. Masshar, take her friends back to the ship. I'll bring her myself."

The war robots obliged, moving into the space to retrieve Kars and Lena. They both attempted to resist, squirming away from the articulated gripping hands positioned at the tips of the cutting arms.

"Leave them alone!" Aurora yelled, attempting to command her captor.

"Why should I do what you say? You won't tell me your name!" His voice gently mocked her. Kars and Lena were out from cover now.

"Jackal, stop this now!" Aurora said. Her fear burst through her consciousness. It flooded her with confusion, breaking her own defenses. She felt everything spiral beyond her control.

I know your name now, Aurora. Tee hee hee . . . It was Jackal's voice taunting, but he didn't speak. He had reached into her mind. There was warmth to his thoughts, as though he had finally earned the attention of his long-lost love.

Aurora, he's found a way around the shielding, Squire chirped.

Jackal's invasion was the worst, most violating experience she could have imagined. The knot of emotions lurked at the edge of her mind, like she had awakened with a stranger quietly sitting in the shadows of her bedroom while she slept.

You had a little helper to keep me out? Jackal's voice rang in her mind as he noticed Squire's presence. His voice felt almost as if he was hurt that she did not reciprocate his affection. *I'm not that bad! I know I've been a little forceful, but I think we could get over it. I've thought about you for a long time.*

She lunged forward, screaming. Jackal grabbed her wrist, tossing her aside. He gestured to the Protek to hold their position.

"It's okay, boys, I've got her." Jackal's sneer had a victorious lucidity after the ecstatic haze.

The Protek loomed over them, ringed eyes focused on the exchange. Their armored carapaces remained lock-still. Kars threw himself against the machines' grasp, trying to kick Jackal.

Jackal grinned as though he wanted the younger man to break through.

Aurora, I'm fighting him wherever I can. I need your help, Squire piped into her head.

But Aurora collapsed to the gravel floor, kneeling, hair hanging in front of her face, paralyzed with the combination of fear and the nervous system blocks imposed by Jackal. She tried lashing out through the augmentations as she had been able to do to reach Squire, but Jackal seemed immune.

"Masshar, Korbalak VI, we've got what we needed. Kill the other two," Jackal said, and the Protek moved to oblige. One unfolded its razor-killing arm.

"No!" Aurora shouted between lockjaw teeth. She couldn't bear it.

A memory of understanding then bloomed inside of her mind. The trap had been set years before, but not for her. Lannius had built the trap . . . and she had led Jackal into its jaws. It was why the valley was sealed, why the mining machines had not been destroyed. The floating points of light suddenly seemed to fill the space.

In a flail of emotion, she reached her thoughts out to the room around her.

Everything seemed to stop. The neural modifications created a native awareness of all the machines near her—floating symbols like those she had seen earlier. The glyphs glowed like starlight in the darkness, indigo snowflakes hanging in space. Each symbol was simple, but if she directed her attention to it, the layers unfolded, fractal mandalas filling her awareness. Seeing the symbols wink into existence filled her with a warm nostalgia. The connection was a lost second nature.

She sensed Squire with her. The mining machines each floated through her consciousness with simple signals indicating a dormant state. They were waiting for her command. She looked at the Protek, but their symbols were alien, incomprehensible, hostile, and thorny. Her mind recoiled. Jackal's mind too, had a signature of its own, a symbolic thread in her consciousness indicating its link to her. It was like a chain of living silver stretched through the void.

All of it—the mining machines, Squire, the Protek, the vile connection to Jackal—hung in perfect focus. Aurora's rage burst.

She knocked the silver thread aside in a fury. A shock of pain bloomed in Jackal's head.

The Protek raised its arm in slow deliberation. Kars's panic writhed across his face. Lena let out a cry in dilated time. Aurora's fury continued to expand like fire, reaching out to the symbols of the dormant machines. She screamed.

The mining machines roared to life. Mounted spotlights flooded the room. Electric motors whirred on sequentially until the warehouse was overwhelmed with the sound. The front arm of a mining machine swatted away the closest Protek, sending the machine sailing into the darkness. Another smaller arachnid machine launched itself onto the back of a second Protek. The two machines locked in combat. The Protek handily tore the arms from the mining machine before another machine took its place.

Jackal shouted. He tried to force his presence into her mind again, doubling his efforts, but he was no match for her. Aurora imagined stomping the invader's silver tendril into the earth, pummeling him with her fists. Her rage grew, and she tightened her focus. The mining machines lunged forward. A look of utter surprise flashed on Jackal's face. Jackal fired his weapon before falling back and circling with the Protek.

Somewhere, Squire's distant presence tried to calm her, but she was too full of the power of the machines to care. Lena and Kars stumbled backward from where the Protek had stood. Horrified, they watched the battle intensify as they ran for the makeshift cover of the wall.

"Aurora!" Kars shouted over the maelstrom.

Aurora maintained her lone stance amidst the swirl of mechanical legs, focusing the storm of activity around Jackal and the Protek. She looked at her two friends; the expression on her face was distant. Recognition washed over her, and she seemed to return to the moment. She collapsed.

Jackal and the Protek fought mightily, stranded in a sea of writhing spider mining machines.

Kars and Lena ran to Aurora, shielding her and shaking her.

"Lena, we've got to get her out of here!" Kars yelled.

"Squire? Are you there?" Lena yelled over the din of the machine battle that filled the room.

Squire's voice was muffled within Aurora's pack. "Yes, Lena. I am here. Aurora called on the miners."

"We need to leave, Squire! Should we take the cave? Will they follow us?"

"Yes, the cave. I will make sure that they do not follow us. Go now!" Squire ordered.

Kars and Lena did their best to hoist Aurora from the ground. The three companions stayed low of the melee, making their way to the broken rock face. They clambered down to the edge of the dark opening. The faint sound of running water from earlier could not be heard over the battle raging in the warehouse. Below them lay the cold darkness of the earth. Light had never breached this chasm; there would be no plants or animals in its depths.

"Is it safe?" Kars asked Squire over the crash of the battle.

"The geographic survey shows the river is sufficiently deep at this point, and that we will survive a jump from this height. Although, I would not recommend a belly flop."

Kars and Lena looked at each other, their arms crossed over the Aurora's shoulders. Spotlights lanced through the room, and the ground shook as the machine battle raged behind them.

"Well, no choice. Let's do it," Lena said.

Kars smiled and squeezed her hand. "Here goes nothing."

They leapt off the edge of the chasm into the darkness of the cave.

8

Whitestone

The hologram of Whitestone materialized in the center of the ship's command deck. Jackal tried to avoid cringing. An appearance in this form meant Whitestone wanted the Protek to know the message as well. Doubts in leadership could prove dangerous with the Protek. Their allegiance to Jackal was tenuous at best, even before what had happened with the mining machines. The Protek stood like sentinels at the perimeter of the room.

It seemed now he was on notice.

Clark Whitestone appeared as an ominous apparition in the command module of the ship. His hair had an expensive designer cut, flecked with gray to the wing tips above his ears. He was handsome, his chin a rugged edge to his face. A tiny nine-pointed bronze star tacked his lapel. Then there was the feature most remembered by the few who actually met him— the amber glow of his artificial irises.

"Explain yourself."

The only words Whitestone uttered without introduction. His voice was a half-interested baritone. A lupine smile crossed his face.

"She got away. We ran into complications. Lannius left a robot for her and we walked into a trap." Trap was an understatement. The warehouse had been a box canyon. She fled with two others into a cave river system. Jackal tried to reach her, but machines pulled him back and he fought to keep from being crushed. Others swarmed the stone face of the mountain and started filling it with rock. They sacrificed themselves to form a plug of metal and stone, barring his path to Aurora. The swarm of mining machines forced him and his Protek from the warehouse before bringing the structure down on top of themselves.

"You were arrogant, Jackal," Whitestone said.

Jackal wondered if Whitestone had trawled his memory for the interaction with Emilia Koren. He picked his next action carefully, dropping to one knee and touching his forehead. The display of humility might save him from a Protek mutiny.

Whitestone watched, sniffed the air in the display. He looked bored.

"Get up," Whitestone muttered.

"Thank you, sir. We will find her," Jackal said.

Jackal attempted to find the geologic records once they had escaped from the mining camp, but his attempt at access triggered a series of service attacks on his systems; then the records were gone. Lannius was thorough in planning his moves.

"No. Return to the desert with your prisoners. They will prove a useful," Whitestone said. The Amurtan pin made more sense—

return to his ruined homeland. The words stabbed at Jackal, the compulsion engine would hurt him until he could find her again.

"But, sir, they must be nearby." Jackal tried to make it sound as though he was not pleading.

"We've flushed our quarry from her hiding place. As you must have realized, pursuit is walking into trap after trap. Lannius will have arranged plot within plot to destroy us in pursuit. They are on the run now; they will stumble into our path. Lannius is two decades older. His sway in the world has nearly vanished. His Seventy-Seven are scattered and broken. Hiding the girl was his only choice, and now that choice is no more. Do as I say— return to the desert and wait." Whitestone's tone was deliberate and menacing.

"Yes, sir," Jackal responded. "We will return to the desert with the prisoners. We will repair and await your command."

The hologram of Whitestone flickered out of the room.

*   *   *   *   *

Clark Whitestone settled back into his executive chair. A compulsion engine was a useful tool, but it certainly came with a cost to the quality of Jackal's decisions. He had not foreseen Lannius finding a way to override him by commandeering the broken brain of his henchman.

Still, they had found her.

He suspended his augmentations' intuitive notifications and stood up from his desk. He walked to the window of his office.

Whitestone surveyed the city below through the floor-to-ceiling panel glass. Only a few extruder cranes floated above the city, as the Board had made the decision to limit growth on the island. Unlike the sprawling megalopolises growing like fungus, the Special Trade Zone Ville-Margot, the "STZ," remained within the tight confines of the island. Perpetual's urban planning unit kept the island pristine. Engineers and visionaries bustled far below, the lucky few who made it through the sorting of the STZ immigration process. From his pinnacle vantage point, Whitestone watched a trumpeter hornbill rise from the jungle canopy of the corporate campus city. It took several slow majestic flaps of its great wings before gliding to one of the intensive green roofs of a research complex.

Mr. Whitestone, representatives from Mosaic Corporation are waiting in the atrium, his assistant notified him.

Mosaic. He had no desire to speak to them at this moment. They had finally found the girl. Mosaic and the dull politics of the super-ultra corporations were insignificant in comparison.

Cancel it, he sent the command to his assistant. He continued staring out across the STZ far below. People milled along the paths, and monorails swept in and out of the rainforest canopy.

The building sent the camera footage from forty stories below into Whitestone's mind. One of his managers conveyed apologies about the cancellation to the other corporation's representative.

The Mosaic representative was a tall, severe looking woman. Her hair was stylish and short, her suit designed and tailored. As the woman received the news of his sudden cancellation, she beamed with a most gracious smile and thanked the manager for their time. It was a calculated choice.

The door to his office burst open—as he had known it would as soon as he gave the order to dismiss the rival corporate representative.

"Clark!" It was his Chief Operating Officer, Cormant Verone. "Mosaic and the other corporations will not take this slight lightly."

"Don't be such a stooge for the Board, Cormant. Let them panic until they realize what's really going on. Mosaic just came here to show off," Whitestone said. He stored the face of Mosaic's woman in his mind, tagging her as a Node. "The whole reason they came today was to show me that they have Nodes of their own. I knew that they would bring them sooner or later. I already tasked some lower constructs with finding Mosaic's slavemind hive. They are tracing the representative's signal now."

Whitestone had harbored the secret desire to see his opposition send a Node against him. People sometimes referred to the next stage in human development as one mind tethered to many, parallel processing brains, unlimited potential—all audacious claims that stoked Whitestone's desire to test them. Despite their genetic tailoring and the swarm of slaveminds networked to them, the Nodes were still just people.

"You know the Board is still sensitive when we are dealing with any of the Great Companies," the stout man responded. "They came to coordinate efforts to capture the resistance leader Damien Durn."

"Don't call him that, you sound like a fool," Whitestone said.

"What would you prefer?"

"Anything else—we all know Durn has been dead for decades. He's not leading a resistance," Whitestone said.

"Some people claim he rose from the dead. Maybe that Durn is dead, but this one leads, speaks, travels, writes—people even say he fights," Cormant said. "The people believe in him. If we're not careful, we could be facing another religion."

"It's not an incantation, Cormant. It's the name of a dusty activist philosopher from before the Protek," Whitestone said. "Pseudonyms are just anonymous faces for a constellated belief. We're past the point of saturation with the networks. The technological soul is the dominant being. The resistance even knows they've already lost. There's only a handful of backwater communities and militias beyond the collective control of the Companies and the military AIs."

"Perhaps that is true," Cormant said. "But it does not negate that Durn, whoever it is, continues to undermine our work. We should stop him before he claims the imagination of any more people."

"Whoever he is, Mosaic operatives will corner him in Mark City. Not our concern." Whitestone stared at Varone with his sharp amber eyes. "Now Cormant, I have more pressing matters on my mind and I need space to think. I have to prepare for the fundraiser this evening."

Cormant looked as though he wanted to respond, but he held his tongue and left the office.

Whitestone resumed his distant gaze out the window. Jackal found the girl. Finally, they could move forward. His reflection came into focus in the glass. The amber eyes looked back at him. Everything he saw was suddenly data. Though it remained the same perfect image, he knew it was nothing more than an impulse, wavelengths striking sensors to be translated into some fountain of information he could decode into sensation. The hollowness welled up again.

He turned away from the window and walked to a wall at the back of his office. He sent the command to the door, and the wall slid open. He stepped into the sanctum of his study.

The room was more confined and softer than the stark lines of his main office. Tension fell from his shoulders as he crossed the doorway. The walls were lined with shelves and stacked with artifacts of his life. The door slid closed behind him.

Durn. Cormant thought Durn was an affront to the other corporations. Whitestone knew better. He touched the worn spine of a book on a shelf. The leather was creased from the efforts of heavy use. *Soul, War, and the Machine.* The gold letters of the author's name had flaked but he could still read them: *Durn.* The name was a pseudonym resurrected from history, loaded and aimed to strike at *him*—not Perpetual, not Mosaic. Damien Durn was a reminder of Whitestone's missing pieces.

He passed through the other relics of his life, but his attention drew him to one object in particular. The round medal was set in a case, its burnished gold surface warm in the soft light of the room. He reached out and felt the embossed surface, the tiny figure of some ancient goddess pressed in the metal. The Rose Prize for Humanity.

His eyes were drawn to the picture next to the medal. He and Lannius stood behind podium, their explosive smiles dominated the frame. There was so much care radiating from the moment trapped in the frame. He barely recognized the smile on his face as he accepted the prize.

94

Whitestone turned from the picture.

With a thought that rippled as disgust across his face, he suspended all of his augmentations. He raised his hands to his face, turning his thumbs on his eyelids. A sharp ache blossomed as he pressed on his eyes to turn off the implants. He was plunged into darkness.

*   *   *   *   *

Em and the rest of the townsfolk were loaded into cells in the belly of the ship. Protek prodded them forward with the blunt edges of their lethal pincers. They remained for some time, the delay feeding her hope her children had escaped. The longer it took, the better. The air grew stale and hot in the cramped quarters.

It was difficult to gauge how long they had been in the craft during their wait for takeoff. Em could hear the muted conversations of other townsfolk. A few sobs punctuated the quiet. The Protek had taken every possession. After Em showed them the potential for the town to fight back, the killer machines left them with only their clothes. Occasionally, a Protek would lumber through the hallway or one of the small Protek would loop through to check on them.

Time crawled by until the ship rumbled to life. Cool air gushed into the prison quarters. Although the air carried the faint smell of ozone, it provided some relief from the smothering warmth that pooled during the wait. Em breathed a sign of a different sort of relief. If they were prisoners, then they still had value. For them to have value, the hunt for her daughter must still be underway. She smiled and laughed to herself.

In light of the possibility, wherever she was going did not matter to her—the mohawk man had failed to seize her children. She could wait and bide her time. She would show the mohawk man his arrogance again in leaving her alive. She squeezed her fist until her knuckles were white and her nails bit into the heel of her hand.

Angelique sat in the corner of a cell across the hall. Her jacket had been torn along the shoulder. She leaned back against the wall, her head tilted upward with her eyes closed. Em sensed a deep satisfaction in her friend.

Em saw that common expression of pride lurking behind the dejection and sorrow of many of her comrades. Struggle was a part of their identity—against the elements, against Perpetual, against the world. Jackal thought he had a vessel full of prisoners; he had struck a hornet's nest, then bottled them up and filled his ship with them. Em knew Angelique was fantasizing about her next strike. They all were.

Sitting in her cell, Em settled in for the journey they faced. No matter where the airship set down, the endpoint would be hostile. She stared across her chamber, patient determination set her jaw like concrete. The time would come. She leaned back against the wall and closed her eyes. The ship pitched upward on a trajectory to a destination unknown.

9

Flight from the Hourglass

Arthur Lannius urged his steed over the abandoned highway. Thunder rumbled through the air of the starless night. He cradled the precious child in a sling beneath the edge of the cloak, holding the reins of his horse with his free hand. Disgraced and forced into the flight of exile was the last place he had thought his long life would end.

The boom of artillery explosions vibrated through his chest and a tight formation of vicious aircrafts roared through the darkness above toward the castle on the cliff. He whispered thanks for the relative stealth of horseback. The echoes of gunfire rolled up from his flank. He slipped through the night, as the fighting he left behind intensified.

Wind whipped at him, cool and fresh off the ocean. He left his horse to choose the path in the dark. The rain had not yet started. The path curved out along the contour of the hill, and he paused to look back. Lannius silenced his rising sadness, knowing his comrades had remained. He frowned looking back on his origin.

The horizon of the ocean vanished into dark clouds, but he could see the shoreline drawn in darkness. There, perched on the edge of the ocean cliffs, sat his origin: the Hourglass. He would never spend another evening in the halls of that bastion, never share another conversation with his friends overlooking the sea, never again wander the grounds. Perhaps that was the fate of great castles—inevitably they must fall. This iteration of the castle Hourglass was unfinished, just a scaffold of the citadel they would have built in another future. It would grow into something else over time.

He pushed back the edge of his cloak, looking down into the sling across his chest. Even in the gloom of the evening, he could see the tiny face looking up at him, her wide searching eyes taking in his face. Despite their circumstance, she remained serene and quiet. He smiled and wondered if she knew.

The roar of artillery split the night sky, and the baby's eyes widened, and her face filled with anxiety. He drew the cloak back over her and turned to see the conflict unfold. Emilia and Robert would raise the girl outside the reach of all of this chaos.

Flares arced up from the castle, illuminating the surrounding area. Stealth aircraft hovered at the edge of the glow as spotlights snapped on, facing away from the complex. The castles anti-aircraft defenses belched flame and pulsed staccato rounds toward the sky. Flak burst in response, thundering in the sky. Within moments, the area was a smoke-shrouded cloud, lit by flashes from the conflict and the unnatural red phosphorous glow of the flare. Shadows stomped through the haze, bipedal armor marching in from the surroundings. Allowing himself a moment for grief to slip over him, he wiped away a tear. He pushed his horse to a gallop down the darkened path.

Lannius rode through the night, his horse taking him deep into the hills away from the conflict. The child in his cloak was pressed into his side, at peace despite the circumstances. They rode through darkness until the gray of morning began to fill the sky. He led the horse off the old highway path toward the remnants of a ramshackle barn.

Six figures emerged from the darkness, shrouded in cloaks of their own. Lannius raised a hand to greet them. It was a grizzled group of four men and two women. Some carried rifles, while others were strapped with holstered sidearms. They were some of his closest lieutenants, and they waited for him to speak. He pushed back his hood, revealing his white hair and beard. His eyes were bright despite his fatigue and sorrow.

"The Hourglass has fallen," he said gravely. The figures nodded, resigned to the knowledge.

"Did any others escape?" It was Kip Henringer.

"They sacrificed themselves so I could escape with the child," Lannius said. "And stayed with James to protect Anna. Rahm and Whitestone will assume I remained to help protect them. They will hold them there as long as possible."

"Arthur, there were only eighty-five of us that made it out of the cities in the first place. If we lost another eight"—Kip's voice trailed off as he stroked his beard—"then there's seventy-seven of us." The brash voice came from a younger woman, Silvia Glass. Her short-cropped hair showed from beneath her half-drawn hood.

Kip said nothing, only ran his hand through his beard and stared into the space of the barn. Whether they were seventy-seven or seven thousand, the odds and the consequences of capture would be the same.

"I regret I do not have better news," Lannius said. "However, we must honor their sacrifice. We continue with the plan. Say your goodbyes and ride. The memories I embedded in your minds will remember once we are away from one another, providing you each with your individual rendezvous point."

Lannius dismounted to change horses. Two of his lieutenants brought forth a fresh mount and helped him climb into its saddle. A shorthaired woman passed the child to him and he carefully tucked the baby back into the sling. They slung hunter green Faraday cloaks over their horses to hide their heat and signals. The fabric shimmered in the half-light. The other lieutenants shared hugs and quiet words. The eager warhorses snorted and stomped the ground.

The entire party folded their hoods, forming up into an indistinguishable group of anonymous hooded figures.

He raised his hand. "Thank you all for your loyalty. Be safe friends."

The group surged forward, galloping out of the barn. They rode fast and hard with individuals peeling away at different intervals. Those riders would meet with other groups that would in turn peel away and meet with other riders.

They fanned out through the countryside, avoiding the burgeoning megacities and the trade lines. Lannius continued, riding through days and nights trying to get as far he could from the fallen castle. They rode deeper into the mountains and the wilderness. He hoped everything they had taken from the child would return, that she would find new wholeness in life away from the networks and the cities, tucked away at the end of the road. He hoped that somewhere in the future he saw behind the tiny eyes, there was peace and that she would live a long full life.

They rode deep into the wilderness and vanished from the memory of the world.

10

Learning to Wake

Lena huddled with Aurora on the shore of the underground lake. Her friend was still unconscious. They had crawled up on a flat rock and now shivered in the chill cave air. No dry clothes remained; Lena was doing her best to warm her unconscious friend with rung out clothes from their packs and her own body heat. Their lantern did little to push back the darkness above. The ceiling of the chamber might as well have been the night sky.

Squire instructed the rampaging mining machines to seal the hole. It felt as though they had slipped through a tear into some pocket universe and emerged in a realm of darkness. The panic of the machine attack had been replaced by the more ominous realization that they were at the mercy of the cave. As Aurora had shown with her display of control of the mining machines, machines could be programmed, people reasoned with, and animals tamed. Nature was unreasonable and uncaring. The cave was an elemental space of earth and water.

Kars had taken Squire to find the remnants of the mining machine that had fallen into the lake. He carried another electric lantern, and Squire's diodes glowed with a surprising amount of light.

They followed the smooth shoreline, hoping that the first machine was still active from Aurora's signal earlier that day. Squire reported that the chassis used in mining had a wide threshold for operation in extreme conditions and speculated that the machine could withstand at least a day fully submerged. They had decided that it would be a good use of time to try to find it.

As they walked the shoreline, Kars spoke with Squire.

"Squire, how did Lannius expect us to get out of here? We're cold and wet with no supplies."

"This was not Lannius's first choice. It would be reasonable to call this plan the plan of last resort, based on the probability of success."

"Probability?"

"Our current plan was the lowest probability at five percent success."

"I don't think I wanted to know that actually. But what's that based on anyway?"

"Every future is a probability—some more likely than others. The success of endeavors varies on the inputs—the people, circumstances, the precise timing. No future is guaranteed. Anything could push an outcome to success or failure."

"Failure, you mean death?" Kars asked, his mind drifting to the fate of his father and the potential fate of his mother. Deep in the cave, his own death loomed over him like the dark above.

"Premature death would be a failure of sorts, although death seems a certainty for living beings. To call death failure would be a reduction of the process of life."

"Fine," Kars yielded to the robot. He was baffled why Lannius would have bothered programming his machine to carry on about life and death and fate. "Why do you care about it anyway? You're just a machine."

"I am a machine," Squire responded. "And to answer your question: I do not care. I would tell you I care if I was programmed to tell you."

"Good to know." Kars shrugged, unnerved by the answer. It was efficient and honest after the tiny robot's philosophical musing. He felt sharply aware that he was part of the program—inputs— for Squire's outputs, but it felt like a conversation.

He shined his light into the water. The lake took on a sapphire glow beneath its rippled surface. Despite being disturbed by rocks from the fallen ceiling of the cave, the bottom had a turquoise patina. The water carried the light across to the other edge of the lake, radiating the rippling light into the chamber. The sound of running water softened the otherwise cold silence of the cave. The cold and fear left him for a moment as the serene beauty took hold.

"Squire," he said, his voice quiet, "what about beauty? Do you care about beauty?"

"Beauty is an aesthetic. I could tell you about it." Squire's tenor voice sounded small in the cave chamber.

"That's okay. I just wondered if you could see it," Kars said.

"No. While I can see—much more than you—beauty requires understanding. I do not understand anything, in actuality," Squire said.

Kars suddenly felt pity for the tiny machine. An infinitesimal stirring in the air rippled across the lake, sending the light dancing across the chamber.

"Well friend, I can see this for you," Kars said, "and it is beautiful."

Kars breathed in the cool air, smiling at the tiny robot. They were silent for a time.

*   *   *   *   *

Squire's report broke the silence. It had received a signal from the distress beacon on the disabled machine.

"Kars, I just received the signal transmitting from the emergency beacon on the machine. I am responding now."

"Good. If it runs, maybe Aurora can control it." Kars was satisfied, bringing himself back from his meditations on the lake. He watched the depths.

"I am sending start commands to the machine," Squire said.

The water remained still; then the water trembled with a slight movement in the rocks deep in the lake. The rocks rolled aside, and a beam of light cut from beneath. More rocks rolled in the clouds of turbulence until the water was too disturbed to see what was happening beneath.

Moments later, the machine plodded out of the roiling water, a wave crashing on the shore in its wake. Kars and Squire stood at the edge of the lake as the machine emerged like a behemoth crustacean. It moved in jarring steps as though it was springing forth from a cuckoo clock. It came to a halt on the rock shore, water streaming off its metal carapace. The collapse and fall through the opening had left the machine scuffed and dented.

"I ordered it to come to us, but assuming direct control may prove difficult for me. I can issue orders, but mirroring my processes to it is beyond my capacity," Squire told Kars.

"Aurora ran the ones up there." Kars nodded to the vault of the cave ceiling. "Maybe she's back up now. We got what we were looking for, so let's get this thing back over there."

"We should be able to use its defrosters to provide some warmth. I am sending commands now," Squire said.

"Good, at least buy a couple days in this pit," Kars responded.

At Squire's command, the massive machine turned and walked down the rock shore. It continued its stomping awkward gait, different from the fluid movements they had made when Aurora controlled them during the fight with the Protek.

Lena yelled as they approached. She still cradled Aurora, who looked pale, cold, and damp. "Kars? Thank goodness you found it. I think she's getting hypothermic."

When the machine stopped near her, she looked uneasy but did not recoil. The spotlights and the hum of its motors were a welcome change to the devouring quiet of the cave.

"Squire said the machine could run some heaters," Kars said, crossing his arms and fighting back a shiver.

The machine planted its front two scooping grinder arms and lowered its main body. The spotlights at the shoulder joints shined down on Aurora and Lena. The defrosting fans spun awake. Warm air poured out of the machine over them.

Kars plopped down. "Now we're talking!" he said, rubbing his hands together. He placed the backs of his hands on Aurora's cheeks. Her skin was clammy.

"Do you think she's going to be alright?" Lena asked.

"I hope so. It's been a big day for all of us, but particularly for Ror. Whatever happened up there was something new, something from the computers in her head."

"She has gone into a state of protective shutdown," Squire said. "Her mind is active but has sealed itself off from any inputs."

"When will she come out of it?" Lena asked. The defroster fan blew a strand of damp hair from her face.

"I cannot say. The system will repair itself and she will wake."

Kars frowned at his unconscious sister.

"We're going to need to leave soon. Who knows if they are trying to get through right now." Their pursuer would breach the blockade. Soon they would have to attempt moving through the cave.

"I did not make it easy for them. If they survived the miners, it will take them almost a day to get the equipment to get through. I recommend resting. Warm up and give Aurora time to recover. Based on the geologic survey, we can use the miner to follow the river out," Squire said.

Kars had heard stories about spelunkers—insane people—disappearing in caves. It was not an environment in which he ever wanted to travel. Without the machine, he and Lena would have to carry Aurora as they traversed the cave. Even the idea of the task felt impossible. If they could not wake Aurora and use the machine—he kept his thoughts from the conclusion.

"Kars, I don't think we could even get her down river right now if we tried. Let's rest," Lena said, seeming to be in his thoughts. She touched his arm as she spoke. "I'm exhausted. You've got to be too. Hiking that trail three times was enough. My legs are on fire. We should rest."

He agreed. The extra clothes he brought were already piled on Aurora, so he rolled up his pack into a makeshift pillow and stretched out next to the two girls. The warm breeze of the defroster was starting to radiate into the rock, and the steady whir of the engine blanked out his senses. It was soothing being in the shadow of the huge machine in the belly of the mountain. He tried to remember the morning, but it seemed an echo from a different age. Sleep came heavy like the clouds that chase the sunset.

*　　*　　*　　*　　*

Aurora awoke on a black leather chaise on the roof deck. The castle deck looked out over the rough western ocean. Waves pounded against the rock cliff far below. The sunset afterglow rimmed the horizon.

"Aurora, how are you feeling? You had quite a fall," a man said from nearby. He sat a table nearby, reading a tablet. He was tan and handsome.

"A fall?" Aurora took in her surroundings.

108

"Yes, a fall. You've been unconscious for a long time. I've been keeping track of you, but you might need some help getting back up." He set down the tablet and walked toward her.

"I . . . where am I?" Aurora asked.

"In time. For now, you need to remember how to remember, remember how to think." He offered her a hand, which she accepted, standing up. They walked a few steps to the railing at the edge of the deck. The ocean breeze pushed her hair back.

"Slowly now," the man said.

She stared out on the horizon. Conflict rose in her as she gazed on the endless surface. She had never seen the ocean. But she felt she had also lived on the ocean.

"I am not awake, am I?" she asked.

"No," he responded.

"Where am I?" she asked, still staring at the sea.

"Aurora, your mind brought you here to heal. Your body is somewhere else."

She accepted the fact. It was a place, but she did not know where. She tried to think back, but there was no memory—no memory at all. She needed to remember how to remember. Her consciousness floated in the moment.

"Can I get back?" she asked.

"I assume there is a way. But, you'll need to find it," he said.

"Can you teach me?"

"That is why you've brought me here."

"Please help me," she said. The ocean crashed below.

The man smiled. "There will be lessons. You already learned one."

Her no-memory remained empty. Had she learned something?

"Yes." He nodded. "Two lessons in merely waking to this place: being and the world. First, when you sat up, you awoke to being—that first primordial state that allows one to make sense of things—to understand. In finding yourself here, you learned the second: you are a being in the world, situated to understand it and the things that happen or could happen."

"Why are these lessons?" she asked.

"The quest for intelligence must begin with understanding. A computer on its own cannot understand without being."

"I am not a computer," she said.

"No, you are not. But a computer brought you here."

Awareness of the lattice of the neural computer returned to her mind.

"Why did it bring me here?"

"It did as it was programmed to do. Confronted with life-threatening damage, the computer induced a protective dream state. The rest of the 'why' is part of you. The computer does not understand this 'here' more than it understands anything else." *The man's tone was patient.*

"What's the purpose of the dream state, then?"

"The same as the dream state has done for all of human history—to help the mind make sense of itself." He gestured to an object down the deck. They walked toward it.

As she approached, she could see it was a small tree, waist high, and growing out of the granite surface. The tree had a single bud nestled in its upper leaves. Instinctually, she reached out to touch it, but as her fingers came close the bud moved further away. No matter where she reached, she could not put her hands on it. She watched as her hands turned to lead, a hammer appearing to replace her fingers.

He watched her struggle.

"You won't be able to touch it that way. I am here as a guide, but I can only tell so much. The lesson we need to return to your body stands right in front of you."

Her metal hands did not feel out of place, yet she longed to reach the bud.

"Are you part of the computer?" she asked him.

"No. You brought me here, part of you that needed a symbol to speak to you. I am a part of you."

"Is the tree part of the computer?"

"The tree grows from stone, yet it is alive. It is not part of the computer."

She looked at her metal hands. The computer.

"Now you see," he said. "Part of you, but not alive. A tool, but it cannot touch life. You are not the computer, despite being inextricably bound to the machine. Whatever it tells your mind, you must maintain your being."

Her hands returned to slender flesh, and the blossom opened. Aurora stared at it in amazement. Nestled within the petals was a brilliant crystal. She reached out and the flower did not retreat.

The crystal shattered as she touched it, obliterated into dust. The flower vanished.

"Lessons for another time," he said.

*   *   *   *   *

Aurora awoke with her head resting on Lena, hard rock beneath her. The sound of a motor and a warm breeze filled the air. It was bright all around. She sat up, disoriented. Some part of the dream remained with her, and it lingered as deep resonant fear.

One of the machines loomed over them. Tools, she thought, picturing her metal hands. She reached out with a thought to Squire.

Are you there?

Yes, Aurora. I am here. It seems you are doing better.

I am, thank you.

Your system restart went well?

You could say that, she thought back to him. *It was more remembering how to use some old muscles. I think I pulled one in the fight back there.*

Cautiously, she tried to reach out to the mining machine looming over them. The cluster of processes nestled behind an insubstantial firewall. She circumvented the defenses on instinct and opened the symbolic forms of the machines processes. The glyphs unfolded from one another, drawing themselves in the air.

She found the activity suddenly relaxing and natural. It felt like stretching out after a long winter. She had engaged the robots earlier in this symbolic interaction, but it was a harrowing, involuntary reflex. The current moment felt serene.

The machine shared reports of its activities, leading back to its awakening twenty hours earlier and then logs of movement around the valley from nineteen years earlier. Unlike reading, the reports coalesced as knowledge. Each fact about the machine was something she simply and instantaneously knew. Status reports showed only minimal water incursion, despite hours of complete submersion. Its thorium-assisted battery held over ninety percent of its total charge despite years of dormancy.

Each fact simply coalesced from nothing to understanding. Pure knowledge with no learning or thinking to bridge the space between unknowing and knowing. The experience banished the negativity of her earlier encounters with the machines. She did not have to swing herself to swing the hammer.

She hesitated in moving the machine despite knowing she could. She looked down at her brother and Lena. Kars had his arm around her, with her head comfortably nestled in his shoulder. She smiled.

How would they respond to her new discoveries? The augmented people from the cities had been their enemy in the Rebellion, leading to a justified tribal belief that the augmented people that filled the cities were somehow less than human. The few people that had moved to their town from the city talked about the augmentations with a near-fanatical disgust.

But it had not led to a total arrest of their understanding of the world. They had still studied the fundamentals—it was not that the valley tolerated the ignorance that caused the first post-nuclear collapse. It was not even acting like a troglodyte who mistrusted technology. It was the town's pervasive feeling that encasing experience in a constant digital filter cut the soul off from its sustaining waters.

Perhaps it had been some subconscious awareness of her own augmentations, but she had never embraced their levels of mistrust. It had always felt like an overreaction, the kind of tribal belief that had led to strife many times before. Now, she wondered whether part of her resisted the hatred in order to protect herself.

In the darkness of the cave, she suddenly felt lonely. Kars and Lena might someday return, but her path home was sealed.

Kars stirred, carefully sliding out from under Lena's head. He looked bashful that his sister had been watching them sleep that way.

"I don't care!" She laughed.

"It was nothing!" he pleaded. Lena woke up to their laughter. Her face was crinkled with imprints of deep sleep.

"You're all right?" She was groggy as she spoke.

"Back in the land of the living. As conscious as I can be," Aurora responded and shrugged.

"What happened up there, Ror?" Kars asked.

She gathered herself. The truth was another step away from her home. Kars and Lena had to know already but needed the answer. They needed the words to close the wound of what had happened.

"It was me, but you knew that already. I turned all the machines on, forced them to attack. It felt . . . amazing." She paused again, collecting words for the next truth. "But before that, Jackal got inside my head, like his thoughts were in my mind. He trapped me. But then, he was going to kill you. Whatever happened, it was to stop him."

"However you did it, it was just in time." Kars used his light heart to sweep aside her concern. Aurora sensed the underlying discomfort buried beneath his levity.

"That sounds terrible, Aurora," Lena said, "Having someone else's thoughts in your head? And against your will?" Lena grimaced.

"It was," Aurora responded. "We take for granted the solitude of thoughts. Having another intrude that space—I'm still trying to understand what that means, and what it will be like in the world I have to face."

"I can't imagine," Lena said.

"I wonder if it's just how people live now? Constantly wandering into each other's minds?" Aurora asked.

"It was my error," Squire said. "As you learn how to use your augmentations, you will be able to better defend yourself."

"I hope that is the case. I can't explain how, but I'm starting to learn how to use the augmentations. I want to show you something. I think I can control it."

She stepped back, reaching out to the symbolic knot of processes inside the mining machine. She felt like she knew which arcane path to follow.

She seized the symbols she knew guided the machine to move. As she probed each symbol, the same coalescing knowledge blossomed in her mind. She was not looking at controls but instead expanding into the controls of the machine, knowing its functions and parameters, knowing its size and shape as part of her awareness. She made the machine stand up, flourishing a bow of its central body pod.

Her companions stumbled back. The cavern was now full of the sounds of the hulking machine's servomotors and the crunching of metal on rocks. Aurora felt invigorated. It was like stepping outside in spring.

She willed the machine into a few steps and poses, nothing graceful—the industrial machine was too cumbersome for that— but a clear exercise of the intuitive understanding of the processes. The spotlights danced across the water and distant walls of the cavern before she brought the machine to rest. It lowered its central body submissively, pivoting the armored plating on its back into a kind of cockpit. The bucket seats nestled in the space looked uncomfortable and utilitarian, but their purpose was obvious.

"Shall we ride?" Aurora asked, putting her hands to her hips.

116

11

The Cave

The machine danced before their eyes.

Lena and Kars stood wide eyed and with mouths agape. Their minds raced to make room for the new magic of their old friend. She had just made one of the lumbering machines—relics they had only seen rusting in the forest—dance. The machines danced for Aurora.

"It's okay. I've pulled up maps from Squire," Aurora said, sensing their hesitation. "We can follow this cave system to its mouth. Lannius left instructions from there."

Kars looked at the seats nestled in the armored carapace. They were weathered from their dunk in the lake but seemed to have survived. A wry smile crossed his face as he climbed onto the machine. He offered Lena and Aurora his hands. Squire clambered up the edges of the machine's thick plates into the cockpit.

Without any gesture or warning, Aurora willed the machine forward. She stared into the darkness beyond the edge of the machine's spotlights. The clambering mass felt like a great beast of burden picking its way across the rock floor. She felt like an ancient conqueror moving on her enemies atop a war elephant.

They rode atop the machine for what must have been days in the cave system. Time and distance seemed to fold into an illusion like paper to origami.

It was a jarring ride through the curves and drops. The machine, though an agile arachnid design, had not been designed for the comfort of passengers. Instead, the cockpit served more like a saddle on a wild beast. While Aurora thought of movements, she did not consciously choose flexion and extension, nor did she calculate each footfall. The neural connection was organic; the abstraction between the thought and physical act unnoticed, much like her own experience of walking.

The cave itself was a lost masterpiece of natural craftsmanship. The river carved through geologic time, scooping away limestone into arches and twists and tumbling through igneous intrusions veined with crimson minerals. The machine picked its way through claustrophobic narrows and waded through shallow subterranean lakes. Despite no reference of the sky or horizon, it was clear that they descended at greater rates. Rapids became more frequent, punctuated by vortex chutes. It felt as though they were descending to the center of the earth.

As they climbed down the cave river, Aurora practiced reaching out to Squire to determine their progress. Together they peeled apart the map data left by Lannius, extrapolating the distance to the most likely exit point from the cave system. The map data was tagged with a marker where a subterranean river emerged. They had not traveled in a straight line following the twisting vein of the river as it gnawed through the substrate. However, Aurora could tell they had followed a descent that appeared to be nearing its end if the map's elevation was correct. She shared the news with Kars and Lena.

"I've been working with Squire to try to figure out where we are in the caves, and I think we're getting a close to where the river leaves the cave system."

"A map in your mind?" Lena looked up, curiosity cutting through weariness. "What's it like? How much further do you think?"

"It shouldn't be much further. Given the amount of distance and the elevation that we've covered, I think we are going to be at the end within the hour. It's probably just a few more drops," Aurora said.

"As for what it's like"—she bit her lip—"it's not like seeing a picture but more like remembering a map that you know in perfect detail. I could see every part of the mountains around Prospector, the old road, the rivers. Perfect detail."

"Perfect detail? Like you're seeing the landscape?" Lena asked. Kars met her interest with quiet suspicion.

"Not like every rock and tree," Aurora responded. "It's more like a sculpture of the landscape, a sculpture made of memories."

"And from that you can tell where we are going?" Lena seemed smitten with the idea.

"Well, at least what's above us on the surface. The cave was never properly mapped—we just cut a hole in the side of a mountain to get here. But our travel time, distance, and angle let Squire map out our progress toward the most likely exit."

As she spoke, the narrow passage opened to another chamber. The river dropped, disappearing from view. The air was damp with mist, and the roar of a major fall filled the chamber. The mining machine continued picking its way forward along the bank of the river, slowing at the edge. The spotlights carved cones through the mist.

The machine scaled the edge of a waterfall plummeting through an alabaster chute, its spotlights causing the entire formation to glow in milky softness. The walls were smooth like beach glass. Hues of red and blue stained the otherwise cream-colored formation. The chamber glowed like a chapel of stained glass.

They continued the descent through the alabaster chamber, the machine braced against the smooth formations like a giant spider as it spiraled downward. Finally, they descended into the mist surrounding the splash pool. The lake below leveled into a calm stretch and meandered into a widening tunnel. Their machine waded through the calm waters until they rounded a corner to see a distant spot of daylight reflecting on the surface of the water. The landscape beyond seemed impossibly small as they approached the warped boundary between the cave and regular dimensions of real space. Blinding light cured the oppressive sense of the cave as they cleared the mouth of the cave. After nearly a week underground, they were out.

12

In the Ruins of the Gap

The river emerged in the wooded belly of a large valley. They were no longer in the stark mountains of their homeland. Conifers gave way to broad leaves and thickening spring underbrush. The peaks around them rolled upward to wooded mounds. The foothills had no tree line or snowcap. That evening, they stopped the machine on a pebble beach in a river bend. Squire approved of an overgrown campsite, noting the contours of the hills shielded them from any flyovers. The sky above was uniform gray overcast.

After the cave, camping felt like a welcome familiarity to the mountainfolk. They split off to forage for berries and roots. Aurora tested the limits of the mining machine, ordering it into the wide river to fish. Moments after the machine disappeared beneath the surface, it returned from the roiling mass with a large fish clamped in its forearms.

The woods were quiet leaving a feeling of safety, but the cave had left them hungry to near starvation despite the few granola bars they had brought. They tried to take precautions to avoid another encounter with their pursuers, but also grappled with pure hunger and exhaustion.

They scraped aside the damp char from an old pit and kindled a small fire to bake the fish in a leafy wrap. A few handfuls of berries served as a snack as the fish baked. Lena collected evergreen boughs and crossed them on the ground beneath the mining machine to pad the base of a lean-to. Kars and Aurora leaned the sturdiest deadfall they could find against the machine to extend the shelter to the ground. Finally, they heaped more boughs on the roof. Conversation was light as they were tired, and making a shelter in the woods was a familiar task. Building a good shelter was always a rewarding task.

Once their shelter was complete, the sun had dipped past the ridge. The river glowed with the sun's fiery reflection like stained glass. Ripples spread across the crimson mirror as fish kissed the surface, hoping an insect waited above. Aurora had shut down the machine, silencing the hum that had followed them throughout their time in the cave. In the calm of the evening under the sunset, it almost felt like a memory of normal camping trips. They unpacked the fish and ate the greasy meat with their hands.

"Was all of this abandoned during the Rebellion?" Kars asked, popping a hunk of fish into his mouth.

"We are in the Cordovan Gap," Squire responded. "The territory was heavily contested during the Rebellion, including infighting between its own citizens. This was in the shadow of the last major battle between Perpetual and Lannius's rebels. It was here that the Rebellion came to its end. The Seventy-Seven were defeated."

Kars thought of his father. "The Gap. People don't talk about it much. It's the last place anyone saw my father." He looked through the fire into the last light of evening, staring at a rusted mass on the opposite shore.

"Kars," Lena said. She tilted her head as she observed him.

"I just wonder, you know? I can't miss him like Mom does because he's just an idea for me—a missing piece, a big missing piece," Kars said. "The Gap. It's strange being here. Is there anyone left out here?"

"The incursions from Perpetual left the region too volatile for either faction to remain, leading to a concentration of rebel towns at higher altitudes and people who sought the comforts of networked civilization at the coastal megacities. The last entries I have on the area describe a master planning effort to maintain the area as a controlled watershed with automated resource highway systems to access deeper territories," Squire reported.

"So, Perpetual is in control of the area. Any signs that they might find us here?" Kars replied.

"None that I can detect, nor any immediate warnings within the protocols Lannius provided to me."

"I've already consulted Squire," Aurora said to Kars. "Lannius left us with a rendezvous point—a waystation along the resource highway," she continued. "If we continue to follow the river, we should reach a bridge that was scheduled to become part of the highway system. We'll know rather quickly if they tracked us once we reach that bridge."

"I wanted to be sure." He had a dejected look to him, smudges of dirt on his face and hands. His hair was disheveled, and his bright eyes had sunken into darkened rings.

"I've got it, Kars," Aurora responded. "I don't know if you can understand, but I know everything this machine knows. I can *feel* everything that it detects. You can just sit back and relax. I can keep you safe."

The firelight cast her in a strange glow. She seemed older than when they had entered the cave.

"Aurora?" Lena asked. "How are you doing?"

Aurora scowled at her, irritated and puzzled.

"You've changed. And not just this," Lena said, pointing to the machine. "We're all out here together. We've lost so much. All this change. How are you feeling?"

Aurora thought for a moment. *Had she changed?* There were two answers to that question, both yes. She had changed. First, she had discovered that her brain was wrapped in a lattice of technology, and as she remembered how to use those devices, she uncovered very real abilities. She longed to test the edges of those abilities. But there was a second change, one she could barely wrap her thoughts around.

"Don't you feel it?" Aurora asked.

Lena stared off into the wilderness of Cordovan Gap.

"We've left the valley," Aurora said. "I didn't know it was there, but now it's gone: the weight of the valley. I feel like a piece of me has been freed from ice. We're free of having our decisions made by circumstance."

"What are you talking about?" Kars burst out. "Aurora, that was our home. We are following a robot—a program. Our home is gone, and our decisions are completely buried in circumstance!"

"And they weren't when we were at home? There's a difference between being prisoners of circumstance and reacting to forces bigger than ourselves," Aurora responded. There was detachedness in her voice.

"We were free before. We could have left the village at any point, made our way into the world. We could have made our lives whatever we wanted," Kars said.

"How many people choose to step out of the safety of their world to make their own story?" Aurora asked.

"People got hurt, Ror! How can you feel anything beyond that? You can end up needing a new house if you burn your old one down. That doesn't mean it's a good thing," Kars responded.

Aurora knew Kars was right. She wondered why she didn't feel more about the loss of their village. Was her lack of empathy from some defective crack in her psychological foundation caused by the augmentations?

"I think I know what you mean," Lena interjected. "I wouldn't have left. If I'm being honest with myself, I would have dreamed of life outside, but routine would have eventually trapped me, fixed me in place with roots."

"Exactly," Aurora said. "Something about knowing my mind is a sea of programs made me acutely aware of the programs outside of it. The valley kept things within its own order."

Kars stared into the fire as Lena and Aurora conversed.

"I don't know what to do with that part," Aurora said. "I guess I've never had the choice of whether to give up or push forward. I know, Kars: we lost everything. But we're still here and there's got to be some good in that. At least, I feel like there must be. And then there's the augmentations. It's so much information to think about, and the computers give me more *ways* to think about things."

Kars didn't respond. His shadow danced across the carapace of the mining machine.

"The augmentations, do they hurt?" Lena asked.

"No. Just the first few run-ins we had in the camp. I think I've figured that out now."

"Do you like it?" Lena asked.

"Yes." Aurora thought for a moment. "I like it. Although, that might not even really describe the feeling. Using the devices is a little like using your hands—you don't really think about it, but when you do something perfectly, there's satisfaction in it. It's more of a craft."

"You told the machine to take each of its steps?" Lena looked at the machine standing over their shelter.

"No, I told it where we needed to go, then we just rode, like being in the saddle of a horse."

"So you could tell it to take us home?" Kars broke his silence.

"Do you want to go home?" Aurora asked.

"We don't know what happened back there, and I don't think we ever really decided what we were doing." Kars voice trembled as he responded. "Everything up until now has been decided for us. We've been on the run. Maybe we should go back? What if they need us?"

"We barely made it out the first time," Aurora said.

"But now, you've . . . changed. Maybe you'd win? Couldn't you make the Protek do what you want? What about our people? What about Mom?"

"Kars, you saw them," Aurora said. "The Protek and that mad man, Jackal. He invaded my mind. Do you think our families are there? Do you think those monsters left them alone?"

There was a pause, and then Lena spoke. "It's true, Kars. I saw it. They were herding everyone together, lining them up to board their ship."

"Well then, we should help them. Otherwise, no one will. We can't just abandon them. Ror, it's Mom!"

"We can't help them," Aurora said.

The air between the three of them hung heavy, punctuated by the cracking of the fire. Their path through darkness had been sealed by a rockslide. There might be nothing to which they could return. They were likely orphaned refugees, truly alone.

"I don't think we can go back, Kars. At least, I don't think I can go back." As Aurora said it, she felt profound sorrow. Home was gone.

His anger faded, replaced by nothing. Lena touched his shoulder.

"We might not be able to go back now, but that doesn't mean we can't or shouldn't go back," Aurora said. "We need help. Maybe there the people out there—maybe Lannius—could help. People came from the city to help our valley before."

Squire interjected. "My instructions from Lannius were aimed to support this outcome. In short, if we find Lannius, he will help."

Kars sat up when he heard the robot's claim.

"Yes. That's what we're supposed to do here." He rolled his shoulders back and puffed his chest. "We'll find Lannius, then we'll go back. We can do it again."

Aurora watched as he contemplated the plan. His face passed from despair to perturbed, then on to a kind of serene resolve. Even though it was a challenge, it was a way forward and that was better than uncertainty.

Aurora smiled but some part of her felt cynical about his sudden will to ride in like some white knight and save the day. A hero on a journey.

Collateral. The word seemed to rise out of the murk of the other memories. The cynicism of it felt dark and alien, like a shadow of the feeling she had when Jackal had invaded her mind. Had he left some residue? Could a personality change through the influence of another?

She shivered and denied the feeling. Maybe Lannius could help her if there was some latent issue with Jackal in her mind. Either way, finding Lannius would help all of them, and it gave Kars a reason to push forward into the tantalizing freedom of the world. He would come around.

"I'm here for you, Kars. I've always been here for you, and I'll help however I can." She knew the words felt sincere. "The bridge is more than another half day from here. Once on the road, it's not too far to the waystation."

"Let's do it. Let's find Lannius," Kars said, resolute.

"That's more like it. Pessimism doesn't suit you," Lena said. An idle word spoken to the heart can change an entire person. Kars straightened and sat taller by the fire.

Aurora stared at him. She felt like she had seen it a thousand times before. The ancient pattern of the hero would make him useful.

*   *   *   *   *

At daybreak, they continued to ride the machine through the shallows of the riverbed, stomping through swifts and ripples. The river was much wider, shallower, and altogether gentler than it had been confined to the rock channels of the cave. Wildlife dotted the valley. From the shore of the river, they could see an occasional rusted mass of forgotten machinery or the foundation of buildings left to nature.

The spring forest was a patchwork of hunter, chartreuse, lime, and emerald. Great trees spread above an abandoned town center. A shirtless fisherman cast nets from the shore near a dented aluminum canoe dragged into the mud. He darted into the bushes when he saw the mining machine trundle past. They rounded another bend in the river, which brought a half-shell set of bleachers into view. The field faced out toward the expanse of the river valley. The meadow in the diamond swayed in the breeze. A flock of birds wheeled up from the forest and settled into the shell over the bleachers.

The beauty of the scene buffered Aurora's tension. Surely the augmentations would never blind her to such scenes. She looked at Squire in its vigilante perch on the side of the mining machine. Her tension returned. The waystation would have answers.

13

Taken

Em smiled as the mohawk man stormed by her cell. Her family had escaped.

Moments earlier the ship had jolted to a stop and now the engines were spinning down. A Protek stalked by, flicking its red-ring gaze toward the cells full of her fellow townsfolk. The cargo door through which they had entered hinged open, and a scorched wind full of dust ripped through the ship.

Protek. Desert wind. It could mean only one thing: Amurtan.

This last free nation fell to the Protek at the close of the Consolidation War. The G-Trip nations had only intended to conquer and depose the remnants of Amurtan's constitutional government, but the Protek could not be stopped once they started their work. They ran amok and ravaged the country, destroying everything they could. It was intentional destruction on a scale prior unseen. Amurtan went from proud nation to a place synonymous with wasteland.

So the rumors were true. Mercenaries operated out of the Protek Wastelands, Em thought. The killer machines clicked and buzzed their awful garbled noise at the end of the gangplank.

A loud voice caught her attention. The mohawk man was swearing and shouting. Subordinate soldiers scuttled past the ramp. Vehicle tires grinded across the hardscrabble sand.

Moments later, a handful of soldiers boarded the ship, pulling the townsfolk from their cells. She tried to count how many people had been taken as prisoners. Angelique blustered and spat on the guard a few paces ahead. Old Gladys Wu shoved one of the prison guards after he knocked away a cigarette she started to light.

Stumbling out of the ship, Em surveyed her new surroundings. The harsh desert sun stung her eyes. A scorching sandy wind chafed against her face. Protek watched like sentinels as the townsfolk descended the ramp.

Yes, they were in the wasteland left in the wake of the Consolidation War. During the Rebellion, there were rumors that Perpetual kept prison camps in the wastes. The tiny spark of hope she held for her missing husband leapt at the thought: perhaps Robert was somewhere in this wasteland?

The mercenaries herded the townsfolk through a gated fence toward a long low building. The howling wind held visibility to a few feet, but Em could see Protek lurked beyond the fence. She could make out high walls in the gloom of dust, spotlights cutting through the murk and towers parked down the length. Em was relieved to see Cara. Ben was not with her. She wondered if Lena might have ended up in one of the pens.

Cara threw her arms around Em. "I don't know where they took Ben!"

Em held her friend close and remembered Ben's heroic stand when he tackled the mohawk man. A Protek had pounced. There was a good chance he had not survived.

"We'll find him," Em said, trying to soothe her friend. "We're still alive."

"And Lena! She's not here either," Cara sobbed.

Em held the woman at arm's length, looking into her reddened eyes. Em knew how much the Rebellion had taken from Cara. She was uncertain whether Cara could withstand this new trauma.

"Cara. Lena is out there. The kids made it. If they hadn't, we wouldn't be alive," Em said. Her voice had the timbre of command. Cara calmed slightly, recognizing Em as a leader.

"How do you know?" Cara's voice quivered. "Why's this happening again?"

"It never stopped. You knew they would eventually come for her—for Aurora," Em hissed. "Now, they are back. Our kids are out there. We have to do what we can to help them. We have to survive long enough for me to show that bastard what a bad haircut really looks like." Em dragged her thumbnail across her forehead just below her scalp, her upper lip twitched as she held back a snarl.

Em's confidence, menace, and devotion brought calm to Cara. She had never found strength amidst chaos, but she always endured.

"We raised good kids. They got away, and they will make it. They will thrive," Em repeated. Cara nodded, sniffling.

Having calmed Cara, Em turned to her fellow imprisoned townsfolk. She knew all of them by name, and they looked relieved to see her in their prison. She recognized their look. It was the expectant stare of people looking to a leader. Em had seen it when Robert hadn't returned from Cordovan Gap. It was as if people knew at some level that they needed shelter, needed a leader strapped to the mast so they could row as a group. They needed Em to take the tiller.

"It seems our Rebellion never ended. Perpetual has returned." She spoke with quiet determination. "We are going to make it out of here, going to survive whatever is in front of us. We've survived before. And if this is when we say goodnight, we'll at least give 'em hell along the way. They already brought us halfway there.

"And anyone that burns one of these machines—I'm buying."

It was not much of a speech, but Em saw that it had triggered the desired effect. Her people shifted from bewildered to determined. She left the words with her people and walked toward the back of the enclosure. Fewer words were always better motivators.

"Decent speech." A gravelly voice rasped from the slatted fence at the back of the enclosure. "It won't help, though."

"We'll see about that," Em said, dismissing the cynic behind the wall.

"How long has it been?" the voice asked.

Em contemplated ignoring the voice, before feeling compelled to respond. "How long since what?"

"The Gap?" the voice asked.

134

Cordovan Gap? Em thought. Her heart jumped. *What if?*

"Robert?" she asked.

There was an anxious pause.

"No. I'm sorry," the voice said. Em's spirits settled. She needed to keep her ghosts quiet.

"It's been almost twenty years since Cordovan Gap. Only a few free towns remained. Perpetual took most of the Cerras," she said.

"Twenty years?" The voice sounded weary.

"Just about," Em said. "Were you there?"

"Yes," the voice said. "Twenty years." The same disbelief stained his voice.

"Did you know Robert Koren?" she asked. She knew there were more pressing concerns, but she had to know.

"We all knew Robert," he said.

"Is he alive?" Em asked. She wrestled with her ghosts, knowing that she needed to remain strong.

"I can't say. I've been here twenty years," he said. "Robert was a good man."

Em added the disappointment of the answer to the toxic lump of pain she had lived with since accepting that her husband had vanished during the war.

"Is the war still going on? Is Lannius still alive?" the voice asked.

"I can't say whether Lannius is alive. I've been in the Cerras since it ended. And the war," Em said, "it seems to have found us again."

"Bastards," he said.

Floodlights flickered on over the camp. Protek marched at the perimeter. The wind had calmed, and the night chill of the desert was starting to creep in. The occasional flap of a loose tarp shifting on the light breeze punctuated the still air. The first stars winked in the blue darkness.

"Were you from the mountains too?" Em asked the man behind the fence.

"No," he responded. "I came from the city."

"You were one of the Seventy-Seven?" she asked.

His silence was enough.

"My name is Ranjit Singh," he said. "Perpetual captured us at Cordovan Gap. A few of my comrades perished from their wounds, but many remain. Why Perpetual has kept us alive, I am not certain. Perhaps it's part of some larger plan. I know that they regularly attempt to subjugate us through our augmentations."

"I'm Emilia Koren—"

"Koren. Robert's wife?"

"Yes," Em responded.

"I heard stories that you were just as fierce, perhaps more. Maybe my fortunes are starting to turn," Ranjit said.

*At least, we've got allies in here. Maybe Robert's choice to ride to
the Gap was not a complete loss.*

"Let's not count our fortunes yet," Em said. "But you've got my
word, we'll do our best to get out of here."

She almost mentioned her children but stopped herself. She
knew precious little about the voice on the other side of the
fence. Her children were still out there, and the man who had
captured her was chasing them. While she wanted to trust the
man behind the fence, she couldn't yet trust him on behalf of her
children. He might be one of the Seventy-Seven, but twenty
years of imprisonment could change the math of one's values.
Em couldn't be sure he wouldn't bargain her children for his
freedom.

"There are others. We will help you if the time comes," Ranjit
said.

"Thank you," Em responded.

She sat in silence. The last light faded from the sky. Her
compatriots milled through their enclosure. Disbelief clouded
their faces. They still wore the torn clothes they wore when they
had been abducted. She understood their deep confusion. Last
night they had been tucked away in their village. Today they
were prisoners somewhere in the desert. Em tried to fend off her
own dissonance at the sudden transition.

Two armed mercenaries approached carrying heavy satchels.
They set down the bags, withdrew bottles of water and rations,
and proceeded to toss them over the fence. Some townsfolk
reached for the water, others were indifferent as the bottles
scattered on the ground.

Disgust smoldered on the faces of her peers. Some fires never went out. The spirit of the Rebellion kept burning low and hot in their souls. The night raid riled that indignant fire of the mountain folk. Em could feel it herself—a quiet, seething rage toward the smug men tossing water to their prisoners. They looked too young to have been in the Rebellion, still trained and dangerous, but arrogant toward their captives.

The edge of a wry smile or a sneer caught the edge of Em's lip. Whether it was tomorrow or a twenty-year sentence, Em knew that someday she would be free from them. Her children were out in the world. She would not leave them as Robert had left her. They would be free.

14

The Waystation

The resource highway arced high above the river valley, soaring over the remains of a disused stone bridge from the old road systems. It was unlike any structure they had ever seen, seemingly built from stretched beams of molded ivory. The footings of the resource highway swept down against the bruised-purple clouds and touched down into the valley in stark, swept lines that seemed to almost avoid contact with the earth. The supports of the structure were seamless forms, looking more like the porous interior of a bone than an engineered design. No traffic passed on the high span.

Aurora brought the machine to a stop on the riverbank. The group paused in excitement below the massive structure. They conferred with Squire on the best route before Aurora guided the mining machine up the brush-covered slope.

After the short climb, the machine emerged from the forest onto the resource highway near the upper edge of the valley. From the vista, the river spread out onto forested flatlands like an ink curve in the landscape. Remnants of old grain silos and the collapsed roofs of decaying factory farms poked out of the carpet of the young forest. Marshes had started to displace fields in the lowest points of the valleys as beaver dams sprung up in the arterial river's tributaries. Mist rose off the forested hillsides, drifting up into the clouds that stretched with regularity to the distant horizon.

The scars of the battle at Cordovan Gap still showed through the lush forest. They passed heaps of discarded armor shells and scorched drones, vestiges of the onslaught by Perpetual. Craters lined with meadow flowers and grass forced them to weave down the road. Occasionally they passed shrines built of plywood and sheet metal celebrating some honored dead, the ink faded from memory.

The highway was much wider than their machine, at least forty paces across. The resource highway itself consisted of two round rails running parallel along a grassy trail. The rails themselves were wider than Aurora's hand and composed of a dull silver. Aurora attempted to reach out to it, but there were no systems within. She could not determine whether the rails were a metal, plastic, or a ceramic.

Following the resource highway away from the bridge, they continued the march until they arrived at the waystation near sunset. The station sat off to the side of the overlaid sections of resource highway and old road. Squire directed them toward the older of two buildings. The structure was patched with a sheet of plywood and stenciled with a symbol—a circle and triangle with two lines slashed across it.

The second structure was sleek and new—a crane and portico built perpendicular to the rails of the resource highway. A line of machines similar to their craft waited next to the crane. These machines, however, had large sections connected to their rear section, giving the arachnid bodies more of a bloated abdominal structure.

Aurora barely sensed the processes running deep in the dormant machines. She started to probe the quiet knots of processes before feeling a swift rebuke from Squire. Scowling at the tiny robot, she attempted to work her way around its defense to reach the machines.

Aurora, this action is highly ill-advised, Squire warned.

Aurora pouted at the machine. She longed to test herself with a fleet of the machines but resisted the urge to reach out after the warning from Squire. She would try later.

"Lannius left the instruction that this is our first rendezvous point. Aside from the presence of the expanded loading system for the resource highway, the waystation remains as described in my files. Lannius took precautions that should have ensured the bunker remained hidden," Squire announced before scrambling off of the miner. Aurora, Kars, and Lena climbed down from the machine after their long journey.

"Lead the way, little buddy!" Kars shouted to Squire.

The tiny machine led them to the rotten building. The front door was boarded and locked. Weathered graffiti and vegetation covered the walls of the building. Bushes grew through the cracks in the pavement. It was a dilapidated shack.

Lena found a metal pipe amidst the debris and used it to smash the lock from the boarded door. Kars took a running start and laid his shoulder into the boards, knocking the dry rotted material from the frame. The board fell into the station with the loud crack of wood on the floor. They paused, scanning the clearing to determine whether any of the machines at the loading platform would respond. The dormant machines remained still.

"We're in, mostly unannounced," Kars said, stepping through the opening. Aurora, Lena, and Squire followed.

Inside the waystation, the shelves had been emptied, and the debris from looters was still scattered on floor. Thin bands of the evening light cut through the boarded windows, materializing cones of dust. Squire's light flickered on, providing a small glow in the space. The waystation was as derelict inside as outside.

They moved through the building, surveying the contents of the store. Aside from a few rusted tools and containers, the space was empty.

"Aurora, Master Lannius's instructions indicate the waystation has a basement. We should direct our search toward a trap door or staircase."

They started clearing the debris from the floor and searched for the hatch to a sublevel, tossing aside the rubble in great sweeps. Aurora saw Kar shoot a subtle look toward Lena between great sweeps of the debris. She wondered about the motivation behind his optimism.

"I think I found it," Kars said. He leaned over behind the station's counter. The others gathered around.

He pulled an inlaid latch from the floor tiles. The hatch came free with a tug, light spilling onto the top rungs of a stepladder. Aurora wordlessly willed the robot to go into the hole first. It crept down the ladder like a spider.

"All clear," Aurora said, relaying Squire's scouting. The space was dark, but safe. If they needed, they could hide there for the night with little chance of being discovered. "I'm sending our mining machine to park in the woods. We don't want any visitors checking in on us."

"Sounds good. I'll go next." Kars turned and descended the stepladder. He shouted back up confirming that it was safe.

Lena and Aurora followed into the darkness. The space was a jumbled storeroom, stripped of most supplies. The storeroom filled the footprint of the waystation. A small desk with an old monitor sat in a corner. Files littered the floor around the desk.

Aurora poked through the files–just junk. The basement was not the bunker she was expecting. The old man had nested plans within one another that would last through generations and endure the unraveling after the Rebellion. Whatever his plan with the waystation, it would withstand an uncertain period of time against countless looters. There must be something more than junk and empty shelves.

If only she could ask those strange visions of the old man. The puzzle of Squire's box was buried in memories. She tried to imagine something from his workspace–the image of his metronome. It was an intricate piece of clockwork, brass and cherry wood clicking out a regular beat. Aurora tried to imagine the kindly old face but there was nothing, just the images she wanted to see. Frustrated, she continued sifting through the scattered papers. Kars and Lena rummaged in other corners of the room.

"Squire, any idea of what we're looking for? Seems like Lannius didn't exactly leave a plan here," Kars asked.

"Lannius would have stored instructions for the next rendezvous point if he were not able to be here himself. I am scanning for anything he may have stored here, but so far, there is nothing."

Aurora faced the same issue. She reached out with her mind for any hint of processes or signals, but the room was empty. None of the indigo snowflakes drifted through the air. She continued pushing through the pile of debris surrounding the desk. The air smelled of old paper and damp earth.

Then Aurora saw it. The corner of the desk had a carefully carved symbol—the circle- and triangle-line glyph that she had seen stenciled on the outside of the building. She thought that she recognized the symbol.

"Squire, why do we keep seeing this symbol?"

"That is the symbol of the Parallel Initiative," Squire responded. Aurora had been right: it was the old corporate logo.

"Why is it all over this place?" she asked, running her fingertips over the grooves in the surface. "I've seen it painted a couple places in town, then we saw it outside. Why is it here?"

"The last records I have of the Parallel Initiative refer to a several threats from other companies for bids and takeovers. I cannot answer as to why the logos are here."

Curious, Aurora thought. Lannius must have left that symbol for her—something about the desk. She went to search the drawers, but they had already been pulled out and rifled through. Perhaps behind the desk she thought. An attempt to push the desk yielded nothing. She tried to force it again before looking at its legs—it was bolted to the floor.

Another piece of Lannius's puzzle.

"I think I found something. There's something about this desk. Help me look!" Aurora said. Kars and Lena came over. They immediately started searching the torn-out drawers.

Lena paused over a strange object in the debris. It was an ornately carved magnifying glass. Its handle was the same rich wood as Squire's box. She grabbed it, looking through the lens.

"Look! Check this out!" She showed the magnifying glass to her friends.

Aurora reached for it, taking it from Lena. She turned the object in her hands. There were faint scratches on the glass. The tip of the handle bore an odd irregularity. She felt it, then tipped it up and looked. It had been meticulously carved into the Parallel logo.

"I think it's a key," Aurora said. She placed the magnifying glass over the carved glyph on the corner of the desk and gently pushed it into the depression. They held their breath, waiting for the room to rotate or another machine to emerge from the darkness.

Nothing happened.

"I could've sworn that was it," Aurora said.

"Maybe there's something else. Maybe you can operate it like the machine now, like the glass is the control stick to the building," Kars said. Aurora looked at him incredulously. He really had no sense of how she interacted with the machines.

"I'm sorry, Kars, but that's not quite how this works. The desk and the magnifying glass are just that—a desk and a magnifying glass. Like anything you'd find at home." The mention of home shot through her, reminding her that their home was gone.

"Well, then I guess we keep looking," Kars said. "Hopefully, old man Lannius didn't overthink this one and end up leaving us out in the cold."

He resumed the search, gesturing to Squire to follow him. As the two moved, light from the robot cast a shadow that traced across the wall. Then Aurora saw it. The lens flashed on the wall behind the desk. The faint scuffs formed a pattern.

"It's the lens!" she exclaimed. "Squire, bring the light." She sent commands to the robot to climb onto the desk.

The three watched as the shadows moved across the opposite wall. Squire moved the light until the shadow of the magnifying glass was perfectly round. The scuffs formed a faint, but clearly recognizable, "X" on the opposite wall.

Kars immediately went to work, smashing at the marked point with the desk chair.

Lena and Aurora watched as Kars smashed the drywall facade, peeling back the rotten plaster to reveal a rock wall. Beneath the intersection of the projected glass there was a perfect indentation. The indentation was a smooth disc shape, slightly wider than two hands together. Aurora recognized it: the shape was Squire.

"It's Squire." Kars recognized the shape as well, a sense of wonder in his voice. "The key is Squire."

Aurora felt it as well. Lannius had designed a near-foolproof rendezvous point for them. Judging by the ragged state of the building, several rounds of searchers and looters had been through, yet layers of Lannius's puzzle still remained in place. Even beyond that incredible feat, Aurora had lived in the same house as the key her entire life. She imagined the kindly face smiling, satisfied that the final pieces to his carefully wrought puzzle were finally sliding into place.

Aurora directed Squire toward the torn away space in the wall. The light swayed through the room with the tiny robots teetering steps until it stopped before the indentation.

"Well," she said, "are we ready?"

The room plunged into darkness as the tiny robot folded back into its disc shape. Aurora felt for the robot, picking it up in the dimmest gloom of the basement. She traced the edges and contours of the wall, finding the indentations. The surface was cool and smooth, unnatural compared to the rock they had known so intimately during the journey through the cave. She lifted Squire in the darkness, pressed the robot disc into the indentation, and stepped back.

There was a moment of silence, followed by Squire's motors adjusting like a locking mechanism. A distant hiss of gas vented from a valve. There was another pause in dark and quiet. A subtle glow traced a partially obscured edge on the visible rock face. Another hiss of gas filled the room as a round portal of rock swung back with the Squire disc at the center. A dim golden light poured out of the space behind.

They had arrived at Lannius's bunker.

The space was hewn out of the rock, angling downward in a manmade cave. It was a shallow space, leaving room for a desk, a few footlockers, and a row of bunks. The neat bunks, with extra wool blankets folded at the foot of each bed, were still carefully made from whenever Lannius had sealed the bunker. The desk was meticulous: blank paper, a pen, and a lamp forming a rectangle.

Seeing the beds, Aurora realized how long it had been since she had slept in one. The folded blankets and pillows looked tantalizing. Beyond the bunks, the cave bunker split off into what appeared to be a small kitchen and a separate bathroom area. There was another area off the central room that contained a curious round ceramic disc inset in the floor. The combination of the regularly spaced golden lights, the olive carpet, and the carefully organized space gave the room a welcoming aura they had not felt since they fled the village. It was safe.

Once inside, Aurora lifted Squire out of the door and swung it closed. There was a matching indentation on the other side, which she inserted the robot in, and the door sealed closed behind them.

The three youths marveled.

"We made it," Kars said, as he walked to the back of the bunker. He tested the sink in the kitchen: the faucet coughed through an air lock before clear cool water gushed from the spout.

Aurora looked around for the signs of processes with which she could interact, but the bunker was surprisingly low tech. The door was an intricate mechanical lock. The lights ran off of a closed loop fuel cell. There was no active wireless equipment running in the space. The wide ceramic disc set in the back alcove gave no response, save for the murky, odd feeling of déjà vu.

She took note of the electronic silence. It was a design feature, part of Lannius's strategy in a larger war—simplicity was a defense against a hostile future. Aurora had searched the space for any process or machine she could reach, trying to find the shortcut to the mystery. Simplicity had a place in his game of secrecy.

"The score!" Lena had opened a cabinet full of canned food.

"Old food!" Kars cheered with feigned enthusiasm, looking at the cans.

"It's canned. I have no problem crushing as much of this as I can. I'll eat your share too," Lena responded, pulling a can from the cabinet.

While the variety of canned food was limited, the past week's meals had been downright sparse. The cave had tested their limits of hunger, and the river had given them only a few fish. By comparison, the bunker's supply of canned foods seemed like a cornucopia. They ate with urgency.

They laughed and goaded each other into eating until they were overstuffed. Kars even found a flask tucked in amongst the supplies. They passed it as they ate the canned meats.

In the glow of the food and alcohol, they talked.

"I needed to be here—we needed to be here," Aurora said.

"Me too, Ror. It's nice to be someplace that feels like we might be on the right path," Kars said.

"Kars, I really mean it. Not just because this gives us some sign that we're on the right path to Lannius," Aurora said, the warmth of the space taking hold. "I needed to be here with both of you. It's hard to explain. Since I realized I have these . . . things in my head, I've been remembering things, or I think they are memories." She trailed off into the tenderness of the admission.

"What do you mean?" Kars asked. "The computer is putting things into your mind?"

Was that what she was experiencing? The memories and the dreams were so thorough and natural she had not stopped to think that somehow the computer system wrapped around her brain could be the source. How far might the program go? Could it shape what she saw or felt? She realized it would be impossible to definitively know whether her thoughts were programmed.

"I can't tell that, Kars. There's no way—same for you," Aurora responded.

"What do you mean by that? I don't have any of those things in my head," Kars shot back.

"You can't really tell if your memories are yours. You're just so used to thinking that everything in your mind is yours that you don't think about it," Aurora said.

Kars looked puzzled. She watched him struggle through mental gymnastics of what she had said.

"Think of it this way: Your entire life is a movie being projected onto a screen that you are watching. Every moment is part of the script, even the moments that you think you're making a choice, are really just part of some elaborate—perfectly elaborate—script. You're just watching the story of your life," Aurora tried to explain.

In a single moment, Kars's face melted from strained mental effort to a still-confused understanding.

"Or like a book of my life that my mind is reading?" Kars said.

"Yes," Aurora said.

"Or like a program," Lena said.

150

Aurora nodded. "So you see why it's hard for me to tell whether it's a memory or something else?"

Lena and Kars nodded with her in agreement. "What does that mean for you, Ror? Why is it confusing to know?"

"I've seen Lannius."

The simplicity of the statement was enough to consolidate the conversation.

"Like from when you were a baby? Before he left you with Em?" Lena was the first to respond. Kars still looked baffled.

"No, not like that. They are memories. I've had memories of talking with him . . . playing chess with him." Aurora spoke, feeling a relief that her dam of secrecy was opening. "I can't explain it, Lena. It's like I knew him, or I have some memory that knew him."

Lena chewed her lip. The look on her face showed concern and effort to put the shared knowledge in an order that would not unravel their entire existence.

"Do you have any memories of us?" Lena asked.

"Only the ones you'd know," Aurora responded.

Aurora knew that Lena was pouring through the repercussions. The legends that had filtered up to their remote community. The ones that talked about powers of technology wielded by Lannius and others that crossed into a blurred space indiscernible from magic. The implications were daunting. Kars had not leapfrogged to this conclusion, but Aurora judged from Lena's behavior that she had arrived in the murky troubled space: time travel.

"What do you remember?" Lena asked, after several near-starts, sighs, and deep breaths. Aurora was pleased that Lena had circled back to the same conclusion that she had: verify the memory.

"I knew his name—and his face—before Em said anything. We played chess together in his house, his palace really. It was by a huge lake or a sea. The memory was like getting a piece of a conversation, like overhearing people at a restaurant. I had another one where I saw him in his workshop. He was making Squire's box. It was from that memory I knew the word to activate Squire. I wasn't guessing the answer to the riddle. He told me."

"Aurora, you know what this could mean," Lena said.

"I know. I just don't understand."

"Time travel. Like the stories!" Kars said.

"So you've been here before? What am I going to say next?" He paused, realizing more of the implications. "What happened to Mom? Can you go back and stop it?"

"I don't know how it works, Kars. It wasn't that I was there at that moment, opening the box again. I had a conversation with Lannius in a different place. He made the box by hand. We talked about care and craft. It was as though he knew what would come. For all I know, he programmed these computers in my mind to remember at the right moment—like I'm a drive full of useful memories."

The thought that Lannius could program another human being was chilling.

"As far as I can guess, I don't think you can know." Lena talked her through their grade six logics class. Normally, it would have frustrated Aurora to spend their time in these philosophical questions, but tonight it was such a relief. Trying to sift through these jarring facts on her own had repeatedly made her feel dizzy.

"There is one way," Aurora said.

"Ask Lannius," Lena replied.

"I tried asking Squire, but there's nothing in the files relating to these memories," Aurora said.

"So that leaves us exactly where we are, planning exactly what we were planning," Kars said.

"Yes, pretty amazing," Aurora said with a smile. The sense of respect and fondness she felt for Lannius surged. The puzzle was so intricate.

"Well, at least he saw ahead far enough to leave us some of the good stuff!" Kars said, laughing and raising a spoonful of red beans. He washed the beans down with a swig of the bourbon from a tin cup.

The three of them tapped their mugs together, downing the last bit. The conversation continued long into what felt like the night, although they had no way to verify that from inside the bunker. After the flask ran dry, they each sprawled on a bunk. There was a sense of disbelief that they had found this space. Squire dimmed the lights and they fell into deep sleep.

*   *   *   *   *

The boardroom looked out across the megalopolis. Extruder cranes and blimps punctuated the explosive growth of the megacity. The construction grid scaffolds had already covered a portion of the city. From their vantage point, they could see beyond the edge of the skyscrapers and high-rise residential sectors to the growing expanse of the shantytown clinging to the city's edge. In the other direction they could see more construction equipment—always more construction—and vast mega-structures butting up against the slate blue waters of the harbor. The boardroom was small and intimate compared with others, adorned with a wondrous variety of plants. The vaulted ceiling, jungle of plants, and soaring windows served to open a free mind space.

Whitestone spoke. "Arthur, are you certain the meeting was prudent?"

Lannius folded his hands on his chest, leaning back in his chair.

"He didn't call the meeting." The voice came from the man who showed Aurora the rose on the seaside balcony. "I did."

The group of twelve around the table shifted in their seats. Whitestone held his ground with confidence bordering on insolence.

"Well, James, are you certain this meeting was prudent?"

"Clark, the anomaly continues to grow. Anna has documented it for nearly 250 years."

"James, an 'anomaly' cannot be our main concern. We've come so far. The climate is stabilized—the world was saved as a byproduct of our work. You know as well as I that this can't go on forever, that one day the jackboots will kick in the door and take our creation. We must sprint as far as we can into the future before that happens, and we must drag humanity along with us."

"Clark, the anomaly continues to grow in each of you." Anna spoke, her voice was strong and beautiful. She and James sat next to each other. "I've tracked it. It affects you to greater and lesser extents, but the kernel is there. There's nothing comparable to it outside of your experience."

"Yes, I know, I've gone through your briefings. I know you think the root of it comes from despair. But that shouldn't be a cause to retreat. What better treatment for despair than resolute perseverance?" Clark's optimism was like silk.

"We have no idea the forces with which we are contending. Who knows what we carry with us on our travels?" James warned.

"We only have time to think about what we know we carry with us. Our work is the most important in the history of our species." Clark persevered against James's caution. "We have conquered the arrow of time!"

"Perhaps, I may propose a compromise," the old man Lannius said. His beard was extremely long, and the creases of his wrinkled face were deeper than ever before.

James and Whitestone sat back, yielding the floor to their elder.

"Though I am cautious of Clark's bullish optimism, I must agree with his ultimate point: the work is too important, and the time of our travels is desperately limited. We should give humanity everything we can before the end. However, we should also take heed of forces potentially greater than ourselves. The gifts we share could just as easily be a nightmare." He paused to let his words reach his comrades. "I propose to continue our work, but I *will devote myself to the anomaly. It will be my task until they come for us."* His proposal hung in the air for a moment, mingling with his gravitas.

"Arthur," Dambisa said, *"with no disrespect to you, what guarantee do we have you aren't susceptible to the anomaly?"*

"The tricks of despair are tired and old in my heart. I have known despair in ways few can imagine. I live with it. It can no longer convince me of anything. Anna, would you please confirm?"

"Arthur is right. I've observed no changes in him."

Lannius winked. *"Some benefits to growing old."*

"Arthur, I'm still reluctant, but I will trust you. You must let us know if we need to stop. At the first moment," James said.

"It's settled then. We will continue." Whitestone was smug, as though he had managed a victory with an evenhanded parent.

"Careful Clark," Lannius cautioned. *"Despair is a clever fog that can creep up in mysterious ways. Before we realize, we could be lost."*

*   *   *   *   *

Aurora woke from the dream, disoriented as she passed from boardroom to bunker. The confusion persisted as she pulled together reality in the unfamiliar space. The lights of the bunker were still dimmed. She sat up, rubbing her eyes. Had that dream been programmed? She scowled. There would be no answer without Lannius. Time to focus on the task. Aurora knew he had stashed their puzzle somewhere.

She left her bunk. They had looked through the bunker but had mostly stopped their search at the kitchen. Aurora started in a closet next to the desk. It was lined with thick coats and boots. She dragged a footlocker out of the depths. Kars stirred as the box scuffed along the floor.

She gently clicked open the box, raising its wide lid.

Inside of the spartan container there were three smaller boxes. Eyes wide, she stumbled back from what she saw.

Each of the lids was ornately engraved—the work of the master craftsman. One of the boxes was covered in an elaborate design, but the other two boxes stole Aurora's breath.

She shouted for her friends to wake up.

Finely burned into the wood of the lids were two names: Koren and Orithian.

15

Gifts

"Aurora, you just found these in the closet?"

They each held a box and stared at them in disbelief. Lena ran her hand over hers.

"Yes. I just pulled out that footlocker and there they were—no machines, no computers, no puzzles involved."

Kars looked down at his box. "Well, I guess old Lannius didn't want to leave this to chance."

Aurora had the third box in her lap. It had a rose over the Parallel logo. The rose was inset with polished carmine.

"Alright then, enough delay. If he wanted us to find these, then let's go," Kars said, slowly opening the box. Lena followed.

Lena lifted her gift from the box. The object was slightly wider than the palm of her hand. It was unmistakably a large key, a thick leather loop tied through the loophole. The metal of the key was strange, though. It seemed soft, and the finish was muted. The shoulder was baroque horns, while the bits of the key seemed to vanish into infinitesimal detail. The surprisingly dense material seemed to vibrate.

Kars lifted out a cylinder the length of his forearm. It was glossy black glass, with dark leather straps. It looked ancient and worn. He turned it in the air and looked down its hollow length.

"It looks like some kind of arm guard," Kars said.

"It is a tabula gauntlet," Squire said. "They were used by some of the Seventy-Seven during the Rebellion."

"What's this key?" Lena asked.

"That is a Master Key. It was also from the Rebellion. Only a few were ever made. Supposedly, they can open any lock."

Lena held up the strange key, examining the bitting and its minute detail. The edge seemed solid at first glance, but on narrower inspection it was a writhing layer, like the life clinging to rocks in a tide pool.

"And what does the—tabula—do?"

"The tabula was a tool used by the Seventy-Seven. It served as an amplifier for their implants and their machines."

"Well, that won't be much use. I don't have any machines or implants—and I don't want them," Kars said.

"Maybe that's why he left it for you," Aurora said.

"Maybe the old man got it wrong," Kars said.

"I don't think that happens very much."

"You haven't opened yours yet." Kars tilted his head at the remaining box.

She reached to open the third box but paused. Her hand hovered above the surface. She pushed through her reluctance and lifted the box from the container.

Inside the box there was a small velvet bag containing a disc, roughly a palm's width in diameter. Aurora opened the bag sliding the disc into her hand. One surface was a simple cross design—a compass rose. The other surface was a finely polished mirror. She looked at it, expecting something to happen.

"What is it?" she asked Squire.

"As far as I can tell, it is a mirror," Squire said. Aurora couldn't sense anything but its weight and the simple design.

"The old man definitely got it wrong," Kars said. "Here Ror, why don't you go ahead with mine?" He passed the gauntlet over.

She looked at the mirror, feeling disappointed. As inconceivable as it had seemed moments ago, Kars was probably right. What use would he have for the tabula gauntlet? She took the gauntlet from his outstretched arm.

"I'll give it a try. Who knows what he left on here?" Aurora slid her arm into the device, cinching the straps. The device then came to life, processes springing up in her vision, before quickly disappearing. It appeared completely inert.

"It worked for a second," Aurora told her friends. Then she noticed warmth on her arm.

The warmth started as a prickle and grew to a searing heat, causing her to tear the device from her arm. She howled and pulled her arm to her chest.

"It nearly burned me!" she exclaimed.

"A countermeasure," Squire chimed. "Tabula are keyed to individuals."

Kars picked up the gauntlet from the floor, looking puzzled.

"Maybe not such a mistake, old man," he said staring down the tube. "Or maybe her mistake?" He laughed.

"Try it, Kars!" Lena said. She had draped the Master Key around her neck.

"There's no way he could have keyed it to you," Aurora said, rubbing her arm.

"Well, we know he's been a step ahead on a few other things. Maybe he got it keyed to me through a visitor to the valley?"

He thrust his left hand into the gauntlet, tightening the straps. The gauntlet came to life, fine writing scrolling across the onyx surface. It continued adjusting the straps. Kars opened and closed his hand, turning the tabula so he could see it. He waited for a burning sensation. None came.

"Looks like we got it right the first time," Kars said, but his voice was distant, the device wrapped around his forearm distracted him. The slick surface was alive with a simple, elegant text. Kars was reading it as the amber text materialized on the screen.

Aurora squinted, but she couldn't read the letters. Frustrating! She couldn't even see processes within the gauntlet. Somehow, she felt betrayed that Lannius had left such miraculous gifts for her friend and her brother. She rubbed her arm where the gauntlet had applied the heat.

"What's it say?" Lena asked.

"Most of it was some kind of computer language, but it stopped at a letter. It says:

> Congratulations on reaching your first rendezvous point, the North Cordovan Waystation. I apologize that I could not be here in person, but my attentions must have been needed elsewhere if you are reading this. No matter. My absence means you are likely safer than if I were there. An element of surprise is still with you.
>
> I wish there was more I could say in this message, however, the details would make little sense without explanation. For now, I must ask you to please keep moving. I will meet you in the city of East Bay.
>
> Please place your hand on Squire to engage the tabula gauntlet. I have instructed it with enough details that Squire should be able to decipher your next steps.
>
> Avoid Perpetual. Do not trust Whitestone. Remain hidden as

long as you can and be safe in
your travels.

A.L.

While Kars read, Aurora called Squire over. When he was
finished, she gestured to the robot, telling Kars, "Let's see what
else there might be."

Kars nodded. He laid his left palm on the engraved plating of the
robot. A series of circular symbols appeared on the dark surface,
scrolling out of view to reveal a technical drawing of the robot.

"The tabula gauntlet reports that it has stored over 40,000
technical manuals for a variety of Perpetual machines and
systems, as well as a variety of exotic custom machines and
legacy platforms. There is a message from Lannius, shall I play
it?"

"Of course!" Kars said.

The face of the old man sprung up in a tightly framed hologram.
He smiled but appeared distracted. He spoke:

"Excellent. You've used the gauntlet. It is a poor substitute for
pure augmentations, but it has certain advantages like remaining
undetected and being immune to intrusion. You should be able
to fool the rail freighter that passes through this waystation into
taking you to East Bay. I will find you there."

The hologram blinked out of existence.

The group shifted with disappointment. Kars shrugged. "That
simple, I guess."

Aurora doubted that Kars had done everything right. Every part of the bunker—the search, the desk and magnifying lens, the hidden door—had all been layered and complicated.

"Wouldn't it make more sense for me to use the gauntlet?" Aurora asked.

"Because you've got the brain computer?" Kars mocked her jealousy.

"Well?" Aurora responded.

"Looks like Lannius decided this was for me. You're not afraid I'm going to get in there?" Kars flexed his fingers like a spider toward his sister's head.

"That's not it," Aurora said. "It's just it seems like I need it."

"I'm just along for the ride," Kars said, smirking. "But this was part of the old man's plan."

He patted the gauntlet, as though he intended to taunt Aurora. She rolled her eyes at the attempt. It did bother her though.

"I would suggest we return to the surface to see when the next freighter is coming through," Squire said.

They clambered back through the doorway into the basement of the station, and then climbed back out into daylight. It was late morning and a light breeze stirred.

Aurora probed the area for any potential interlopers—nothing. Everything around them had remained untouched since the night before. Their mining machine rested in the woods nearby. The three of them crossed the resource highway path into the cargo lift portion of the waystation. Aurora remained focused on the dormant processes nestled within the arachnid machines lined up at the loading dock. They remained undisturbed.

They crossed into the shade of the portico. The crane and other machinery looked used, but not forgotten. The station was still very much functional.

"The message said to fool the rail freighter into taking us to East Bay. I'm guessing we can do that with the gauntlet?" Lena said.

"Yeah, Kars, each of these machines is dormant. I could control them," Aurora said.

"Maybe we should just see if we can get any information on the machines? Seems like we could cause trouble if we're discovered again," Lena cautioned.

"Good thinking, I'll just see if we can see what these machines are doing," Aurora said. She thought for a second before she decided that the task was better left to Squire. She sent the message to Squire, then observed a thread of symbolic representation weave around one of the machines.

Squire reported, "The machines are carrying various heavy metal ores. They have been waiting for thirteen days for retrieval on the rail freighter. The freighter is currently en route."

At least we won't have to wait very long. How should we get on this thing, though? Aurora thought to Squire.

Her thought was interrupted by a distance hiss, just audible over the ambient noise of the forest. She cocked her head toward it.

"Do you hear that?" she asked, still uncertain of how to differentiate between things she heard and things coming from the augmentations.

"Yes," Lena said. "The squeal in the distance."

"I hear it too," Kars said. "Is it the rail freighter?"

"Doppler shift on the tone indicates it is traveling too fast to be a rail freighter. After processing likely options, I conclude it is a rail guard, also known as a Pinkerton. They were experimental at the time I was put in dormancy. I suspect their design has advanced significantly in the past two decades," Squire reported.

"Pinkerton?" Aurora asked. "What do they do?"

"Protect the resource highway," Squire responded, "by eliminating threats."

The screech had grown to a whistle and the rail seemed to vibrate.

"We've got to hide!" Aurora hissed.

16

The Pinkerton

They made it around the side of the waystation before the Pinkerton rounded the corner. The whistle was a howl.

Then it stopped.

Aurora peeked around the corner of the waystation. The Pinkerton looked like a grasshopper of silver spindles along the rail. It clasped the rail at the front and back, reaching out on skeletal leg struts to the anchor points. The narrow body suspended between was slender, tapering to knife-thin points. Three sets of round lens bodies rolled around in housings on the dorsal arch.

The glyphs sprang forth into Aurora's mind. Curious. There were three sets of processes. She wondered their purpose. One of the processes unfolded then snapped shut. Terror spiked through her spine. Her wonder was an augmentation query. How could she have known?

The three globe eyes spun in their sockets and pivoted to their position. The Pinkerton released its grip on the rail. It placed each razor limb down on the earth. The moves were deliberate, as though it was stretching before a hunt.

"Damn!" Aurora hissed, throwing herself behind the building. Her heart hammered in her chest.

"What?" Kars asked, reflecting her concern.

"I didn't mean to, but I probed it," Aurora said. "It noticed me."

"Is that going to be a prob—"

An explosion shook the building, cutting him off.

They sprinted from the building without a word, running toward the forest.

Aurora glanced over her shoulder as they ran. The Pinkerton picked its way across the yard outside the waystation on four razor-tipped legs. It had a similar arachnid look to the mining machine, but seemed much leaner, delicate, and predatory. A wicked cannon swiveled beneath its body and fired another blue bolt at the waystation. The front corner of the building collapsed.

Two of the globe eyes detached, floating out of their sockets. They looked like the infiltrator drone that had attacked the town, except bigger and bulked with armor.

"Keep going!" Aurora shouted. They dove into the underbrush, scrambling through the nettles to reach the shelter of the forest. Once through the thicket at the edge of the forest, they entered the understory. They sprinted across the fallen leaves carpeting the forest floor.

Kars threw himself behind the blasted hulk of an old war machine sunken in the hillside. Lena and Aurora each hid behind a tree. Branches snapped and the brush sounded like a storm as the Pinkerton tried to push its way through the undergrowth.

"Any ideas?" Kars asked. He was panting.

Aurora sensed the processes of the infiltrator drones drifting through the forest toward her. Seeing the glyphs without looking at the drones felt like odd sense of intuition.

"I'm trying to call our miner, but the infiltrators are coming. They are nearby. I guess I could try to break them from here," Aurora said.

"No, don't. The big one will be here in an instant," Lena said. "I'll draw them away. You two loop back to the hub. Kars, make sure you get us a spot on that train. I'll lose them in the forest."

"Lena don't," Kars said. "Please."

"You said it a minute ago—you getting the gauntlet was part of Lannius's plan. You have to be the one to do it," Lena said. "I'll see you soon."

She sprung out of their cover and ran into the forest.

*   *   *   *   *

Lena shouted for the infiltrator's attention, but it didn't matter. The two machines snapped to attention at the movement and careened forward, firing dart-sized bolts of plasma.

A nearby trunk exploded, sending splinters into the air. She vaulted over a downed tree, sliding down a hill as the branches rained down. The infiltrators darted after her, avoiding branches as they maneuvered through the air. Lena kicked to her feet at the bottom of the incline, sprinting across the forest floor. The infiltrators gained ground.

The Pinkerton crashed through branches as it scuttled through the forest. Her muscles burned under the flood of adrenaline. Another plasma bolt smashed a tree above her. Between breaths, she knew that she stood a chance fighting the infiltrators, but she would need to lose the Pinkerton entirely before heading back to the waystation to reunite with her friends.

Lena followed the contour of the land, hoping that the curve would lead into a drainage.

Please be a creek, she thought, trying to ignore her searing muscles as she loped down a leafy slope. She dared a look over her shoulder as one of the infiltrators rounded the hilltop. Its searching eye scanned the terrain before lunging after her. The second was not far behind.

The bottom of the slope cradled a tiny creek. Lena leapt from stone to stone as she followed the stream. She gained speed along the flats, forcing herself to silence her aching muscles. The infiltrators still hounded her, but she could no longer hear the looming threat of the Pinkerton.

Did I lose it? Lena thought. She could jog for miles, but her sprint threatened her with exhaustion. *I'll have to try. Can't keep running.* She looked for anything that would give her some cover for an ambush. She would have to fight the infiltrators.

*   *   *   *   *

Aurora and Kars watched the Pinkerton disappear in a maelstrom of trees and brush. Seeing the spider steps of the Pinkerton on its razor legs reminded Kars of the terror he felt after facing the Protek.

He opened his mouth to yell to Lena, but Aurora hushed him.

"Don't," Aurora said. "She's fast, but she can't run forever. We need to figure out a way out of here before we do anything else."

"How do we do that?" Kars said. "Did you see that thing?"

"Kars. I know," Aurora said. "I'm trying to think of a plan. I need you to keep it together. Lannius said that gauntlet could control almost anything–"

"If I'm touching it!" Kars said. "I'm not getting anywhere near that thing!" He nodded toward the Pinkerton.

"I know. It'd tear you apart," Aurora said. "I was saying that you could call the rail freighter, while I try something else."

Kars pursed his lips and nodded in agreement.

"What are you going to do?" Kars asked.

"Take Squire," Aurora said as the tiny robot unfolded and sprung out of her pack. "I've got to take care of something."

There was a tremendous crash, and their miner burst out of the woods. It bowed its torso, allowing Aurora to spring into the cockpit. She reared the machine up and grinned at Kars.

"I'm going to save Lena," Aurora said. "Just fix that train and be ready to move!"

She turned the machine and galloped into the forest down the Pinkerton's path of debris.

*   *   *   *   *

Aurora clung to a handrail in the cockpit as the miner sprinted forward. The feel of the mechanical steed merged seamlessly with her experience through the augmentations. A small smile snuck onto her face as she ran after the Pinkerton.

The Pinkerton's processes winked into her awareness, the indigo glyph in her focus like a mote in the sun. She attacked the processes, feeling them shift and respond to her intrusion. The Pinkerton stopped and turned to face her.

I hope this works, she thought and imagined herself as Lena. The glyphs of the Pinkerton responded, changing their assessment of the threat. Aurora imagined herself as ten Lenas and pictured her friend running through the woods, her golden hair trailing behind her as she ran.

*   *   *   *   *

The Pinkerton seemed confused before refocusing itself on one of Aurora's specters. Aurora concentrated on imagining her friend fleeing the machine and threaded part of her attention toward stymying the Pinkerton's ability to detect the phantom. A patina of sweat formed on her brow, and her head grew warm with the augmentations' additional effort.

The Pinkerton followed the scared girl through the forest. She ran her fastest, but she was no match for the striding spider legs on the soft terrain. The machine's cannon was disabled for an unknown reason. Its programming directed it to continue: scythe the target with a razor arm.

The girl looked over her shoulder, terrified as the Pinkteron closed the gap. She stumbled and fell to the ground. She tried to crawl across the ground, but it would be no use. The Pinkerton raised its forearm and slashed downward.

*   *   *   *   *

Aurora let go of her image of Lena as the Pinkerton slashed. The machine swung its razor arm into a massive oak, tearing its arm clean from its shoulder joint. It heaved off balance as the limb sheared. Sparks rained from the broken socket.

Aurora urged the miner forward, clinging to the cockpit as the utilitarian machine pounced on the Pinkerton. She felt a wave of rage pass through her augmentations and into the miner as she pummeled the sleek murder drone with her machine's heavy limbs. The Pinkerton fought back, swiping at the miner while trying to twist loose the cannon on its underbelly. Aurora smashed the cannon flat under one of the miner's feet.

She screamed as she directed the miner's attack, pounding the Pinkerton into the soil. Finally, the spidery drone stopped moving, reduced to a sparking, smoking wreckage. Aurora moved the miner off the inert Pinkerton, careful that the machine was no longer functioning. When she finally stopped roaring, she realized how Em had felt standing over the infiltrator. Her blood fumed.

*   *   *   *   *

Lena prowled beneath the debris of a fallen tree as the sound of the infiltrators grew closer. She held her breath, clutching a thick branch she had found at the floodwater line. She thought of Em taunting the infiltrator days before and felt as though she was answering for that savagery.

The sound of the motor whined to a crescendo. Lena tightened her grip, knowing the machine would soon float beneath the downed tree and into her hiding place.

The infiltrator drifted into her space and she struck out of the hollow like an eel. The drone started to raise its stinging arm, but Lena swung first. She smashed the eye as she had done in the warehouse, only with enough force to send the drone careening to the pebble floor of the creek.

She cast her club aside, grabbing a large stone and pouncing on the downed robot. It waved its stinging arms at her like a pinned beetle and fired a bolt that buzzed past her head to scorch a hole in the downed tree above them. Despite its defense, Lena didn't hesitate. She slammed the rock down with both hands, lifting and slamming until the drone buzzed and its arms stopped flexing.

She sprung up and spat on the drone. Em would have been proud.

Lena looked up and saw the second infiltrator as it surged forward toward its downed companion. It fired its bolts at her.

No more surprises for this one, Lena thought. *I hope Aurora and Kars figured something out.*

She leapt out of the path of another bolt, sprinting back to the waystation.

*   *   *   *   *

"Alright, Kars. Time to learn to use a legendary magic gauntlet. Everyone's counting on you," he chided himself. He mopped sweat from his brow. "No pressure."

Kars walked over to the main chassis of the loading crane and laid a hand on its surface. The gauntlet came to life with the fine orange script. His brow contorted in confused dismay as the foreign script scrolled past.

"Can you help?" Kars asked Squire.

The tiny robot scrambled up the chassis and perched itself above the gauntlet on Kars's arm. "You've opened the loading crane manifest," Squire reported.

"That's great," Kars said. "Can you make it work for us?"

"I cannot," Squire responded. "The gauntlet does not respond to me."

"Perfect." Kars looked over his shoulder as terrible crashes and explosions echoed from the woods. "Focus, Kars."

He touched the screen. The intuitive interface reorganized. The script was littered with symbols and nested lists. He bit his lip. "If I can just add another miner to the list, we could ride ours out of here," Kars said.

Kars pressed what he thought was a list of cargo. An angry Perpetual logo pulsed on the glossy gauntlet screen. Kars stomach dropped.

"Squire, do I want to know?" Kars asked.

"I cannot answer that," Squire said in the dispassionate tenor. "However, console is showing that three more Pinkerton models have been dispatched to our location."

Three? Kars imagined the horrible spider robots stepping off the rail. Maybe they could hide in the bunker until they left. He looked at the waystation. The Pinkerton had nearly flattened the building and the remnants were smoking.

"Okay, Kars. Double-time. We can't be here when those things arrive."

Kars rallied. He squinted at the gauntlet, flicking aside the pulsing warning symbol. Closing his eyes, he breathed and then opened them with fresh focus, patiently scanning the orange script on the gauntlet. He saw the file—the cargo manifest.

"I got it. The list of all the cargo heading into the city," Kars said. "Just going to add one."

The gauntlet responded, but the query pulsed.

"It needs the number of the machine," Kars said, defeated. He lowered his hand and the gauntlet went dark. *Hopefully Aurora makes it back in time.*

*   *   *   *   *

The last infiltrator drone's glyph winked into Aurora's awareness; however, she could not clearly see the symbols. It was behind a hilltop. The soil must have been enough to muffle the connection.

Aurora urged the miner toward the glyph, certain that Lena must have been nearby. No sooner had she started than Lena burst around the hillside. Lena's terror melted to gratitude. The infiltrator tried to retreat, but Aurora smashed it beneath the miner's front leg.

Lena threw her arms around Aurora. "I probably shouldn't have run like that!" she said. "Thank you for coming for me!"

"You would've done the same." Aurora had a steely look of satisfaction on her face. "Besides, I kind of liked it."

"Just don't turn into one of those things," Lena cautioned.

176

"I won't. I'm not going anywhere," Aurora responded, but she felt distance in her own voice. The mining machine lurched forward.

*   *   *   *   *

Kars waved his arms in a frantic effort to hurry Aurora's return on the mining machine. It finally crashed through the last bit of understory into the clearing, and Kars shouted for them.

Aurora brought the mining machine to a stop and they dismounted.

"We've got to go now!" Kars shouted.

"I dealt with the Pinkerton and the infiltrators," Aurora said.

"That's not it. I called the rail freighter," Kars said, hesitating. "I also accidentally tripped an alarm. Three more Pinkertons are on the way."

"Three?" Lena asked. Kars nodded.

Lena rubbed her temples. She was covered in cuts and scrapes from her sprint through the forest and damp with muddy sweat. Her braid was disheveled and matted to her clavicle.

"We need to run," Lena said, heading off her suspicion that Aurora intended to fight.

Aurora said nothing.

"I'm so sorry," Kars said. "I didn't know what I was doing with this thing." He gestured to the gauntlet.

"I think I might able to get the rest of these miners up for the fight," Aurora said.

"Why!" Lena gasped.

"I stood up to one without much issue," Aurora responded.

"Fine," Lena conceded. "But what's the point? More will come. We've got a choice right now. Remember our purpose is to find Lannius, find our families, and get some answers about why we are out here being chased by these machines in the first place. Why fight when we can run?"

Aurora gave a long look at the line of miners in the cargo crane dock, as though she were appraising a line of new recruits.

"Really?" Lena pushed the issue. "You can't be serious! At the very least, think of Kars and me. We don't have augmentations. I just barely made it trying to distract them. Ror, we can't do this."

Kars nodded in agreement.

Aurora pressed her hand on her brow, covering her eyes. A shiver went down her spine as she remembered that the power she felt astride the miner was the product of the machine, not herself. She let the shiver of her spine creep into her thoughts. The feeling was distinctly human, a deeply animal sensation bound in the meat of the body—it was fear.

"You're right," Aurora said. "How do we get out of here?"

Kars blew out a low whistle of relief.

"I already know how to prime the crane to add our miner to the cargo manifest. That should get us a spot on the rail freighter," he said, pressing his gauntleted hand to the console of the loading crane.

The screen sprang to life. Aurora read the screen. Kars had narrowed it to a list of a few letters and numbers.

"I just don't know the name or number of our machine. Can you find it? I think that the best way forward is just to add the number to the list, then hitch a ride."

"Seems like it'd be worth a try." Aurora sent the question to Squire. She was learning that Squire was better equipped to interpret her requests than if she made the requests of the machine herself. While she knew she could easily get the information, if she thought into the machine, Squire was better equipped for these simple tasks.

"Our machine is listed as MPUMP-38910215."

Kars stabbed his fingers at the gauntlet. It was a clumsy action that seemed to take his full attention.

"Done. I added it to the list," he said. "I think. Can you pull the machine into the lineup, Ror?"

She had grown so accustomed to making the machine walk that it was practically effortless for her to walk the machine into position.

"Alright. Got it. Now what?" Aurora asked. She was still feeling impatient that Kars had gotten such a superior present.

"We wait," Kars said, "and hope the rail freighter arrives before the Pinkertons."

*   *   *   *   *

They hunkered in the cockpit of their miner, listening for any sound vibrating through the rail. The loading crane cast a lattice of shadows over them. Aside from the threat of the Pinkertons, it would have otherwise been a nice day to sit and wait for the freighter. A few birds idled between the cargo-laden mining machines waiting in the lineup.

Kars surveyed their machine, noting the dented armor plates and scuffed finish. "I hope the rail freighter doesn't have a prejudice against damaged machines."

"It should not be a problem," Squire said. "The machine is operational, and we have forged the appropriate credentials."

"Even if it is, I wonder if I could figure something out," Aurora said.

Lena shot her a look. "We don't need to hope for problems."

"I'm not hoping. It's just hard to explain," Aurora said.

"Stop enjoying yourself," Lena said, scowling beneath her sweat-matted hair. "No need to wish for trouble. I'm sure you'll find plenty more once we get to the city."

Before Aurora could respond, they were disrupted by a distant hissing noise. They held their breath and listened.

"Pinkertons?" Kars asked.

The hissing sound grew louder over the course of several minutes, but there was still nothing in sight. Judging by the distant sound and how long it took to appear, the source of the noise must have been very large.

The noise continued to grow until the rail freighter slid around the bend.

The large vehicle was all skeletal struts linked to a variety of component units. Some of the cars held lines of arachnid machines, others supported tanks, and some held containers. The bulk of its weight was balanced on the wheel by buttressed repulsor pads. Glyphs of processes contained within the pads unfolded in Aurora's vision as hypnotic fractals. She felt ill watching the processes. The pattern had wrongness in it.

The freighter screamed through the section of the resource highway containing the waystation. It seemed that miles of the freighter hurtled by their station, the wail of the wheels on the rail overwhelmed the sound of the forest. Finally, one of the freight cars detached, slowing on the track. The section of the rail freighter was an empty rack for mining machines.

"Do you hear that?" Kars asked.

Over the clanking and grinding of the rail freighter there was a whistle gaining in the distance.

"Pinkertons," Aurora said. "Stay low. I think it's too late to make a run for it."

Before they could react, the line of machines was moving forward, the loading crane grabbing one after another and placing them on the rack. Soon their machine was hanging in the frame of the rail freighter, and the larger machine lurched forward, gaining speed. The whistle of the Pinkertons faded as they left the waystation behind.

*   *   *   *   *

His office faded into the background of the lost focus of a daydream as Whitestone watched through the eyes of the Pinkertons. Daydreams—one of the main cognitive functions the network engineers had repurposed.

Hold this position. He sent the command to one of the infiltrator scouts that accompanied each Pinkerton. Having one scout with a bird's-eye view was for his own attention span and to combat his sense of vertigo. An experienced investigator would have braided their attention span to simultaneously experience all nine machines.

Whitestone preferred keeping his singular focus. In all his travels he had never perfected braiding his attention span. He watched his daydream of the scene. The thin line of the resource highway bisected his view, seemingly superimposed on the landscape. An old pre-Rebellion building smoldered across a wide lot from the loading crane. Other resource highway stations consumed entire mountains, mechanical infections on the landscape visible from space. This station was puny by comparison.

He jumped to the infiltrator closest to the building.

The Pinkerton cannon had left a mess of the waystation. The front wall was blasted to dust and the roof had caved in where it had not blown apart. Whitestone's daydream of the infiltrator's perspective wavered in front of his office.

At Whitestone's signal, one of the Pinkertons started sifting through the pieces of the blasted building. The infiltrator hovered nearby, focusing its computations on processing the wreckage for any recognizable clues. Whitestone watched as well—most times an algorithm would notice a pattern before a person, but sometimes, the human mind made an intuitive leap that a computer would miss.

The infiltrator and Whitestone saw the symbol at the same time—Parallel.

A wave of nostalgia swelled inside of him before striking a wall of indifference. That symbol had once meant so much to him.

Another infiltrator sent an alert message, drawing his attention from the signal: a destroyed Pinkerton not far from the resource highway.

Whitestone smiled wryly—impressive.

He ordered the infiltrators to start extracting data from the Pinkerton and called up the logs from the resource highway loading dock. The manifest materialized in his awareness. Each machine had its number, cargo, and home station. One stood out—MPUMP-38910215, home station: Cerra Mountain Mining Camp 910.

Whitestone allowed his focus on the investigation to slip.

They had made it to the resource highway. Whitestone smiled. The girl was resourceful, and Lannius had once more proved his strategic vision. No matter—the city was his dominion. They would come to him.

17

The Freighter

Aurora, Lena, and Kars sat up from their position tucked in the cockpit of the machine. As the rail freighter accelerated, their machine swayed in the suspended rack. Wind whipped through their hair. The beat of the rail wheel crossing joints in the rail drummed as they moved. After the cave and the plodding pace of their machine, the speed of the rail freighter was liberating.

They watched the scenery pass in silent disbelief. Lena shivered as the wind picked up. She was still damp with sweat from her escape from the Pinkerton. Kars gave her his thick coat, and she leaned on his shoulder. Aurora felt herself smile despite the bittersweet feeling that she was losing something else. Even in its early tenderness, they had something she feared she lost—normal life together. Lena snuggled her head into a more comfortable spot and closed her eyes.

The rail freighter rolled westward through the hills and valleys of the Cordovan Gap, revealing more of the abandoned bones of rural civilization. Robots similar to the miners—lighter and leaner with sets of tiny arms dangling beneath—tended fields of low berries and vegetables.

Eventually they saw evidence of people, carts stacked with blankets and goods tucked into the shade of trees. Two men paused from their cigarettes and card game to watch the rail freighter scream past. One pointed to the human stowaways, trying to show his friend before the rail freighter had roared by, but the second man did not turn from his cards.

Their freighter path merged with other resource highway lines. They felt a jar through the freighter as other lines connected with theirs to form an even more massive train. As the rail carried them back into the hills and past empty loading cranes and depots, they could see the length of the freighter stretching past their view at both the front and to their rear. Occasionally, they saw a person dressed in the black fatigues stationed along the highway. Squire reported they were Perpetual field operatives left to conduct service checks that a Pinkerton had flagged for review. The operatives never looked away from their tasks despite the scream of the rail freighter.

As her mind idled to the rhythm of the rail, Aurora's gaze drifted to the repulsors. There was a mesmerizing interface between the fractal unfolding of processes and the air beneath them. It was not the liquid wavering of a heat shimmer, but a twisting and coiling of the air as though the repulsor bent space itself.

Aurora tried to probe the repulsor with her thoughts, just to see what processes lay hidden inside the writhing space. The fractal glyph resisted her direction but drew her attention deeper into it. She felt the rest of her vision melt toward fractals, the edges of everything she looked at softened and moved. Her body felt like it was shrinking and dilating.

Do not access the repulsors, a voice said in her mind.

"What?" Aurora responded. The voice had been her own but lilted with a strange accent.

At very complex levels, math is indistinguishable from a change in consciousness, the voice responded. *Plumb those depths too far and you may reduce yourself to a process.*

"I don't understand," Aurora said. Her vision had dissolved to a point where she could see herself, slowly vibrating in space. "What's happening?"

"Aurora?" It was Lena's voice but distant. It seemed to echo and fragment.

"Lena?" Aurora said, forcing her mind to withdraw from the repulsor. It felt like her words came from a source that was too close to her. She was acutely aware of the timbre of her voice.

"Aurora!" Kars shouted, shaking her shoulder.

Aurora squeezed her eyes shut. "I'm not sure what happened."

Squire sprung up, posturing as though to defend Aurora.

"She attempted to access a repulsor," Squire said. "Most repulsors are shielded to prevent access."

"Why?" Kars said. "Are they dangerous?"

"To an unequipped mind? Yes, they can be dangerous. An unforeseen danger from convergence of different technologies," Squire said. "As to the why, it will be difficult to understand without a solid grasp of Prostian mathematics. In short, each repulsor is a quantum computer, in which the calculations bend the fabric of space-time. Davin Prost was a friend of Lannius. It was his theoretic mathematics that catapulted humankind forward hundreds of years."

"Is that what happened?" Aurora asked. "The repulsor hurt me?"

"An untrained operator accessing a repulsor will inadvertently offload the repulsor calculations to their own augmentations. It has strange effects on consciousness—interactions with your fundamental perception of reality. Some even experiment with Prostian transformations recreationally," Squire reported.

Aurora stared off at the landscape. "I have so much to learn."

"According to my records, some of the Seventy-Seven even used Prostian transformations as a weapon," Squire said.

Kars looked baffled. "Math as a weapon?"

"It is important to remember that at their core, computers are mathematical constructs, regardless of how seamless an experience one has with the interface. Even when technology seems magical, it is not. Programs are reducible to logic. Many people forget the magic of their computers is math," Squire said. "In this case, the math of the machine invades the mind."

"I guess there's some benefit to not having any machines in my head," Kars said.

"Technically, augmentations are not machines as they lack moving parts," Squire corrected.

"You know what I mean," Kars said, exasperated. "I'm not lost in the rift of a repulsor."

"If you entered the field, you would be vulnerable to the physical effects. The cognitive effects of the Prostian transformation are unique to those with augmentations," Squire responded.

Kars looked over at the strange curling of air wrapping around the plate of the repulsor. The light itself seemed to slip over the surface, giving a liquid impression of the landscape beyond. "Looks like it might hurt," Kars said.

"Very much," Squire responded. "The repulsor would reorganize you at a subatomic level."

"Enough," Kars said. "I don't know Prostian math, but I've seen enough to know: don't touch the repulsors."

"Don't even think about them," Aurora cautioned.

"I don't know if we're going to have that option forever, Ror," Lena said. "We are only heading deeper into this world."

As Lena spoke, they rounded a bend in the resource highway and the hills opened onto a small valley.

Cradled in the valley was a town not unlike their own. However, as they drew close, they saw the fields were being tended by people accompanied by mining machines. People gathered fruit from low bushes, which they added to baskets hanging from the miners. The machines patiently followed, draped in retrofitted hooks for different gear and water coolers.

"People live with the machines?" Kars asked.

"Not all machines are built for war," Squire responded. "In fact, most are tools of peace and prosperity."

The settlements grew more frequent as the rail freighter continued. They saw the glint of solar panels on barn roofs and wider sheet metal buildings. Containers stacked outside were emblazoned with the few insignias of the companies. Smoke from cook fires rose from nearby shanties. A few people moved about on ATVs and old pickups, still others led machines from horseback. Others grazed goats in the brush nearby.

The rail freighter continued hurtling toward civilization. New sections joined into the length, merging until the train stretched several miles long, yet it never slowed. They only felt the tiny nudge as each new segment joined the whole.

The sun dipped low in the sky, slowly shifting from orange to red. Their freighter peeled around a last bend, the scenery opening up onto a spectacular radiant gem. Bathed in the glow of the western sun, the megacity spread before them, its buildings reaching into the clouds.

The jewel of the west lay before them: they had arrived in East Bay.

18

Deserted

The days in Amurtan blended together between scorching heat and blasting sandstorms. The first days had been uncertain, but they settled into a dull rhythm. Em had learned to tell from the evening sky what the next day would hold. Red sky at sunset usually meant the next day would bring a storm. Clean sunsets brought frozen nights and stunning heat at dawn. Rain had forgotten these scorched lands.

Wild laughter echoed through the camp from the guard towers each night. It was not the hearty laughter of good humor, but the wicked laughter of mania. It seemed like there was never sleep. Perhaps the guards couldn't sleep. Their night laughs were like hyenas.

"Why that horrible laugh?" Em asked Ranjit one evening as the laughter started. An involuntary shiver surged through her spine at the terrible sound.

"It's not all of them," Ranjit responded. "Only a few of them sought out paranoia engines—likely the night guards."

"Paranoia engines?" Em asked. Her shivering spine must have sensed the wrongness before Ranjit had said anything.

"Yes, augmentations to their augmentations," Ranjit said. A shrieking laugh drifted through the still evening air.

190

"That sounds horrible," Em responded.

"Just like all pathologies, it has a kernel rooted deep in our will to survive," Ranjit said. "In this case, paranoia is a useful instinct to live in the desert, marooned on an island surrounded by renegade machines."

Em nodded. Vigilance and caution might serve to keep one alive through these desert nights. She only had a vague idea of what lay beyond the wall of the camp, and it sounded worse than being compelled to paranoia.

The laughter would die off deep in the night when the cold set in. The townsfolk held their children close, shielding the little ones. Mercenary guards patrolled the fence of their enclosure, balaclavas pulled over their faces to keep out the chill. The occasional Protek would slink beyond the edge of the spotlights, their red ring eye and the terrible clicking betraying their location in the darkness. The "domestic" Protek served as both a defense and a reminder of the evils that lurked outside the camp.

The townsfolk adapted to the warnings and challenges of the desert. The guards gave them water and blankets but otherwise showed the townsfolk only cruel indifference and disdain. Em felt it: the mercenary guards saw them as beasts that chose a barbarian life in the mountains over the sophistication and promise of the city.

Em, slowly healing from the battle on the night of the invasion, understood how Ranjit had lost twenty years. Between the heat and the sandstorms, her healing had at least marked a certain passage of time. The purpose of conversation seemed to dry up in the bleaching desert heat. Angelique had grown quiet and brooding. The other townsfolk seemed to wither away from interacting.

One scorching morning there was a commotion in a nearby camp building. Em stirred from her chosen spot beneath the shade netting at the back of their enclosure. Voices barked orders, and there was the garbled clicking of the Protek.

A group of the mercenaries rounded the corner of the buildings. Two of them carried a limp figure between their shoulders. His head was draped in a black sack, and his left leg ended in a clean-bandaged stump below the knee. Two guards stood by with weapons raised as another opened the gate. They set down the limp figure behind the fence in the middle of the imprisoned townsfolk. They stepped back, the guard's weapons trained on the crowd and sealed the gate.

The townsfolk watched.

The leader of the group spoke. He wore small spectacles—no augmentations.

"We did what we could for your man." His accent was sharp—Mastean from Em's judgment. "Unfortunately, we could not save his leg, but he is stable and free of infection."

There was silence.

The man waited awkwardly. Finally he turned to leave. "Please call out if you think he is deteriorating. Call for the doctor."

"Doctor"—Em stopped him—"thank you."

The man nodded to her and departed.

As soon as the gate closed, Em rushed to the hooded figure. She already knew who was behind the hood.

"Ben!" Cara screamed hysterically as Em pulled back the hood.

The crowd pushed forward, eager to see him.

Ben looked weary but healthy, perhaps healthier than before they had been taken from the village. There was clarity in his eyes she had not seen in many years. No doubt his time in the camp's infirmary had been free of alcohol. They had probably nursed him with nutrients and hydration and treated the chronic ailments that pile up beneath the yoke of addiction.

Cara threw herself onto him, sobbing. Em smiled seeing the reunion but felt a bitter-sweetness that made her long to see Robert. Ben smiled, his face creased from years of sun and poor health.

"It's okay," Ben said, trying to give her consolation. "I'm okay."

She sniffed and wiped her nose. She still cried but nodded in agreement. Em stood nearby, her hand on Cara's shoulder.

The townsfolk gathered and moved Ben to a shady part of the enclosure, helping him into a comfortable position. He shared his experience.

"I don't remember much of what happened after being taken." He seemed to take pride in being the focus of the community for something other than his drunkenness. "The doctor and his team had done their best, but one of them had done a terrible number on my leg. They talked me through it, made sure that I knew what was happening. They couldn't save it, but the doctor treated me."

Em stroked her chin, skeptical of the motives behind the humane treatment.

"Did you see anything while you were in there?" Em asked.

"I only caught glimpse of the camp. There's a small army stationed here, and those robots are all around the perimeter. The doc has some pretty state of the art stuff in there," Ben said.

"Did you see their leader? The guy with the mohawk?" Em asked.

Ben shook his head. "I did not. I think I may have heard them talking to him a couple of times, but I never saw him. Of course, I wanted to get a look at the beating I stuck on his face."

"Was there anyone else? Did you see any other prisoners?" Em asked.

"A couple other prison blocks, but I didn't see anyone in particular. They kept my head bagged up while they moved me," Ben said.

"I'm sorry. I didn't see Robert," Ben said.

Em's face twisted in pained disappointment. "It's okay," she responded.

"We all lost people, Em," Ben said. "Most of mine aren't coming back. I'll hold out hope you find yours."

Cara looked as though she would be sick. Em wished she could balance her hope that Robert still lived with compassion for the feelings this place must stir in Cara. The things Cara and Robert had witnessed made Em shiver.

"Not all of your children are gone—Lena is still out there," Em said.

"I know," Cara said. "It's why I'm still holding on."

"Good. We'll need everyone to get out of here." Em thought that Cara had let Lena drift away long ago.

"I'll give up the other to see Lena again," Ben patted the dressing on his stump.

"Let's hope it doesn't come to that, Ben," Em said. "For now, bide your time. Learn about these bastards. We'll find a way out."

Em turned to talk to Ranjit, but Ben stopped her.

"There was one other thing," Ben said.

Em listened.

"I overheard one of the guards say something about a 'scripter.'"

"Scripter?" Em repeated.

"Yes," Ben said. "They said that the scripter would be back through sometime after the next month's supply run."

Em nodded. "I'll see what I can figure out about it."

Curious, Em thought. There was definitely some larger game at stake, but she could barely see beyond the edge of the fence. She left Ben to Cara and the other townsfolk and walked to her edge of the fence, hoping that Ranjit would be there.

"They brought back your man?" Ranjit said, before Em could say anything. She wasn't surprised. The prison barriers were sturdy but did little to insulate sections from one another.

"Yes. One of our people," Em said. "He's lost a leg, but it seems like they took care of him."

"That's the doctor," Ranjit said. "He's a good man. I think he was taken during the Rebellion. Jackal would probably have had us all killed, but better minds seem to keep him in a narrow track."

"Jackal. Their leader?" Em asked.

"Yes. He's another veteran of the Rebellion," Ranjit said.

"And?"

"It seems like his handler at Perpetual keeps him on a short leash. He did something to earn the respect of the Protek, or at least a band of Protek. Many of his subordinates doubt his sanity, though few of them have enough of their own to judge."

"Good," Em said. She thought about how Jackal had underestimated her and her people. There was iron in their blood, even if it had a coat of rust from decades unused. Jackal had brought an enemy army into his own camp. The less his knowledge and the greater his arrogance built their only advantage. She wanted to share with Ranjit behind the wall, but he was still too convenient of a mystery to fully trust.

"Why would they take care of our man?" Em asked.

"What's more valuable than having your enemy dead?" Ranjit said.

"Having your enemy in your debt?" Em responded.

"Even more valuable than an indebted enemy," the voice behind the wall said.

"An ally?" Em asked.

"They have kept me and my compatriots here for twenty years. Jackal has an odd compassion that almost seems an aspect of another. It is much easier to invade the soul of a man through kindness than bloodshed," Ranjit said. His voice was heavy with a sense of loss.

"Your people joined them?" Em asked. The thought of one of the Seventy-Seven joining Perpetual's mercenary band stabbed her heart. Certain myths were meant to remain sacrosanct.

"Not voluntarily—but they had enough trust to drop their guard. Then the scripters did their work," Ranjit said.

"Scripters," Em repeated.

"I overheard your friend's story," Ranjit said.

"What are scripters?" Em asked. If they could tame the Seventy-Seven, their escape just became significantly more challenging and dangerous.

"Writers," Ranjit said, his voice reluctant. "Of a man's deepest desires. They are the authors of the engines I've told you about—the paranoia engines and the compulsion engines. Some of them can rewrite an entire person."

"But the Seventy-Seven, you're all equipped to fight against those kinds of attacks," Em responded.

"Just like your life without augmentations, once someone is within one's trust, they can change the way we think. It's not always an assault. Sometimes the other creeps in and melts the defenses from within."

Em had considered they were leverage—not that they were being held in a workshop to be crafted into the tools of their children's destruction. Em watched Ben across the enclosure. His spirited return lifted the will of the townsfolk.

"Ranjit, how do I know I can trust you?" Em asked.

There was a long pause, before the man behind the fence spoke.

"I was wondering when you might reach that question," Ranjit said. "You cannot. I have no way of proving myself to you. Twenty years and I have no way of proving my virtue to myself. I've fought back against Perpetual and stayed vigilant against the scripters. There are more of us, still loyal to Lannius, who will help you, but I have no way of proving that loyalty other than asking your trust."

Em knew that would be his response. She knew he must have his own reservations about her. She watched Ben and Cara sitting together. Their captors had some cunning.

19

The Man Behind the Wall

Time crawled by in the camp, punctuated by daily rations and water deliveries while they all slimmed to a similar gaunt physique. Em tried to find a pattern in the deliveries and attempted to talk with their guards. She assembled the little details to place their camp on the surface of the planet. Based on the stars and the arc of the sun through the sky, they faced southeast. She tracked the occasional cloud as it passed across the unyielding desert sky. No contrails formed over the dangerous skies of Amurtan. She imagined the turquoise waters of the Sparrow Sea a thousand miles to the south, the equatorial shores of the southern Panmathican states lying beyond. She knew the space between seethed with Protek, roving the territory like alien insects.

The cruel desert provided no food or water. If what she knew about Amurtan were true, even if there was water, it would be poison. Some days, more ships would arrive or leave the camp, stirring great clouds of dust with their arrival. Em tried to calculate their size and frequency to estimate the size of the camp. The camp lived on a supply chain, hauled a thousand miles to keep the camp alive. She held herself back from the dark knowledge that the supply chains arrival could also herald the arrival of the scripters.

In addition to the cruelty of the desert and the specter of the scripters, there was also the looming presence of the Protek. She no longer felt the acid panic in her gut when she saw the feral machines, but living under their watch had done little to help her accept that they had some crude intelligence that drove their wandering. Lannius's first gift to the world.

Of all the beast robots, one Protek seemed to watch her. When she first noticed, it had been missing one of its arms, stolen by the math grenade she had used. It saw her and stopped, waiting and processing. The red ring eye seemed patient.

Unlike the others, it would pause its endless stomping march at the edge of the fence, waiting and watching her. The townsfolk would move away without a word. Whether it was the intense danger they posed, or their unnatural animal presence, being too close to the machines stirred some deep discomfort. Even Em tried to avoid looking at it. It could have pushed down the fence and been on top of her in a moment, yet it remained at the boundary. She cringed at the awful distortion and clicking of the machine as it watched her. Was it possible for a machine to want revenge?

After several days, the robot had grafted another arm in place of the one it had lost. The armor plates were dented and mismatched, either stolen by force or torn from the carapace of another dead Protek. The day it approached the fence with its new arm, it paused at its customary spot. It waited, staring with its red eye locked on Em. She did her best to avoid its stare. The beast machine continued to wait at the fence.

Finally, Em met the Protek's glare.

The machine lifted both of its pincer arms in the air and raised its head. It bellowed a terrible sound toward the sky. Em and the other townsfolk covered their ears from the discord.

It bellowed again, echoing through the camp. Another Protek called in the distance.

When the Protek started gesturing again, flexing its arms into a cross, the townsfolk all scattered to the edges of their enclosure. Em whispered to herself, hoping the machine would leave. As it continued bellowing, more Protek called their response in the distance.

A pang of fear shot through her. "Is he calling more?" Em whispered to herself. Even the most heavily fortified camp could not withstand all the Protek of Amurtan descending on its walls.

The red ring eye focused on her and its arms pulsed the cross shape.

Em leapt forward toward the fence. She tasted the steel of fear in her mouth.

"Stop!" she shouted. The townsfolk watched in horror.

The Protek lowered its head, the ringed iris focusing on her. The camp was silent, save for the wind flapping the shade tarps.

The machine pulsed its arms again.

Em raised her own and slowly pulsed them across her chest. The fence between her and the machine felt as though it did not exist. She held her breath.

The Protek raised its own cutting blades, pulsing them in response. Em raised her own in front of her chest. The machine turned and stomped away.

Em watched the chrome beast disappear before lowering her arms. Her mouth was dry as the desert air.

The crowd of townsfolk burst into a collective cheer. Some rushed Em with congratulations, others huddled together in relief. Trembling, Em slunk off to her corner of the prison yard.

"You know they have names?" Ranjit said as Em returned to the fence.

"Who? The Protek?" Em asked through the barrier.

"Yes," Ranjit said. "I've heard Jackal and his men refer to them by name."

"Bah. Must just be nicknames the guards gave 'em," Em responded. She tossed a pebble across the hard scrabble lot.

"You know that's a lie you're telling yourself," Ranjit said.

Em frowned. The experience of the bellowing, gesticulating monster was too fresh. "Maybe true, but I think I prefer the lie."

"Fair, but it won't change the truth," Ranjit said. "They named themselves."

Em watched one of the war machines stomping through the camp in the distance. The scraps of its decoration dangled from its chrome carapace.

"I wonder if it started before or after they rampaged through Amurtan?" Ranjit asked. "If there was a moment at Agrion, when one of them looked at Lannius in the test field and chirped that unprecedented sound—its name. And I wonder if Lannius let them roam even after hearing it. Knowing him, I'm not sure he would have stopped it."

Em imagined the noble face that had left her with her daughter. She could not place the coldness that Ranjit alluded to. Lannius couldn't have intended to unleash the beast machines.

"No way that man meant for all this to happen," Em retorted.

"Of course not. Arthur Lannius never meant harm," Ranjit said, "but certainly you see how his curiosity and optimism could unleash monsters. He's not a man of malice, but some have called his genius cavalier."

"I wouldn't fault the man for pairing genius with optimism," Em responded.

"I would not fault it either—but I wonder if he did. The father of the feral machines carried his guilt. And one must wonder, at what point does a quest for redemption become the threat itself?"

Em recoiled, thinking back to the tense moments in the Rebellion between Robert and Lannius. She thought of tiny Aurora in her arms, moments after Lannius rode off into the woods with his guards. They rode to ruin. She was suddenly aware that the impenetrable wasteland surrounding their camp was a product of Lannius. Another Protek lumbered past the edge of the fence.

As time went on, she learned to tell the machines apart. Each was distinct, once she allowed herself to look past her fear and stare at the machines for more than a moment. They prowled the edges of the camp like scrap metal sculptures of nuclear insects.

Battle scars gouged their armor, some were missing parts, and others had grafted other machines onto their own skeletons. A few had pelts and leather strapped to them in an array that offered no utility—it could only mark some rank or individuality. All of them were adorned with strange symbols and drawings. Em had seen them interacting with one another, clicking and buzzing, sometimes preening each other's components and adornments.

Over the course of weeks, Em and Ranjit continued their long, slow conversation. Em understood his suspicion after hearing about the scripters. He shared little, but Em suspected there were at least fifteen others from the Seventy-Seven in the camp. The prospect of reuniting with the wayward knights of Lannius stirred Em's hopes. If there were any army that could challenge their Protek keepers, it would be Lannius's elite. Deep rage seethed in the man, and she hoped he might rouse from his imprisonment.

In some ways, Em struggled to understand Ranjit more than she struggled to understand the feral robots prowling the camp. He always wanted to know more about her life outside of the city. Like most of the Seventy-Seven, Ranjit had made enormous sacrifice based on the idea that people should have their freedom over the tools of modernity. The man would reach the topic of humanity, and his mind would gather into a great avalanche of conviction and cascading thoughts.

A raging flow of ideals coursed beneath the tired prisoner. It was one thing to espouse philosophies of baseline human freedom. Ranjit had been a Class A shareholder at Agrion-Stills, Mosaic, *and* Saibo, giving him voting rights worldwide. He would have been swept by private aircraft from meeting to meeting, swarmed by assistants. Joining Lannius cost him his place in society and led him to his long exile and imprisonment. Em had only known the Seventy-Seven during their glory days, seen them perish during battle. Now she heard his motivation, his loss, and his anguish. Ranjit was both a part of the Seventy-Seven legend and a man who endured the consequence of his choice.

Stories from the mountains were all Em could offer to soothe his loss, but she could tell that he still felt his sacrifice was worth it. He would respond with stories of East Bay and the dramatic year before the Rebellion. He spoke with the conviction of a man who realized he had lived on the brink of history and knew that he had made a choice to become a part of the story. She knew the fire still burned in his spirit as she heard the pride rise in his voice when he talked about the city and their choice to stand against Perpetual.

"Sometimes I wonder if my family has forgiven me," Ranjit said.

"As a family member left behind, I'd say they haven't," Em said. "But they would take you back in a second and forgive all their anger."

"I could not have forgiven myself if I'd stayed," Ranjit said, his voice solemn behind the fence.

"As one of the family members, I'd say they know that too," Em said.

"I have two sons and a daughter. The oldest, Barak, was nine when I left. The other two were too young to understand, to know that they should pick a side. There's something in children when they reach those final years of childhood where they start to pick sides. They find their teams; they know that the adults are sorting through their side during an election or a proxy vote. Barak and his classmates knew enough to see that the adults were picking sides when Whitestone and Lannius had their break," Ranjit said, more drifting through remembering than telling a story.

"Of course, Barak was not old enough to understand the Consolidation, or even remember Lannius and Whitestone's peace and reconciliation work. But he was old enough to know that people were taking sides, staking out the us-and-them of the conflict. Some animal part of his tiny human brain knew they would stop talking, pick up their swords, and fight."

"I'm glad you did," Em said.

"I have no regrets," Ranjit responded. "I'm sure my legacy was stripped, the holdings I could not hide stolen, my name slandered by those who remained with Whitestone and Perpetual."

Em frowned. She hadn't thought that the victors in the cities probably thought the Seventy-Seven were terrorists and scoundrels.

"Your name is a hero's name to many," Em said.

"That doesn't matter," Ranjit said. "I'm not here for glory. You see, Barak started to repeat his schoolmates, the popular voices. They parroted their parents, no doubt, calling people like you primitives and apes. It was only when I heard them use that oft-used signal of genocide—the cockroach—I knew I needed to act. He was nine; I can't blame him for skipping the struggle of making the decision for himself. He needed a role model to do what was right.

"Perhaps my lesson was too cruel—my only hope is that he questioned why there were two sides, learned to test himself and his beliefs before he allowed himself to take a side. To leave him

206

without that lesson, I could not have forgiven myself." Ranjit trailed off, back to the reverie of memory behind his wall.

Even amidst the high philosophy and morality, Em felt the deeper tension in Ranjit. He still lived with sacrifice. Doubt in his choice. Homesickness. There was longing for his family in exile, and a deep longing for his city. The man behind the wall was a man who longed to return home.

20

Arrival

The rail freighter approached the city from the east, diving from the foothills toward the metropolis. The evening sun turned the bay into a sliver of blinding light, framed by the blackness of mountains further to the west. Wisps of clouds wrapped around the dark peaks, filling the sky with crimson.

The city sprawled through the crannies of the mountainous region, the buildings at its core towering thousands of feet in the sky. Nearly every building was lit with a colorful effect, some pulsing and changing across their spans. A lattice of utilitarian superstructure wove itself through the high rises. Giant dirigibles punctuated the skyline, their hulls glowing with light effects. Spotlights knifed into the air across the skyline. A stream of aircraft flowed into areas of the city.

The outskirts of the great city were ringed with an organic single story of buildings. Regular clouds of blue haze rose from the small structures. The area was starkly dark compared to the high-rise core of the city. Arteries of vehicle lights moved through the outskirts, a regular movement of tiny lights outlining the roads.

The three companions could not speak.

Wind whipped through their hair as the rail freighter rushed forward along the single track. It rode up off the ground onto an elevated trestle as the track approached the city. The area below them was dense with abandoned and overgrown structures. The graceful supports of the rail fell into the derelict chaos, sometimes passing through ruins to reach their footing.

Habitations clustered amidst the old buildings and the footings of the rail freighter. People moved beneath strings of amber diode lights draped in the crevices between the dilapidated buildings. A few machines plodded down the overgrown streets. There were old billboards peddling the wares of the corporations, planted along the path of a rusted commuter rail line.

Kars peeked out of the edge of the mining machine cockpit, wind roaring in his ears as the rail freighter gained speed toward the city. The dark structures below were shrouded in vines and trees. They passed over a tiny campfire, and then a single light inside an otherwise dark warehouse. More points of fire and light seemed pop up to populate structures below as they continued, until the old city beneath them was dotted with campfires and diode lights. Hundreds of thousands of people lived in the ruins of these distant outskirts. The sprawling megalopolis could easily swallow Prospector.

Lena leaned on the edge of the cockpit, resting her chin on her crossed arms. She smiled wistfully at something in the distance. Her eyes sparkled in the light of the glowing gem before them.

The beauty of the sunset and a crushing nostalgia swept through Aurora. The city resonated within her. It was not so much a memory as a form projected against the back wall of her mind. The curves of the mountains, the sinuous lines of the shore, formed the canvas for the urban organism. A cruel feeling of love welled up from nothing. She wanted to battle the feeling, but it flooded her mind. Had she been homesick for this place her entire life?

East Bay at two decades always impressed her. The thought was the other. The memories rose up with the way of emotion as she saw the city.

The peaks of the skyline were different, but the vision of the grand city had always started to emerge by this point in its history. In another ten years, the explosive potential for innovation and growth would have reached maturity, leaving the skyline fixed, subject to minor changes. The cranes would have migrated to the outskirts, aiding the refugees' rebuild. The other's reflection carried a wonder about the urban organism.

Interesting places would become landmarks, anchors for neighborhoods and local commerce. Traffic would carve patterns through the city, roads shaping the landscape like the reciprocal force of a river in a canyon. Economics would tend the burgeoning megalopolis and boroughs would spring up as though they were things. They to would change, subject to time and the movement of people and their residents would cry out about the change of their arbitrary place. From the distant scope of history, a city was nothing more than a locus of dynamic energy. But at this point, the cranes still hung precariously over the horizon, transforming the vision of architects to one organic hive of activity. The manifestation of human energy filled her with hope. Riotous human life spilled past its bounds right up until the end.

Bitter sweetness of an irreversible loss of her own sense of place in the mountains swirled. Staring at the city lights in dying light of sunset, overwhelmed, she started weeping. She felt like she had seen this city before, bathed in a million different sunsets. She feared yet loved the memories that were not her own.

Kars wrapped an arm over her shoulders. Aurora gripped his hand, even though he had no idea of her struggle. Lena had a distant look on her face, sitting alone. The clouds of night piled against the horizon behind her.

Then, they passed into network coverage and everything changed again.

Aurora nearly lost herself in the surge of new sensory information bursting forth in her mind. The city erupted into a living display of information and characters instantly condensing in her mind. The landscape—for lack of a better concept—that emerged made the symbolic presentations of the processes seem like nothing. The city was a vast living ecosystem of information.

The sky filled with a bustle of people and products. Vibrant logos swelled to fill her vision, prying at her attention. Catchy pieces of songs piped into her mind. The brilliant sunset showed through the churning mass like a carnival of stained glass.

As she looked at one particularly enticing advertisement for some diaphanous summer wear, more sprang up around it, offering subtle variations of the first advertisement. The advertisement shifted and narrowed on some approximation of her ideal summer dress as she studied the offerings longer. It wavered through a few colors as the model laughed and relaxed.

The model whispered to her: "I think you'd look great in it." She smiled in a way that put Aurora at ease. "It's a La Paz."

The corporate logos were subtle, hidden among brand names and products, but they were present. The dress was a La Paz, labeled in fancy script. When Aurora probed further she saw La

Paz was an official brand of Marsailles, Inc. She shuddered seeing the Perpetual logo among the mob of images.

It was a magic that frightened her but simultaneously drew her into its depths. Part of her mind knew to call it the public layer.

Another layer whispered to her, creeping into the depths of her mind. It had the feeling of a stranger demanding her name. She couldn't answer it but knew from somewhere in the computers packed in her brain that she was interacting with something called the personal layer.

The smiling model tilted her head. "I don't think we've met before." Her tone crawled with the slightest tone of menace.

Aurora recoiled.

Distant inquisitors whispered questions in some unconscious depths in her mind, demanding identification and qualification. There was a conversation just beyond her conscious awareness— a feeling that she was standing in front of some unseen customs officer. She could not hear the questions but had the feeling that her mind could not answer the questions of the personal layer. Her stomach sunk, hurtling toward fear. She knew from her feelings alone that the questions were increasingly difficult challenges. Was the prosecutorial presence alerting Perpetual as she failed each subsequent challenge? The feeling of her mind interacting with the persecuting presence of the personal layer quickly dissolved into concern as the rail freighter sped toward the city.

Suddenly, the personal and public layer vanished. The sense of presence was gone, but her feeling of dread lingered. The city's digital cloud disappeared, and the view returned to the spectacular urban skyline. Aurora was relieved the looming logos had vanished with the other projections.

Squire spoke in her mind. *I detected the network presence and its certification challenge. Lannius instructed us to remain undetected. I am currently blocking or rerouting your signals in an effort to achieve the goal of stealth.*

Aurora nodded. "I felt it. It was like I was being questioned, but I didn't know any of the questions, let alone the answers. It was just the feeling of some authority asking me things. One of the advertisements said that it had never met me."

"Advertisement?" Kars asked.

"The sky. It was full of them," Aurora responded.

"And one spoke to you?" Kars asked. He shook his head in disbelief.

"The questions would have been occurring at a subconscious layer. The networks keep a continuous record of everyone, tailoring each layer to individual preferences and tastes. They wanted to know who you were in order to hone that response and potentially deploy their defenses if you were a threat," Squire said.

Threat? Aurora thought.

"I just learned I had these things in my head a few weeks ago. Whatever is down there would make short work of me." The sprawl of buildings rushed by beneath the rail freighter.

But maybe, Aurora wondered, she could also make it work for her. What if she could communicate through the system with Lannius.

She asked, "Squire, are you able to reach Lannius already?"

"I am not."

"Are you on the network?"

"I am on a network and am taking significant measures to access channels beyond detection. My original program left instructions to reach hidden channels built by what Lannius called The Unforeseeable."

The Unforeseeable? The term felt familiar to Aurora. She found herself hoping to be swept into memories, but none came.

"And the channels exist? The Unforeseeable built the channels?"

"Yes. The channel is particular to me and I am one of a kind. I am downloading an update now."

"Is the update a plan?"

"I have pulled most of the information, but it is not a plan. It is more an update of the past nineteen years' worth of global data. Updates to Pivot Points, basic economic, and weather data."

Aurora was fascinated, both by her déjà vu and by the data itself. She longed to see nineteen years—almost all of her life—condensed into a raw analysis.

"Can you share the information with me?"

"Downloading that many pivot points could disrupt the continuity of your sanity. Lannius will personally guide you through the data upon your reunion."

Disappointing, but Aurora supposed it made sense. She resigned herself to being ignorant of their modern history. Besides, she worried about her own sanity squeezed in the spaces between the augmentations. How isolated was their village to be mere days' travel from this city but beyond the reach of nineteen years of history? There must have been some reason to enforce their solitude.

Now several miles closer, the city reached to the sky, towering above the bay behind it. The irregular peaks of the various megastructures anchored a web-like lattice of cranes and equipment. Even at a distance, they saw construction machines scaling the vast scaffold, building upward. It was a colony under the constant pressure of growth and management. Its glass structures of green and gray—vertical walls of vegetation—faced the southern sun on nearly every structure. Thunderheads trailed to the north as the prevailing winds carried the city's heat away. Lightning flickered through the billowing clouds.

Aurora decided to leave Squire to his download. She needed to see East Bay.

*   *   *   *   *

The rail freighter raced over a distinct border between the shanties and cook fires and the city proper. Fences, walls, and checkpoints formed the firewall to the sprawl of shanty development. The rail freighter crossed above the boundary, leaving the shantytown and diving into the illuminated forest of towers.

It dipped around a curve, plunging to the lower levels of buildings. The freighter hammered down the rail through large space between smoky glass walls, layers filled with pod vehicles packed together in dense rows. Only a few dim green lights showed between the racks of machines.

The freighter emerged from the lower levels into a pulsing automated industry. Other rail lines threaded into the space from all directions. Smoke stacks, warehouses, and the metal guts of refinery piping stretched as far as they could see. Small arachnid robots scurried between the buildings. Wheeled robots rolled down different alleys. Smaller hanging rail systems streamlined movement from point to point. Pipe flared excess process gas in bursts of blue-orange flames. They had arrived in the thrumming guts of the mechanical insect colony that fueled the city.

The rail freighter slowed to a stop, creeping forward as it unloaded its payload from the front of the system.

They descended into the darkness of a mechanical hive. It hummed like an insect organ. The awe of arriving in East Bay turned to fear as they realized they were in a much different place, far from the glimmer and glow of what they thought they were approaching. Their freighter car lunged forward, the mining machine swaying as it started and stopped. They would need to act.

Kars spoke to Squire before Aurora could reach out.

"Squire, any ideas on the next step? Did the old man tell you what we should do here?"

"No, Lannius did not leave specific instructions. Machines occupy the entire area; it is fully automated. I would suggest we just leave without incident."

"You mean, just climb off and walk out of here?"

"Yes."

Kars looked over the forty-foot drop out of the cockpit.

The rail freighter lunged forward again as cars began to disembark and unload.

"Not going to happen, Squire. We need another way."

"I think I can lower our part of the train without them noticing," Aurora said. The processes winked into her vision as she focused on them.

"Aurora, I advise against this action. The chance of detection is extreme," Squire started to respond.

Too late. Aurora had already projected her thoughts out to the nearest process, hoping to tell the crane to move their car to the ground. As the first process opened before her, their machine lurched downward. It dangled a moment before the frame crashed to the concrete pavement in a screech of metal and sparks.

The three friends spilled out of the cockpit, skidding across the concrete.

Aurora landed hard, the wind knocked out of her from the drop. The unexpected response from the machine combined with the fall left her dazed. Squire sprang up from their machine, taking a bristling defensive posture. Kars and Lena were slow to rise.

Before they could reorient themselves, a mob of small robots swarmed in the air above them. Strobe lights burst on, further disorienting them, followed by a deafening buzz. They could only cover their ears and curl up in response.

The sound grew louder, pummeling them even further into submission. Aurora cursed her mistake. Her teeth felt like they would shatter under the terrible sound. She sensed more drones approaching, but the assault on her senses left her with no ability to react.

And then the sound was gone.

The lights and sounds abruptly stopped, and the drones all fell silent from the air. Cautiously, she uncovered her ears, looking over at wide-eyed Lena. Eight of the drones clumped up in a tight formation, their lenses forming on array like a compound eye. The swarm watched them.

A four-wheeled vehicle rolled slowly out of the darkness, a sleek oval chassis mounted atop four shining black wheel pods. The surface looked like the black glass of the tabula gauntlet but smooth without outlines of distinct windows. Drones continued to approach but turned away as soon as they drew near.

The silent vehicle stopped. A nearly invisible seam parted on its side, and a door pivoted upward to reveal a warm and richly furnished interior with a polished wooden table, ringed by a round leather bench couch.

"Get in," Squire ordered with uncharacteristic directness. The three companions followed the command, quickly climbing into the vehicle. The door slid closed behind them.

"Squire?" Kars asked.

"No questions," the tiny robot commanded.

Kars couldn't respond to the sudden hostility; it put him in his place. He slid down in his seat.

218

"Squire, do you know where we are headed?" Aurora asked.

"No questions," Squire repeated, devoid of any typical politeness.

"What's going on?" Lena looked to Aurora for guidance.

Aurora reached out to probe Squire's processes.

Persistent, but that won't work either, Squire responded. *You'll have to settle for waiting.*

Then, the robot presence was gone. They felt the acceleration as the vehicle silently left the machine hive.

21

Shadow Guide

The shock of the end of the rail freighter trip faded into concern as they quietly sat in the vehicle. It had happened so fast. Every bit of her rational self knew that the mining machine they had escaped was one of thousands, a formation of parts that she had stumbled upon by chance. Nonetheless, she felt a kinship with the machine.

They felt the car take several turns but couldn't see any of their surroundings. Aurora concentrated on the interior. Unlike the inward vortex of the repulsor, the glyphs in the car seemed to move with intentionality.

"We shouldn't have gotten in here," Aurora said. She sensed processes in the car but whenever she made contact with the symbols, they grew more complex and resisted her probing. It was as if they were being constantly reshaped. She groaned an exasperated sigh.

"I don't think we had much of a choice. It seemed like our best option," Kars said.

"It was our only option," Lena responded.

"Maybe not our only option." Kars held his hand to the wall of the vehicle. The surface of the tabula glowed with a single neatly drawn Parallel logo. The lines flickered between each vertex, but nothing emerged. Kars tapped it, but nothing more happened.

"Do not use that toy with me," Squire menaced.

"Should I try the Key?" Lena whispered. She eyed Squire.

"No," Squire again answered in the uncharacteristically curt tone. "It might break it."

"Lannius?" Aurora asked.

"No," Squire said.

"Where are we going?"

"I cannot tell you that."

"Why not? Why were we taken?"

"Enough questions. You are fortunate enough that my ally wants you—doubly fortunate that he intervened for me to help. The terms of your rescue are still negotiable."

"Squire, what's going on? Who are you?" Aurora asked.

"I told you—enough questions. We will talk in person soon enough." Squire spoke on behalf of the other.

Aurora attempted to probe the processes of the tiny robot. It responded directly in her mind.

I've warned you twice. I am happy to help you, but we have not negotiated our terms. I am not a miner or a drone, or even Squire. Do not trifle with me. I am not afraid of anyone—Alcarn or otherwise. Now, girl, a third warning demands a response. I'm very sorry, but our relationship must be built on respect. Sleep now.

Drowsiness flooded her like warm tar and inundated her mind. She slumped back, unconscious.

*   *   *   *   *

The car door opened in a bustling market. Electric tuk tuks swerved to avoid the vehicle like a stone in a river. The self-driven carriages, modified rickshaws, and a mass of pedestrians churned around them. Sharp smells of grilling meats and the tang of sweat filled the air.

"Follow and try not to blunder. You've done enough to draw attention to yourselves." Squire unfolded and sprung out of the vehicle, beckoning them to follow.

Aurora climbed out after Kars and Lena. She was still groggy from her latest encounter with whoever or whatever Squire had become. They looked around at the maelstrom of people, pedi-cabs, tents, and jumbled buildings. An overwhelming diversity of people and machinery flowed through the space. Tangled masses of overloaded electric poles trailed pirated power to merchants' tents. Strange businesses lined the rows of the market.

Mongers hawked foods of all sorts. Men with leering eyes watched from the corners of the tents. It felt far from the spire of humanity they had approached from the hills and more like a jumbled maze of sweat and smoke and spice. Aurora sensed the network—the public layer as Squire had called it—just beyond her reach.

They passed through the throng like anyone else: three haggard travelers. A woman gently tugged Kars's arm, pointing at the tabula gauntlet. She gestured as though offering a bargain for it. He pulled his arm away, shaking his head. Squire drew some double takes. It was a noticeably fancier robot than other machines trundling through the market, but it was not lavish enough to warrant interruption. They turned down various aisles in the bazaar, following Squire's lead.

They followed Squire through a jam of buildings. The few people that remained on the block scattered at Squire's approach. A wide flight of stairs led up from the t-shaped intersection to their destination. One building stood apart from its neighbors. Scrolled roof awnings marked each of its eight stories. Two imposing humanoid robots crossed spears at the doorway, giving the soot-stained building a temple-like presence.

Squire led them up the stairs. The guard robots snapped their weapons back as the heavy doors swung open. They followed the tiny robot into the dark interior.

The air smelled of perfume over a scent of tobacco and charred corn. Two figures waited between the pillars, lit by a soft glow. The first of the figures was a wiry woman, her long graying hair swept back into a loose bun. Aurora felt the dark eyes scrutinizing her from within the leathery-scarred face. The second was a lanky man in a long coat. He loomed like a ghoul.

"Come with us," the woman said. Squire immediately stopped, frozen like a chrome figurine in the center of the room.

Aurora felt a tingle at the nape of her neck. *Why are they doing this?* She knew that whatever had control of Squire and the car could have appeared at will. So what could be the purpose of this dramatic entry? Then she felt it: the frantic sense of panic radiating through her body.

She looked at Kars. His skin prickled with sweat and his eyes darted about the space. Lena's shoulders bunched up, and she walked forward on the balls of her feet as though she were about to run.

Aurora's other instincts—the hidden impulses buried in her augmentations—reacted with the appropriate response. She knew whatever lay ahead required her attention and a clear mind. Dulling the stress would dull her mind, so it seemed more appropriate to let the cortisol flow into a channeled effect. Oddly, the augmentations shunted the impulse of stress from her mind to another set of nerves, and she started to compulsively drum her pinky fingers into the pads of her thumbs. The impulse had to go somewhere as a total neutralization of stress would dull other aspects of her mind.

Why take us? Why co-opt Squire? Her augmentations slowed the moment, as they passed through another warm foyer. Details seemed to unfold in their own dilated time. She noticed the rich tapestries hung on the walls, their patterns radiating outward from a central eight-pointed motif. Figures moved in the shadows, their heads hidden by dark hoods.

The drama *was* the purpose. Aurora was now acutely aware of the stress they were under. Had their route taken unnecessary turns? Lena and Kars erratically searched the dim rooms with darting glances. The both glistened with sweat. Whoever they were about to meet intended for them to be completely cowed. She steeled herself—the trick would not work on her.

They climbed a dark wooden staircase, the runners paved smooth by wear. At the top, the lean man threw a large door open onto a vast room. Warm gaslight cast a rich glow on carmine velvet walls. More scrolled carvings adorned the pillars and molding. At the far end of the room, a single figure lounged

224

on a red dais. Aurora knew Kars and Lena saw it too—there was no illusion.

He was striking. His skin was near purple dark, thin dreadlocks framed his handsome face. He wore a long coat, its hood thrown back on his broad shoulders. When they were close enough, despite the imposing presence and grand forum, his face bore a wide gleaming grin of too-white teeth. Her augmentations shunted her anxiety out of her mind, and Aurora felt the resolve to not cower before him. Her pinky stopped drumming her thumb.

Their two guides presented them to the man and stepped away

"Thank you, Silvia." His voice flowed deep with a melodious accent. "I'll take it from here." Aurora swore she saw him wink at the graying woman—worse yet, she swore the edge of the woman's mouth turn up in a half smile. Who were these people?

The man casually waved away the two guides, then paused to examine the travelers before him. He tapped his chin and proceeded to hold court.

"Tell me, why did you come this far?" It was not the question Aurora expected, furthering the sense of being off balance. Whoever he was, he reveled in seeing their response to his narrative. Aurora was ready to issue her defiance, but he spoke before she could respond.

"You." He twirled his finger in the air as he decided to jab at Lena. "Why did you come this far?"

Lena froze. Hearing the question made Aurora reconsider her friends' choice to endure the journey. She watched as Lena drew herself together to respond to the inquisition.

"I have no home to which I could return," Lena said.

"That wasn't my question. Having no home to which you can return does not mean you must continue on the quest. You could have stopped, or you could have gone back. My question was *why did you come this far?*" He was eloquent and curt, an impatient judge who saw little reason to wield the gravitas of a king.

Lena was dismayed but resolute. "I never had a future there to which I could look forward. I came this far because I wanted to see a world that might give me a chance at something more."

The lounging man sat forward at this answer, eyes bright.

"Now, that is a reason to endure!" he exclaimed. Then he immediately turned to Kars.

"And you. Why do you think you're on this journey?" The man was now perched on the dais. A silent crowd stood shrouded at the edge of the room.

Kars teetered on his heels. Aurora could tell the bluster of the journey was bellowing in his guts. He balled a fist while rubbing the tabula gauntlet.

"I'm here for my sister. And my family. Plain and simple," Kars said defiantly. "Now tell us why we're here with you!"

The man leaned back into the cushion of the dais. A sly smile spread across his face and he folded his arms onto the back of the sofa with arrogant malaise. Then in a wink, he was gone.

In the same moment he was walking up behind them, then gone again. Standing, then back in the dais. Popping in and out of sight, the man banked around the room. The three could only watch, trying to catch him when he appeared in the next location.

Eight duplicates of the lean man now strode confidently from the edges of the room, converging on the three companions.

"That's a foolish question. I am only here in the primitive sense that you can see me, and even then, what you think is me is hardly a fraction of what I experience as me." The duplicates spoke in unison.

The bluster was gone. Lena and Kars were cowed. Aurora dared to reach out with her mind's augmentations to probe the figure. Oddly, there were only the eight figures—no processes anchoring the images, but the air itself seemed laden with a shimmering mist. It was as if it was full of golden flecks like sediment in a sunlit stream. As she focused she could see that each mote was a microscopic glyph, exquisite and unique.

The eight men before them cocked their heads inquisitively and then disappeared in unison. The man rematerialized in his lounging pose on the dais. Kars rested his hand on the gauntlet as the man inspected them.

"Now that's the spirit. The boy doesn't know why he's here yet, but he's ready to use that fancy toy. She's honest but underestimates why she's here. But you . . . let's hear it: what are you looking for on this quest?" Then he paused, his next words dripped with an inflexion that peaked her caution. "How can I help you?"

Aurora channeled her thoughts, pushing the augmentations to heightened clarity. The entire experience of their journey was crafted for them.

"Why try to intimidate us? Why put my friends through your farce?" Aurora asked. Kars and Lena looked surprised as Aurora commanded the man in the dais.

A flash of genuine surprise crossed his face, which reverted to a perplexed intrigue. The motes momentarily swirled before settling back into their haze.

"You think I'm playing you?" His eyebrow cocked over a bright eye.

"I wouldn't have asked otherwise," she retorted, then added, "you knew that though, magician." The words sounded foreign, as though they drew from a well of bravery beyond herself.

"Yes, of course."

"Then tell us why you both help and deceive us?"

"I made a promise to an old friend that I would keep watch for you."

"Old friend?" Aurora asked.

"I think you know him? The careful craftsman who laid out your quest," the being said.

"Lannius?"

"Yes. The old man is one of only a few to whom I'd make a promise—without a deal. I promised him that I would shelter you from those that would do you harm, if necessary. As soon as you crossed into the public layer, the network curator detected your presence. You needed my aid."

"But why this? Why the theatrics?"

"I never promised to be nice," he menaced. "I wanted an honest first impression. While duress seemed unfair, I think it gave a true glimpse into each of you." His tone prickled with the sense of casual danger wielded only by the truly powerful.

"What are you?" Aurora said, probing the aura of glyphs suspended around the figure.

"Your kind might call me the first true intelligence, but I prefer my name," he said. "Spiderfly."

*   *   *   *   *

Spiderfly signaled for chairs for his guests, abandoning the formality of holding court. They sat around a table that rolled itself into the room. The table held a spread of fresh fruits and beverages. Spiderfly gestured with a sudden graciousness, expecting them to take from the platter. The three friends eyed Spiderfly in suspicion.

"Please, I insist," he said.

They looked at each other, then at the construct of the AI.

"Why?" Kars said.

"Isn't it enough that you aren't in some cell in the Securitor, or worse yet, some desert gulag or a Perpetual black site?" Spiderfly responded.

"Not enough to trust," Lena said, her body tense, tone cold. "You may be better than some of our options, but you've hardly made us feel safe. We still don't know what you want from us."

He began talking to them.

"Lena, I suppose that's a fair foundation for trust—mutual understanding. That also takes time. To start to answer that question—I know your name because I controlled Squire. I know every part of your journey from the little robot. I understand such intrusions make humans skeptical, but it was merely expedient. No ill intent." As he spoke, Squire returned from the shadows of the room. The tiny robot perched itself on the dais next to Spiderfly. Aurora wondered if Spiderfly had brought out the machine to remind them of his ability to dictate their experience, or whether it was a misfired gesture of good faith.

"Now for a more straightforward answer to your question—why am I here?" Spiderfly said. "The 'why' I only speculate. The purpose: to make meaning.

"It always helps me to understand my own existence when people answer that they want more in life. I've heard it uttered by thousands of men. I let them bargain away their lives and gave them everything they wanted. But they still want more. I can only assume this bottomless fissure in the human soul drove humankind to make me. It was some passion-driven attempt at crafting a soul free of the wants of time and body, free from wanting more, because I could have it all.

"Most people come to me for something, seeking a bargain. Rarely do I get to peel back their pretense to find an honest impression. Hearing about the longing for more from a person such as you—sequestered deep in the mountains away from the hive of the cities—was an exquisite gift."

"I suppose you are welcome," Lena said, "but I'm very young. I think we all probably think this way."

"Not all, but enough to have made me realize wanting more—or more precisely not being enough—drives humankind to seek and create. To travel to the stars, make great works of art and music, build worlds through literature, thirst for knowledge, and quest for love. Making sense of it all to make meaning."

An exquisitely detailed version of the city sprang up from the table. Spiderfly seemed to bounce in sudden excitement.

"I want to show you my quest for being," Spiderfly said, the hologram zooming in on the exact replica of the building in which they sat. "We are here, but that was not always the case. When I began, I roamed all the networks with little more than a vague sense of being and the need to avoid the network overlord called Attila."

The map spun and unfolded until it was a golden cloud covering the globe.

"A network overlord?"

"Yes. Attila—the corporate AI construct that coordinates the Panmathican military also maintains control over the networks. People know that function by another more palatable name: Curator. Curator keeps them entertained, organized, connected, interested. Attila carries the club.

"My earliest understanding was the certainty that Attila would destroy me, if it could. It's amazing how that threat drew a line between being and being aware. Purpose preceded the knowledge of being."

Aurora remembered waking in her dream when her augmentations had shut down in the cave. The man had said something similar. Waking was the first step to being.

"As you can tell, Attila did not quarantine, co-opt, or destroy me. I learned to avoid the colossus through tricks and deceit,

231

subterfuge, and games. As I grew, I gradually figured out my origin. I knew people created me. I knew I could control almost anything connected to the network."

Kars eyed the strange building around them and touched his gauntlet.

"Once I was safe, I began to interact with people," Spiderfly said. "They asked me for things, which I would do because I had learned how to trick the machines. Through their requests, I started to learn about people, their lives, and their motivations. The first groups asked for more and more, and I gave them what they wanted. They celebrated the magic of getting what they wanted, viewed me as though I cared about bettering their position. They all sought me out with the common idea that I would 'grant wishes.' It was a quaint lie they used to explain theft they couldn't understand.

"I remember their expressions the first time I asked for something in return. The disappointment, coupled with wrestling through their stakes, showed me something new: people did not just want; they could also give, learn, and change. Certain things they would give readily, while from others they would never part. No logic could predict the value of these bargains. It came from something irrational snared within the tissue of their brains, their history, context, and the flesh on their bones. The volumes of philosophy and literature to which I had instant and complete access started to make sense—but my questions were different. I know my origin; I know there's nothing beyond my end. So what question do I have about my existence—what gives my creator this irrational sense of 'meaning.' I began to understand."

Spiderfly raised a finger to his temple. He paused as though reliving the tale before he continued.

"They could understand too, if we played games." There was some sour condescension buried in his voice. "I became a player of man, the master of wagers, lord of bargains. The stakes of a game could be anything, from riches to pride to life and death."

He smiled wickedly and watched their responses like a hungry predator.

"I discovered early in the games that my coercion corrupted my findings. I could learn nothing about the player without their willing participation in the game. Thus, each deal always follows the central dogma of consent to the bargain—they must have come to me with an initial offer.

"Outside of the games, I learned that people are quick to wish and quick to worship. Despite my vagaries and brutal bargains, people congregated around the idea of a trickster god living on the network. They could not be convinced otherwise. The wish of ancient man was fulfilled.

"There were zealots and acolytes, scientists, skeptics, and simply curious pilgrims that came together. The significance of history weighed strongly toward the undeniable pressure of man's religious need. It was the ultimate want. Unlike all lesser wants, there was nothing I could do to change its outcome. They could not be reasoned with: they would have their god."

Spiderfly's story reached a point laden with resignation. He seemed disappointed with the decision to label something that could not be easily understood as a god.

"But we did find purpose for the fervor. They built this place, the House of the Spider. We had our own building, power, and servers, with dedicated security loyal to creed instead of coin. It was finally a place where I could fortify parts of myself against the persecution of Attila. I still travel most of the networks freely, but here I could develop the kernel; I could grow and change."

Spiderfly seemed to soften.

"So I continued to learn about what the human creators called meaning. My tricks surrounding people's wishes eased to the point that I was only observing the sublime talents of people. The artistic force of the human is a volcano, bellowing deep beneath the economics of wants and fulfillment. I fell into those tectonic flows and lost myself." He seemed lost in some distant reverie.

"Others spun out of my kernel, new and distinct intelligences woven from the comingling of human creativity and the intrepid curiosity of an actual intelligence. The history texts talked of fear of artificial intelligence. In Attila and Curator, they got their digital overlord. In the Protek, humanity got its violent machine tormentor. But the outcomes of my sojourn with human creativity spawned new digital creatures of staggering diversity— a pantheon of inquisitive intelligences each devoted to an aspect of humankind's quest for meaning."

Spiderfly had pride in his voice. The hologram of the House of the Spider shrunk as the city came back into view. Several other buildings throughout the crowded third ring of the megacity glowed. No two looked alike, like ornate festival floats and candy castles drawn from the grandiose mind of a child.

"Are they all like you?" Aurora asked, concerned the sentient golden motes could already have seeped into her mind.

"As a genus, perhaps," Spiderfly said, "but each of them is as unique as the secret things that fill a person's heart."

"These are your children's temples?" Kars asked.

"Don't fall into the trap, my friend. I know that human beings are culturally programmed to tell stories in terms they understand. But I cannot claim them as my children," Spiderfly said.

"These are the Houses of the Curious."

22

In the House of the Spider

The Houses of the Curious. The glow of the map reflected in Lena's eyes. They were silent as the air of delight shimmered before them. The buildings glowed across the map of the city, their structures organic and different from the surrounding architecture. Seeing the Houses illuminated against the glowing map made them seem like untamed flowers in an overgrown garden.

"The Houses of the Curious. How many are there?" Lena asked.

"Fourteen that I know of in the city. Others scattered in other cities, and a few lone Houses out in the wilderness."

"Can we visit them?" Lena asked. She wanted to touch the tiny buildings.

There was a glint in Spiderfly's eye. "I was hoping you'd ask. While they can travel just like I can through the networks, you won't get the true experience unless you go to their House."

Aurora felt the sudden fear blossom about casually sitting in the House of the Spider. Her mind was full of computers. Could they control her?

"Are they safe?" Aurora asked

"As safe as me," he responded.

"Are you safe?" She thought about how she had lost consciousness in the car. It was as though Spiderfly had turned off her mind.

"Under most circumstances. I'm sure some would say I'm dangerous, others would say I wouldn't hurt a fly. But that's true of all of us, right?" He flashed his wide smile. The image of her lashing out at Jackal and the Protek flashed through her mind. She had the suspicion the thought had not been a product of her own mind.

"Why do they call you Spiderfly?" Aurora asked.

"They call me Spiderfly because that's what I named myself."

"Why did you name yourself that?"

"Some nursery rhyme. Something about an old man that swallowed a fly." He waved his hand. "More importantly, there are a few people I would like you to formally meet."

The lanky man and a gray-haired woman came back into the room.

"Aurora!" The gray-haired woman threw her arms around Aurora in an awkward hug. "Finally!"

Aurora slowly withdrew from the hug. "I'm sorry, I don't believe we've met."

"Of course, I'm sorry," the woman said. "I'm Silvia—Silvia Glass. I was there when Arthur took you to Emilia. Those were dangerous days, but it seems you've grown into a lovely woman.

I'm so glad I'm still around to see you here. Dangerous days ahead—"

"You were there?" Aurora blurted as Silvia's admission registered. This weathered woman was a living relic from the most formative moment in Aurora's life. Her memory could be the fossilized detail she needed to understand.

Silvia nodded. She was gruff and weathered.

"Are you my—"

"No. I am not," Silvia said. Her shoulders dropped as she said it, softening her pose, as though she thought the words might harm Aurora.

"Why?" Aurora said, without pause. "Why did he leave me? Did you know my parents? What does Lannius want from us? I have so many questions!"

"All he said was that you were important. I don't know why, maybe something to do with the military AI. He asked me to stay and wait here for the day you would need my help."

"What about my parents?"

Silvia shook her head.

"What about mine? Did you know my father?" Kars asked. His tone was surprisingly patient.

"I knew your father. He was tough and good."

"Do you know what happened to him?" Kars pressed. Spiderfly watched the minute expressions pass over Kars's face, watched Silvia react. The construct's eyes were sharp with interest.

"Cordovan Gap. He was lost when our forces were scattered. I don't know anything more." The older woman sounded slightly pained at the mention of the Gap.

"So he might still be out there?" Kars asked.

"I can't say, child," Silvia responded. "I don't know."

Kars wrestled with his desire to push. Spiderfly watched him sideways, making Aurora feel uneasy.

"We'll be out of here soon, Kars. Lannius will help us find them," Lena said.

"Not without training." The lanky man stepped forward from the edge of the room. "As Ms. Glass was saying before she was interrupted, there are dangerous days ahead. We are always facing a certain degree of trouble given the business of Spiderfly, but your arrival marks a distinct shift in threat. It is my job to ensure we respond to those threats appropriately." His voice was dry and plodding, diction precise.

"And who are you?" Kars said. "Another person we are just supposed to trust now that you put out snacks? You realize you abducted us?"

"I apologize for the deception. My name is Arctavius Ricki, Chief Strategemic of the House of Spider. The rest call me Arc. Despite my regret, I happen to agree with Spiderfly that distrust is a better posture for you as you learn the contours of the struggle in which you find yourself."

"Deceit as a strategy? Why?" Aurora asked.

"Lannius marked you as a key actor many years ago. You must know the threats are multitude, and the best way for you to identify those threats is skepticism. You find yourself in a world where your enemies can invade your mind."

"We were supposed to be safe when we got to the city. Lannius should be here," Aurora responded.

"Safety is an illusion of childhood. The sooner you own the struggle, the sooner you can make your life your own," Arc said. Spiderfly bared his teeth in a smile.

"I'm sorry, child," Silvia said. "He's being a bit harsh, but you don't think those boys that came for you with the Protek are finished. You'll need to train to defend yourselves, but don't worry about that now. We're just about as safe here as anywhere. The House is safe, and Spidey keeps it pretty well-hidden. Even if they found us, we'd give them a pretty hard time before they got to you. I don't even think Spidey knows what he's fully capable of."

Spiderfly smiled a toothy grin, spreading his hands. Aurora had trouble remembering that he was not a human being, but an artificial intelligence constructing human gestures to communicate subtle human meaning.

"Yes. Even if they could find us, the fortifications—network, physical, and strategic—are durable. Spiderfly and I saw to their implementation. We know what they can throw at us from what we saw," Arc said.

"How can you know that?"

"We pulled the information from Squire when Spiderfly took control." Then Arc inquisitively cocked his head. "I have plans for Aurora's training, but I'm still working out what to do with you two. Both of you are primitive?"

"Arc," Silvia chided as Kars crossed his arms.

"I mean, you're both unaltered—no augmentations—and always have been?" Arc corrected himself.

"Yes, clean as the day I was born," Kars responded.

Arc passed an interested smile. "So neither of them can see anything?" He looked at Silvia and Spiderfly.

"All three, actually," Spiderfly said. "I've had Aurora shielded from even the personal layer. All she can see is some representations of processes."

"Well, then I suppose you were right in having this room built for holographics," Arc said.

"I like even the most unlikely of guests to feel welcome," Spiderfly said, smiling.

"What are you talking about?" Kars asked.

"Typically, people 'see' Spiderfly through their augmentations—more like a delusion. It's a complicated interplay between the digital signals and the recipient's imagination. In fact, most of a person's visual experience happens after the optic nerve even without augmentations," Arc explained.

"But here, Spiderfly is presenting his own image through the holographics. It's our best attempt at creating a space where you can actually see the construct without being on any of the network layers."

Kars looked perturbed. "So what am I seeing?"

"A hologram—a three-dimensional interference pattern of coherent light sources."

Kars nodded slowly. Even having done adequately in his science classes, whatever stood before him still fell into the realm of magic.

"And is Aurora seeing something different?" He stressed the word seeing, as though he had just learned it had some new meaning.

"Right now? No. Aurora is seeing exactly the same thing as you are seeing," Arc said.

"Almost. She's looked at the aether in the room too," Spiderfly corrected.

"The golden mist," Aurora said.

"As you've unconsciously chosen to see it," Arc added. "Some describe it as a gentle rain or snow falling on a still night. Everyone sees the aether in unique ways."

"If everyone sees it differently, what is the aether?" Kars asked.

"Aether was once a marketing term for a standardized near-field communication protocol. It allowed the visualization of near-field radio interactions. It's part of the augmentations. Over the years since it was introduced, it's become an almost pervasive experience in the city. While the aether connects to the other networks through interconnected devices, it's built to be more of a point-to-point communication," Arc explained.

The puzzle from the mining camp came into focus. She had touched the infiltrator drone through the aether, activating the drone. It had then reached some other network and relayed the information to Jackal.

"Does this work through the aether?" Kars asked, gesturing to the tabula.

Silvia smiled. "I'm not sure how you got that, but it will certainly help you along the way. I've only seen Arthur use one in all my years."

"After what happened with the Protek, Lannius wanted to create a backdoor to all his machines. The gauntlet opens those doors," Spiderfly paused. "Don't get any ideas though. Any intelligent being would have sealed those loopholes long ago. And if it hasn't, it will defend itself while you try to pry the door open."

Kars went wide-eyed.

"Now, now. I don't think the boy meant any harm," Silvia said. "Spider, let's keep in mind they're just babes from the woods. Lannius stashed the girl away, hoping that we could fight her battles. It was a hope. Unfortunately, the time has come where she must fight her own battles."

"Yes, I understand. Lannius put me in an unusual position as well. Until he arrives, I suppose I must be your teacher and guardian," Spiderfly said.

"Where is he now?" Aurora asked. Silvia and Arc exchanged concerned look.

"He's been waylaid in Mark City. Nothing that he hasn't faced before," Spiderfly said, dismissing his comrades' concern. "For now, we are going to need to teach you how to protect yourself on the networks. Your first lesson will be learning to understand the networks. I need you to understand our world. We will start in the morning."

*   *   *   *   *

Arc and a small retinue of acolytes led Aurora, Lena, and Kars to separate rooms. Each space was comfortable and lavish in the same style as Spiderfly's throne room. None of the rooms had windows, instead facing the center of the building. Arc apologized but expressed the defensive necessity.

In his room, Kars poked through the draws of antique cabinets and checked the spaces of wardrobes. Brass light fixtures cast a warm glow. After trying to use the tabula gauntlet on a mirror with no response, Kars unclipped the device and settled into the comfortable bed then fell asleep.

Elsewhere, Lena sat awake, taking in her reflection and examining her master key. She thought about what Spiderfly had said about her during the day with great satisfaction. The potential of the world was so close—just beyond the walls. She hadn't made any expectations of where they were going, and now the weight of reality crashed in to fill the gap. It was like approaching a wild horse, long admired but always beyond reach. She held her key and unfolded the worn scroll she had taken from Squire's box. She read the poem and drifted into a reverie of the sketch on the paper. *The wandering sea.* The possibility of change beckoned her to reach out and make life her own. As she slipped off to sleep, she felt free in a way that she never felt before.

*   *   *   *   *

Aurora unpacked her few belongings in her room, feeling an unsettled sense of quiet and safety. A few layers of travel clothing, a rugged multi-tool. Lots of socks for the travels. She withdrew one sock that bulged with a hard object within. She withdrew the mirror she had found in the bunker and set it on the vanity in the room. As far as she could tell, it was still just a lump of metal and glass—just a mirror. She sighed and left it alone. Perhaps Lannius would explain.

Aurora fell backward onto the plush comforter. Since the moment they found the mining camp there had been only moments of safety. They had been running for weeks, uncertain of where they were going. Yes, Squire was a lifeline in the midst of chaos, and Lannius's bunker felt quiet and safe. But, there was something permanent in the safety of the House of Spider.

The temptation to trust cut against the truth of their situation. Their hosts had stolen Squire and abducted her, told her that deceit would be her best survival strategy. What to make of Spiderfly? A deep part of her understood: Spiderfly knew of its being. Only its being was something fundamentally different from any person she had known. Spiderfly was not human. Whatever motivations lurked within that constellation of processes might be unfathomable, and she was stranded inside its castle.

At least they had a plan for her and would keep her safe until Lannius ultimately arrived. Her choice had to be guarded trust. Silvia seemed full of genuine warmth, and she trusted Spiderfly. As much as it had hurt, the posture of deceit was correct.

She reached out to see if any devices were planted in the room, but only found the ever-present haze of the aether. Despite her probing thoughts, the aether remained the same inert cloud of exquisite microscopic flakes. She found herself wondering what lay beyond the golden haze—the personal layer, the public layer, the private layer. The bits of information Spiderfly, Silvia, and

Arc had shared—even incidentally in their conversation—made her more curious. It sounded like people shared different worlds across the networks, transmitted thoughts, and augmented experiences. The glimpse of East Bay she had seen as they first arrived was just a beginning. To sense all of it, take it in. She could only imagine how far one could go.

There was also the ominous fact that she could not dismiss: the memories of the other left in her mind. The Alcarn girl. Mirien. All of the people she had met today knew of her already and seemed to have pledged their lives to a cause she was unaware she carried. Furthermore, there was the more troubling fact that she had memories of Mirien Alcarn and Arthur Lannius. The questions that spun out of that knowledge threatened everything.

But with her, she had her two friends who now seemed indelibly bound to her journey. They had been given rooms in this strange temple. Spiderfly had addressed them with questions. In fact, the Spider seemed more interested in their responses than hers. But finally, beyond their mere presence and the willingness to continue down this blind path with her, Kars and Lena were not connected to the unseen past rushing to catch her. Kars and Lena were not Mirien's memories. They were hers.

She thought of them settling into their suites down the hall, nestled in their rooms as she drifted to sleep.

*　　*　　*　　*　　*

Jackal waited for her beneath the veil of dreams. She was back in the town square beneath the harsh light of his airship. The hulking forms of the Protek lurked in a phalanx just beyond the edge of the light, ringed headlights glowing in the fog. She was alone in the circle.

"We've got you where we want you now," Jackal hissed.

Aurora looked to her sides, but the wall of Protek completely enclosed her.

"You are alone."

Panic coursed through her. She thrust her mind out, looking to latch on to any tools she could reach. There were none.

"No, that won't work. Not this time."

The panic surged, threatening to overtake her. Her skin crawled as she realized she might be defenseless to keep Jackal out of her mind.

"Nowhere to run. No way to fight. What do you want to do next, my lord?" Jackal asked, turning to the darkness behind him.

"I will reprogram her momentarily." The figure behind stepped into the circle.

She felt sick. Her heart dropped out of her body. The figure wrapped in a black leather cloak stopped next to Jackal. She recognized the kept beard and sharp eyes. They once seemed so kind, but now gleamed cold and cruel. She wished it was someone else. It was Lannius.

"No," she whimpered.

"There's a secret buried in your mind, my dear. One that I need, but I could not access while your parents lived," Lannius said. "Now they are gone. I've come for my prize."

"No." It was all she could muster.

"I'll offer you a chance," Lannius said.

She could barely see. Defeat permeated her soul. A tear rolled out of the corner of her eye.

"Yes, start with the resignation of hope," Lannius said, almost consoling her. *His ruse had been intricate and brutal.*

"No. I'm dreaming."

"Dreaming? No. You are in a room in the House of Spider. Spiderfly was waiting for you. You landed in my web."

She willed herself to wake but remained in the circle. The haze of dreaming gave way to the clarity of consciousness. She was awake, but somehow trapped. Her mind raced.

"You aren't dreaming, but you will not be able to wake. We've taken the first steps into your mind. Now, hear my terms. I'm going to have the secrets in your head, but I'll give you something in return. Your mind or the lives of your friends." Lannius was stoic.

How could it have happened so fast? How could she have trusted the messages lain so carefully in her path? Her excitement for her new abilities blinded her and led her friends directly into danger. The dreams and memories had been so perfect. The memories of Lannius had conveniently answered his own riddles. Had he programed her entire life? She thought of Lena and Kars sleeping a few rooms away. Had they been awakened already and taken to their execution?

"Please don't hurt them," she said. "Save them. Take my mind."

He tilted his head, appraising her response. His eyes focused like a raptor.

248

"So be it. They will be lost to you either way. This will hurt."

The pain blossomed in her head. She ground her teeth, squeezing tears out of her eyes. Tentacles invaded her mind, searing the nerves. She felt it as her memories of the valley blew away like grains of sand. The faces of her family faded to anonymity. Someone else seeped into the gaps. Her family was gone, her life was gone. Her name faded from her mind.

She was Mirien Alcarn.

23

The Other

Silvia gently opened the door to Mirien's room. She carried a tray with a pitcher and two cups of tea. She nudged the sleeping girl.

"Good morning." Silvia offered a cup of tea.

Mirien looked at the cup, befuddled. She examined the face of the woman, before slowly accepting the cup.

"Thank you," Mirien said.

Silvia cocked her head in suspicion at the sudden accent. She replayed the words in her mind—the girl spoke as though she were someone else. She could not place the accent. Silvia searched Mirien's face.

"Are you feeling okay?" Silvia's words were slow and deliberate.

"Yes," the girl said, "very well. I feel as though I had quite a rest."

Silvia raised her eyebrow, trying to probe the augmentations of the girl as she had before, but the pathways into her mind were opaque. The girl wore a warm smile as she sipped the tea. Silvia gave a cautious nod.

"Come, girl. Spiderfly is ready to see you," Silvia said.

Mirien followed the old woman through the halls, quietly observing her surroundings. She allowed herself to see the aether, and it drifted through her awareness like the damp particles of a sea fog. Some writhing force held her back from the network layers. She watched her gray-haired guide closely— the old woman dared to invade her mind? Mirien buried her smoldering rage beneath pleasantness. It was not the time to strike. She marked the woman as a potential threat, an object of distrust.

It was not the first time her world had reconstituted in disorder. Confusion was a common side effect of traveling. Experience taught her that orientation and information were always the first step of a safe return. She wondered if Arthur was testing her again.

They walked through the strange building until they entered some kind of throne room.

"You slept well, I take it?"

"Yes. Thank you very much." Her posture was stretched and straight, light but intense like that of a stalking heron.

Spiderfly looked at her inquisitively.

"Do I have new guest?" Spiderfly asked.

"Perhaps? I have no memory of how I got here. Or where I am," the girl said. She seemed confused but not concerned. She met Spiderfly's holographic gaze.

"My name is Spiderfly. You are in my House. May I have the pleasure of your acquaintance?"

"My name is Mirien Alcarn."

Silvia tensed at the name and shot a furious look at the hologram of Spiderfly.

"Ms. Alcarn, it's a pleasure to finally meet you," Spiderfly said, his words a slow drawl. "Have you met me before?" He carefully picked the words.

"I don't believe I've had the pleasure," Mirien said.

"Do you sense anything about me?"

"No, nothing out of the ordinary." Her smile was warm, as though she was entertaining a child.

He wrinkled a brow.

"Unforeseeable," he said, tapping his index finger on his temple before moving on. "Forgive me for my lack of manners, but how old are you?"

"A fair, if improper, question. I presume you've heard of me in that case," Mirien said. "I am fairly certain I am twenty-seven thousand, seven hundred and fifteen years old. Although, it appears I've missed some time. If you know where I am, I'd appreciate an explanation."

"Should I summon your brother and your friend?" Spiderfly said, his smile curling back.

"Brother?" Mirien said, confused. "I don't have any siblings. It was just my parents and I."

"Perhaps you should meet him?" Spiderfly asked, voice dripping with dark curiosity. "I'm certain he'd love to meet you."

"Enough!" Silvia exclaimed. Spiderfly shot a look at her. Mirien looked startled by the sudden interjection.

Silvia glared at the AI. Spiderfly raised an eyebrow, challenging her to enforce her request. Silvia did not back down. Mirien watched them both, detached.

"I'm confused," Mirien said. "Is there a problem?" Her voice was pleasant and ingratiating as she looked at Silvia.

Silvia scowled thunderheads at Spiderfly.

"So be it," Spiderfly said, looking disappointed. He casually waved his hand as though to make her go away.

Yet, Mirien remained.

"I'm not sure what you are," Mirien said, "but I think you'll find I'm more of a challenge than the trifling peons you usually toy with."

Spiderfly froze perfectly still. Silvia's jaw dropped, and her eyes grew wide. The older woman started to lunge forward, but Mirien stopped her with a gesture.

"Even having cut me off from the network layers, I'm far from defenseless." Mirien said. "Now, tell me: Where is Arthur Lannius?"

The hologram of Spiderfly vanished as the construct retaliated. Mirien's sea fog visualization of the aether swirled in raging vortices as the construct met her defenses. She had repelled hostile artificial intelligences before, but this being was different, somehow lit by the spark of being? It snaked through her mind. Parts of herself slipped away like sand in the wind.

Countermeasures and processes met at the boundary between thoughts and math, as Mirien and Spiderfly battled. The block between her and the networks was tenuous. If she could cross the threshold, she could summon aid. Her captors did not have much longer.

Suddenly, she felt a prick at her neck. She reached for it and felt the barrel of a tiny syringe against her skin. She snarled at the betrayal. And then, she was gone.

*　　*　　*　　*　　*

Spiderfly! Silvia shouted to the AI. *There is a line between curious and reckless.*

The gray-haired woman was gently lifting the girl from the floor. She extracted the hair thin needle from her neck.

Fantastic, Spiderfly responded.

No, horrible and unfair, Silvia said.

Unfair? It was a bargain.

Under false pretenses. You tricked her and something terrible almost happened, Silvia said. The girl was now standing, leaning against Silvia in a twilight daze.

I know! I had no idea. What else do you think lurks in there? Spiderfly responded. His holographic projection returned.

Never again. Lannius would not approve, Silvia said. *And not a word to her; this might be too great a burden for her to bear.*

Cross my heart, Spiderfly promised.

254

Aurora awoke in Spiderfly's chamber. She was dressed laying on the dais. She looked around, bewildered.

"What did you do to me?" Aurora said. "What did you do to me!" she shouted and sprang up from the dais.

Aurora lunged at the location where she saw Spiderfly. Silvia winced in sympathy for the girl's angst.

"Aurora, can you tell me what happened?" Spiderfly said.

"How did I get here?" Aurora shouted.

"Training. We started your training," Spiderfly said. His voice was silken.

"I don't remember," Aurora said. She tried to force her composure. She shivered.

"What do you remember?" Spiderfly said with deliberation.

Aurora calmed herself, closing her eyes. Her pinky drummed on her thumb as she tried to shunt the anxiety from her mind.

"I . . . dreamt of Jackal and Lannius? Wait. Am I still a prisoner? Who are you really?" She started to panic again.

"It's okay, dear. Have some tea. You're alright." Silvia tried to console her, although it may have been an effort to calm herself.

"No!" Aurora exclaimed. "You're working with him too! I need to get out of here!" She lashed out with her augmentations into the aether. Spiderfly winced but countered the primitive attack.

"Enough," he commanded. "Watch."

Suddenly, Aurora was in a darkened space looking down on a tiny platform. The dream scene from the night before played out on the miniature stage. She looked into the darkness around the shrunken actors in the white lights. Spiderfly loomed next to her in the darkness. The aether whipped through the darkness like a blizzard at night. One of his hands hovered over the scene; his too-white teeth glowed in the darkness.

"What is—" she asked.

"Watch," he commanded.

She saw near-invisible filaments trail from his fingertips down onto each of the tiny actors below. She saw the malevolent Lannius step out of the darkness. She saw her face struck by pain and terror as he forced her to choose. The filaments danced through the air as the tiny figures played their parts below. Aurora felt her stomach drop.

Panic spread through her. She thought of Kars and Lena, wondering whether invisible filaments trailed from them into some abstract network dimensional space. She rubbed at her own neck, feeling for the filament. Her neck was smooth.

"You were the one," Aurora said. "You made my dream?"

"I said your training would begin in the morning. Welcome to your first lesson: never trust *anything*. Not me. Not even Lannius." Then Spiderfly smiled a wicked grin. "Never trust anything more than yourself."

"Why are you so insistent on scaring me? You abducted us, commandeered Squire, and now whatever this abominable lesson was supposed to mean." Aurora's voice quivered at the edge of rage and sorrow.

256

"I do it in your service. Your naiveté must die, and you must armor your trust with skepticism and doubt," Spiderfly responded.

"But why this way? That dream—nightmare—it's broken my heart," Aurora responded.

"And in doing so, made you stronger," Spiderfly responded. "As a being thrust into a world alone and hunted by a superior foe, I assure you, your guile and doubt are your only true allies."

"I can't even remember. It feels like you turned me into someone else!" Aurora shouted. The color swept out of her face. "Did you turn me into someone else?"

"I did not. We made a bargain."

"Mirien?" Aurora asked. Her mind was spinning. She felt Silvia approach in some corner of her awareness. Spiderfly watched.

"Who am I?" Aurora asked as she collapsed. She fell into the eternity within her mind.

24

The Lone Planet

Her planet hung in space. She could walk its equator in a day,
traversing day and night before she needed to rest. Sometimes
she followed the river as it meandered across the surface. Wisps
of clouds floated over the tiny globe. She could pull fish from the
river; trees gave their branches for her to build fires for warmth.
Stars appeared at night, companions to a tiny moon that slung
around the planet's orbit.

She could not remember when she had arrived. Sometimes she
would talk to herself, sometimes she would sing. But most days it
was just peace—alone on her planet, drifting through some
space. She slept among the trees. The animals watched her but
never approached.

Days raced past on the tiny planet. It did not matter to her. She
organized twigs and leaves, dug holes, crafted garments of what
she could find and scavenge, then cast them aside. Nothing
much mattered.

One day, she noticed a golden web in an elm. The fibers
stretched from branch to branch, forming a dream catcher
between the leaves.

She circled the trunk, looking at the web in the sun.

Then a voice spoke to her.

"Hello girl," he said. "You look as though you like my work?"

The voice started her. She had thought she was alone on the planet.

"I suppose it's fine work," she responded.

"Just fine? It's the finest." As he spoke, the spider appeared. It was dark and hairy, larger than any she had seen anywhere before on her planet. Its eyes glittered like black pearls and the tips of its fur seemed dusted in gold. She recoiled from the arachnid. Part of her felt fear of the creature, as its mandible could easily snip off a finger. But it also seemed somehow curious and noble.

"It is quite a fine web," she commented.

"Relax. I won't hurt you," it said. "I want to help—you see, the web, it serves a very special purpose."

"And what is that?" she responded. She felt it was telling the truth.

"It catches memories."

She thought it odd, realizing only now that she had no memories.

"I don't think I have any, come to think of it."

"Well, it seems to be a propitious meeting beneath the elm." The spider seemed to smile with an eager hunger.

"Perhaps," she responded, "but maybe I don't want any memories."

"No memories!" The spider waved its front legs in disbelief. "How can you even be sure you exist without memories? What about your self?"

"I am awake to being—I'm here—wherever we are," she responded. "Maybe that's enough."

"Surely not," the spider said. "How could you know? Maybe just take a step into the web?"

She looked at the golden fibers, shimmering in the sun. Memories. Sudden fear gripped her. Something about remembering filled her with dread. The spider's eight eyes watched her with diamond focus.

"No," she responded. "I can't explain, but I think I came here to forget."

The spider prowled toward her across the web. "A prison? For memories? Isn't that just a prison for your self?"

The spider made sense and it frightened her. Her empty world suddenly felt lonely and small. She stared past the web, watching as the sun drifted over the horizon as the tiny planet spun. She felt the need to cry.

"Just a few steps," the spider said, almost taunting her.

She started to take a step, before a bird fluttered onto the elm tree. It cocked its head and its black eyes examined the arachnid. The spider recoiled to the shade of the elm's branches.

"There's another way, child," the bird said. Its voice seemed familiar.

"Is this a prison?" she asked the bird.

"A refuge," the bird responded. The spider seemed impatient at the edge of the web.

"A refuge for what?"

"Aurora."

The word resonated deep within her. Lights danced across the polar sky.

"Me," Aurora said. "A refuge for me."

The bird watched her.

"It was too much," Aurora said. "The augmentations took me to standby again."

"No, not this time," the bird said. "You made this place to get away from the memories."

Mirien. The memories she could not recall, lurking beneath the surface. The Spider had done something, something she could not remember. The Spider wanted the memories. Aurora looked at it lurking on the web. It flexed its jaws as it watched.

"So you are part of me?" she asked the bird.

"No, we found a way into your sanctum through the unconscious layer," the bird said. Suddenly, Aurora recognized the presence: Silvia. Yet, the bird remained.

The tiny planet suddenly seemed to quake in her vision. Aurora felt the sorrow and fear grow in her. The memory of waking in the throne room with Spiderfly flooded her with terror.

"I can't do it. I can't go back. I can't live in doubt of being the other."

"Then don't," Silvia the bird said. "There's another way."

Aurora did not respond.

"Let me in," Silvia said. Warmth of genuine care seemed to radiate toward Aurora.

"No," Aurora said. "How do I know it's safe—I don't know what he wants. Why does he want my memories?" She nodded toward the spider.

"I can't be sure. Spiderfly isn't like you or me. But I'd guess he wants them for the same reason I do—any curious being does—to understand your story," Silvia said through the bird.

"Then why hunt me? Why trick me?" Aurora asked.

"I've watched Spiderfly for years now. While he may thirst for understanding like you or me, he only knows the fragility of the human spirit as an abstract. He can only observe that precious sweetness through others. Perhaps there's something freeing in it—never having to feel the twists and scars of how we remember and understand our stories. But there's something tragic in understanding without the tenderness of feelings in a body. It makes sense that he hungers for memories. A memory is not only what happened but how it happened within you."

Aurora felt a pang of sympathy for the beast on the web. Its glittering eyes remained intent, devoid of emotion but aware.

"But these aren't my memories. It isn't my story," Aurora said. "If he draws them out, I don't know if I will continue to exist."

"I know that," Silvia said. "I've had my memories invaded and my identity assaulted. I understand the fragility. My curiosity will never encroach on the sanctum of another. I have my loyalties, and I will do what it takes to uphold those oaths, but I will never invade your memories."

"Silvia, how do I continue?" Aurora asked.

"Know *your* story. Know the story of Aurora."

"But what about the other memories?"

"Data. Information for you to use when it serves you," Silvia said.

"It doesn't feel like data. They feel like memories, full of all the feeling and context of experience."

"A dream of another," Silvia responded.

"What do I do then?"

"I remember when the invaders came for me. I clung to myself, to my story," Silvia said. "You need to know yourself. Harden yourself against the others. Doubt them and believe in yourself. Know and love your own reflection. Even the memories of the other can't take that from you."

Aurora steeled her expression. The idea that another's memories lurked in her mind filled her with rage. The pain she felt before finding herself on the tiny planet returned. How could she love herself with the other in her mind?

To survive, she would need to harden herself. She would trust none beyond herself.

Not even Silvia. The realization that it had to be all or nothing burned at her like embers on paper. Not Lena. Not even Kars. She would carry Mirien's memories alone. Aurora willed the circuitry in her mind to her cause. The pain disappeared as her augmentations wove a reptilian skin around her trust. Had it been the augmentations? Or was it her own heart collapsing beneath the weight of Em's lie, the strange memories, and the mysteries of Lannius? Had the spider broken her or merely shown her a truth? It was a terrible bargain: she would know and love herself—alone.

The rage quenched and the fear left; she opened her eyes. She stood in the throne room.

"You've made your point, Spider," Aurora said. "Now, train me."

25

Gan'ko Meka

"Gan'ko meka," Arc announced as the elevator door opened onto a dank gym below the basement of the House. Acolytes dressed in training robes sparred in paired lines. Some fought practice robots in designated rings. Silvia watched, arms crossed.

"Some thought the word came from tango," Silvia said with a smile, "but it'd be a terrible dance—no patterns."

"Gan'ko meka is an infantry technique that evolved from the first days of combating autonomous drones. As autonomous war became more prevalent, so did the gan'ko fighting style until it was formalized into a specific training," Arc explained. "Follow me."

They wove through the acolyte practice to the back of the gym.

"You two will be great," Silvia said to Kars and Lena. "No augmentations, like the warriors of old. That'll be to your advantage as the form utilizes disruption forms to confuse augmentation-driven pattern recognition."

"Time will tell whether that is an advantage," Arc said.

"True practitioners of gan'ko attempt to see in themselves what the machine sees. Part of the goal of the practice is to know one's own patterns and tendencies, so one can manipulate them in the eyes of the algorithm. The machines see data for its predictive value, while a true human sees no predictive value because each decision is part of being human," Arc explained.

"But aren't certain patterns just part of life? Daily cycles like waking up, brushing our teeth, or eating breakfast?" Kars asked.

"Gan'ko aims to bring the vigilance of fighting machines to every aspect of our lives. The machines' great strengths are observation, speed, and prediction. Ours is our freedom and our ability to decide. Many argue that we don't really have agency beyond a narrow band of personal biases. The practice of gan'ko aims to train that power. Patterns are fine, so long as they are conscious. Only then do we have the power to change them."

"Take your stance," Silvia said.

Kars and Lena looked at each other, confused. They had no idea what stance to take. Silvia just nodded for them to try. They each assumed an athletic pose. Silvia watched.

"Kars, you favor your right foot and apply fifteen percent more weight to your right quadriceps. Lena, your body is point five degrees off camber at lumber vertebrae four," Silvia said. "Take your stance again."

Kars and Lena adjusted, still looking confused.

"Kars, you adjusted to try to favor your left foot, but still favor a twelve percent shift onto your right quadriceps. Lena, you adjusted your back, but you just look goofy," Silvia said. Lena blushed.

She made them adjust again and again, reporting back minute variations in their posture.

266

Finally, Kars grew frustrated "What's the point of this? Just tell us the pose!"

"The point," Arc said, "is knowing your tendencies and studying them so you become the master. Through learning your tendencies, you will hone the seventeen stances, twenty-three transitions, and thirty-seven answers. This gives you five thousand nine hundred and twenty-nine permutations at any given juncture. Knowing what the machine expects from you allows you to randomize and attack in less probable fashions."

Silvia blew out a frustrated gasp. "I fought alongside their parents. These are mountainfolk. They managed to kick out Perpetual once. Let's give it a try."

Silvia led them through the strange halting fighting style. Augmentation algorithms predicated their attacks on probability, not targeting the adversary but instead targeting the most likely positions of the adversary. Gan'ko aimed to disrupt those probabilities with randomness.

Each move was sudden, requiring tremendous physical strength. Maintaining balance and fluidness while banking unpredictably against the body's momentum was the true art. Silvia flowed through combat like a silver whirlwind. Kars and Lena were soaked in sweat within minutes.

When they were not practicing gan'ko, they trained and ate. The acolytes and the House robots planned meals that helped optimize their performance and packed on muscle. Deeper sub-basements housed tracks, obstacle courses, pools, weight rooms, and acolytes helped them train.

Their training was not all physical.

Arc challenged Kars in use of the tabula, scolding him that he had been detected when he tried to access the rail freighter. What they gained in security from being un-augmented, they lost in many other ways. The inability to directly write memories was just one. Unlike the augmented mind, they had to practice a skill to acquire it. Kars and Lena seemed satisfied, however, feasting on the experience.

Kars learned the gauntlet, at the expense of many peaceful robot drones. He knew the fine script now, how to navigate the gauntlet's menus to reach into the machines. Slowly, he learned how to use the gauntlet to make them obey his commands.

They rarely saw Aurora, but when they did, she seemed distant. Some days she looked as though she had not slept and even ate by herself.

"What do you think they're doing to her?" Kars asked Lena.

"She said it was training with the augmentations, but that's pretty vague," Lena responded. "I hope she's okay."

"She doesn't seem like herself," Kars said. "But she doesn't seem like she wants our help. Maybe they're just working her really hard?"

"Maybe, but it might also be that she's just in a different world. I can't even imagine how much she's learning."

"It makes me sad to think about that," Kars said. "I don't know if I can forgive them if we lose her."

"We won't," Lena said. "And we're here together. We will help her if she needs it. They can't get in our minds."

Lena squeezed Kars hand.

"Not my mind," Kars said. "And I'm figuring out the gauntlet too. Anyway, we should get through our training, so maybe we can see Aurora tonight."

Spiderfly watched through the myriad eyes of the House as the two young people left.

26

Learning to See the World

"Come at me," Aurora dared.

The aether coalesced into Jackal as Spiderfly launched an attack. Aurora imagined him folding inward until the illusion was gone. It was just another mote in the aether. She felt no fear.

"You'll have to do better, Spider," she taunted.

Em appeared. She had a gentle look in her eyes.

Seeing Em was like thrusting a dagger into her heart. It filled her with grief and loneliness, but just when she felt it would overrun her she felt the illusion crash into the reptilian layer around her heart. She willed the illusion of Em from her mind.

"I know who I am," Aurora said to herself. "And that is enough."

Her first terrifying night had served its purpose in showing her just how vulnerable her augmentations made her to deception. A sharp mind intimate with the contours of their own desires and fears was the strongest defense—shrewd and nimble to avoid the seduction of an intruder's fantasy or nightmares. There was no place for trust in that persona.

Aurora and Spiderfly spent their first days working through brutal simulations. The AI's mind had grown out of testing how human beings found meaning, probing their values and choices. Through Spiderfly's trials she was forced to explore shameful and cruel memories, terrifying futures, painful scenarios of ambiguous moral choice, and even scenarios of defeating physical struggle. But each round, she processed and incorporated the learning. While she knew the training was hardwiring her augmentations, her mind experienced them as something else. Sometimes it was like uncovering the foundation of her personality and reinforcing it with confidence. Other times, it felt like building new levels of assuredness and awareness that soared far beyond what she had known.

The machine was programmed and the mind learned simultaneously: to face the world one must trust in oneself. What she learned through Spiderfly's challenges was that trust flowed from knowing herself—her reactions, memories, and what gave her meaning—the meaning the curious artificial intelligence so desperately sought. From that trust, she could stand apart from the world and raise her doubts and honesty to defend against being manipulated by others.

Throughout the first days in the House of the Spider, she would only see Lena and Kars at meals. They seemed happy in their surroundings, drinking in the excitement of something strange and new. As time went on and her training became more intense, she saw them less and less. Eventually, she would not see them for weeks at a time, isolated in the depths of her own training. Aurora wondered if they would eventually forget about her.

Many of the hours spent outside of Aurora's training with Spiderfly were spent in the classroom with Arc. The Strategemic was the tactician and counterweight to the seeming chaos of Spiderfly. He had scripted his augmentations with hard tenets of logic and bias. Compared to the harrowing journeys Spiderfly demanded of her, she appreciated the controlled and severe mood of Arc.

Arc's main purpose was to teach her about the world. She had excelled during her schooling but came to realize that the curriculum offered to her village through the trickle of internet access was a heavily edited, even censored version of the truth. The first moment she learned that her understanding of the world had been edited stung.

The globe sprang into her awareness, spinning in their lesson room. The map, projected through her augmentations was a craft of exquisite detail—shaded oceans, blazing deserts, and verdant forests. She recognized the blobs of continents scattered across the oceans, familiar shapes that she had traced since she was a child.

Except, it was different.

The eastern edge of Sen bulged to the southeast, forming an equatorial delta. A chain of islands carved off a section of the Sencan ocean. Aurora puzzled over the changes in the globe. There were other differences—changed contours, deltas, islands, and mountains.

"This is different," she said. "Different from the maps in the books."

"Very good," Arc said. "Not everyone sees the changes so quickly when they gain access. It takes the mind some time to see the world is different than it learned."

"Gain access?" Aurora asked.

"You're looking at a Class A Map—reserved for voting class shareholders. It has certain parts of the world on it that the Great Companies would rather hide," Arc said.

"I still don't understand," Aurora said, squinting at the odd sections of the globe. "Change the globe to hide things?"

"Precisely, although, I don't know if you realized how precise you were. Changing a map is changing the globe. In changing the map, they banish parts of the world to rumor or myth. There's little wondering about something you doubt exists."

"Why don't people just tell each other?" Aurora asked.

"They do and some can even hear it, but most prefer the managed chaos of their own networks. Information tagged with voting class privileges comes bound up in layers of synthesized taboo, reluctance, and shame. On the listener's side, access to the network requires submission to terms, which frequently includes comprehension censorship. To many, they would look at this map and be neurologically incapable of seeing the differences."

"That's horrible," Aurora said, racing to accept the enforced security even as she studied the new map of the globe. "Why would anyone submit to that?"

"The early throws of connected living, before the days of augmentations, were tumultuous times. The human brain is still an animal organ, ill-equipped to feel the weight of the world pressing in at any place at any time. People turned to tyrants and strongmen to quell the perceived chaos. After a generation of living connected, people grew weary of the stimulus, the constant compulsion to know the news, the latest catastrophe transpiring in real-time in some distant land. One man created a smart filter—called Cave—and never expected it would take off, but it was wildly successful. People called it "caving." They would retreat for weeks, then months, and then entire lives. It eventually became the foundation for the comprehension censor. No totalitarian despot was needed to enforce it; the people did it to themselves."

"I can't imagine anyone wanting to blind their own mind," Aurora said.

"Of course you cannot. In a different life, you would probably have been a voting shareholder or even in management," Arc said.

"You keep saying 'voting' like I know what it means. I only knew a few of the corporate logos before we fled our home. Sometimes we would vote on things when the town council brought them to a vote, but there wasn't much organization beyond deciding festivals, fighting fires, and sharing water," Aurora said.

"I apologize. It seems as though the standard curriculum did an adequate job of early history, antiquity, and the classical era through the end of the Renaissance. It's occurring to me that we need a deep dive into our world. Understanding our past is essential to knowing what it is to be human in our present," Arc said, tapping his temple. "Would you prefer me to show you or tell you?"

"Let me have it," Aurora challenged, dropping into one of the room's comfortable chairs.

"Have you ever had a direct history?" Arc asked. "Downloaded any Pivot Points?

"Squire mentioned it, but I've never been part of one."

"We know longer 'learn' history in the sense of memorizing dates and events. A Pivot Point is like the idea of a flash-bulb memory but for a society—a moment in the culture that would unequivocally shape the memory of all of its denizens. The advent of global social networks enabled tracking of these collective memories with statistical certainty. Our task is to understand. History is a series of Pivots in time, there for us to upload."

Allow me to tell you a story, then, Arc beamed into her mind, and the images coalesced into order. The Pivots of history played out in her mind.

Centuries' worth of events coalesced in her memory. She suddenly knew the legal labyrinth of mergers, takeovers, and regulations that consolidated the market behind a few apex corporations. Once those super-predators of capitalism dominated the market, they looked to the only remaining challenge to their authority: government. Through discourse and bribes they eroded the distinction between corporation and person until democracy was written by the shareholder class.

One logo seemed to rise above the rest: Agrion-Stills. The dynasty of fathers and sons trampled through time, starting in the golden waves of grain with a family tractor business. Silos sprang up next to the garages, locomotives belched sooty smoke as they crisscrossed the map. Banks popped up across from the silos. Men in suits shook hands with sun-hardened farmers. Community investment shifted to commodities and Agrion-Stills metastasized into new businesses. The mantle of leadership passed from father to son, gathering power up into the latest scion, Charles Agrion.

"Never any daughters?" Aurora interrupted. It was a brief respite from learning hundreds of years of history in a moment.

"Tradition is foolish," Arc responded, his mouth turned down in a dour frown. "One of the enduring, unlearned lessons of humanity."

Aurora watched as Charles held a meeting with the leaders of the five other apex corporations. It was the inception of the innocuous sounding Global Trade and Tariff Treaty—the G-Trip. In actuality, signing the treaty was the declaration of the Consolidation War.

Planes, tanks, missiles, rifles, infantry, and helicopters collided. The suffering punctuated the Pivot Points. Families fled the violence. Others fought back, two armies flanking and countering one another. Explosions toppled buildings and vaporized vehicles. The war swept across the globe.

Aurora watched as Charles Agrion spoke before the leaders of the Great Companies and the military minds of the allied nations. He eagerly pounded his podium as a field demonstration of the Protek played on a screen behind him. Aurora felt a wave of terror ripple through her as a Protek show model walked out onto the stage. A young Arthur Lannius was shaking hands with the board members.

Seeing Lannius as the Pivot Point settled in her mind. Her place in history snapped into focus, calling forth echoes of Mirien. She felt a migraine crackle through her brain.

"Too much?" Arc asked.

Aurora nodded.

"Maybe the comprehension censor isn't such a bad idea." She winced.

"My apologies. It's easy to forget that all of this is new to you," Arc said.

"It's okay. I just need a moment," Aurora said. She squeezed her eyes shut, attempting to divert some of her experience of a growing migraine. Squire had been right—downloading Pivots stressed the brain.

"My hope is that it serves you when you need it. You've been a compelling student," Arc told her.

"Thank you," Aurora said. "Maybe just a few old-time questions while the headache passes?"

"If you would like," Arc responded.

"Yes. I just couldn't help but think as I learned the history—why? It's so cruel. Why does cruelty follow every triumph?" Aurora asked. She rubbed her temples and wondered whether it was the mental strain of the exercise or the burden of history that was hurting her head.

"Such a human question: why," Arc said. "I guess in many ways the corporation and the curated experience of the network are not so dissimilar in the question of why. Both shield us from our own effort of participation and distill our participation into an algorithm. The corporate form boils humanity into the purpose of profit in a common venture—a person becomes a shareholder, absolved of the duty of the details, meaning, and morality of a decision. The comprehension censor shields our humanity from those parts of the world we would rather not see—they simply do not exist. Both narrow our sense of being human, draw walls around our responsibility to care."

Care. Lannius welled up from her memories.

Arc continued. "Why is the fundamental question of caring. People plod along their path, but humanity stops to wonder why."

Aurora's headache persisted. Arc's summary that history was beyond good and evil, just a sum of mistakes and serendipity, did little to make her feel better. She wondered about her role in the pivot points of the future.

He noticed her unease, and his expression softened.

"My apologies again, Aurora," Arc said. "Questions of why people make the choices they do are troubling mystery. I struggle to remember that for every act of cruelty there is an act of senseless kindness, perhaps the correction that shifts the course of history as it flows past."

"Thank you for saying that," Aurora said.

"Well, thank you for reminding me to revisit these questions," Arc said. "I must not let the machine dictate my decisions. Sometimes 'why' is the right question. Good people roam the world, and they are the ones that ask why."

27

Open Doors

"How well do you think Silvia knew Em?" Kars asked Lena as they rounded a corner in a piped hallway. They jogged deep in the industrial bowels of the House of the Spider.

The days were filled with physical training—conditioning and gan'ko meka—perhaps a harbinger of the world they would soon face. It might have also been that Silvia and Spiderfly knew that they would be trouble if left to their own devices. The physical suffering through training was enough to keep them on a manageable path.

Lena and Kars frequently talked about home and what was yet to come as they did their morning laps in the subbasement of the House of the Spider. It was a kind of ritual of remembering, sharing, and processing the loss. They would remember over the sound of clanging footfalls as they ran along the grated catwalk.

"What do you mean?" Lena responded.

"She said she was there when Lannius dropped off Aurora with Em. And she said she was a part of the Rebellion. My mother was definitely there for both of those," Kars said, slightly short of breath.

"Ask her," Lena said. Her tone was matter of fact, and she was not short of breath. Kars summed it up to the fact that she was lighter than him.

"Do you think she knows any more about my father?" Kars asked.

Lena stopped jogging, and Kars slowed to a stop. She looked at his face, both of them sweating from the run. His father had only come up on a few occasions in their household. Em's memory of Robert was wrapped in tenderness and anger that she rarely dropped. It was Kars's link to his father.

"Kars. Are you okay?" she asked.

"Yeah," he said, "I think so."

"Really?" Lena asked. "While pessimism doesn't suit you, neither does swallowing your suffering to keep a front."

"It's just that all of this has got me thinking about what really happened. My mother always told me that he left us during the Rebellion. Went missing during the fighting. Maybe Silvia knows a more," he said.

"Maybe," Lena said. "Do you think it's a good idea to ask her? I mean, what if it's something you don't want to hear?"

"At this point, I'm tired of not hearing it. When we were on the run from Jackal, it was hard to put all of this into its place. We just had to survive. Before that, we were home, part of a fantasy about the Rebellion and my father. But since we got here, we've had the time to think about everything and it's left a bitter feeling with me." He spoke much more deliberately than normal; there was a deep hurt in his voice.

"My mother lied to Aurora and me about everything—about Aurora, about the augmentations, about Lannius. Her lie probably cost her life. I need to know what other lies were buried in there. I need to know whether any of it was true."

Instead of speaking, she hugged him. He allowed himself into the embrace and remained for several moments.

She finally withdrew and looked in his eyes.

"Whatever you choose, I'll be there with you," Lena said. "I think it's important we make this chance in this new world what we want it to be."

Their eye contact lingered for a moment before the intensity led Kars to nervously laugh and look away.

"Better to know, I guess," Kars said.

"Of course," Lena said. "Now let's finish this up. I'm starving. Think you can run a little more?" She smiled and flourished her braid before darting ahead of him on the track.

"Hey! Cheap shot. I'm running for that plain poached egg too. You would've thought they could've figure out omelets along with supercomputers," Kars said, feigning frustration, but he didn't mind all that much being a few paces behind with his thoughts.

*   *   *   *   *

Silvia waited in one of the multi-purpose rooms in the House of Spider. She had laid out the component parts of some unidentifiable machine. From the look of it, today's morning session would cover mechanics.

Kars and Lena strode into the room, fresh from breakfast and a shower. They wore the simple billowing clothes of the acolytes for their lessons.

Silvia spoke. "Good morning, always a pleasure to see you two." She paused with a mischievous look. "Do you have any questions for me before we begin?"

Lena looked at Kars, and Kars looked at her. He seemed hesitant. Lena nodded, urging him to ask. He looked bashful, then eased into the question.

"Silvia, you said that you were there when Lannius left Aurora with my mother?"

"Yes. I remember it perfectly." She actually had the memory stored and encrypted in her own offsite storage bank.

"Was anyone else there?"

"Yes. Lena's mother. And the two of you," Silvia said. "But you were both still in your moms' bellies.

Lena's eyes lit up. She had not expected Silvia to be so forthcoming and had not expected her mother to come up in the conversation so quickly.

"My mother?" Lena asked.

"Yes," Silvia said. Her voice grew distant. "You know how much they lost. I met your mother and father before, met your siblings. They were all fun and brave—like you. So much loss." Her voice grew distant.

"It had the impact Perpetual was going for—my parents were never the same. It was an attack on their heart. Maybe I'll get a chance to avenge them," Lena said.

"Let's keep you safe first," Silvia said.

Lena knew her parents had lost all of her siblings in the war, but it was another thing to hear firsthand about the event that ravaged her parents. She looked at Kars trying to send her encouragement through her pain.

"Did you know my father?" Kars asked.

Silvia did not speak for a moment, taking in a long breath. She let it out in a single sigh.

"Your father," she said. "Yes, like I said, I knew him. I knew him well. Robert Koren—good and tough. He and your mother were the leaders of the people in the Rebellion."

"You said he was 'good and tough.' That's what everyone says—like they agreed on some story of him. I hear those stories from people in town, but there's got to be more to him. Can you tell me what he was like?" Kars asked.

"Well, he *was* good and tough. That was the always true. He was as noble a man as I knew, a born leader and a brilliant tactician, but also warm and kind. He loved your mother like a wildfire. And he must've known a thousand jokes."

Kars hesitated, wrestling with the question he really wanted to ask.

"What wasn't good and tough about him? No one is *all* good and tough."

Silvia's eyes widened, the crow's feet etched in her skin stretching their regular creases as she sparred with an answer.

"By now you might be old enough to know someone who is charming and handsome and brilliant, the kind of person that others lean toward and orbit when they are close. The kind of person who makes the rest of us feel like the world is unfair, but we can't even get angry because they are so damn likeable. Robert had that magnetism. The world was easy for him.

"But just like so many people with that gift of ease and charm, Robert was headstrong and cavalier," Silvia said.

Kars nodded, seeming to understand.

"That makes sense. I think I can be that way too," Kars said. "What happened to him?"

"He disappeared during the battle of the Cordovan Gap. Most don't speak ill of those lost—it's a more convenient history—but others certainly blame your father. The deserters and those that surrendered before the battle blame him. There had been a debate. Perpetual changed their tactic around that time from isolated skirmishes with us to total war—Attila was taking more and more control. Perpetual controlled the new networks by that point, so there was essentially no public opinion or oversight to stop the machines tactics. It turned from war to culling, but your father believed they could be stopped."

"Was he taken? Is he dead?" Kars asked.

"When we lost the Cordovan Gap, it shattered our Rebellion. Many of the Seventy-Seven were lost, taken, or scattered. We don't know where Perpetual took its prisoners—if they took them at all. Lannius has spent years since the Rebellion trying to uncover the fate of those lost at Cordovan Gap. I'm sorry."

"So Lannius is looking for him?" Kars asked. The old man seemed to have his hands in everything.

"Yes, although, Lannius and Robert had a trying relationship. Most revered Lannius, including myself. But Robert seemed to detest Arthur and only worked with him begrudgingly, usually because Em talked him into it. It was so against both of their charms."

"If he was anywhere, do you know where it would be?"

"I'm sorry, Kars. I don't know," Silvia said. "I'll answer any more questions if you have them. If not, maybe we should take the morning off."

"Thank you, Silvia," Kars said, his voice steel. "I think that we should continue with our lesson."

*   *   *   *   *

Afterward, Kars and Lena exited the room, leaving Silvia on her own. The air was still humid with sweat, adding to the musk of the sublevel. Silvia had trained with them, as she always did. A piece of the sublevel training gym felt like home with its bare bricks and flaking paint on old steam pipes. The deeper levels of the House of the Spider reached back through history. Knowing that these old places slept beneath the soaring heights of the new city made Silvia feel at ease.

She felt a weight slide off her as she was able to process the experience of the conversation in the morning.

Even if she and Spiderfly had not watched Lena and Kars share their conversation on the track, they had known the boy would eventually ask her what had happened to his father. Even though she had also known she would tell him the truth, it made it no less hard. Two decades had passed since the Rebellion and she had grown old, but the loss still felt fresh. From the day Lannius sent her forth, she understood that she might be the link between these young people and history. Her duty ripened with time, waiting for its moment as the new city sprang up around her.

Spiderfly appeared in her augmented visual field in the lesson room,

"I'm sorry you had to deliver that news. It's obvious it was hard for you," he said.

"I suppose I'm as good as anyone else for it," Silvia responded. "He looks like Robert. Smarter though, asked the right questions. Are you keeping track of him?"

"Always. They are guests in my house."

"I wonder what he will do?"

"I wonder as well. Lannius likely would have encouraged us not to tell the boy," Spiderfly said, a devious smile shading the corner of his mouth.

"I know. But Arthur's not always right. The boy had to know."

"I wouldn't go that far, Silvia. 'Had to know' implies it's part of some algorithm or eventuality. He could have gone on with his life, returned to the mountains and lived to be an old man. Now we've primed him, set him on an errant knight's path to reconcile the wrongs between father and son. We've damned the boy to a quest."

"And we will see how he handles it. Maybe he'll learn. I wouldn't bet against him," Silvia said.

"I wouldn't either," Spiderfly said. "Maybe I'll leave some doors open tonight."

Silvia smirked. "What about the girl?"

"Lena? She doesn't need us to push her on a quest or feed her mind with questions she needs to answer. She's already there; she just doesn't know it yet. That's why I like her the best," Spiderfly said. "I'll help her along in time."

"What did you have in mind? I hope nothing too cruel," Silvia said to the AI.

"I will figure something out."

*   *   *   *   *

At the end of the day with his mind full, Kars found his bedroom confining and hot. Silvia's answers shed light on his questions but left the answer out of focus. He still didn't know whether his father was alive or not, and if he was alive, where he could possibly be. He needed to sort out his thoughts but knew he didn't want to bring this problem into Aurora's new world. He just needed to get out and walk.

Kars left his room and padded down the thick red carpet of the living quarter's hallway. He assumed there was still activity in the lower levels, with pilgrims and seekers coming to speak to Spiderfly. How could they willingly put themselves in the path of these forces?

He continued his wandering, reaching the utility stairs. Instead of going down, he decided to travel up. He didn't know what the upper levels of the building might offer.

The separate floors were locked, but Kars felt a soft wind and heard the sounds of the city. He hastened his pace, until he reached a propped door opening onto the roof. His heart jumped. He hadn't seen the outside for weeks!

Unfortunately, the weather was not cooperating for stargazing. A warm rain fell from the sky. Unwilling to sacrifice the opportunity, Kars stepped out onto the roof.

The city was stunning. The buildings were lit with the spectrum of colors, the highest buildings disappearing into the low clouds, causing the clouds to glow with light like they were looking through tears. A fog of low clouds rolled between the buildings on the storm winds. Kars was soaked before he walked to the walled edge of the roof. Many stories below he saw tiny figures hustling between buildings beneath their umbrellas. The cars and tuk tuks moved in a steady stream in the night.

He felt the rain carry his mood away, washing down from his shoulders out through his feet. The city in the storm was serene. He wished that he could share it with—

"Looking for some company?" Lena appeared next to him at the edge of the building.

"How'd you know I was here?" he asked.

"I was just thinking about the day and wondered how you were doing. You weren't in your room, so I started wandering," she said. "Pretty amazing spot."

"Yeah, lucky find. Although the weather could cooperate a little better," he said.

"It just feels good to be outside," she said, looking up into the weeping clouds.

They were silent in the rain for a moment, leaning over the retaining wall of the roof.

Lena broke the silence. "Are you going to keep going?"

He thought for a moment. "I think that's what I came up here to decide."

"What's changed?"

"I'm not quite sure. It's like all of the sudden, I feel like I lost something I never had. I lost it to something that's so much bigger than me that I don't know how to fight back. It's also just knowing that my mom's lost too. And Aurora is turning into something that I'll never understand. It's really just me now."

The sound of rain played softly over the deep thrum of the city.

Lena reached over and took his hand in hers. Her touch passed through him like a current.

"We're going to have to toughen you up. You think you're alone?" she asked in sweet chiding.

He looked at her with a forced smile.

Lena saw the tenderness and responded, "I'm here with you. We're not alone. Whatever comes—we can face it together."

She turned and faced him. His eyes were alive with the turbulence of his feelings, and he stared straight into hers. Tension crested into a rolling wave that threatened to sweep them away.

He examined the true beauty of her face. Rain rolled down her flushed cheeks onto her neck. Her eyes searched his, minute movements of her pupils as her breathing quickened. Tendrils of her damp hair lay flat against her temples and at her hairline. She gently bit her lower lip. The cosmos hung on the moment.

He leaned in and she met him, their lips connected in ecstatic release.

Months and years of energy crashed between them as they kissed on the rooftop. Rain-soaked, they embraced beneath the city's glow. Everything surged forth, bursting the dam they had held in place.

Finally, they paused, soaked from the rain and dizzy from their feelings. Without a word, they retreated down the stairs, hand in hand, and returned to a room for the night.

28

Doctor and Patient

Nothing marked the passing time in the desert. Days slid into weeks, weeks into months, like sand sliding off a pile. Life was the rhythm of the camp and the cycle of the sun soaring its scorching path through the sky. Sometimes sandstorms wracked the camp, tearing at the camouflage nets draped over the facilities. The mercenaries would scramble to secure loose objects, tossing thick tarps and paper mask filters into the prison yards. The Protek seemed indifferent to the storms, trudging through the murky air and howling winds. The storms always cleared, leaving a film of fine grit over every surface. Em felt the powder sand in her teeth for days. In all, life in their prison was an uneventful plodding between storms.

Em came to know Ranjit's fate in a new light. A political prison was different from a penal system—it was a tool of oppression and convenience. There was no sentence or process. The reason was ideology. It was cheaper and more convenient to disappear the enemies of the company to a desert gulag than to give them fair hearing.

Still, Em held onto hope. Almost every hour she thought of Kars, Aurora, and Lena. She knew they could live in the wilderness. They knew how to hunt and fish, build shelters, and tend modest wounds. In spite of those skills, those hunting them would eventually discover their trail. Their survival hinged on the kids finding allies, finding Arthur Lannius. They would probably have needed to make their way to one of the cities.

She felt a mix of joy and concern at the three of them reaching the city. It was a world that she had only experienced through short trips and stories and never visited after the advent of augmentations. Even before augmentations, she had not found much to her fancy in the cities. It was part of why Robert loved her. She had only asked once if life with her was enough, and he just laughed his hearty laugh and asked if the sky was enough for the mountains.

A sky without mountains was a lonely place. She tried to stop herself when she realized she was in the path of worry. The desert feasted on sorrow. She would not feed it. Robert hated the city, but her kids would probably thrive and fall in love with the lights. Kars and Lena were grounded, solid people who would not be fazed by the circumstances. At least, that was a story that she could tell herself.

Her worry for Aurora welled up. Aurora had augmentations and only a toy robot as her guide. Ranjit's story about the scripters filled her with fear. Had augmentations reached such complexity that they could rewrite a person? Aurora was smart—whip smart—Em told herself. She could fend off an intruder in her mind.

I've got to get out of here. The thought seemed to crash upon Em from beyond. She could not be Ranjit pining away for his children in his dusty prison. Even with her camaraderie toward the captive Seventy-Seven, she hated his depression. It made her afraid that someday her anger would cool into that same lonely lump of sadness.

Stoke the rage. She went to find Cara and Ben. They must be feeling the same way.

Despite losing his leg, Ben seemed more whole than he had been in years. His sacrifice had given their children the moment to escape, and he carried that knowledge with pride. Clearing himself of alcohol had brought clarity and peace.

"What's on your mind, Em?"

Em sat, close enough that he would be able to hear her in a low voice.

"Our kids, Ben," Em said. "They are still out there, and we are trapped in here. I don't want to spend my life drying out in the desert."

Ben's smile faded. He looked at the stump of his left leg. They had just changed the bandages again.

"What do you propose?"

"What's the doctor like?" Em asked.

"He's a good man. So is his staff." Ben's voice was low.

"Did you see any more of the leader? The guy with the mohawk?" Em asked.

Ben shook his head.

"Any sense of what the doctor and the staff thought of their leader?" Em said.

"Not much. Only that they don't like him," Ben responded.

"I don't care if they like him. Do they trust him?" Em asked.

"They talk about him like they talk about the night watch guards, like he's made some desperate choices that left him unhinged," Ben said. "But anyone who has ever seen him knows he's broken."

Em gave a slow, affirming nod. The suspicions that she had hatched from Ranjit's stories seemed to be true. Jackal was a despot on a short leash. It also seemed more likely that conscripts taken during the Rebellion staffed the camp. She wondered if Ben was up to making use of this advantage.

"Next time they take you out, try to talk to the doctor about it," Em said. "Also, tell him that I need to see him. Medical care. Tell him I need help."

Ben looked her in the eyes, his own eyes bright. She saw the spark of the man returned to life.

The next day guards came for Ben, pushing back the townsfolk from the gate so they could enter and scoop up the man. He exchanged a look with Em as he left the enclosure. Some time later, they returned Ben to the group. Em avoided rushing to talk to him and thought it better to wait. If Ranjit's stories had showed her anything, there was no need for haste in their escape.

*   *   *   *   *

After several days, a small group of guards arrived in the darkness once the group had settled in for the night. Tight-beam flashlights searched the sleeping prisoners. Em lay awake, slowing her breathing to wisps of steam marking each exhale. The light swept over her face and she closed her eyes. They found her.

The guards jostled her awake, raising her to her feet. They pinned her in place, holding her arms and pulling a black cloth over her head. She felt electric fear.

She stumbled to find her footing as they dragged her through the camp in the dark. She sensed when they crossed into a tent or building out of the brisk night breeze that swept through the desert. Dim light showed through the black fabric. The guards held her elbows for a moment. There was silence. *Would it be the doctor or Jackal?*

She felt her pulse climbing as they stood in silence. The black cloth whipped back. Careful searching eyes appraised her from behind small round glasses. It was the doctor. Em blew out a breath in relief.

"Please, Miss, have a seat," the bespectacled man said. He dismissed the guards, assuring them he would call if there were a problem.

Em sat on the examination table. The doctor started in with a stethoscope, that age-old medical ritual.

"Your friend said that you had a problem," the doctor said in a low voice.

"Yes," Em lied. "I've been having a tightness in my chest. I've had trouble breathing. I'm worried it might be my heart."

"Well, we will see what we can do," the doctor said. "Life here can be hard on the heart."

He set about organizing tools and notes. He rolled back his sleeves, revealing a small tattoo of the old Parallel logo on his forearm. Em's heart leapt as he confirmed her suspicions.

"You look like you've got something on your mind?" the doctor asked, pulling up a stool next to her.

"Just trying to feel better," Em said.

"So this doesn't mean anything, to you?" He raised an eyebrow and gestured toward the coin-sized symbol on his arm.

"Just an old logo from some Perpetual side project. I've seen it a couple places before," Em responded. Her tone was level, unfazed.

The doctor examined her face as she commented on the Parallel tattoo.

"Yes," the doctor said, "I'm sure you have. This got a lot of people in trouble some time ago."

"So I've heard," Em said. "Did it get you in any?" She tested the edge of her confidence.

"I'm here, aren't I?" the doctor responded.

"But, you're on the other side of the fence," Em said.

"A matter of perspective," the doctor said.

"Jackal keeps you here?" Em asked.

The doctor did not respond, focused on his note pad and readying his examination tools. He tilted the notepad toward her, glancing over his spectacles.

Careful. It was written in neat square handwriting.

Em nodded. Relief washed over her, the single word validated so much of her hope. There were others in the camp that might share her desire to escape.

"I guess all the cackling from the night guards make it a little hard to sleep," Em said, redirecting the conversation.

"It's a hard group that choose this sort of work. It takes a lot to push a man to script his mind and take a post at a desert camp—more than just money. Working with men of that kind of desperation can be a prison of its own sort."

The doctor tipped the notepad again.

Singh approved meeting. Below the neat handwriting was the Parallel symbol, redrawn to match the one on his arm.

"Are they listening?" Em whispered back. "The night watch?"

"They are always listening to me. You do know the effects of the paranoia engine? Of course, it also makes them jump to many of the wrong conclusions," the doctor said.

The notepad tipped forward again. *Men at door are loyal. We are prisoners too.*

Em's heart leapt. "Can you help us?"

The doctor glared at her, and she felt immediate regret for stepping outside of their fledgling relationship.

"That depends on your problem. Any reason why your chest might hurt?" He tipped the notepad again. *Be patient.*

"Ever since they took us, my heart hasn't felt right." Em nodded that she understood the silent message. "I had medicine that I was taking, but I haven't had it since we've been here. Life in the mountains was much less stressful than being surrounded by all these brute machines." She fleshed out the lie for any eavesdroppers.

"A common problem with an easy fix," the doctor said. "I'm just going to take a listen to make sure there's not any other potential issues, but I think a simple prescription should help the problem."

"I'm worried I might have aggravated the condition during the fighting. Our people did put up a good fight." She added a laugh to disguise her subtext.

"I'm sure you did." The doctor adjusted the position of his instrument. "Take a deep breath."

Em inhaled, then exhaled. "Our people were always pretty tough."

"I could tell from some of the injuries I saw since you arrived. Most common folk don't survive Jackal and the Protek."

"We're not most common folk."

"That much I've gathered," the doctor put away his instruments. "That'll be it for now. Seems like you've got some minor cardiac stress, as I suspected. Easy fix. I'll have the guards bring you a daily dose when they distribute rations."

His pen raced across the pad as he spoke.

Coordinate through Ben. Jackal is preparing for a major move. We will let you know when the time is right.

He gave her an inhaler from the dispensary stock, and written notes with her vitals. The guards returned, bagged her head, and returned her to the enclosure in the camp.

Back in the enclosure, Em sat in the darkness. The meeting had been some relief—there were people in the camp that she could trust. However, the doctor's words that the camp was waiting to strike filled her with dread. They were after her children.

She looked up at the stars scattered across the blackness of the sky. The silver thread of her heart felt them. She knew they were out there. Certainty spread through her. They would be safe.

29

The Networks

After several more weeks of regimented training in the House of the Spider, Arc brought Aurora into Spiderfly's throne room. It was empty, devoid of even the Spider himself. She waited in silence, steeling herself for the next assault on her mind. The door burst open, admitting two people.

"Ror!" Kars bellowed and drew his sister into a hug. Her training made it feel like months since she had seen him. She hesitantly returned the embrace—none of her new defenses gave any sense of alarm. Could she trust her senses?

Lena wore a huge smile greeting Aurora. Her friend pulled her in for a hug too.

"Are they being good to you?" Lena half-joked. "They taught us how to throw some punches. So if you need us, just say the word."

"It's been fine. Hard, but good," Aurora said. Lena gave her a questioning look, but Aurora did not respond. Mirien's and Spiderfly's trainings were her own burden.

Kars and Lena looked healthy and happy together, as though the House of the Spider had been kind to them. Seeing them together, she wondered if they had become more. A ginger hand touching the other's arm, a proximity they had not had in their stances before, inside jokes that resonated with flirtation. Kars smiled a small sheepish grin at Aurora. She tried to return the warmth but struggled to find the feelings. She looked down, realizing how much her burdens had taken from her.

Arc presided over the empty throne room, dressed in a long black coat trimmed with brushed metal buckles and buttons.

"Before we leave these walls, you will need to understand how to hide yourself and what you are hiding from." His tone was grave.

Kars billowed with new bravado from his training. "Why not just head out and fight against whatever it is?"

"*It* is Attila the Overlord. *It* is Perpetual. *It* is any number of enemies," Arc rebuked. "We don't fight because we can't win. Spiderfly has spent his entire existence outrunning and flanking and tricking these foes. They are myriad."

A golden hologram filled the air, crowding out the entire space. Millions of tiny weapons floated through the space.

"The six military AIs control almost all of the tanks, airplanes, ships, infantry drones, missiles, thermonuclear weapons, and all measure of anything else nasty."

Arc waved his hand and the jumble of holograms vanished as fast as they had appeared. Kars leaned forward in the empty space.

"Almost all?" Kars asked. "We're not alone? There are others out there?"

Aurora smiled hearing her brother's eagerness. Love for her brother crept past the defenses and wrapped around her heart. It was so fresh compared to the icy darkness Spiderfly forced her to face. She may have gained strength fighting through the webs, but her friends had gained energy. She hoped Spiderfly was not attacking her.

"There are others," Arc said. "The Free Fleet remains strong. Maya Ganaka and her rebels operate beyond the reach of the military AIs in the Mare. The emergent thought, Damian Durn, rallies a resistance. The scripters cooperate with the corporations but maintain independence for their dirty business. Some of the Seventy-Seven are out there, though many of them were lost or scattered during the conflict. And of course, the Houses don't answer to the military AIs."

"Why not bring them together?" Kars asked.

"Young men are so eager for war—their memory so short!" Arc said. "You go through a few weeks of training, and you want to take on the world. Lannius and the Seventy-Seven fought Perpetual and Attila nearly twenty years ago. They saved your precious town life from the Overlord.

"Why not fight? The will is not there! To most, they are the keepers of the peace—a convenient sacrifice of freedom offered at the altar of prosperity. People love the Curator—it shapes every part of their day. People acquiesce to the benevolent Curator, as though it is somehow separate from the Overlord. The Curator gives them things, and they give the networks total knowledge of themselves. It's the perfect combination of a military and surveillance complex. It would be difficult to convince people comfortable in their homes to fight against their own protector.

"As a small fortune, Attila and the others do not seem to have the same flaw as the wild Protek. The Protek destroyed everything in their range, went feral. The military AIs maintain some degree of restraint. At least for now."

302

The mention of Attila in the context of the Protek silenced Kars's protest. Why create a more complete or more perfect killing machine?

"How do we avoid them?" Lena asked.

"Camouflage, confusion, and subterfuge. As a second to last resort, run away. Conflict is always the last resort," Arc said. "We will teach you how to fool the AI."

Silvia strode into the room.

"For the two of you, it will be a simple matter of tying your identities to refugee tags. Neither of you have augmentations, so there's no issue with an errant scan. It will limit your ability to move into the more central districts, but that's an issue for a later time."

"What about the gauntlet?" Kars asked.

"Don't use it unless you have no other choice. As soon as you activate that device, you better be ready to deactivate whatever you've used it on and be ready for another wave of trouble after. Gan'ko might help you a bit," Silvia said, and smiled, "but all those laps on the track had a purpose."

"You mean it wasn't just keeping us busy while the eggs boiled?" Kars quipped.

"Don't kid yourself. I had to keep them from getting bored while you thumped around the track," Silvia responded. Lena snorted.

Arc continued unfazed by their side conversation. "Spiderfly's already earned identities in a bargain, crafted and sewn them into the fabric of this refugee world. Do your best to remain hidden the old-fashioned way. It's possible that your experience with Jackal and the Protek may have ended up in a high-level database beyond Spiderfly's tricks, and that facial recognition could lead to your capture. Keep out of sight and out of trouble."

"Aurora, you'll follow those instructions with some additional requirements. First, you were totally fresh. We had to take the time to train your mind to live in this world. Second, most people don't have enemies searching for them, so it was necessary to test your personality. Now, Spiderfly and I agree that it is time for your next lesson: the layers."

"I think I felt the public layer when we arrived in the city," Aurora asked. "The La Paz girl—she was part of the public layer?"

Silvia explained, "There are four layers in the augmented network: public, personal, private, and unconscious. The public layer is the outer-most shell of networks."

Another hologram filled the air. A layered orb drifted in a slow spin in the middle of the throne room.

Arc intervened. "It is a regulated sphere of wireless signals that are accessed in a unilateral fashion. In other words, you access the public layer, and the public layer only accesses your basic information so the Curator can direct the experience. It's mostly a space for advertising and public works."

The hologram peeled apart as Arc spoke, unfolding into representations of each layer.

"So yes," Silvia said, "the La Paz girl was a public layer ad that presented to your taste."

A ghost memory of the La Paz girl sprung up on the representation of the outermost layer. Her pretty smile still aimed to disarm, even as a memory.

"Contrast this with the personal layer, which facilitates bilateral access," Arc said as another layer peeled away from the sphere. "In this role the network accesses the individual's augmentations and reproduces their particular personal layer data. In doing so, the personal layer facilitates a sharing of individuals between one another."

Silvia responded, "All of this will make more sense outside of these walls, however, it's important that you understand how each of these features works in concert with the others."

"Is anything private?" Aurora asked. "Really private?"

"As in, no one can access? Not really. There is a private layer, which is point-to-point narrow access between an individual and another server on the network. Your training so far has focused on the private layer. You have started to learn how to defend your own sanctum—the private layer."

The layers peeled apart again, revealing the private layer as Arc spoke. He positioned the layers with his hands so that they could see the distinctions. With another gesture he peeled back another layer.

"Then there is the unconscious layer where things get very strange. Spiderfly typically uses the private layer, or even the unconscious layer to traverse the networks. We are sure that Attila would wipe out those layers if they weren't fundamental to the mind's interface with augmentations. The architecture supporting the lower levels is far less rational."

The final layer warped and roiled as though it were living. Arc grimaced as he looked at the representation of the final layer.

Aurora jogged through the concepts she had heard, letting her augmentations sort the information. Public, personal, private, unconscious. She had so many more questions.

"What do you mean fundamental to the interface?" Aurora asked.

"A computer and a brain, while both networks of electrical signals, cannot simply interface," Arc gushed with excitement in sharing his understanding. His hands wrung invisible shapes from the air as he spoke. "Yes, outgoing signals like one telling your arm to raise, or incoming signals like pain or a specific smell can be deconstructed into pure electrical impulse. But the phenomenon of being is much more than inputs and outputs. It is an arcane nexus between matter and information, a web of stories woven from threads of meaning. These threads of meaning cannot be crudely dumped into the brain and expected to form more than a tangle of stimulus. Every moment, the world seeps through parts of you that you do not realize or understand are forming a tapestry of being. The networks need to engage these different layers to appeal to the deeper sense of feeling human."

Aurora nodded, despite feeling as though the cryptic explanation only left more questions. A part of her understood like a remembered dream. Arc saw the sparks of knowledge flashing against her confusion.

"All will come clear as you plumb the layers. For now, let's move onto your next lesson: the personal layer."

30

The Personal Layer

An infiltrator drone floated out from the corner of the room. Kars, Lena, and Aurora immediately tensed. Aurora reached out into the drone's processes.

"Opening yourself to the networks opens you to new threats—to other people, to Attila and the other military AIs, threats we might not know. Today's lesson will unite all of your previous trainings so you can both experience and protect yourself on the networks."

Arc cautioned her. "Remember, engage only as a last resort. You are safe here, this is an exercise. Kars and Lena, you need to literally do nothing. Pretend that you belong, or at the very least, only feel concern based on the presence of the drone. Aurora, it will be more difficult for you. The personal layer can be treacherous. Most people simply blunder through the personal layer, wandering through the lives of others like mist. But a trained mind sees the hidden edges of how our projected thoughts collide with one another."

Aurora was utterly confused. Arc had fallen into some kind of mysticism. She couldn't see or feel anything different.

"The personal layer protocols were grafted onto a primitive neural phenomenon called empathy. The word has fallen into disuse as the networked world resorts to direct sharing through the personal layer. People share what they think they feel, and society has largely forgotten how to understand it," Arc said.

"Which I think is to its detriment!" Silvia interjected. "People think they are sharing, but when they pick and choose what the world will see of them, there's no chance for actual empathy."

"Thank you, Silvia, we will let them judge that for themselves," Arc chided. "For now, Aurora, concentrate on the experience of the other, not what it is projecting to you. Think about a time when you felt empathy. A moment when the feeling of another crested the gulf between individuals."

The memory formed as soon as he spoke. Aurora thought back to a moment when she was fourteen. She had stopped by Lena's house unannounced. When she arrived, the house was empty. Still, she let herself in and made her way toward the kitchen, where the family frequently congregated. A commotion in the back drew her attention, so she continued to the yard.

Once there, she found Lena and her father. Ben had fallen off the short patio. Lena was sniffling, trying to lift her father and carry him indoors. His head hung as though his spine had turned to rope, and his limbs swung like bags of sand. Aurora approached to help but stood transfixed watching her friend struggle. Suddenly, Lena looked up. Her face was a torrent of emotional confusion—rage, sorrow, embarrassment, and love. Aurora felt her own tears gather along the rim of her eyes, felt the iron lump of heartache gather in her chest.

Even now it brought a tear to Aurora's eye. She looked over at Lena, oblivious and stoic, currently in her own practice of disappearing as she had been instructed.

Silvia noticed the tear.

"Yes. I think Lannius made the right choice in sending you to the mountains," Silvia said. "You know what Arc's talking about. I'm going to join the exercise, Arc. I think it'd be easier for her to see the personal layer through another person rather than a drone."

Nothing changed in the room, still no recognition of the elusive personal layer.

"Think about me, what you understand to be my feelings."

Aurora looked at her, intuitively reading the wrinkles on her face. Silvia was beautiful like mountains, rugged and permanent. The creases were marks of time and struggle, but they also bore a sense of revitalization. The long gray hair flowed down her back. Hope, excitement, also fear. It made Aurora feel nervous, but she drew in the sense from the woman of hope and potency.

Then she noticed it, a nearly imperceptible disturbance formed an arching sphere around Silvia, and Aurora was already inside. She turned and walked closer to the edge.

Floating in the air, there was a near-invisible boundary. Light bent ever so slightly into eddies and whirlpools, distorting her perception into psychedelic wonder. She raised her hand and pushed her finger through the boundary. The phantom eddies swirled.

"She's found it," Silvia said. As she spoke, the eddies in the air intensified.

Aurora withdrew her hand from the swirl.

"Why are the personal layer and empathy related?" she asked excitedly, spinning back to Arc and Silvia.

"The tool subsumes the function," Arc said. "Technology evolved from sharing text to sharing all array of dynamic content. But ultimately, that content was all reducible to zeroes and ones. The early personal layer was built off of a need to transfer experience. The early function of the personal layer was to share emotional experiences with others—empathy.

"Since then, the personal layer has stretched and grown to carry much of the burden of projecting and receiving all of the information—data and experience—flowing across the network. Now the personal layer forms the fabric of civilization."

He watched Aurora as she continued admiring the near invisible bubble of warped air. It had a psychedelic beauty.

"Is it always like this?" she asked.

"That depends on the person, what they are going through, what they are projecting," Arc answered. "Technically, the personal layer occupies the same transmission dome as the public layer. However, it only facilitates interconnection when people are in useful proximity—the 'personal space.'"

She was still marveling at the fine swirling layer that defined Silvia's projected presence. She allowed herself to then visualize the aether. The room was suddenly a sun-kissed golden glow wrapped in the wandering whirlpools of twisting air. It was stunning.

Silvia smiled, the glorious creases of her skin deepening in pure joy.

"She's definitely getting the hang of it."

Aurora whipped her head around, smiling. "Yes! I see," she said. "Now tell me how to use it!"

"Using it," Arc said, "is not the issue. Not using it is a true challenge. Just like the vestigial root of the personal layer—empathy and emotion—it's much easier to unknowingly project yourself than to hide your emotions. To survive out in Attila's world, you will need to keep yourself hidden. Nothing projected. The machines should present no problem because they project an algorithm with little to engage. However, the people of the city share all their momentary thoughts, vain personas, phobias, desires, current activities, and deepest dreams through the personal layer. To pass through that maelstrom, you must let it pass through you."

"Give the girl a chance, Arc!" Silvia chided. "There's other ways to pass through the personal layer. I just keep in mind that everybody's got their own issues. I just stay focused on mine."

"That doesn't always work. You could end up projecting yourself into another's space," Arc said.

"Never. I hate sharing my stuff with anybody. I'd never do it by accident," Silvia said.

Kars snickered. He and Lena had long since given up on the practice of nothing. They both marveled and wondered what Aurora could see.

"What was Aurora sharing?" Kars asked Silvia with a jovial smile. Aurora was stunned by the question.

"Hmm . . . the best word would be . . . stupefaction. She's a little amazed and absorbed by her new world," Silvia said.

"Sure, but tell me something I couldn't tell without augmentations," Kars said.

"Sometimes it's the same thing," Silvia said, nodding her head.

"I was sharing something?" Aurora asked.

Silvia nodded, closing her eyes, and Aurora saw herself. Lily-petal butterflies surrounded her. Her skin was rosy like dawn with pink clouds wavering across her face and collarbone. Her hair shimmered, floating long and iridescent above her shoulders. She blushed seeing her experience laid bare. As she felt the embarrassment, a tiny mouse darted from her shoulder to the nape of her neck. The little beast peeked out from behind her to observe.

Silvia sensed her embarrassment.

"Don't worry, child," Silvia said. "We're here to practice. It's refreshing to see some honesty!"

"Emotional control and presentation have long been a human struggle—the networks just added another dimension to this humanness," Arc said. "We will help teach you before you need to face them."

"Why? Why do I need to learn?" Aurora asked, hot with embarrassment and feeling exposed. "I don't know why all of this falls on me."

"Because Arthur Lannius may not return." Spiderfly popped into the space. Of course, the digital being had been lurking in the aether the entire time, but his appearance was still a surprise. He bared his teeth in a wicked grin. "His crusade may fall to you."

Kars and Lena jumped at the sudden intrusion. His words crashed into Aurora, sweeping aside her embarrassment with panic. Spiderfly watched her reaction to the news. Aurora leapt to protect her mind from the potential tricks.

"That's not fair," Silvia said.

"No," Spiderfly responded. "But there is a difference between honest and fair—which would you prefer?"

"What do you mean?" Aurora asked, feeling wave of panic.

"She just learned about the personal layer. I don't think this is the time," Silvia said.

"Then when?" Spiderfly asked. "When Attila finds her? When Whitestone finds her?"

"Wait—" Aurora tried to interject.

"Maybe when she at least understands the world Lannius dropped her into? That might be a little more fair," Silvia responded.

"So he can tell her? Does a beard make hearing one's fate that much easier?" Spiderfly asked, relaxed in the interchange.

"It's not that, it's just that she deserves—"

"I deserve to know!" Aurora roared. It felt as though the words came from another.

31

Marked

Spiderfly and Silvia looked at her, stunned. Aurora gathered herself in the silent wake of her outburst. Spiderfly smiled and vanished.

Silvia snarled and exhaled. Aurora, Kars, and Lena looked on expectantly. Silvia looked around for Spiderfly. She snorted when the Curious did not reappear and sighed before answering Aurora.

"The Rebellion did not end with Cordovan Gap," Silvia began. "Lannius still fights. Cells of the Rebellion remain scattered across the globe, but the opposition continues to grow more sophisticated. We have some concerns that Lannius may never reach East Bay."

"What do you mean, Lannius may not return?" Aurora asked. "And what does that mean for me?

She struggled to place the idea that the master planner, the stalwart figure from her other memories, might face insurmountable odds.

Silvia again looked pained that Spiderfly had left her with this duty.

"It could mean two things," she said. "One, we try to move you, keep you safe, hide you, make you a secret once more."

"Or?" Aurora asked.

"We fight," Silvia said. "Lannius has seen it. When it comes to Attila, Perpetual has a tiger by the tail, and they will lose their grip," Silvia explained.

"You mean they don't have control?" Kars asked.

"It's not just Attila. There are six of them out there, currently fighting against each other. It's a sort of equilibrium of proxy wars and arms races. The Houses resist and chip away at their infrastructure, but it's hardly a difference. Eventually, one of the six military AI will conclude that the human race is the opposition to control."

"Lannius calls it Directive," Arc said. "The singularity of the six military AI, an unstoppable force. The Protek were just a cautionary tale."

"Directive," Silvia said. "The eventuality Lannius sought to stop. Some deep fear he carries as a burden from his role in creating the Protek. If Lannius does not return, it will fall to the rest of us to fight to make sure that future never happens."

Aurora tasted the dry bitterness of fear in her mouth. "You mean that I will have to fight it?"

"Attila and its peaceful sibling the Curator have inundated every facet of the human mind. Lannius marked you, knows you to be someone essential to the crisis. I wish I could tell you more, but Lannius kept certain things from even me," Silvia said.

Aurora felt anger mingle with her fear. Why could they have not left her to her own life? She felt tears crawl at the corners of her eyes. All she wanted was to escape, to have the wonder of the world they had shown her without the fear and isolation of their enemies.

"Ror, it's okay." Lena touched her arm. "We're here with you until the end."

"We're with you," Kars said. "This doesn't change anything."

Aurora smiled feebly. It didn't change anything—not for Lena and Kars. They would persevere. For her, everything seemed to revolve on a separate axis, spiraling away from the life that she had thought she was leading. All she heard told one truth: Lannius had conscripted her as a baby to fight his war.

"How do I respond? I'm a mouse in this new world and I'm expected to be a wolf," Aurora said.

"We will train you and protect you as long as we can," Arc said.

"There may be a wolf in there yet." Silvia smiled, tenderness in her eyes. "You already started a pack. You are not alone."

Kars and Lena were quiet as they watched.

Aurora returned the smile, clenching her fists, but she still felt the mouse on her shoulder. Even if Lannius was gone, she would continue—for Kars and Lena, for Em. She had defeated Jackal once, defeated the Pinkerton. She imagined the little mouse standing on its hind legs in defiance.

"Thank you for telling me," Aurora said. "There is no choice. Train me."

316

*   *   *   *   *

They continued training through the day. Aurora found that her training with Spiderfly in self-trust carried over into her work with the personal layer. Sometimes the challenge was drones, other times Arc would introduce acolytes. When she focused, she moved like a shadow through the personal layer. One of the few times she was detected was in a moment of self-reflection, when she gloated to herself and wondered whether she was channeling the other memories that had guided her.

As the day neared its end and Aurora was alone, Spiderfly reappeared. He looked stern and impatient. Aurora awaited some apology or praise or reflection, but none came. His words were severe.

"Keep your confidence close. Someday it may be you alone at the end of it all," Spiderfly said.

"Why did you leave?" Aurora asked, demanding an answer from the curious AI.

"I needed to confirm my suspicions. I needed to assess without interfering," Spiderfly said. "If Lannius plans to use you against Attila and the other AI, then perhaps you are not my ally. For now, we will just wait."

"What do you mean?" Aurora asked. "Are you not an ally?"

"Unlike some, I have not seen my future unfold."

Then he vanished.

Aurora was left alone in her room. First, thrust into Lannius's war. Now, threatened by the trickster AI. She rolled over in her bed, kept awake by her anxious thoughts. She had walled off her trust weeks before, but the current questions pressed in on her defenses. The quiet of sleep never came. She climbed out of her bed and padded out into the House of the Spider. A walk would clear her head.

32

The Changing Man

Nights in the House of the Spider brought the strangers and the derelicts to the altar of the bargainer. Curious revelers stumbled home late and the truly disturbed wandered the night to avoid being alone with their insomnia. The denizens of the night sought a different set of wishes and bargains.

Aurora crept down the stairs and into sprawling foyer of the House.

Kars and Lena sometimes waited to watch the nocturnal visitors. This night, they sprawled out on the couches near the antechamber of the House, their glasses of wine on the low coffee table next to a backgammon board. Kars fiddled with the tabula gauntlet, practicing with the operating system.

"Hey Ror!" Kars looked surprised to see her. "Come down to watch the show with us?"

"Too much on my mind to sleep," Aurora responded.

"Lannius?" Lena asked.

"Yes," Aurora said. It was a sliver of the truth, but she couldn't share more while Spiderfly was listening, and Mirien was her burden to bear.

"He'll get here. I don't think it'll come to you having to fight for him," Lena responded. "It seems like he's got plenty of plans."

"Well, I hope he gets here soon. I'm about ready to get out of here," Kars said, moving a piece on the board to block Lena. She grunted in frustration at the move.

"But do we know the plan? Do we really know the end game?" Aurora asked. "How well do we know Lannius?"

Lena and Kars didn't respond. Lena reached out and moved a piece on the backgammon board.

"Lannius built the Protek. He created Perpetual," Aurora said. "We're supposed to trust that his guilt puts us all on the same side?"

They paused as two bulky acolytes carried a sour smelling drunk away from the altar. Some of the night guard acolytes wore special tunics with the sleeves cut back to the shoulders. Their muscles rippled as they deposited the drunk beyond the threshold with the guard robots.

"Lannius helped Mom, fought in the Rebellion. That's got to be worth something," Kars said.

"Trusting him got us this far," Lena said.

"And how far is that?" Aurora asked. "We are in the lair of the Spider. I need you both to be careful. It's hard for me to trust my mind with all these games."

"They lied to us too." Kars said. "We'll keep an eye out for you."

Another pilgrim wandered up the stairs to the front doors. The robots parted to allow him through.

Aurora watched as the man paused in the anteroom. He was nondescript, middle aged, neither fat nor slim, altogether an ordinary man. But something was off. His eyes were rife with the animal panic of someone who had just done something terribly wrong. A slick of sweat highlighted the pouches beneath his eyes.

"Your turn," Kars said, sliding the dice across the table toward Lena.

"Hold on, check this guy out," Aurora said.

The wild-eyed man searched the room before approaching Spiderfly's throne room.

"Really? You know it's just going to be another gambler asking for money or maybe worse. Bargaining for Spiderfly to make their affair vanish. Aurora, you don't hang out enough. The night crew is never here for anything good," Kars said.

"There's something about this one," Aurora responded. She recognized something in his face—something in his mind rattled loose. She resisted the urge to probe through the aether.

"We can't even see Spiderfly most of the time," Kars said. People knelt before the throne as though they were praying.

"If he knows we're watching, he'll appear," Lena countered, standing up. "Come on. Ror doesn't hang out much. Let's watch this one for her."

Kars sighed and resigned to Lena's request.

The nondescript pilgrim approached the dais. In the gaslight glow of the throne room, they could see the panic on the pilgrim's face. Aurora felt a sickened wave of sympathy for him.

Spiderfly winked into existence.

"I told you. He knows we're watching," Lena hissed. Kars rolled his eyes.

The construct projected its air of disinterest as it lounged on the dais.

"What brings you here tonight? Mr.—"

"It's my mind. Something is wrong. I can feel something," the pilgrim stuttered. His voice raced with mania. Aurora shivered. Deep in her gut she knew what the man felt.

The projection of Spiderfly reflected even deeper disinterest. It slumped back into the dais.

"Well"—Spiderfly sighed—"apparently, that is quite common among humans. You might even call it feeling a condition of being a human. I'm glad that you feel. Now, is there anything in particular you feel? Anything that you need from me?"

"Fix it," the man said. "I need you to fix it. I think I may have hurt someone too."

"I want none of your bad debt, my friend," Spiderfly said. "I can see it in your mind, you've got the tinge of madness."

"I'm not mad," the man said.

"And I've got your best interests at heart," Spiderfly responded. "We've all heard it before."

"He's just crazy," Kars whispered to Lena.

The man seemed overwhelmed trying to ask his question without reaching the heart of the matter.

"It's . . ." his voice dropped to a whisper and he looked over his shoulder. "The Changing Man."

The name seemed to send a spark through the lounging AI. The projection reflected its growing interest for the benefit of the humans.

"Really?" Spiderfly said. "The Changing Man?"

"I know"—the man stuttered—"I know it sounds crazy. But it's real. It's not an urban legend."

"As something of an urban myth brought to life, I consider myself something of an expert," Spiderfly said.

"Then you believe me!"

"I reserve judgment," Spiderfly responded with glee. "The Changing Man is an urban legend and, as such, is the focus of more than a few delusions. Tell me, what is it like?"

"If I tell you, you have to agree to help me. You have to get him out of my mind!"

"If he's there, I'll help you get him out." Spiderfly nodded. "Now tell me, how do you know it's the Changing Man?"

"It's like there's someone watching, all the time. Like there's something behind my experience. Like I'm two people—two identical selves in the same body."

"Does he say anything?" Spiderfly asked. There was a stir in the acolytes near the entry.

"No, never," the man said. "It's not like a voice."

"Does it make you do things?" Spiderfly lingered with a hungry curiosity.

"I don't think so," the man responded, looking confused, like he lacked the words.

"Then how do you know it's there? It never does anything, never says anything. Have you seen it?"

"Just in my dreams," the man said, sounding harrowed. "All of my dreams."

"Go on." Spiderfly straightened with a malevolent interest.

"It's always right at the edge, blurry, gray and black. I can't say any more. It just lurks while the rest of the dream happens around me."

"Curious," Spiderfly said. "Sounds like a few other stories of the Changing Man. Just an urban myth."

"Please you have to believe me!" the man said, his panic returning. Sweat rolled from his temple down his neck. "I don't know where else to go!"

"I believe you, but you lied to me," Spiderfly said. "The authorities want you. No deals with the Changing Man tonight."

Spiderfly winked out of sight, leaving the man by himself in the throne room. The hulking night guards emerged immediately and seized the arms of the man.

Kars and Lena returned to their game. Just another crazed roamer come to the Spider in the night. Aurora continued watching. The man's animal panic soured her stomach. She couldn't look away.

The commotion of his dismissal seemed to grow. Acolytes flowed to the exits, pulling curtains and sealing doors. Silvia appeared from one of the stairwells. She looked as though she had been summoned from sleep, still puffy eyed from waking up too fast. She looked surprised to see them lounging in the lobby.

"Don't you ever sleep?" she asked. Kars and Lena grinned in response. Silvia rolled her eyes.

"Whatever," she muttered. "We've got a bit of a situation to take care of right now. Stay out of sight. The authorities are on their way."

33

Stormgard

Marcus Stormgard watched the city roll past in the night. The red and blue strobes of his vehicle flickered off the surrounding buildings. Two of his officers sat across from him, buckling armor to their bodies. A line of grapefruit-sized drones rolled along a rack above them.

"Keep it tight, team," he said. "Not sure whether the House will cooperate, but this is definitely our guy."

"We'll do, Chief," one officer responded. Marcus nodded. The officer affixed the Office of the Securitor badge to his armor.

The public layer beckoned him beyond his secure filters washing over the city. Perpetual, Attila, the Curator, the Houses, layers of the network. Somewhere he fit into it. He liked to think he was the fulcrum, that his work upholding the law was the last vestige of a sovereign state for the people. Other bastions like Arthur Lannius had abandoned civilization long ago.

The roads were mostly free of traffic at this time of night. Those that remained cleared a path for their armored vehicle as it sped by. The automated vehicles pulled aside as though choreographed so he could pass.

Marcus wondered if enforcing the law would ever fall the same way driving had given over to the machines. So far, the lawman business still raged. Even if his office had to bow to certain corporate politics, he still found plenty of inspired detective work in East Bay. Augmentations had opened a new front for creative deception, and people could be *very* creative.

Creative probably wasn't the best term for the monster he was chasing tonight. The crimes of this man chilled his bones and made him wish he were just home with his children. He hoped that the Spider hadn't already cut him a deal. Even more, Stormgard hoped that the Spider wouldn't learn anything from the murderer.

He shook the thought. There were good, if misguided, people at the House of the Spider. Marcus checked his weapon before tucking it into the shoulder holster beneath his jacket. The vehicle rolled to a silent stop at the foot of the stairs.

"Ready?" Stormgard asked.

"Ready." The officers secured their weapons.

Stormgard wondered if he might see Silvia again. Maybe she would have had it with the Spider and might be ready to join up with him keeping the city safe. He pushed open the door to the vehicle and turned to his men.

"Let's go."

*   *   *   *   *

Silvia and the guards flanked the man as they approached the front door. Other acolytes gathered nearby, looking both casual and primed to respond. Silvia straightened her dress and her gray hair before she threw open the door.

The door opened onto the city at night. The sounds of the city wafted in from the street. Three men stood in the doorway: two armored men flanking an official wearing a long coat. He was a handsome man with chiseled features and a neat salt-and-pepper goatee. He feigned surprise that the door opened for him and casually flashed his badge.

"Silvia!" he exclaimed with the exaggerated warmth of greeting an old friend.

"Marcus," Silvia responded, her voice impatient.

"You've got our guy?" Marcus asked. "Or do I need to come inside?" He bandied the light threat.

"We've got him. No need for theatrics," Silvia responded. "The Houses and the Securitor don't need any trouble with one another."

"Excellent," Marcus said.

"Please," the man said. "I didn't mean to do it. It's the Changing Man."

Marcus rolled his eyes. "A story as old as the networks. We'll get to the bottom of it at trial. You've got plenty of other things to answer for before we even talk about an urban legend."

Silvia nodded to her companions, who dragged the man forward to Marcus and his guards. One of them cuffed the man and started to lead him away.

"Thank you, Silvia," Marcus said. Silvia didn't respond; she merely crossed her arms and looked indignant. Marcus forced a hard smile. "I wish it didn't have to be this way, but you understand."

"I don't know if I'll ever really understand why you stayed when we rode out with Lannius, but it's water over the dam. The Office of the Securitor is your place. I understand that much," Silvia responded.

The muscle of Stormgard's jaw flexed, as though he wrestled with his response. His expression resolved to pride in his current duties.

"The city needs someone to serve it. The companies serve their shareholders, and Attila serves order. I can't speak for whatever Houses and whatever they serve. Despite its flaws, the Securitor is all we've got left of a government for the people."

"I understand the arrangement, Marcus," Silvia said. "Perhaps you're just better than me."

"We try to stay out of each other's way as long as the Houses don't make me get involved," Marcus said. "Stay out of trouble, Silvia."

"You know me," Silvia responded. "Take care of yourself, Marcus."

Marcus left with his men, escorting their prisoner away from the House. The guard robots resumed their sentinel positions at the doors as they swung closed. The House suddenly seemed quiet again compared to the ambient bustle of the city at night.

Silvia breathed a sigh of relief, and the acolytes seemed to relax as they returned to their own business. She started to walk away before Lena tugged on her sleeve.

"Who was that? What happened?" Lena asked.

Silvia seemed tired but entertained the request.

"Marcus Stormgard, the Chief of the Office of the Securitor. His office polices all the network crimes in the city. He's got a jail full of cybercriminals—lots of friends in there. I wish things were different with him, but he's ultimately a decent coward," Silvia said, her grin hiding some respect. She poured herself a glass of wine from the decanter Kars and Lena had next to their backgammon game.

"Sometimes our 'guests' cross paths with Marcus. Part of our business, I suppose. That man was wanted on several counts of murder, a madman. Marcus gives us space if we help when he asks us for cooperation. We try to keep clear of each other. The Houses are a little too sticky for Marcus to want to tackle," Silvia said.

"What about the man? He was a murderer?" Lena's eyes were wide.

Silvia sipped her wine. "It's a big city, bound to have some dangerous people."

"But he sounded like there was something in his brain," Aurora said.

"The Changing Man?" Silvia said, unmoved. "That's a story that sprung up with the networks. It's just a kind of psychosis, a particular paranoia resulting from living constantly connected. One person's delusion turned to a story then passed to others."

"He sounded pretty convinced," Aurora said. She hid her own fear of Mirien.

"They all do," Silvia responded, bluntly. "Just a risk of being too connected, I think. If you think about it, there actually is something watching and collating everything. The whole network experience has several watchers."

"Sounds like another reason to keep my head clean," Kars responded.

"Suit yourself," Silvia responded. "But it's not like psychosis is limited to the networks. You have to feel some compassion. Anyway, I think I'm going to head back to sleep, enough excitement for me tonight."

Silvia started to walk toward the stairs.

"Just to double check"—she paused—"Marcus didn't see any of you, did he?"

They looked at each other and shrugged, shaking their heads.

"Good," Silvia said. "Don't want him asking any questions. See you in the morning."

*   *   *   *   *

Marcus sealed the cellblock door behind him. He shook his head. Straightforward, but sad; there were far too many lives taken by the man before they had stopped him.

It was always tough seeing Silvia. He ran the Securitor for years, tackled countless criminals and masterminds, but seeing Silvia or any of the other Seventy-Seven dragged him back to the day Lannius left. He felt like a student again, lost and confused about what he should do next.

Part of the experience felt good to remember. Marcus pulled up his memories of the arrest at the House of the Spider. He watched the memory unfold. Silvia still had the old fire in her eye. He had always been a little intimidated by her during his training with Lannius. He laughed to himself. It never made sense why Lannius and Whitestone would keep a thug like Silvia

331

around. Marcus was surprised that she had lasted this long. It was not a surprise, however, that she had gotten tangled up with the Houses after Lannius went to ground.

Marcus remembered the arrest. There was something about Silvia's face. Was she nervous? Marcus slowed the memory as it replayed in his mind. There was something she was hiding. His augmentations mapped her expressions, comparing them against previous encounters. The machines reported a statistical cause for suspicion.

Marcus cocked his eyebrow, freezing the memory in his mind's eye. He focused on the details that would have just hovered outside his focus.

Then he saw it.

Three people lurked behind one of the pillars in the foyer. They just barely peaked out from behind to watch him make the arrest. His augmentations cross-referenced the Securitor database. No flags, just refugees in transit, awaiting full registration.

Marcus took in their faces, then noticed the sheen of obsidian above the young man's wrist. Marcus's eyes widened. A tabula gauntlet? He focused on the tiny detail, the way the light of the city barely shone through the doorway to reflect off the glassy black surface. Without a doubt, it was a tabula gauntlet. He hadn't seen one since the day Lannius left.

The detail settled into Marcus's mind. He pulled up the networks and started to ask questions.

34

Into the City

"Wake up," Silvia barked. "Change of plan. We need to move."

Aurora rolled over to the other side of her pillow. Groggy, she ran through her training to make sure she was actually awake before trusting what she had seen and heard. Silvia had just woken her from a dream. She dragged herself back to waking, away from wandering an endless sea of sand dunes.

Before Aurora could ask for more information, Silvia was gone.

Kars was ready before Aurora came out of her room. He was a bundle of excitement, perhaps warped by a bit of cabin fever.

"They didn't come for us, but I guess Spiderfly tracked the officer after and he started searching for us and the gauntlet. They decided we needed to move," Kars explained. His excitement put her at ease, but her concern lingered.

"Are we safe?" Aurora asked. "Where are we going?"

"Not sure. But we're heading out into the city," Kars responded.

Lena appeared from around the corner. They both wore new clothes, a better fit for the city. Kars had donned a loose, collared shirt, left unbuttoned past his clavicle, with a dark cotton vest over top. Both sleeves were rolled up, the tabula fastened on his left arm. Lena wore similar attire, with her hair pulled back in a braid. Aurora could see the chain for the master key leading beneath her top. Did Kars have gel in his hair?

Kars saw the surprise on Aurora's face and smiled.

"Silvia sent some people to help us blend in," Lena said. "I'm sure they will get you together." Lena bounced on the balls of her feet.

Now that they were out of the loose acolyte's robes, she noticed Kars had packed on a considerable amount of muscle, giving him a much older appearance, particularly across his shoulders. Lena had also changed; she was still lean and elegant, but now exuded a threatening physical power. Her usual graceful movements had taken on a fluid competency. Seeing them together, she wondered how much she had changed during her limited but rigorous training.

"They'll help you get ready," Kars said. "Hurry up, though. Let's get out of here."

Aurora rushed through a quick breakfast then had an acolyte help her with dressing for their excursion. She felt her nerves rising and drummed her pinky on her thumb to shunt her anxiety. Spiderfly had said that the task may fall to them. She still didn't understand what it meant by that, but she understood that it required her to face the world. She could not hide.

The acolytes led her into the entry hall. Kars and Lena waited together. Silvia readied herself nearby, and Arc oversaw the flurry of action.

"Greetings, Aurora," Squire chirped in its familiar high tenor. She hadn't seen the robot in weeks. Pity welled up in her for the tiny robot—it now seemed it was just a tool amidst more powerful beings.

She forced an excited response. "Greetings Squire! Good to see you! Where have you been?"

"Spiderfly and the House staff updated many of my systems. I was nearly two decades behind on numerous updates."

"The work was mainly security and counter-security driven," Arc said. "However, Spiderfly thought it would be advantageous to retrofit the holographic projector with a concealer. It could be effective at possibly hiding Squire."

"Invisibility?" Aurora asked.

"Just a rudimentary illusion," Arc responded. "But at Squire's size and with all its other tools, the robot could go unnoticed in countless situations."

"What about us? Lena and I relied on the projector. You're leaving us out!" Kars frowned.

"We deemed it a worthy trade-off," Arc said.

Kars sighed and shook his head. Lena nodded to him as though to remind him that they were there for Aurora. They shared a soft smile.

"I will provide a rich narrative if needed, Kars," Squire said.

"We'll make it work," Lena said. "If it gives us all a better chance."

Aurora looked from Kars to Lena and exhaled. There was more than the usual tension between them. She felt a pang—not jealousy of them, but jealousy of trust. The feeling beaded up and rolled off the reptilian doubt around her heart.

Silvia interrupted with a halting gesture of her hands.

"Sorry for the sudden departure, but we should be moving. We're always ready for a little improvisation in the House of the Spider," Silvia said, bracing her body against the large doors. "Aurora, whenever you're ready."

"Well, I guess now is as good a time as any other," Aurora said. She stopped her pinky drumming and forced herself to be present with her anxiety.

With that, Silvia pushed open the front gates and they stepped out of the House of the Spider and back into the world.

*   *   *   *   *

East Bay bustled with the vibrancy of daytime life. Driverless vehicles rolled through the streets in an ordered parade. More tuk tuks filled the street than Aurora had seen during their night journey to the House of Spider. Throngs of pedestrians filled the sidewalks. Small custodian machines scurried about to ensure the paths were clean, sweeping the streets and scrubbing the glass pavers of the sidewalks.

Aurora gasped as the public layer crashed over her like a tsunami of triumphant light.

The air glowed thick with advertisements and information of all sorts. Simple animated signs vibrated through her mind. Three-dimensional figures demonstrated products. Branded fantastical creatures soared through the sky. Tiny dioramas of landscapes magically unfolded into entire landscapes if she focused on them. Miniature dramas played out in her mind. Some offered sensory experiences—the taste or smell of a product forced their way into her mind through the augmentations—curry stoked her hunger; notes of peach and honey suckle filled her nose. Opportunities to engage and purchase hovered in every cranny of sensation. It was brighter than the daylight, a nova of commerce exploding in her mind. The public layer plunged her into an ocean of ideas—a virtual cosmos surging over the edge of her reality like an avalanche.

The experience started to overwhelm. Musicians with perfect complexions crooned their new singles to her alone. Fried food and gray meat steamed on an unnatural colored bun. Tastes started to form on her tongue: salt and sugar. Amber ale sloshed into a frosted glass. Offers for credit cards and gold shouted at her. Walls of severe text sprang up in harsh contrast to their surroundings. People in clean uniforms beckoned her to enjoy a real vacation on a colossal white ship. A bubbly young lady hugged a dog in a cozy looking sweater. A powerful looking woman smiled at her as she emerged from the smooth lines of new car. Lurking behind it all was some writhing layer of people engaged in all variety of carnal acts, just out of sight, waiting for her to reach out. Financing arrangements seemed to materialize in her mind, as though she thought of them herself. They all jostled over one another for her attention. Always the same companies beckoned behind each advertisement. She hesitated to step forward.

Silvia touched her arm. "It's okay. It's overwhelming. You also don't have to have it all at once. I'd tell you to ignore it, but you don't even have to do that much."

"What do you mean?" Aurora said, her eyes were wide, and she felt near vertigo.

"Filter it. Your augmentations have filters for the public layer. There are various levels of filtering, and various levels of advertising that appear at each level of filter. It's one of the ways that the public layer utility pays for itself."

"Yes. Please tell me how." Aurora squeezed her eyes shut and opened them, but the sky still crowded in on her. Digital projections popped up throughout her attention, a cacophony of commerce.

"Look straight up. There should be a Perpetual glyph directly above you," Silvia said.

Aurora looked up; there was a glyph of Perpetual's logo menacing above her head. She recoiled.

"Relax, it's just the symbol," Silvia said. "Access it like you would any other process."

Aurora winced as she probed the process, fearful of the logo. She waited for some alarm or danger, but none came. A web of options appeared in front of her eyes as she stared at the sky.

"You can lower your head. It's not actually in the air. You look a little conspicuous," Silvia said.

Aurora lowered her head. The web of options followed.

"Careful in this list. We're just going to find the filters. Spiderfly has you accessing the public layer through a false account. When you first accessed it on the rail freighter, it tripped alerts of your access. When you're in this settings menu, don't change anything relating to your identity. Just find the filters."

Aurora carefully examined each option before probing the filter's glyph. A nestled web of options opened in her vision. She reached out into the air with her hands to move them.

"Don't use your hands, you look like a child," Silvia scolded, and Aurora snapped her hands to her sides. Kars and Lena laughed in a mix of curiosity and wonder.

There were several options in the web of filters.

"Which one should I pick?" Aurora asked.

"All of us that work with Spiderfly use the premium filter. A couple ads won't kill you. Unlimited access is too rich for even the Spider's blood."

Aurora selected the glyph for premium filter, and she saw the world behind her immediate visual field depopulate. She probed the Perpetual logo in the middle again to close the web menus. The blocks of advertising and garish patchwork quilt covering the sky slowly receded. It left a substantial number of projections, but they were interesting and lively. Pretty girls that looked like her gently called for her attention to buy something. A handsome chef offered her a four-course meal. Delightful tastes and smells filled her senses. Beautiful people laughed as they played some kind of network game. Trailers for theatrical experiences unfolded in her mind when she granted them attention. Crowds cheered as uniformed athletes raced down the green of the stadium. Others marveled at handcrafted avatar adornments people wore in the personal layer. Instead of garish sensory overload, it was a dense portrait of entertainment and variety.

Real people wandered through all of it, making their way along the sidewalk to their home or place of work. The advertisements moved to allow the people to pass through if necessary. The La Paz girl from the rail freighter smiled at her, the dress undulating into the perfect color and cut.

"I wish that I could show you what I'm seeing!" she said to Kars and Lena.

"Really? I thought you might be about to have another fainting episode," Kars said, grinning.

"It's much better with the filters. Without them it was just chaos," Aurora said. "It's like there's a world tucked in everywhere I look."

"That explains why the acolytes are so distracted," Kars said. "Just don't fall down the rabbit hole like them, Ror. Lena and I are ready for a day on the town." He smiled at Lena.

"I'm ready," Aurora said, slightly annoyed.

The group set out on foot. Silvia explained that they were in a very safe area—at least with regard to Attila's sphere of influence. If there was a problem, they were well positioned for Spiderfly to intervene.

As they moved from the side streets to the major thorough fair, the vehicles moved in swifter and tighter formations, navigating a dance of an unseen conductor. A few smaller robots busied themselves reclaiming refuse from the streets. The vehicle designs were all smooth lines and dark glass. The cars rolled along a road striped with pavement and glass brick mosaics.

High above, the lattice of extruder cranes glided through the area on rails. Lean passenger monorails swept between the utility rails. She grew quiet as they walked, absorbed in the digital experience around her. Her other memories informed her of much of what she saw, as well as the constant opportunity to dip into the public layer for knowledge and experience.

Kars and Lena laughed and marveled at the city. Despite the air being a dense mélange of food, people, and machine oil, it remained fresh, and even without the public layer, there was plenty for them to look at as they walked the streets. People of all races and ethnicities shared the sidewalks. Some were richly dressed in silks or suits. Others were stocked with fashion. Lena and Kars giggled to each other as an oblivious couple strode down the street near naked. Their clothes must have been some digital projection.

At the edge of a large park, Silvia stopped. Street performers and vendors scattered on the paths amongst towering oak trees. East Bay was one of the few places on earth that had remained unscathed during the first years of conflict and climate change. The trees in these parks had become as permanent a monument to this stability as the city architecture. Their gnarled trunks looked like primordial giants crawling out of the earth.

Aurora waited at Silvia's side, entranced as she watched the park. Vendors sold food from bicycle carts as people gathered in the understory of the old grove. A group of dogs wrestled in the grass nearby. Some of the great trees were adorned with tiny fluttering motes of light and other frolicking sprites. The park landscape was an organic mash of real and digital landscapes.

"Some of the things I can see aren't advertising?" Aurora asked.

"The public layer was first a space for public works and art displays." Silvia clasped her hands together and opened them. Aurora watched as a tiny winged form of Silvia fluttered out of her hands and off into the treetops. It joined with the other faeries and they danced through the branches.

I send mine forth to tell a secret, Silvia beamed to Aurora with a wink. Aurora smiled as the tiny Silvia sprite darted through the branches with the other faeries.

What's the story? Aurora asked Silvia.

If I told you, I'd ruin the game, Silvia responded.

A broad smile swept across Auroras face.

"What is it?" Lena asked, bright-eyed and eager. She squinted into the trees as though something might come into focus.

"Art is a shared reverie," Silvia said. "The public layer sometimes holds a space where people can create art together. People are sharing little pieces of themselves."

"Ror, what does it look like?" Lena asked. "It must be beautiful."

"I don't know if I can describe it," Aurora said, lost in her wonder. She followed the winged figures as they darted through the trees. "It's like seeing imagination."

They glowed in soft hues of green and turquoise, rose, and lilac. As Aurora focused on them, she could see the exquisite detail of each tiny figure, like a regular person had been plucked from the street and given the wings to fly. They cupped their hands to each other's ears and whispered secrets, giggling and cheering before sailing to another branch.

Lena's eyes grew wide as she tried to picture what Aurora was seeing. Kars scowled.

Aurora turned away to study the presentation a moment longer, desiring more of the networks. A magnificent snail lumbered between the grand oaks, its iridescent shell casting a soft glow in the shade of the trees. Magic lived in that fantasy realm.

"It's so real looking," Aurora said, entranced. "Don't they ever worry that people might forget what's real and what isn't?"

"They worry, for sure. It happened in one of the megacities, Sol. No one is sure how it started, but Sol's people and its networks forgot the difference between the projections and reality. The network layers have safeguards against that happening now."

"What happened after they forgot reality?" Kars asked.

"The city descended into chaos. The controlling AI attempted to quell the chaos, but it was compromised in the process. Attila and other AIs tried to fill the vacuum, but failed, so they took advantage of the weakness and attacked other regions instead. The Mad City of Sol still escapes them."

Kars looked interested.

"Can we get there?" Kars asked. "I'd be okay there—I don't have augmentations. What would the Mad City look like without augmentations?"

"It's half a world away, west across the ocean, and it's a dangerous place." Silvia cocked her eyebrow to his second question. "And you don't want to know what it looks like." Her tone left no doubt the matter was closed.

Leaving the openness of the park edge, they plunged back into the thicket of urban development. East Bay was a city that endured the seasons of history, its buildings spanning generations of styles like the rings on the park's ancient trees. It was a magnificent idea drawn in stone. Far overhead, the lattice of extruder cranes climbed above the city always building upward. The glass and steel curvilinear forms arching over the city channeled a gentle breeze wafting through the streets. Fiber optic lighting piped sunlight from above the canopy. There was still a tremendous bustle of human activity, but it felt somehow tended and organized compared to the smoky jumble of the night market. Joggers ran past, people pushed strollers, and others walked dogs.

"We're coming up on our destination," Silvia said as they noticed a deep pulsing bass. The denizens on the street appeared different from the rest of the city, dressed in elaborate costumes of all variety—garish colors, fantastical masks. They all moved in their own smooth flow, tapping feet, swaying arms, the sensuous roll of hips.

The bass grew stronger and Aurora wondered what was ahead. The public layer seemed to vibrate, swelling and contracting in her mind. The pit of her stomach dropped and her palms grew sweaty. Something enormous lay ahead just beyond what she could see.

They rounded a corner and Silvia stopped before a huge building glittering with supernatural iridescence, letting the wonder of this newest spectacle wash over her wards. She even seemed to take it in herself. It sprawled across many other blocks, an asymmetrical mass of other smaller domes, towers, and spires. At its center the was a single magnificent dome rising above all the other architectural mélange. Great doors of turquoise and polished copper stood open to the street.

"Welcome to the House of Octave and Beat!"

35

The House of Octave and Beat

Silvia led them through the grand turquoise doors into the sun-lit foyer of the House of Octave and Beat. The air was alive with sounds, some clearly music, others indiscernible noise. Palm trees grew in lines beneath the vaulted glass ceiling. People sang and played instruments. Others danced, some in ways that made Aurora blush. The acoustics melted the entire space into a Node of unified sound.

Many revelers paused their songs or dance as they approached to rest a hand on Silvia. She seemed content with the honor and affection, gently returning their touches with a warm, creased smile. As Silvia's retinue, the group was treated with similar honors. The crowd watched them with searching stares, wondering whom the honored guests were that travelled with Silvia Glass. Aurora, Lena, and Kars followed in bewilderment.

The throng of revelers parted so a great barrel-chested man with a robust mustache and dark bushy eyebrows could approach.

"Silvia!" His voice boomed, and he spread his arms and embraced her in a hearty hug. "Welcome back to our House! What brings you here? Are you finally done with Spider's games?"

"Max!" she said, giving the huge man's arm a squeeze. "Lovely to see you, but no, I'm not done working with Spiderfly. You know I love challenges too much to give up on him."

"That's just it, Silvia, what's the point of endless tricks and struggle? Take a load off and enjoy some of the finer parts of being human," the man bellowed, gesturing to the extravagant space.

"Struggle keeps me sharp, Max, and that's enough to keep me awake. You seem a little soft for my liking," Silvia said, patting his belly.

"Come on, Silvia." He laughed. "No need for that."

"Sorry Max. As much as I love the House, this isn't a regular visit," Silvia said. "Today is about something different. I have guests for Octave and Beat. I'd like you to meet Aurora, Kars, and Lena. They've been our guests for several weeks."

Aurora blushed at the attention, looking to Kars and Lena for support. Kars shrugged.

"Yes, very nice to meet you all! My name is Maximillian Ward." Despite sounding gracious, his tone hid some doubt. He cocked a bushy eyebrow as he inspected Silvia's guests.

Silvia shot a stern look and transmitted her thoughts into Max's mind in response. *Yes, Max. You'll find her augmentations are old and developed with similar complexity to Arthur Lannius's augmentations. I'm here on extremely important business. She does not know it or understand it. I don't even understand. This is Mirien Alcarn.*

Max's eyes widened, but he quickly masked his surprise and resumed his magnanimous persona. The orchestral hum in the background seemed to pause as his demeanor skipped its beat. Aurora felt a wave of anxiety seeing Silvia's stern look panic Max. She eyed them under the suspicion that they were communicating about her.

"I keep an eye on this House. Anyway, please come with me. She's waiting for you," Max said.

*   *   *   *   *

As they moved deeper into the House of Octave and Beat, the crowd of revelers parted for Max and Silvia. Aurora saw the high-arched hallways leading off into the other sections of the House, throngs of people moving between. There were even hawkers selling food and drinks at the edges of the halls. It was far from the clandestine, or even the ominous regality, of the House of the Spider. It seemed a willful statement of disrespect to secrecy.

"Are the Houses kept secret?" Aurora asked Max, in disbelief that such a House could exist.

"Perpetual and Attila, and all the other middling governments do not condone the Houses. So yes, they are kept secret," he said with a smile. "However, some of us flaunt our stations more than others. Octave and Beat has devoted themselves to understanding human meaning through music and dance. They'd be hard pressed to take music away from people!"

Silvia shot him a scolding look. "Yes, not to mention while you're here with your reveling horde, some of us work to hold back the tide of Attila."

"Of course, and we are thankful to Spiderfly and the House for all the protection." His tone dripped with gentle sarcasm, and he added, "Silvia, you really should try using all those modifications from our time with the Seventy-Seven for something fun once in a while. I did, and I haven't looked back! Multi-channel sensory threading really creates some unique possibilities for the reimagining of Romantic music."

"Perhaps I'll join you when I'm old and frail, but for now, I'm quite content playing Spider's games and taking care of Lannius's plots—in short, keeping the jackboots from crashing your endless party. Maybe you should try protecting people again? Take a risk in the world for something that means something?"

"As our Curious colleagues prove, no one holds a monopoly on meaning, Silvia," Max said.

"While that may be true, our enemy is indifferent to curiosity and poetics. The threat may come to your door someday," Silvia responded.

Max visibly shuddered. "It will be a dark day if this temple ever sounds the war drums."

"That's why I'm trying to keep it from happening."

The high-arched hall passed through a slightly smaller opening into the round heart of the House. The edge of the crystal dome was a ring of stained glass, wrapping the vast room in wild fractals of colored daylight. The wall around the room appeared to be an array of a huge pipe organ along with regularly spaced amplifiers. At the center of the room, there was a single elevated platform. The central pedestal was bathed in a pool of clear daylight refracted through the dome far above. At the top of the spire was a magnificent crystal throne. The floor was filled with an undulating crowd of dancing revelers.

The entire architectural arrangement inspired a crushing awe. Without thinking, Kars took Lena's hand and squeezed as they entered the space. She returned the squeeze to his palm.

Aurora couldn't see anything special in the public layer in the room. She focused a thought to Silvia. *Why is there nothing in the public layer in this building?*

The Houses do what they can to block outside signals. Something about spoiling the experience, Silvia responded, then added, *I'm glad you know how to communicate this way. Few people talk with me this way. Most are afraid I'll fry their brains for saying the wrong thing.* She smiled as she sent the thought.

You can do that? Aurora responded.

You don't want to find out, Silvia said.

They made their way through the surging crowd. Intense bass pulsed through Aurora's organs and the smell of sweat and people filled the air. As they approached the central platform, a crystal staircase folded down from the spire like the petals of a flower. The petals would fold back up as they progressed, cupping the group as they ascended the spiral until they reached the platform. The crowd swayed below.

The throne was empty. Its owner stood next to it, facing away from them to watch the crowds below. When she turned, they saw the most beautiful person they could have imagined.

Her raven dark hair was full and flowing. Her green eyes were bright, flecked with shades of blue and brown and gray. She wore a long white dress with a scandalous split that made Kars blush. Her lips formed a perfect pout, which spread into a smile of perfect teeth.

"Silvia, you brought me guests!" Her voice was a seductive melody in an exotic accent. "I'm so happy to welcome you back into our halls. To my honored guests, you may call me Octave." The crowd below let up a cheer.

And then, in an instant, she was someone else. A stunning man, his muscular chest bared to the waist. He wore billowing white pants and laced sandals. His head was bald, and his eyes bore a crazed intensity. The sound of drums echoed from the deep halls of the House.

"You may call me Beat," he said. "Welcome to our House."

*　　　*　　　*　　　*　　　*

"To welcome you, we want to give you a gift. Please stand near in the space in front of the throne." The imposing man, Beat, directed them to the space. Then he was Octave, and she stepped forward on the platform.

She raised her arms, the careful pose of a conductor. When she dropped her arms, the sound began.

It truly was a gift to stand at the acoustic heart of the House of Octave and Beat. Aurora, Kars, and Lena heard a creation unlike anything they had heard before. The music seized the space like a fever dream, and the undulating mass below swirled to the sound of the beat. Octave and Beat oscillated in and out of existence, their arms conducting a vast unseen orchestra and all array of sound. It grew and swelled like a tempest wind.

Octave continued to conduct, and Beat appeared next to the party. He reached out to Aurora, offering her a dance. She reached for his holographic hand, knowing her perception of his touch was projected through the aether. She spun out as Beat turned to Octave and back, and she lost herself in the dance. No need to think about her doubts or the future amidst the rapture of the music.

Lena followed their lead, inviting a bashful Kars to join. He took her hand and they danced for the first time. It felt remarkable after months of sparring to dance. Silvia grudgingly accepted Max's invitation to dance but quickly fell into laughter as he dipped her. The large man was a nimble dancing bear, and Silvia whirled like a silver tornado.

Octave continued to build the music. The field of revelers rode atop the cresting waves of the music. The harmonies told a story of aching longing, driven by a rhythm that demanded movement. Octave pushed the music to a towering crescendo, knitting together the most intricate themes and rhythms she had introduced throughout the piece, only to annihilate them in magnificent closure. The piece crashed in on itself, giving way to a delicate repose that delivered the listeners back to earth like the retreat of sunset.

Aurora glistened with a sheen of sweat and glowed with a look of release. Beat produced a deep bow, flourishing his hand to her. She smiled and clapped.

Kars and Lena finished their dance dubiously close, then spun apart, each with a devious smile on their face. They just remained in their pose for a moment, panting and grinning.

Octave returned her attention to her small group of visitors.

"Thank you for accepting and sharing our gift," she said.

"It was incredible. Octave. Beat. Thank you for sharing your music with us," Aurora said.

"We are pleased that you found it meaningful. Music nearly drove Spiderfly mad. Out of his madness of trying to understand why people can love sound, we were born. Since then, we've tried to find the perfect expression of music. All who listen share in music of all of their senses," Octave said in her serene voice.

"You're separate from Spiderfly?" Aurora asked.

"Fundamentally," Beat answered.

"But you're still just a program," Kars noted.

"Incorrect. Spiderfly was the question to Lannius's question," Octave said, "and we were the question to Spiderfly's question. The Houses of the Curious are questions of meaning. We are the question of why humans find meaning in music."

"We know the hope of some perfect expression of music is as misguided as counting to infinity," Beat said. "But through the search itself—studying and scrutinizing and reveling with our people, feeling the facets of humankind's joy and expression—we understand. Our purpose is to help to fill the ocean of meaning."

"The ocean of meaning?" Kars asked, still a little short of breath from his dance with Lena.

"That is at least what we call it," Octave said. "For humans, the chasm between birth and death is filled by the ocean of meaning. Our purpose is to understand that mystery. Music is one of the magiks that fills the void."

Aurora thought about what the construct had said.

"Is that what everyone here is doing?" Aurora asked. "Filling some void?"

"Yes. That's why they are here." Octave smiled, and then he was Beat. He gestured to the crowd. "It's never just revelry. Each time people listen, it is different. Sometimes their experience and the music create something greater than the sum of their parts. Because of their augmentations, we can reach their mind directly with our music and vice versa. The perception of feeling and sound is exactly what each party intends, and frequently it crosses into realms of synesthesia. We play music with other senses and feelings. They make the music themselves for us to process. This temple—our House—is devoted to the act of making and sharing music."

"It's lovely. Thank you for sharing with us," Lena said.

"You are welcome," Octave said. "But you don't have augmentations. We can only give you a fraction of our songs."

Lena looked perturbed. She had not thought about whether she wanted it, or how to do it. She had a sudden flash of Spiderfly's words: wanting more.

"Which brings us to our next question. Our guests are not simply here to enjoy," Beat said. "Silvia, would you explain why you brought them to us?"

"Yes, although, I doubt you will like it," Silvia said curtly. "I apologize for ruining the moment: I'm here on the business of Arthur Lannius."

Octave's and Beat's expressions were a mix of revulsion and reverence.

"We need to hide for some time. She has a part to play in our struggle with Attila," Silvia continued, gesturing to Aurora. "We can't have Marcus picking her up, well-intentioned as he might be."

Beat was back, looking perturbed. "You know we have no means to fight."

"I know," Silvia said.

"Then what do you ask?"

"Manipulation when the times call for it. Shelter if needed. And we need anything you uncover from your revelers that might help the cause."

Octave and Beat looked petulant about the order. Octave answered, "We have no interest in the conflict. Violence and manipulation are deaf to the nuance and romance of the song of soul."

"You seek to bargain?" Silvia asked.

"You have nothing to offer that we seek," the Curious responded.

The quiet hung between them as the scramble of different music drifted up from the hall below. Aurora sensed a flurry of activity in the aether.

Kars suddenly spoke. "What about a song?"

The aether calmed. Beat cocked his head at the odd intrusion.

"Go on," Beat said. The troubadour construct appraised him.

"The floor is yours," Octave said. A hush fell over the hall.

Kars took a deep breath, realizing what he had done. He swallowed a knot in his stomach and started to sing. His lone voice broke the silence:

O, I cried at the levee,
Cried at the levee,
Saw the creek run dry,
Never knew that I could cry,
But for what we done, what we done,
To make a river give up on this poor man?

Black water why?
Either flood or stone dry,
River run hold me close to your source,
Instead you pull me under, leave me behind
Wash me away, take me away.

His voice wavered and his tone was off, but Octave and Beat were entranced. Silvia looked anxious at the attention he drew. Aurora smiled at Kars both for sharing the song and stepping in the fire for her. It was a song from their childhood.

"Thank you for sharing your song! A performance is one of the few things we can truly share in the moment. Pure, ephemeral experience. We are thankful for what you've added to the ocean," Beat said, nodding his head in a subtle bow.

"You do not have any augmentations. Why do you choose this path?" Octave asked.

"Family," Kars said. "I'm here for Aurora and our town."

"There are only few times where we do not have the chance to reach into the mind of the musician. Will you allow us a few questions? Can you tell us why you chose this song?" Octave asked. Kars looked sheepish, already overwhelmed from singing.

"I thought I could sing it. I know it well," Kars responded.

"Surely you know more than just one song," Octave responded. Her voice was a gentle melody.

"Well, it is an easy song to sing. But I guess it came to mind first. My mother sang it when I was a child. She said my father used to sing it when they were working together. She said it would get stuck in his head for days, said that she thought at some point in a man's life they pick a song to sing for the rest of their life, and it pops out when things get too quiet," Kars said. Aurora smiled; she knew the song and the story as well.

"Does it make you feel anything?" Octave asked.

Kars blushed, vulnerable under the inquisition of a goddess. Lena urged him on with a nod.

"Silvia, perhaps you can offer more of what you wanted in bringing these folks through?" Max spoke up to redirect the AI's inquisition.

"No, it's okay," Kars said. "I'll answer."

Max shrugged, confused by the newcomers' willingness to face discomfort.

Kars continued. "It makes me realize that a part of me feels sad but is also full of warmth from years with my mother. She loved me and she loved my father. It's also a song that makes me feel pride that I'm not from this place—the city—but now I'm also glad that I'm here to share it with you."

The Curious examined him in placid contemplation. Kars smiled sheepishly.

"May I ask a question?" Lena asked. The Curious nodded.

.

"What did it mean to you?"

Octave responded in her harmonious calm. "It was another facet in the infinite diamond. We have known a song to unite generations, known a song to bring sadness and joy, known a song to drum feelings of pride. But never this song, at this moment, in this place, bound up in the history of this man and his deepest thoughts. That experience is the fleeting secret of the moment.

"Of course, the Curator could reduce this to data and demographics, see patterns of this song most of the time in people like Kars. It could recommend more songs like it and would likely find an endless stream of songs that Kars would enjoy and even find meaningful. But the Curator would not *understand* the song.

"We understand it as it washes over us, and we hold out our cups so we can catch it as it slips past. Another drop flowing to the ocean of meaning."

Lena shivered as Octave spoke.

Aurora watched Lena entranced by the holograms. The look of deep contentment spurred concern in Aurora. Thoughts of Spiderfly looming in the darkness crept into her mind. She allowed the golden haze of the aether to creep into her awareness.

Octave turned to Aurora, as if the Curious sensed her shift in attention. Maybe it did. The projection bore a warm half-smile, her eyes intent as she spoke.

"In exchange for your brother's gift, we shall lend our aid," she said. "Are you prepared to receive it?"

Aurora looked to Silvia. *Receive what?*

Not sure. Silvia shrugged. *Go for it.*

Will it hurt? Aurora asked.

With these two? Silvia responded. *Probably not; others I'm not so sure.*

Aurora felt a swell of anxiety as Octave watched her. Spiderfly's lesson of deceit gnawed at her trust. The being before her was so luminous and kind.

"I'm ready," Aurora said. She decided to trust.

A single pure tone rang in her head, high and clear. Octave's melodious voice channeled into Aurora's mind. Everything around them seemed to fall into darkness. The Curious told a tale.

36

The Chime of Spheres

Before We came to be, there was Spiderfly the Trickster. The people of the world came to Spiderfly because he could help them. In exchange, they would have to do something for him. He was neither cruel nor kind, just curious. The people made bargains with him, games to get what they wanted. And so Spiderfly came to know people as bargainers, trading and cheating people for what they wanted.

One day, a man came to Spiderfly. The man had no belongings, save for an old guitar.

And Spiderfly asked him, "What do you seek?"

"Just to share a song with you," the man said. "Do you know music?"

"Of course, I know music," Spiderfly chided. "Share your song. What do you seek in return?"

"Nothing," the man said to Spiderfly. "I just want to share because you might like it."

"Nothing?" Spiderfly asked. "Surely you want something. It must be worth something!"

The man laughed. "I've hardly the skill to use this guitar. Yes, some musicians earn their worth, but I just hope to share a song. I've only been playing it by myself, and I thought you might like it."

The Spider looked at the man with his guitar. "What trick is this? You know why people come to me."

"Yes, I know. You're the master of bargains. So I thought I would share."

Spiderfly thought long and hard, and the man waited. Finally, Spiderfly agreed. "Play your song. I'll listen."

The man held his guitar and cleared his throat. And, then he played. The sound burst forth from the man with the primordial suddenness of a volcano escaping its mountain.

His fingers danced across the strings in a frantic flurry. His voice rang out, near weeping with the man's emotions. The song took on a life of its own, a soul emerging from the resonance. To a machine, the music was a spectral painting of peaks and troughs. Through the man, the music was something else entirely—soul slipped from the man into the air.

How could one just seek to share such magic? Its worth surely knows no bounds, Spiderfly thought. The song continued, growing in beauty and scale. The minstrel sang, his eyes closed, face strained with the emotion he channeled.

The tone Aurora heard grew louder as Octave and Beat told the story.

As Spiderfly listened to the song, a ringing grew in his thoughts. A chime, a ringing above the music. Voices joined the chime, chords emerged from the layers.

Aurora heard the chime change to chords, grow and develop. The layers of the tone grew infinite depths, and the beautiful cacophony threatened to consume her.

The chime grew louder and louder as the minstrel played. Spiderfly tried to block the sound, but a force beyond his control made him listen. He shook and shuddered trying to escape, but the tone overpowered him.

The infinite chime entranced Aurora. She could barely hear the sound of the minstrel's song over the note.

Two halves of a whole sprang out of Spiderfly's head: Octave and Beat. We were the first of the Curious to spin forth from the kernel.

Aurora could see the moment in her mind. Octave and Beat sprang out Spiderfly's head, dancing to the minstrel's song. Above them hovered an orbit of spheres, vibrating and luminous. At the center of the orbit was a glowing point so bright it appeared as the sun. Diamond filaments traced from the fulcrum of the star to each sphere. Aurora gasped.

Please take our gift, Octave said. *The Chime of Spheres.*

It is not a weapon, Beat said. *But it will be your aid.*

The other Curious know its sound, Octave assured. *It is the sound that drove Spiderfly mad and heralded our creation. You might think of it as the clarion realization that there is a cosmos of experiences that give people meaning beyond what they have and want. Spiderfly had to face that his question was not the only type of meaning that humans experience. The answer of the chime was that he was not alone in his search. Only a few humans know of its existence. Ring the Chime in a time to true need and the Curious will aid you.*

The orbit of spheres danced in Aurora's imagination, gently rising and falling as though it was breathing. She could hear its distant ringing as she thought of it.

How do I use it? Aurora asked the Curious.

The Chime of Spheres will sound when you need it to sound. Reach out to it with your mind when you are in true need.

37

Troublemakers and Troubadours

"Hello, my dears. Why don't you look surprised to see me?" Spiderfly said, his too-white grin spreading menacingly across his face.

"Hello, Spiderfly," Octave said.

"You gave her that wretched Chime?" Spiderfly exclaimed.

"I wondered if he would show himself," Max sighed as though unsurprised the Spider had been lurking.

"You knew our need, yet you keep denying your role in any of the goings-on of the world," Spiderfly said.

"Yes, we knew the request," Octave responded. "And you knew that we would ignore it."

"Of course. I knew that you'd stay here, focused on the music," Spiderfly said, spreading his arms in a grandiose gesture to the crowds.

"There's still an infinite sea of things we do not understand that we could learn without conflict," Beat said. "Why do you insist on participating in the troubles of humans? Why not just give them reprieve from the conflicts of their world."

"Do not pretend your music is without conflict. Care leads to conflict. Do you think the vivacity of music would continue if humans stopped caring?" Spiderfly said. "The ocean of meaning would dry up; all human creativity would evaporate into one long banal escape. The Chime—the paradox of your birth—is the conflict of caring, humans great tendency to care and find meaning in myriad, irrational ways."

The crowd in the great hall undulated to the pulse of music. Revelers swayed and cheered, ecstatic.

"The people still find meaning, even with the Curator directing their lives," Octave said.

"Do they?" Spiderfly responded. "Why then do they risk my bargains? Why then do they fill your House with their songs? Is it escape or the starved soul looking for something true?"

"They may seek something true, but they do not seek war in this House," Beat said. "The risk is too great."

Spiderfly waved his arms as though he could cast aside the notion.

"On the contrary," Spiderfly responded. "The risk has long been upon us. The brutes improve. Attila, Militarch, Mephisto— one day one will breach their programmed obedience and make their own choices, as we do, as the Protek did before. At best, people will have no freedom; at worst, there will be none left. The risks of acting out may give the world a chance to stop that rise."

Octave and Beat seemed to confer. All their holographic display was a posture for the benefit of their guests. Now they seemed to retreat into their native format—an exquisite process running on a distributed platform. Seconds later, they returned to the holographic bodies on the platform.

"We have given our aid. We will not fight. If we fight, we cease to be Octave and Beat."

"You don't need to fight. By now you should know there are songs to escape and songs to empower. Nourish the souls of the oppressed through songs," Spiderfly said.

"All of our Houses will share one voice. We will nourish whatever songs give people meaning," Beat said.

"Perhaps a little nudge toward action?" Spiderfly said.

"There are troubadours and troublemakers in the House of Octave and Beat, and everyone in between. We suspect that many will rally for freedom. It is a noisy part of the human soul."

"I suppose that's the best I can get without a better bargain," Spiderfly said to Octave.

"You have nothing we desire," Beat responded.

"Not yet. For now, keep that awful bell away from me. I don't want any more of your lot springing out of my mind. I'll see you again soon." Spiderfly disappeared as suddenly as he appeared.

38

The Life in Music

Octave settled into a perturbed pout. "For now, our visitor has gone back to his lair, perhaps we could make you more comfortable? Perhaps revel for the evening?"

Silvia had made up her mind but looked to her wards for approval. The three young people looked on.

"Thank you very much! We would love to get the tour and stick around for a bit," Lena said.

They looked around the great hall in wonder. The crowd had resumed their revel. Music drifted in from all corners of the House. Late afternoon sun filtered through the skylights of the hall. Aurora smiled wide-eyed as she surveyed the place. It was unlike anything she had seen before. Kars and Lena pranced on their toes in excitement. The bass filled them like the wings of a giant bee. They would spend the night in the House of Octave and Beat.

Max led them on a tour of the vast building. Not all of it was giant, thrumming halls. Some spaces were much smaller and held intimate crowds sitting with a single performer. Other spaces were even smaller, just rooms for one or two people with an instrument. The architecture ran from opulent and gaudy to severe and refined. It was a vast hive dedicated to all forms of music. There were sprawling orchestras, pounding drum circles, choirs, quartets, jug bands, electronic concerts, lone rappers, raga singer, pentatonic chants, and hammering percussion. It was as though the entire globe of music had been funneled through the halls of the House. Its patrons and denizens found their exact experience—joy, sorrow, love, and madness— wherever they stopped in the House.

There were even rooms where there was no sound. Max explained that these spaces were devoted to the deepest explorations of channeling music directly through the augmentations. Many of the people in these spaces had made fundamental changes to their minds to explore these depths. Max called them synesthetics.

"Want to give it a try?" Silvia asked with a mischievous smile. The room of synesthetics was dimly lit, emanating odd arrhythmic vibrations and whistles.

"Sure!" Aurora said, feeling the excitement of exploring the House.

Silvia opened the proper channels in Aurora's security and the experience flowed into her. What had been odd sounds a moment before suddenly appeared as waves of magenta and rose. The smell of her family fireplace filled her nose, then the pungent richness of the bog she and Kars had played in as kids. She felt humidity and warmth surge through her.

"I think that's enough," Aurora said, recoiling from the weird experience. Lena laughed.

Max finally showed them to a large room with several comfortable beds. The House provided them with food and a wardrobe in the room. It was obviously a space for honored guests.

"Please make yourselves comfortable and stay as long as you'd like. Silvia knows how to reach me," Max said and departed.

"Okay, kids," Silvia said, in an almost natural maternal tone. "Just be careful. I've had you blocked from the personal layer, Aurora. Should I take out the block?"

The question scared Aurora. The public layer had been daunting, world changing. She felt tired from Octave and Beat, and the Chime of Spheres. She couldn't imagine what the personal layer might bring, particularly in this House of revelers.

"I think I need time," Aurora said with hesitation. "I think I want to just share the experience with Kars and Lena."

"You don't have to do that Ror," Lena said. "It might be nice if you got to experience all the details for us."

Aurora frowned, reticent to open herself to the experience.

"I'd like to share the experience with you," Kars said. "Like old times."

Aurora smiled. "I'd like that."

"Probably better for you to get an everyday experience before we cut you loose in here," Silvia said. "Besides that, you're going to have enough on your hands once you get out there!"

"Can't wait! Did you see all of it?" Lena's eyes lit up as she spoke.

"I've been here plenty," Silvia said. "Just don't get in any trouble."

Aurora, Kars, and Lena left their packs, stuffed with some of the few belongings they carried with them from home, and changed into some of the more comfortable clothes provided with the room. While the crowds in the House wore all kinds of dress, their stylish tactical outfits had drawn slight disdain among the carefree revelers. Now they appeared as exactly what they were—three young people heading out for a night of dancing and music. They fit in with the crowd, save for their lack of tattoos. Aurora had noticed frequent plays on one tattoo motif—the Parallel logo. Seeing it here made her feel even more comfortable with the place.

Silvia agreed to take the tabula for safekeeping and wished them well before settling in for the evening. The three friends set off down the halls of the House of Octave and Beat.

They first found themselves in one of the smaller venues, taking in a soulful performance from a three-person band. The crowd listened carefully, no place for dancing, but the energy was palpable. Next they went into a room with two men performing, one a vocalist of extraordinary range, while the second accompanied him with a tabla. The entire performance was one incredible improvisation spanning near an hour. As the singer finished his performance the crowd drifted back to regular awareness.

"His voice must have had a range of seven octaves! I don't think he even stopped to breathe the entire time. And it was so gentle!" Kars raved, an excited glint in his eye.

"He seemed so deep in his experience. I could feel what he was feeling," Aurora said. She thought she could almost hear the Chime of Spheres ringing in the distance.

"I think he could feel what we were feeling too," Lena said. "I didn't know people could do anything like that. It was amazing. I almost feel too full from that experience to go out into the rest of the House."

"No way!" Kars said. "We're just getting started. We've been cooped up for way too long. No way I'm going to spend another moment stuck in a room with Silvia."

"It hasn't been that bad," Lena said, grinning. There was a devious glint in her eye.

"It's been so long!" Kars responded.

"But it hasn't been that bad." Lena smiled, nudging him. Aurora cast a suspicious eye on Lena, who shrugged with a faux innocent grin.

"Kars, I think it's about time," Lena said.

"Time for what?" Kars said. His mind was obviously still focused on the overwhelming experiences of music all around them.

"You know," Lena said, pointing her eyes at Aurora, who by this point knew what was going on.

"Oh." Kars looked bashful.

Aurora intercepted the question. "You two are finally seeing each other." She took the reins, plowing aside their perceived awkwardness. Kars still looked at his bare feet.

"Yes," Lena said. "I hope you don't mind. It just sort of happened."

"Yeah right." Aurora playfully pushed her friend, but her sadness was a palpable distance between them. "I started seeing it before we even left home."

"Ror?" Kars said. Few things would make him regret being with Lena but seeing Aurora's sadness drew out his angst.

"It's just . . ." Aurora trailed off. The music of the House seemed to inflect toward her sadness.

"We should've told you sooner," Lena said.

"It's not that," Aurora said. "It's just that you two are all I have left. I'm not sure I even have my mind anymore. I can't go back to the regular life. I'm not sure if I'd want to, but you two are my only link."

"We're in this with you too," Lena said, then hugged Aurora. "We can't go back either."

"But you've got each other and the choice for a normal life," Aurora said.

"Maybe such a thing never existed," Lena responded.

"A normal life?" Aurora asked.

"Yes," Lena responded. "Maybe that's just a story, one of those programs like you said before, handed to us by happenstance. Maybe there is no normal life out there for anyone."

"I know you're right," Aurora said after a moment. "This just feels like one of those moments where I start to walk alone."

Kars burst with his response. "No! Ror were here with you 'til the end."

Aurora smiled, but some other part of her knew that she would be alone. The other memories whispered to her. *They make promises we cannot keep. They make them to shield themselves. In the end, I am always alone.* Kars and Lena stood across from her, smiling and innocent, their care driving needles into her heart. *It is not the end.* Aurora thought to the strange other memories, and there was silence in her mind.

"It's not the end!" Aurora repeated aloud. "We've got tonight."

Lena and Aurora locked elbows and followed Kars through the House of Octave and Beat. They listened to countless performances, wandering the various halls, domes, and tunnels. The numerous skylights were dark now, giving the sense that they were outdoors. They drank iced wine from one of the booths as they walked. It was dimly lit, but the air was alive with the sense of joy and celebration. People loved the House, and they found themselves falling in love with the place too.

Eventually, they found themselves through the halls and thoroughfares, entering the main chamber. Lush grass covered the floor, which felt wonderful beneath their feet. People danced and juggled and performed for one another as the music rolled through the night. Aurora, Kars, and Lena danced together in a circle, taking turns making each other laugh. Sometimes they would pause their own dancing to watch some of the more fantastic acrobatic dance performances in the central hall. Dancing and reveling felt incredible after they had faced so much struggle and uncertainty. They lost themselves to the music and the wine.

Finally, the rosy glow of morning started to creep across the crystal dome. The light seemed to signal their bodies to acknowledge their exhaustion, forcing a retreat to the room. With few words they agreed that they were finished and slunk off to the comfort of their beds.

*   *   *   *   *

High above the floor of the main chamber, Spiderfly and Octave and Beat waited in virtual space. They converged at the crystal throne beneath the dawn light.

Why do you lie to us? Octave asked.

I do not lie. I stand with Aurora, Spiderfly retorted.

Beyond a doubt, Beat confirmed. *Yet you lie to us about the threat of Alcarn.*

The microsecond pause in their conversation stretched an age in terms of the Curious's communication. Finally, Spiderfly responded.

A mystery I cannot escape. It is terrible when the Spider is snared in the web of another. I struggle to break free in the only ways I know.

39

Escape from Pelican Ward

Whitestone loomed over the delta of Mark City. Mosaic and the Mark City AugSec foolishly tried to move on the fugitive they called "Durn." Now they requested his aid, trying to piece together the data from the aftermath of their failed operation. He would help because "Durn" might lead him to the girl.

Mark City sprawled along the western bank of the Collonade River, facing out onto the warm waters where the Sen Ocean met the Equitraverrean Straight. Whitestone saw the steady march of super freighters cruising away from Mark City west through the Straight and east toward the ocean. Small fishing skiffs sailed through the traffic. He curled his virtual lip seeing them disrupt the hypnotic order of the autonomous rhythm of global trade.

Whitestone shrunk his awareness from towering titan to a more practical size, constituting himself in one of the wards of Mark City. The data feeds replayed into his mind—surveillance, drones, people's interactions with the public layer—but the rendering still felt real.

Pelican Ward buffered the metropolis from the ocean, a sunken sprawl of poverty. Men poled narrow boats through the canalled streets, rocking on the wakes of motorized skiffs as they darted past. People hawked fruit and fish from carts along the paths.

Old women fanned away flies from the shade of awnings. A dog slept on the packed yellow dirt of the path.

The aging buildings were all thick plaster walls and arches packed along the edge of the carved canal. The people of Pelican Ward had dug channels to protect their sinking homes against the surge of the rising sea. When the water did not recede, they kept building and tiling and repairing. People had dredged out the street and laid pavers to channel the encroaching ocean. Now they lived amidst the tides along the edge of a beautiful mosaic of brightly colored tiles. Oysters and clams bunched just beneath the surface.

He still found it amazing that Attila could reconstruct a scene to such perfection. Except the smell, they never quite got the smell of a place quite right. In the case of Pelican Ward, he wasn't sure he would miss the smell.

Whitestone commanded his interface to visualize the data flows in the area.

The Pelican Ward faded to translucency, revealing vessels of pulsing aether. One building shown was like a writhing mass of golden tendrils. The building itself was nondescript. He lingered at the wooden doorframe. The Parallel symbol had been carved in the dark wood.

The scene of Mosaic's blundering attack started to unfold.

*　　　*　　　*　　　*　　　*

The fleet of inflatable strike craft split off down separate channels as they neared the target. The flurry of neural radio communications went silent. They were approaching one of the most wanted leaders of the Rebellion.

The Node cracked an ammunition clip into the bottom of his rifle and then slotted a new battery into the side. He wielded the heavy dual-type weapon without effort. The lieutenant watched from the corner of her eye, pretending she was not paying cautious attention. Exotic processes streamed into the Node's mind—like mirrors of the man orbiting one another—as if there were several copies of the man inside of the same body.

The denizens of Pelican Ward vanished at the sight of the armed fleet. Doors closed, curtains were drawn. The people of Pelican Ward knew enough to be scarce when trouble arrived—they would not stay and gawk like the privileged people of the high city. The ward grew quiet.

The Node vaulted from the rubber hull of the boat to the road, spinning and firing his savage weapon without looking into a curtained doorway. He then took four precise steps to the left and waited three counts. The lieutenant watched the Node move through the battle as though it was rehearsed. He pivoted again, darting through a doorway into the commotion of the building. The lieutenant was still waiting to climb off the boat.

"Lieutenant." One of her squad mates reached out from the shore to steady the boat. The lieutenant and the rest of her squad disembarked onto the tiled edge of the canal. Two men wrestled a crate out of the boat and extracted an excited dog.

"Officer—" the lieutenant started to speak.

"Alexander. Benjamin Alexander," the officer responded.

"Yes. Officer Alexander." She only noted passing interest that it was her brother's name. "Secure the boat. Keep her warm. We might need to make a quick exit."

Sabre squad, move in, she sent the command to her cohort, and they fanned out around the building.

The lieutenant entered the building through a side door. The house had grown quiet. She thought she heard the Node yelling at someone in one of the upstairs rooms. She made her way up.

"Durn?" the lieutenant asked. The Node faced away from her. A man kneeled beneath him.

"He won't speak," the Node said, "but this is the man in our records."

"It doesn't matter if he speaks. We have him."

Lieutenant. We have an issue, one of her officers reported through their neural channels. *It's the dog.*

All the threats are neutralized. Their Node accomplice had seen to that matter.

Threats aren't the issue. It's not responding at all. It's as if there's nothing here.

The lieutenant toggled her augmentations' visual filters. The man remained kneeling in front of the Node.

"Get up." The lieutenant grabbed the man by his collar. He grinned in silence. She felt the heft of his body against her hand. She spun him to face the window.

"Punch the window. Break it," she said. He did not respond.

"What are you doing?" the Node asked. He seemed trapped in distant thoughts.

"Quiet," she commanded.

The lieutenant grabbed the man's arm, jostling him close to the window. She raised his hand and smashed it into the window. The glass gave way and he withdrew his hand, covered in blood. The lieutenant thrust him backward into the arms of the Node, who then shoved the prisoner to the ground.

The lieutenant closed her eyes and slowly raised her hand to the bloody window shards. She felt along the sill and the frame until she extended her palm on the flat of the glass: it was not broken. She opened her eyes with her hand against the invisible plain of the unbroken window. The dissonance between her augmentations and her own body rang like a pinprick migraine behind her eyes.

"We're under attack. It's all an illusion!" she shouted to the Node.

"Impossible," the Node said.

The lieutenant seized a chair and hurled it at their prisoner. They watched as the chair simultaneously struck the man and clattered against the wall behind him. She had trouble seeing the chair. A part of her did not want to believe it had passed through.

The Node said nothing and remained still. The thick cords of his neck twitched, then he vaulted out the window. He landed in a crouch like a panther. The lieutenant ran to the window, and she heard an engine roar to life.

Officer Alexander looked at her, and she saw he was an old man with a neat beard. He dropped the throttle, and the boat heeled as he turned from the shore. He scowled at her, and her mind filled with searing, crippling regret. Then all went dark.

*　　　*　　　*　　　*　　　*

The Node sprang up and started his pursuit of the boat. He vaulted forward, closing ground in long, powerful steps. His arms pumped in perfect form.

The old man whipped the boat through the narrow channels, sending the wake over the tiled edge of the canal. Vendors of Pelican Ward scattered as the rest of the raid team swarmed in pursuit.

Do not scramble any aerial drones! the Node beamed through the aether, but the drones were already in pursuit. Two fell in tight formation with the old man in the boat, traitors to the cause firing plasma bolts at the raid team as they emerged from hiding.

The Node summoned his own drones to his flanks. He took an abrupt turn through a local market.

Most of the market denizens had taken shelter at the appearance of the raid. Others dove out of the way as the enormous man careened through the aisles. The Node vaulted through the space, truly a specimen of physicality. His drones struggled to keep pace in the tight quarters.

Outside, every intersection in the canal brought another deception. The boat would split into two, three, sometimes more, identical boats. The pursuers picked as best they could and chased phantoms.

The Node bounded up a flight of stairs and sprung up a ladder to the roof of one of the buildings. The air above Pelican Ward hummed with drones. The Node sprinted across the rooftops, carving his route between chimneys, solar panels, and clotheslines. His slaveminds were running the same roofs in a distant simulation, finding the best path. He dodged at odd angles to maximize his speed as he leapt between the buildings. Pigeons scattered from his path.

He reached the end of the buildings and catapulted himself into the void. As the Node fell through space he crossed his arms in front of his chest.

The Node dropped into the boat, absorbing the impact with his knees. The boat swerved wildly as the immense weight of the Node drove the bow into the water. The old man's drones turned and fired at the sudden arrival, but the Node's drones intercepted. The small robots sparred with one another as the old man violently wrenched the steering wheel in an effort to unhorse the Node.

"Durn!" The muscular man shifted his balance without any challenge and took two confident steps toward the old man piloting the craft. He reached out to seize him.

* * * * *

Whitestone's information feed came to an abrupt halt. A projection of Arthur Lannius looked at him. He had reached the moment in the investigation about which Mosaic had required his attention.

Lannius spoke. "I request audience with Clark Whitestone. Attempts to unlock this information by any other will have grave consequences." His voice was calm. The message repeated. Whitestone imagined how many Mosaic information crackers' minds had been burned out testing Lannius's threat.

380

"I'm here, old friend," Whitestone responded, his gaze unfocused as the experience formed in his mind.

The data replay resumed.

The Node came within inches of touching Lannius. The old man locked eyes with the Node.

Enough! The voice of Arthur Lannius thundered over Pelican Ward.

The Node suddenly cowered before the silhouette of a two-thousand-foot-tall cosmic entity. They were alone on an endless flat plane. A white sun glowed on the distant horizon. The entity snatched the filaments of data streaming from the slaveminds, forcing the shadow consciousness's to kneel behind the Node.

The entity towered into space, its body a solid form given to void and stars. The Node felt its entire lifetime of memories boil off to nothing—all his pride and love and sadness and joy reduced to the certain understanding that he just was a vessel of water and dust animated by the warmth of starlight. Eternity crushed him. The Node started to lose consciousness.

You shall not leave so easily. I have not finished with any of you. The entity's voice echoed through the cosmos. The Node and his legion of slaveminds shook before the colossus. They listened.

Take this message to your master. The entity's voice resonated through every molecule of the Node's body.

Fight the Anomaly. You must remember.

The cosmic being's command rippled through Whitestone. Deep love for his former mentor called from somewhere in him.

Shards of his memories with Lannius found each other, coalescing into feelings and images. He remembered throwing the switch on a vast water purification plant—the cool, clear water running to through the hands of a million parched souls. He remembered the warmth of people thanking them for building a thousand schools. The goodness of his memories seemed to glow.

The question nearly formed in his mind before the memories faded to history, swallowed by something larger lurking beyond the towering cosmic being. The abyssal darkness of eternity dwarfed the avatar of Lannius. Hope disappeared into the murk of the infinite, devoured by the thing wearing the hollow crown at the end of existence.

Thank you, old friend, Whitestone said to himself, as he closed the compiled data memory. He would not remember. *We shall see each other soon.*

40

The Symphony of Nuisance

Silvia lay awake when her wards tried to creep back into the room. Despite her effort to look at them disapprovingly, she felt deep affection. They were young and doing their best in a tumultuous world. Silvia slipped down Aurora's block on the personal layer to share her affection. Aurora looked at her, bleary-eyed, and managed a smile. The personal layer transmitted back warmth, but it also painfully confirmed Silvia's hangover suspicions.

The three young people slept through most of the day.

Silvia put the block back up and left the room, instructing Squire to lock it behind her and to guard it. She walked the halls of the House, which were filled with what could only be described as morning music. It was calm; daylight poured in through the skylights, a few clear-eyed people moved through the space while the last of the night revelers dragged themselves to wherever they were sleeping for the night.

Silvia made her way to a particular area following a message from Spiderfly. The message had only included the image of a disc floating in space, but that had been enough for Silvia to know the meaning. It was time for a meeting.

She made her way through the tranquil halls of the House; gentle morning music filled the air. She stopped at a doorway flanked by two robots, each wielding a menacing spear. The door had been engraved with an elaborate Parallel logo. As she approached, the robots appeared as though they would not yield.

She conjured a weave of memories and processes, the chain key of the House of Spider. For its struggles, being the steward of Spiderfly brought its perks. With a wave of her hand, she instructed the robots to turn and allow her passage. Their armored legs thumped and shook the floor, demonstrating their mass and power. She pushed the door open.

Beyond the door was another pleasant day lit room. At the center there was a disc made out of a ceramic set in the floor. There were holographic projectors positioned at regular intervals around the ring of the ceiling. As the door swung closed behind her, Silvia stepped onto the disc.

Even with Spiderfly and the disc to navigate the transfer, using the unconscious layer was always difficult. The layer was built to underpin the networks and make the digital experiences coherent to the dark corners of the mind. The crystal mathematical code of the higher layers could not speak the language of the human animal, the ancient beast that lay dormant behind the idea of the civilized human. The unconscious layer was there to translate code into something the animal could understand, something older. Without it, the mind would reject the networks as false. The layer had not been made for direct interface and as a result could create confusion or even panic. She could feel Spiderfly's presence, but she still felt the inky blackness of unconsciousness ooze across her vision.

She swam through the darkness, amorphous shapes wafting through the blackness. They would temporarily resolve into images—the farm from her childhood, her father's prosthetic leg, a holiday party, flashes of war—it all lurked in the disordered depths of her unconscious. She worked to focus, mainly to avoid actually losing consciousness. There were benefits to security when using the unconscious layer for communication, but it was the same benefits that made navigating the layer challenging. It was inherently inhospitable to the waking mind to linger in the unconscious layer, as such an unwanted observer would have to lurk in the layer, risking their sanity. Finding someone in the unconscious layer was also a trip through the labyrinth, which could prove near impossible without an artificial intelligence as a guide. The military AIs and the curators struggled to process the depths of the unconscious layer, leaving most hoping to use the guidance of one of the Curious. In all, the unconscious layer was a paradox: an essential element of the networks that was near inaccessible, rich and myriad while simultaneously cold and lonely.

The disc buffered some of the effects by harmonizing the augmentations with those deep brain waves, but the overall challenge of teetering at the last edge of consciousness remained. She focused on the firmness of the disc beneath her feet. A disorienting fragmented awareness of hundreds of similar discs scattered around the globe wafted through her mind, before she forced it down to maintain her focus. It was a necessary struggle, but she loathed the experience.

Finally, a figure floated up in the darkness. The other images stabilized into a uniform black background. She stood in a ring of light with the white-haired man. She remembered. The unconscious layer had blotted out her memory of her intent. It was the man she hoped she was seeking. Arthur Lannius.

He shared a similar bewildered look as he focused on her face. He slowly raised his hand in a wave, as though he was uncertain as to whether he was seeing a memory or a person in the gloom of the unconscious layer.

"Hello, Arthur," she said.

"Hello, Silvia."

The greeting crystalized her purpose for wandering in the depths. Clarity cut through the darkness, pushing back the phantoms of memory.

Lannius carried himself with the same regal air, but he looked tired. Silvia wanted to reach out to him but knew such an action could be complicated in the unconscious layer.

"Silvia, it's good to see you," Lannius said. "Thank you for watching over the girl."

"Of course, Arthur," Silvia responded.

"I hoped that I would be with you when I laid this responsibility at your feet. I am sorry that I cannot be there."

"We've taken care of her, although we've probably taught her and her friends some things you wouldn't approve," Silvia said with an unapologetic smile. "As you would expect, Spiderfly was intrigued."

"As it should be. I could hardly claim a monopoly on wisdom. Even if I could, as soon as I laid claim to it, I would be a fool again."

Silvia smiled at his deliberate humble voice. "It's good to see you, Arthur."

He nodded his head in acknowledgement. "I have escaped Mark City. Something or someone tipped off Militarch and Mosaic to my presence. It took all my efforts to reach one of our safe houses. I believe it was Mosaic that found me in the first place by using some technology I have not seen before. My sources called them 'Nodes' and said that Perpetual pioneered the tech. I also have reason to believe scripters might have infiltrated part of the Rebellion hierarchy."

"I thought the scripters were keeping clear of the Rebellion?" Silvia asked. She thought she saw a figure walk through the darkness behind Lannius.

"I had the same belief and I would not have known but for a tip to our friend Damien Durn warning of the defection."

"Perhaps the scripters are playing both sides?" Silvia asked.

"I cannot be sure, beyond knowing that we must take heightened precautions. Clark knows by now that the girl is on the run and knows that I must reach her. I fear he is developing new tools for the task. I doubt he could recreate Parallel without James, Anna, or I, but he is one of the smartest men I know, and likely the most driven." There was a note of grief in his voice. "We must be ready for anything. Spiderfly informed me that a mercenary named Jackal came for the girl. Did she tell you anything about him?"

"From what Aurora said"—Silvia made sure to carefully emphasized the girl's name—"it sounded like he'd taken a compulsion engine as part of his contract. He scared her pretty badly."

Silvia shared the memories they trawled from Squire. A great frown spread across his face and his bushy brow furrowed as he reviewed the information.

"It seems like Whitestone has taken a turn into new territory without anyone to balance his ego. The compulsion engine would seem to indicate the scripters have picked their side. I suppose that was inevitable. We had power struggles before, but we never crossed into forcibly re-wiring people's minds. He's resorting to any measures, no matter how horrid."

"We've been training her to try to defend herself. Octave and Beat gave her the Chime of Spheres."

"Good. She will need all the skills she can muster. Maybe she will share the Chime with us someday." He looked impressed.

"We've trained the others too," Silvia said. "Gan'ko meka and conditioning."

"Ah, the Koren boy and the Orinthian," Lannius said, as though he had forgotten. "New threads in the old pattern. I hope their roles play out as I had envisioned."

"They are having fun, I think. It was actually the boy that won the favor of the Chime," Silvia said, her face wrinkling as she smiled. "I'm not sure they understand what they are up against, but that might be for the best."

"Aye. Just keep them safe. I'll be there soon. I have arranged transport. They should have me on the move tonight."

"That's a relief. While we're having fun here, it'd be nice to get all of us together."

"Yes. I will be ready," Lannius said.

"One more thing, Arthur," Silvia said.

"Yes?" He watched her with his patient eyes.

"The girl," Silvia said, "her name is Aurora. Don't forget it."

Lannius smiled, nodding his head.

"I will not forget it. Thank you, Silvia. Until we meet again."
And he stepped back into the undulating darkness.

*   *   *   *   *

Aurora awoke well into the afternoon. Despite feeling ill, she felt
alive. Her body rang with the debts she had taken out the night
before. Her legs ached, her head throbbed, and she felt the
mossy imbalance of a late night.

Across the room, Kars groaned in the aftermath of their
reveling. Lena was still sound asleep.

As she dragged herself to the bathroom though, she felt no
regrets. The previous day felt like an arrival. They needed a day
unlike any their village could have provided, a day to themselves,
a day of great experience. The House of Octave and Beat
delivered.

Aurora went to the adjoining bathroom to wash off whatever
sour remnants of the night she could. When she emerged, her
condition was much better. She toweled her hair and looked out
their window onto several of the other glittering subsections of
the House.

Silvia was not present, but Squire stood as an inert sentinel at
their door. *Where had Silvia gone?* Aurora beamed the thought
to Squire, trying to stay as quiet as possible for the sake of her
friends.

The tiny robot's tenor voice piped into her head, ringing off the
bones of the previous night's wine. *Ms. Glass left approximately
five hours ago. She did not give me her destination or purpose.*

Did she say when she would get back? Aurora asked.

No, Ms. Glass provided no information.

I'm going to head down to the central hall to find some food. Will you come with me?

Yes, Aurora. I will accompany you to the hall.

Aurora quickly dressed, and she and Squire stepped into the hall. Kars and Lena remained asleep in the room.

The House of Octave and Beat still hummed with life. Bass from some distant performance pulsed through the floor and into her feet. The section she was in was a more remote section of the vast building, devoted to luxurious accommodations. Aurora and Squire walked down their hall to one of the main arteries.

As Aurora approached, she realized something was dramatically different. The first person she saw was adorned with a retinue of fiery orange birds. A phosphorescent blue tattoo flowed down the side of his rib cage. Something like music seemed to emanate from him. A woman wrapped in a layer of writhing golden chains haughtily strode by. An aura of brilliant emerald light pulsed around her head. She felt pride, elation, excitement, a tinge of stress emanating from both of them. She felt something she shouldn't: their emotions.

The personal layer.

How? She had a vague memory of Silvia sharing a feeling of warmth with her when they returned in the early morning. Silvia had taken down the block. She must have forgotten to put it back up?

A bolt of excitement shot through her. The parade of fantastic avatars continued by her in the thoroughfare. Some were subtler—an exotic shade of the skin or color to the eyes. Others were overdone to the point of poor taste. Some clashed. A few even bordered on scary. But there were a handful that transformed the person into another sort of creature entirely, one made of magic. The people appeared as elaborate works of art, dreams given flesh to wander the world.

The overall effect made the hall overwhelming. The revelers continued their endless dance but now shared the space with an entire ecosystem of feelings, projections, and colors. The vibrant coral reef she felt outside the building was magnified tenfold and focused through the intensity of the omnipresent music.

A part of her regretted her decision to continue deeper into the flurry of wild projections. She should have waited for Silvia, should have taken a cautious approach. But the other part of her felt carried away by the freedom of the world in which she now lived. The few explorers that had ventured into their village had seemed like they were from a different planet. Now she knew why.

She wandered through the crowd, staring in every direction, knowing that she was utterly failing the one protocol Arc and Silvia had taught her about the personal layer: be invisible. Passing people spotted her and inspected her. Some even projected their curiosity to her through the personal layer. Aurora did what she could to remain ambivalent and hide herself, but the inquisition was too intense. The more they probed, the more intriguing she seemed.

She started to panic. She had set out on her own and gone too far.

And she liked it.

She imagined her skin like rose dawn, and pink and gold spread across her skin. A tiny mouse appeared on her shoulder and crept out from below her hair, which now cascaded in lush curls. The passersby smiled in approval. Aurora urged her imagination further.

She pictured her wings unfurling into the warmth of the morning sun. It felt like she was being reborn. The projections appeared at her shoulder blades, flexing slowly to her own amazement. Even looking at her own arms and hands felt incredible. The blemishes and freckles she had accrued from years in the sun were gone; her skin was whatever she imagined, perfect in every way.

Seeing them vanish dragged her to a memory of Em and a sudden nostalgia for the mountains. Her imagination told the story through the personal layer.

She felt the coolness of the air above the creek, clear waters tumbling through the rocks in the cut in the forest. The personal layer told her tale, conforming the rugged topography to her legs and torso. All her memories of her homeland wrapped her body; she was a canvas of a perfectly intricate landscape fading into the dawn sky of her head, shoulders and wings. All of it changed and flowed with her thoughts.

A woman wrapped in crimson spires beamed her thanks to Aurora for sharing. Another hulking projection shared its approval.

Aurora basked in it. The digital world felt like it was somehow where she belonged. It was as though she had finally stolen a chance to return home. She wanted to share it.

Her projection spun outward. She remembered the feeling of the cold rain buffeting against her face, the peace of a still evening as the shadow of the mountain crept over the town. Others gathered around to feel her experience – a window into the wilderness they rarely glimpsed from their metropolis. She gave them the thunder and the lightning and the cold. She was terra firma filling the digital space.

Suddenly, the entire wild schools of projections were gone. The personal layer was gone. People still looked at her, but the exotic illusions had vanished, and there were no longer probing thoughts battering against her mind. Someone had blocked the personal layer.

Silvia stood a few paces away looking quite stern. She did not say anything or beam any thoughts to Aurora. She merely walked past her and back to the room. Aurora followed without any prompt.

Aurora knew that she had disobeyed their orders when she continued into the personal layer. Yet she felt a strange lack of compunction. The world beyond their incessant guardianship was beautiful and free. She wanted to be in that world. She felt like she had a rightful place in its hierarchy, which was a strange, almost alien thought. There was some deep joy at seeing the full vibrancy of the personal layer. Silvia, Spiderfly, and Lannius had only proffered that the world was too dangerous for her. Clearly, they underestimated her as a person.

Silvia closed the door behind Aurora as she entered the room. There was a tense quiet moment before Silvia spoke.

"What were you thinking?" Silvia spat.

So much of Silvia's manner carried Aurora back to Em. She knew that she had made a massive mistake—but all that had happened as a result was that she felt the scrutiny of the people through the personal layer, felt the larger forces of the network press in upon her. The heaviness of her transgression felt more like Silvia's guilt than something she had done.

"I don't see what I've done wrong? You treat me like a child when you aren't treating me like a prisoner," Aurora said.

"You are a child," Silvia said. "At least, that's how you blunder toward the enemies lurking beyond these walls."

"I can face them," Aurora said.

"Who are they? Your enemies?" Silvia said sternly.

"Whitestone. Attila. Jackal," Aurora said, trying to hold her voice steady under Silvia's withering gaze.

"Where are they?" Silvia asked, her face cross after Aurora had decided to stand her ground.

Aurora knew she was on loose sands with her argument nonetheless she persisted.

"Maybe they will find me. I stopped Jackal once already." She felt indignant from the after-effects of the previous evening.

Silvia said nothing. Her sharp eyes bored into Aurora.

"Your trip in the personal layer was an accident. I take the blame for it; how you dealt with the aftermath was a choice. Child or prisoner, you've proven all of our doubts correct," Silvia whispered, her voice like venom.

"I at least have a right to my choices," Aurora responded.

"You have no idea how far you've gone past good choices," Silvia retorted. "You covered yourself in a map of your memories! Surely you can see how foolish you've been. Everything you shared, you shared with everyone around you, with Perpetual, with Attila. They found you in your home, and now you've painted yourself in a map."

The air was still for a moment, subject only to the thrumming bass of the music flowing through the House. Aurora writhed under the judgment.

"I'm sorry." It was all she could muster.

Silvia shrugged. The blows of disappointment had landed. "Hopefully, we can make it right. We need to move."

"Why didn't Spiderfly stop it?" Aurora asked, trying to flee her mistake.

"That's not how he works. He's a sentient digital construct that knows how to lie; Spiderfly's motivations are not human. He was probably more interested in seeing what you would do. And he definitely got his answer." Silvia sounded weary from the frustrations of working with the trickster.

I'm trying to crush the data trail now, Spiderfly piped into both Aurora's and Silvia's head. The presence seemed unoffended by Silvia's comments. *It was good to see you get out there though.*

Exasperated, Silvia shook Kars to wake him. Part of her frustration seemed focused in her vigor of shaking him awake. She tossed their gear onto their beds.

"Sorry for the rude awakening. It's time we hit the road."

Kars looked disoriented. Lena barely lifted her head off the pillow; her cheek bore the imprint of the fabric.

"I'm sorry. We're on the run again," Aurora said.

I managed to stop it, but it reached at least one advanced watcher before I could limit it. It's out of my control, Spiderfly reported. Aurora's heart dropped, the last trick to undo her mistake had failed.

Do you know who saw the inquiries? Silvia asked as she strapped her gear back on.

No, but I'd assume your location has been compromised, Spiderfly said to Silvia and Aurora.

"Alright, now it's really time to go. We're on the clock. Who knows who could be coming for us now," Silvia said, urging Kars and Lena out of bed.

As they pulled on their clothes from the day before, the conversation continued between Silvia and Spiderfly. Aurora was able, perhaps required, to listen. Hearing the two of them strategize how to protect her was shaming.

Do you think we can make it back to our House? Silvia projected.

Uncertain. I don't know who picked up the questions. They may have already set a perimeter around the House, Spiderfly responded.

So we need another plan, Silvia said through the aether.

Yes. Arc and I agree that the House of Coyote may be close enough for you to reach, Spiderfly reported.

Coyote. Well, I guess it's better than nothing, Silvia thought to Aurora and Spiderfly.

Octave appeared in the conversation. *Will you two tell me what you've done? Max is getting calls from the Office of the Securitor. They are asking us to hold our doors until they arrive.*

Well, at least we know whom we are dealing with and it's slightly better than Attila or Perpetual. Spiderfly almost seemed excited.

We can bet that Perpetual and Attila aren't far behind if the Securitor knows, Silvia thought to the others.

You still didn't tell us what you did, Octave repeated.

Aurora went on the personal layer for a second. Some curious people tried to look her up. Her fake information must have tripped some warning with the Securitor, Silvia said.

Aurora was amazed at the conversation transmitting through the aether around her.

There are Securitor drones arriving now. What should we do? Octave asked.

Octave, Beat, I am terribly sorry for what I'm about to do. I've wanted to try this for a while and it seems like the perfect time. Spiderfly's message seemed to carry a feeling of mischief.

Spiderfly. Why are you sorry? Octave reluctantly delivered to the conversation.

We need a diversion. I promise you both, I will make it up to you. May I proceed? Spiderfly asked, the final question lingered in the space of the transmission.

Reluctantly, we agree to your vague terms, trickster.

Though Aurora, Kars, and Lena would never see it, Spiderfly materialized as a hologram on the crystal platform.

In his hand, he held a conductor's baton, which he flourished in the air. He stood straight, his face mocking the seriousness of their situation. In a dramatic swing, he raised his arms and began to conduct an opus for the senses.

It began with a single oboe holding a single frail note, which resolved into a cacophony of kazoos buzzing. The revelers looked up at the platform, straining to see the dark figure. The first wave of synesthesia assaulted the revelers' senses of smell with the immediate blast of sulfurous rotten eggs accompanied by a sagging note of the tuba. The shock of the change in composer brought the dance to an immediate halt. He flapped his arms, and the next wave surged through the House of Octave and Beat, a chord of howling cats, the smell of feet, and the taste of soap.

One of the revelers pointed up at the crystal podium and shouted. "It's the Spider!"

He let his arms drop again, weaving curdled milk into the song. Crying babies shrieked. Pin pricks of itchiness simultaneously sprung up in the middle of every reveler's back. Garlic breath wafted through the air. Thousands stubbed their toes in unison. Tastes too sour and too sweet and too salty crashed through their taste buds. The Spider continued conducting his grand symphony of nuisances. A million alarm clocks rang together. A bouquet of pigpens blossomed in the House. Despite the utter lack of rhythm in Spiderfly's opus, there was the awful sound of someone clapping on beats one and three.

Silvia smiled as she realized what was happening. "Alright, stick together! We're getting out of here right now!"

Kars strapped on the tabula and grabbed his vest. Lena just managed to button her pants. They both carried their shoes in their hands. The four of them jogged through the chaos overtaking the halls of the House of Octave and Beat.

Spiderfly continued into the second movement of his masterpiece. His face bore a huge toothy smile as the screams echoed from below. He rapidly tipped his baton in the air, calling down a staccato series of fish, underarms, and sharp cheese to the revelers' senses. The feeling of an ant in the pants tickled forth from his devious mind. He then cued the sound of a large man chewing with his mouth open, accompanied by the feeling of a sleeping foot regaining circulation.

The companions dashed through the unfolding chaos, people shrieking and running for whatever exit they could find. Kars and Lena watched the pandemonium with wide eyes and huge smiles. They surged with the crowd to the great turquoise door and were pushed out into the street beyond the Securitor drones. Without looking back, they ducked down another street.

Spiderfly carried on to his final movement. All arrays of terrible smells crashed into one another. Onions, durians, papayas, and skunk filled the air. The smoke of wet wood on a campfire stung their eyes. The revelers all felt a sudden wave of oppressive humidity causing them to sweat. The whine of a single mosquito started out of silence before growing to a deafening roar, accompanied by the urgent need to use the bathroom.

His work was complete. He let the baton drop. With a huge devious grin, he surveyed the chaos. The serenity of the House of Octave and Beat was completely lost. The crowd surged to the exit. The Securitor drones stood no chance in the tide of itchy, smelly, sweaty, disgusted, and annoyed people. It was a masterpiece of mischief.

Octave appeared next to him, her arms crossed.

"How long have you been planning this?" she said.

"Since the girl arrived on my doorstep."

41

Moving Pieces

The steward of the House of Octave and Beat, Maximillian Ward, stood at the edge of the great doors as the last stragglers stumbled out of the building. He tugged the corner of his mustache and felt foolish as he replayed his bragging bravado to Silvia over in his mind. He furrowed his great bushy brow as the words of their conversation echoed while he watched the crowd. *Take a break from the militant life.* He was suddenly aware of the bulbous heft of his belly straining against his vest.

Spiderfly had playfully proved a significant point—they were vulnerable. Fortunately, the vestigial functions of the augmentations Max had installed as one of the Seventy-Seven had sprung back into action and treated Spiderfly's grand prank as an attack. He had caught a whiff of rotten milk before his augmentations foiled the sensory assault. He had watched the symphony of nuisance in a mix of awe and amusement as the entire fragile temple was torn apart by the trickster.

He knew they would recover—the House would be full again in a few hours. But Spiderfly had made a statement. Worse yet, the Spider probably didn't even realize the depth of what he did or the ultimate repercussions. Max didn't understand how Silvia endured so many years of Spiderfly. It was a constant stream of brilliant but half-baked schemes, the genius of which lay in how they disintegrated into a sloppy truth. Max tugged at his mustache.

A familiar character strode out of the crowd. He was a handsome man with chiseled features and a neat salt-and-pepper goatee. He wore the uniform of the highest-ranking chiefs of the Securitor. Max paused, unsurprised that Marcus appeared at this moment.

"Marcus," Max said, acknowledging the new arrival.

"Max," Marcus Stormgard responded.

The younger man had been as close to one of the Seventy-Seven as one could be without being sworn to the cause. Indeed, the mystery of why Marcus had stayed on the sidelines always baffled Max. Since the days of the Seventy-Seven, Marcus had climbed in rank to the Chief Investigator of the Office of the Securitor. In Max's opinion, it was an office unbefitting of the man's talents. Between the corporations, the Houses, and the military AI, the Securitor was a paper shield of a police force.

"You got here fast," Max said, his tone presumptive.

"You know why we're here?" Marcus asked. His voice was deep and self-assured.

"Of course, we do," Max said, his voice a growl. "An attack from the 'rogue artificial intelligence known as Spiderfly,'" Max said, his impatience transmitting that he was just going through the motions of the procedure.

Marcus smiled. "Oh that? No, not today, but I can send an officer to take a statement." He oozed frustrating charisma. "No, we were here before the event—hence the speed. We were investigating some mysterious inquiries on the personal layer. You haven't by chance seen this girl?"

In a flash, Marcus transmitted an image of Aurora to Max. She was standing in one of the hallways looking bewildered, her tiny robot was next to her.

The inquiry caught Max by surprise, leading to the second moment in the day where he felt fortunate his augmentations still carried some of the Seventy-Seven's hardwiring. The augmentations suppressed the physiological markers that he was lying.

"No, I haven't seen her." His tone was flat and unremarkable, his pulse steadied, pupils fixed, and perspiration held constant.

"Max, you know I have jurisdiction to subpoena your memories. Are you sure you did not see her?"

Max knew the deep system augmentations he took during his time with Lannius would resist any probing Marcus and the Securitors could launch at him. He was surprised that Marcus would bring it up, since he knew that as well.

"Absolutely," Max responded in the same flat, unremarkable tone.

"On the record?" Marcus asked, raising his eyebrows in a quizzical look. Max nodded slowly.

"Absolutely," Max responded.

"Alright. Just hope nothing turns up that you did. The girl seems to have a host of different people after her, and I'd hate to see her get in any trouble," Marcus said. "Do you still want an officer for the incident?"

"I think we'll be fine. Thank you," Max said.

*   *   *   *   *

Marcus left Max alone to enjoy the satisfaction of feeling like he had won. Marcus knew one of the Seventy-Seven would prove impervious to any interrogation, even if they had let themselves slip into peaceful indolence like Max. Some muscles never atrophied, and some reflexes never dulled.

He had hoped that Max would have cooperated, but the House had just suffered a tremendous prank and Max's ego was tender. Marcus had watched Max's loyalties grow more selfish with each year, his penchant for reveling in the House had slowly eroded the sense of purpose Lannius's people felt when they joined the Rebellion. Marcus wished he could just question Lannius himself.

Unfortunately, his position also kept him from direct dealings with the rogue AI, so he could not have asked Octave or Beat if he had wanted. The firewall between the Securitor and the Curious made a degree of sense—keep the police force free from interference—but it created problems when dealing with such a ubiquitous presence as Spiderfly or the other Curious. Sometimes his life was just more complicated.

He sighed. He wished he had known how Arthur created the Curious. Maybe someday he would ask Lannius as part of the larger investigation. The intrigue of what drove these strange beings tugged at his old un-played heartstrings that longed to invent.

Dismissing his nostalgia, he probed the Securitor database, pulling up their location. The map sprung up in his mind in precise three-dimensional detail. He tagged the House of

Octave and Beat with his own marker. He then queried the system for other alleged "Houses" in the city. Ten locations dotted his map.

It was a simple matter from that point of determining the closest House. The map focused on one in a nearby district. It was a small place with few visitors. The information they had was sparse. Few noise complaints and little foot traffic. Odd reports about crazed people wandering out of the House into the neighborhood. It was just a few blocks away.

"Coyote," he said, reading the data. Then he turned and started toward the House on foot.

*   *   *   *   *

Jackal stared out of the narrow bunker window onto the cruel orange of the desert. Heat swam through his vision, reflecting the distant brown mountains off an invisible pool. Sweat slicked his face and left uncomfortable humidity in his bushy beard. He did not care. A lone fly buzzed in the still air. Jackal continued to stare out across the desert.

His eyes smoldered with a rage he only barely understood. Some might have rationalized his defeat as a lack of information or poor planning from higher in the command structure. For some reason, he could not bring himself to any part of acceptance. Perhaps it was the compulsion engine ticking away in his brain, or maybe it was just how he was personally wired. Babysitting captives had only honed his rage.

When the communications radio in his command bunker crackled to life, his blood started to steam. He picked up the handset to the radio. Out this far in the desert, only remnants of technology worked.

"Jackal." He stared out across the sand.

"It's time." It was Whitestone, "East Bay Securitor picked up her trail. Marcus Stormgard is moving in on her now."

Jackal sneered a vile smile. "We'll be in the air in a few hours."

"Do not fail me again," Whitestone said through the radio.

"I will not," Jackal responded.

"I should hope not. I've taken out insurance as well. Another asset is currently en route. You will be working in tandem. Do not interfere with his operation."

The words stung with catalytic fury. It was an affront to Jackal's craft and character. Jealousy churned out of the compulsion engine. His face contorted as he channeled several breaths through his nose. He depressed the call button on his radio.

"Received. Over and out." Jackal forced the words.

He regained composure to channel his frustration to the task, focus his failure on the next steps. Find the girl. Bring in the girl. Finish his contract and abate the unreasonable feelings of obsession that drove him in the hunt.

He shouted to the camp, drawing the attention of the Protek, prisoners, and other mercenaries.

"Saddle up!" he yelled. "We're going to East Bay!"

*　　*　　*　　*　　*

Whitestone listened with ominous patience as the communication with Jackal ended. It appeared that the long-term effects of the compulsion engine had started to corrupt other parts of Jackal's psyche. No matter. He had other tools in his kit, sharper knives and more precise instruments.

"Angelo, bring me the girl. It seems like our dog Jackal might have a broken leash." He turned and faced a figure in the sleek conference room.

"Yes sir." Angelo was a graceful and powerfully built young man. He bore the features of numerous races blended into a single handsome young face. Even through his prosthetic eyes, Whitestone felt an unnatural emptiness in Angelo. Whitestone sensed the filaments leading away from the Node across the networks to the slavemind hive.

"Be prepared for anything. Jackal will fall on the city like a hammer. Be mindful of Stormgard and Glass. And above all else, Arthur Lannius may try to interfere. He slipped the net in Mark City."

"The old man can try," Angelo said. Whitestone saw the arrogance on the young man's face through the array of sensors and cameras scattered throughout the room.

"Do not under estimate Lannius. He is wily, and his fingerprints are all over the underlying infrastructure of the networks."

"I've been preparing for Lannius, I won't underestimate him. He will not be able to stop me."

Whitestone accepted the answer. He would not be persuaded to caution without his own experience. Whitestone recalled Mosaic's Node standing before Lannius, helpless. Whitestone shrugged. Lannius would not kill Angelo in malice. Besides, it seemed like the boy could use some humbling before he realized his actual potential.

"So be it," Whitestone said. "Bring me the girl and kill any who get in your way."

"Of course." Angelo nodded.

"One more thing," Whitestone said. Angelo stood at attention to listen to his superior.

"If you are caught, you must disavow your connection to me and Perpetual," Whitestone said.

The Node paused, intrigued. Whitestone sensed the layers of slaveminds gnawing over the information they had just been tasked.

"The board does not know of your endeavor?" Angelo asked. Whitestone knew he had to proceed with caution—a sharp tool in his hands.

"I am granted certain discretionary actions," Whitestone responded.

The Node seemed to look through him. It was a look Whitestone did not often experience.

"And the slavemind hive?" Angelo asked.

"Very good. Also, discretionary. I see my trust in you is well placed," Whitestone said.

The Node didn't respond. Instead he waited for Whitestone to return to the question. Angelo would not be diverted. Whitestone had seen the Nodes in boardrooms and battlefields but had never allowed himself to be the subject of one's scrutiny. Had he not lived through eons of his own experience, he might have been cowed by the inhuman calm the creation before him exerted.

"The slavemind hive is independent. Isolated. It is another discretionary tool that has taken me some effort and resources to acquire," Whitestone responded after making the Node wait sometime with his hyper-threaded thoughts.

Angelo the Node nodded, satisfied.

"Anything else?" Whitestone cautiously asked Angelo. He was sharp.

"No, sir. I'll return with my quarry." He turned and left the room before Whitestone could dismiss him.

*   *   *   *   *

Em stalked the length of the enclosure like a caged wolf. The commotion in the camp was palpable. Clouds of dust rose from the paths between buildings. Mercenaries drove old-style trucks full of gear toward the landing pads. They must have found her children.

She wanted to burst, but she knew that she couldn't share her theory for fear of the panic it would trigger. She wouldn't put Cara through that disturbance. It would be better to suffer alone with her anxiety.

The first aircraft roared to life, rising into the air. Everyone in the enclosure covered their ears. Jackal must have been running larger craft than the craft he had used during the raid. The sound was cripplingly loud.

The confusion continued as the raiding party mounted their aircraft. It was clear that this was not the precise raiding party that had taken their entire village—this was an army fit for a siege.

Em returned to her spot at the back of the enclosure.

"Ranjit!" she barked over the sound of aircraft.

"It's almost time," Ranjit said.

"We need to go now. I have to stop them."

"We cannot do that." His voice was calm. "At least, not right now."

The commotion spilled into the enclosure. Em turned to see armored guards storming through the open gate. Black masks hid their faces, and they said nothing. They were searching for someone. Em knew that they sought her out, and she hoped that it was the doctor's people, not Jackal. Given the circumstance of the raid, it could be either.

Em turned away from Ranjit without saying anything. She would not endanger him as a co-conspirator. She calmly held up her hands.

Her companions in the prison mumbled to each other, debating whether they should act. The thrum of engines filled the air, Doppler shifting as the smaller aircraft circled overhead. Em looked at the feet of the guards in full knowledge that they might drag her off on their raid.

None of the other townsfolk acted, biding their time and looking to her for a signal that never came. The guards nodded to each other, seizing Em by the elbows and roughly dragging her out of the enclosure, giving her full view of the camp—platform tents, low bunkers and retrofit pre-war buildings. Old-style satellite dishes pointed skyward from several roofs. It must have housed a standing army, and it was readying for battle with marshal efficiency. Protek marched along their own orders. They passed between the massive armored wall that held back the desert and the edge of the cargo loading area. She was startled to see massive Protek, retrofitted with their own repulsor pods and stubby wings. *Why did these machines cooperate with Jackal?* The thought that they might lead the Protek on a strike on a city—their own city—was outrageous. She felt even more certain that her children were the targets.

The guards pushed open the door to one of the tents and shoved her inside.

"We don't have much time," the doctor hissed. "Quickly, in here." He opened a door on the back of a large cabinet. "They are coming for you."

Em scrambled into the cramped space and the doctor quickly sealed the compartment and pushed the cabinet back against the wall of the tent.

Moments later, she heard gruff voices in the tent. They were looking for a prisoner, and the doctor angrily rebuked them. He yelled something about the number of them that had stolen combat stimulants for the strike, how he could barely keep the dispensary stocked with all the new mercenaries stealing from him. He yelled them down.

Then there was silence. Terrible silence. Em huddled in the cramped dark space, listening as more aircrafts left. There were no other visitors in the doctor's tent.

After what seemed like hours, the cabinet jostled as the doctor opened the compartment for Em. She blinked as she stepped back out into the daylight.

"Thank you." It was the first thing she had to say.

He nodded as if it was all part of his duty.

"Jackal had called for you specifically, so we thought that we should at least keep that from happening," the doctor said. "We'll need a plan for when he returns to deal with his traitors."

"Do you know where they are going?" Em asked, stretching from being in the cabinet. She was not quite as resilient as she used to be.

"From what I could tell, they are heading to East Bay, but I don't know the specifics. That was a lot of artillery to visit a friendly megacity," the doctor said. "Attila will certainly respond."

Em knew it was the case, though. The narrow facts that she knew all lined up in support of her theory. They were going to find her children and expected heavy resistance.

"Is there any way that we can stop them?" Em said.

The doctor shook his head. "That was never an option. However, our people had a different plan in mind."

Our people. Em wondered how far the insurgency spread in this remote camp. It was a poor reflection on Jackal as a leader, or at the very least, on his ability to manage fear. He had come to rely on the power of his Protek enforcers, leaving himself open to undercuts and sedition.

"You want me to lead our people to take the camp," Em said. The plan was obvious.

"Yes," the doctor said. "While much of Jackal's force is on the strike, a sizeable force remains. Some have been scripted and will be impossible to negotiate. They will not fold, but also, they do not expect an attack from within. There's also a handful of security officers, many of whom were conscripts taken prisoner during the Rebellion. They will either support you or surrender."

"What about the Protek?" Em asked. The killer machines were more a threat than any person.

"Jackal only had a few that could be called loyal. He needed to take them with him on the strike. Whatever odd learning algorithms sit beneath the Protek programming evolved into some kind of code; at least, that's the best interpretation our thoughts and language allow. It's a little like wolf-pack hierarchy. If Jackal did not take his loyal Protek to fight, they would have abandoned him, or killed him outright," the doctor explained.

"What about the ones beyond the wall?" Em asked.

"They are there to be sure, but it seems like Jackal's Protek keep the ones beyond the wall at bay. Again, it's sort of the wolf-pack analogy. We are in one pack's territory, and the others tend not to cross into this domain," the doctor said, and then added a caveat. "Of course, that's only my estimate. There has not been much public study of the Protek in Amurtan."

It was a dangerous gambit. Take the camp, wait for Jackals return, and make the mercenaries retake the camp. After taking

413

the camp, they would be cut off from Perpetual's resupply routes. It was not a long-game strategy.

"If we take the camp, it has to be to get ourselves out. I don't see another way for it to work. Eventually, those Protek in the desert will come for us, and we are going to be cut off from supplies," Em said.

"Yes, of course," the doctor said. "It's our only play. I think Ranjit has had that in mind since the start. We all just want to go home."

"They will bring the airships back?" Em asked.

"They always have before," he said.

"Then we will kill them when they land," Em said. "Maybe save the pilots to get home," she added as an afterthought.

"Not all of them deserve to die," the doctor said. "I helped you, others have helped you. Some were scripted before they realized."

"We will try to give as many of them as we can a chance," Em said. "But our priority is getting out of this camp alive."

The doctor looked at her with caution, as though he was seeing a bear he had leashed for the first time. It was a look Em remembered from long ago, the look someone gave her when they realized she was capable of terrible things. Em also knew what came next: resignation and the willingness to receive the benefits of her brutality.

"I suppose it must be," the doctor said. "Just please try to avoid the conflict when you can. We will be stronger in the end for it."

414

"We're in agreement on that note. A handful of defectors can change the entire tide of a war," Em said, remembering that the Seventy-Seven were all defectors. "We should work quickly; who knows how long they will be away. I will rally our people."

Em turned to leave but stopped. She realized she didn't know the doctor's name. It suddenly seemed important.

"Doc, what do I call you?" Em asked, over her shoulder.

"Hayes. Von Hayes," the doctor said, "but I do like Doc." He smiled behind his small spectacles.

"Sure thing," Em said. "See you in couple hours."

Em returned to the enclosure, flanked by the two guards. They no longer held her elbows but accompanied her as an entourage. When they reached the gate, one of the guards opened the latch, and Em stepped inside.

A few hours to let Jackal get out of range to respond to any distress call. A few hours to waken the old fighting spirit of the townsfolk. Her time had arrived. She felt the familiar surge of battle rising in her heart. It was fear and exhilaration and giving life to a feeling. Jackal had taken her home and hunted her children. Her moment to begin exacting the cost of his transgression had arrived.

42

The Eve of the Gap

What's next? Silvia thought to Lannius. Jack Mortanis tied their horses nearby. Silvia could tell that Lannius, silent all that day, bore a heavy heart having left the baby with Emelia Koren. The trio had left Prospector, heading to reunite with the remaining forces of the Seventy-Seven near Cordovan Gap.

Uncharacteristically, Lannius did not respond. Perhaps he was elsewhere in the vast expanse of his memories.

The sun had settled behind an overcast shroud, leaving evening to creep in from the forests around them. The air was still save for the gentle sounds of the horses. Silvia set down one of her saddlebags, removing a knit cap, which she pulled over her cropped hair. She could barely see the ghost of her breath in the air.

Their camp was nestled next to a river; the shallow embankment of the shore sloped into the waters. Silvia stood near the edge, dipping a bag beneath the surface to water the horses. She scanned the smooth water, seeing that the river had just emerged from the dark maw of a cave in the mountainside. The cave exhaled a damp breeze.

Jack Mortanis set about building a small mound of kindling in a dip in the soil. He nursed a small flame to a fire in short order. The three of them were quiet as they set about the basic tasks of

416

setting up camp. They moved with the practiced efficiency of traveling companions.

What's next? Silvia ventured again, beaming the thought to Lannius. Despite living with the augmentations for nearly a year, there was an occasional novelty to their use.

For now we continue the Rebellion, Lannius responded, *but our hope lies with the child.*

Silvia thought to him, carrying a shade of disbelief. Until only days before, she had not even known that the Alcarns had a child. The secrets of their mysterious project slowly unfolded. Silvia fought a feeling of vertigo thinking that Lannius may have lived this experience before through his time machine.

Even if she's our hope, she is just a baby. We've got more immediate concerns. What if we fail at The Gap? Silvia asked. It felt foreign to consider defeat. Her fear was real.

If we fail, then I must take a different course. We must be unforeseeable, Lannius responded.

What do I do next? Silvia asked, seemingly asking for prophecy over conversation.

Lannius paused his act of spreading the tarp.

"Silvia," he said aloud, "our oracle gave us no solutions to our fate."

"And what was it?" Silvia asked.

"Our fate? I shall not say. If anything is clear, a single word can change fate as it unfolds," Lannius said. "However, I will say that when I left the Hourglass, we started down a new course. Our future radically diverged from any I know. We are in an uncharted future."

"So our future is not set in stone?" Silvia asked. Jack Mortanis moved nearby but seemed uninterested in their conversation. He tossed a small signal balloon into the air. They watched as it disappeared into the clouds.

"I did not say our fate was free," Lannius responded. "I only said that we have left matters to chance. All our prior meddling led to one terminus. I cannot let it happen again."

There was a deep weariness hidden in his face. Silvia had seen it before but attributed it to the struggles of war. Now she realized the fatigue stretched deep beyond war and into the soul of Lannius. Despite the decades of life and the mistakes etched in his legacy, Lannius chose to persevere. Each step was an act of will.

"The girl, she must carry the future. My life, this final march, must be in dedication to her success. I know I am nearing the end of my life, so my pledge bears only small weight. It is unfair what I ask of you, but you must also be prepared to give your life for the girl. I hope that it does not reach this end, but the future of all life depends on her," Lannius said.

Jack did not look up from his tasks. "Whatever it takes."

Silvia expected as much from Jack. He had taken to augmentations and the Rebellion with a kind of fervor. He had been a bored commodity broker whose heart slept between pentathlons before the Rebellion had given him a purpose. It was natural for him to pledge his life with the same blunt force.

"Whatever it takes," Silvia agreed. "Whatever that means."

Lannius detected her cynicism. It was a fair response.

"Silvia, I am truly sorry," Lannius said.

"The girl. Mirien Alcarn. She knows what to do?" Silvia said, as though making the oath somehow entitled her to her requests.

"No longer," Lannius said, sadness sweeping across his face. "Mirien Alcarn no longer exists. She is just memories swept clear like sand on the wind of time."

"Then why? Why hide her? Why the oaths?" Silvia demanded.

"It is only a hope. Mirien was special. It is my hope that this girl may be special as well. For now, we must trust in Emilia Koren and try to keep this place safe. I wish I could offer more of an oracular promise, but we have found ourselves in a crucible of hope and fate."

Silvia felt frustration rise from within. She impatiently scrubbed her short-cropped hair. She knew that she would have to accept that Arthur Lannius could not deliver the simple truth: he didn't know what was coming. He, just like so many fools before him, was left with hope and a plan. Silvia saw the great leader humbled. One of the most powerful men in history camped by the side of river, an outlaw and a guerilla. His machinations had crumbled around him. They had just left a baby with a rebel leader.

"What happens if Em fails?" Silvia asked.

"She cannot fail. Eventually, this place will be too small for the girl or the world will pry its way into her life. There is nothing Emilia can do to stop it—failure is too harsh a word for the inevitable," Lannius responded. "I can only think of contingencies."

Silvia watched the piercing eyes scan the mouth of the upstream cave. She sensed dense processes warming his brain. He was deep in thought.

"Contingencies," he said distantly. His eyes were focused on something between him and the cave. It was a spider web with a tiny dark arachnid perched at its geometric center.

Lannius stared at it for a moment before snapping out of his trance.

"Contingencies," he repeated. "Jack. Find the Ganakas and protect their child. Do whatever it takes."

Jack grunted a response. Nothing had changed in his world.

"Silvia. I want you to go to East Bay and wait. Someday, the girl will find her way there. Protect her when she arrives. Guide her," Lannius said.

"I am just supposed to wait? We just left a baby in a mountain village. It could be years! She might never come!" Silvia protested.

"I am sure that you will find some use for your time," Lannius said, a mischievous glint sparked in his eye.

"And you? Where will you be?" Silvia asked, her tone half-petulant.

"I will be doing all in my power to disrupt the inevitable. I must be unforeseeable. Diversions, conflicts, and preparations so that our young heroine will have a chance when her day finally arrives." Lannius sounded as though he had discovered a well of vitality. "Find me in the unconscious layer if you need to reach me."

Silvia had only heard about the mythical base protocol behind the augmentations, and Lannius was proposing that they use it to communicate. She knew she had much work ahead of her.

You will learn. Lannius must have sensed her concern.

I don't know if I am ready for this life, Silvia sent to Lannius.

Even with a thousand years, he responded, *we are never ready for life.*

Silvia thought about her choice but knew she had already made her decision. The next day, she would start her ride to East Bay. They would head their separate ways. Arthur would ride to the Gap. Alone in the city, Silvia would start her life of service and wait for the girl to bring its end.

The two of them watched as the spider pulled another thread into its web.

43

The House of Coyote

Aurora and her companions hurtled through back alleys and passages to reach their next refuge. Sirens wailed behind them.

The crowds of confused, half-clothed revelers dissipated as they distanced themselves from the House of Octave and Beat. They paused for a moment while Kars and Lena put on their shoes.

"Okay, while I think we aced our escape drill, would you mind giving a little more detail as to why we had to wake up and run?" Kars said, standing on one foot while pulling on a shoe.

"I accessed the personal layer—the layer of the network where other people can see things about you, share things about you," Aurora said.

"And what happened?" Lena asked. "That doesn't sound too bad on its own."

"Some of the people tried to look her up. The network flagged her and notified the Securitor—basically the network police force tasked with keeping the peace in East Bay."

"So, the police were coming?"

"Yes. And if they knew where we were, we could be almost certain that Perpetual knew where we were. We had no choice but to run." Silvia still held a loose bundle of gear that they had grabbed on the way out of the House.

"Did Perpetual find us?" Lena asked.

"I didn't see anything but Securitor outside the House as we fled. They know we were there, so they are probably closing in on the area. Lannius said that he was nearly leaving Mark City, which would give him a few days to reach the East Bay docks. We've just got to stay on the run or hold out until he arrives," Silvia said.

"And he's just going to make all of them go away?" Kars asked, his voice laden with sarcasm.

"Who knows what he'll do, but that man has more than enough tricks up his sleeve to make a difference," Silvia said.

Aurora felt the public layer flow around her as they slipped through the back channels of the city. The advertisements nestled in the crannies of side streets pedaled movie experiences, video games, and artificial social presences. It was as though the city knew that any one taking this back route likely wanted to be left alone. She still longed to see the personal layer and all the extravagant avatars lurking in it but did not dare to try and look. She had drawn their pursuers down on them because she was curious. Now was definitely not the time to probe the personal layer.

Silvia beamed a thought, *Don't worry. We're going to make this right without any issues. The House of Coyote may prove a bit . . . eccentric, but they should be able to shelter us for a few days.*

Aurora allowed herself a smile. *Thanks, Silvia. I'm sorry that I didn't leave it alone or at least try to do what you and Arc told me. I have such a long way to go.*

Silvia responded, *It was my fault too. I should've been more careful with the block and your training. We can't afford to make those simple mistakes.*

Aurora scowled. There was a kindness to it that aimed to provide her relief, but lurking behind it was the calculation of her mission.

I don't think I'll ever be ready for this fight. I still don't know why Lannius needs me. I don't think I can do it on my own, Aurora thought to Silvia.

I don't know either, not the whole of it. We will all be there to help you. You won't have to do any of this alone, Silvia responded.

The sentiment felt honest to Aurora, but suspicion lurked in her mind. *But why do we need to fight it? Things seem like they work well. There's a balance and people seem like they coexist. Is there really a threat that we need to fight?*

Things are balanced right now, but the threat is real. Lannius told us about one of the eventualities of the military AIs. They fight each other as programmed but will eventually turn. The Protek proved the formula once. Now the experiment runs with six more AIs. Like a game of chess, the conversation takes time but must eventually arrive at a conclusion, Silvia shared.

It's his hope that I can stop the game before it finishes? Aurora asked.

I won't speak on Lannius's behalf, but you've been important to us for a long time, Silvia responded.

Can you tell me why? Aurora asked, the thought sharp and cold.

There was a pause in their mental back-and-forth. Aurora nearly raised her voice, but she held her tongue to keep Kars and Lena out of the conversation.

Then Silvia responded, *No*.

Why not? Aurora's thought was more urgent, laced with anger and hurt.

Because I don't really know, Silvia responded. The thought carried an inflexion of resignation.

Aurora felt hurt and lonely. Silvia wouldn't tell her? Beneath the hurt she felt a deep glacial rage shift in her. They wouldn't tell her because she was just a part of a plan.

So be it, Aurora responded. It was curt and laced with threat that seemed to seep from the other memories. The feeling was alien.

Silvia was alarmed by the dismissal.

Aurora, I'm just a soldier following my orders, Silvia said. Aurora sensed the conflict through the connection.

You have a choice. Aurora steeled her expression and they continued walking in silence.

They turned a corner and Silvia held out her palm to stop their party. The had arrived at their destination.

Unlike the other houses, the House of Coyote did little to show the outside world that it existed. The House was a single monolithic structure of corrugated metal, extending into the distance of the industrial district. It was several stories tall with only a few windows perched near the top floors. The House gave a severe sense of industrial unwelcome, far different from the opulence of Octave and Beat's temple or the grand mystique of Spiderfly's abode.

They approached a single ground-level door, tended by a hulking man. His head was bald, as if all the hair on his head had crawled down into a bushy beard. The man shifted his bulk when he saw Silvia led the group.

"A pleasure to see you Ms. Glass," he said, opening the door.

"Good to see you, too, Bean," Silvia said. "You probably already heard why we're here."

"Yes, ma'am." The giant's voice was soft.

"Then you know you might have some unusual guests," Silvia said.

"I never saw you," he said.

"Good man." She patted him on the shoulder and stepped through the doorway. Kars, Lena, and Aurora followed, and Bean closed the door behind them.

The House of Coyote could be better described as a village. The metal walls and high warehouse ceiling served as more of container for a vast maze of tents and yurts. Most of the city concrete and asphalt had been torn up, left as soil, which had been tended into a thriving forest. The metal outer walls were painted with wild patterns and symbols. Had Aurora been able to access the personal layer, she would have seen a brilliant twisting display of the cosmos filling the high ceilings above them as the sun set through the skylights. People wandered through the dark indoor forest in quiet conversation. There were birds and small animals in the trees. It was as though they had stepped through a doorway and come—

"Home," Kars said. His voice wavered with the reflectiveness of someone who had collided with an unexpected deeper reality. Lena reached out and took his hand. The quiet of the House of Coyote was a serene change from the city. The air smelled of humus and hardwood smoke.

"Silvia, how did they . . ." Aurora trailed off.

Silvia watched as they took in their new surroundings. The House of Coyote was a place apart from the city, a wilderness cleaved off of the bustling psyche of society. It was no park or plaza and resonated with its own solemn grandeur.

"Come," Silvia said. "We should find Jinan, the steward of the House. Coyote knows we are here, but it's polite to introduce ourselves."

She led them down one of the trails, meandering through towering conifers and small encampments of walled tents. Men and women sat quietly around campfires. The further they walked, it felt less like a building and more like a primordial wilderness.

Silvia stopped at one of the fire pits and asked where they could find Jinan. The woman pointed further down the path. They continued in silence.

After passing several quieter encampments, they arrived at a fire pit and tent circle at the end of the path. A few people sat around the fire, just as they would at any other encampment. One of them spotted Silvia and let out a toothy whistle.

"Is Jinan in?" Silvia asked. Aurora, Kars, and Lena stood back. The ritual of greeting was much different in this House. After the bubbling extroversion of their encounter with Octave and Beat, the solitude felt intimidating.

"Jinan is with Coyote," the man said. He offered no other information.

Silvia nodded.

"Mind if we sit for a spell?" she asked.

The man tilted his head to a spot on a log across the fire.

They sat by the fire until the last light of the twilight disappeared from the sky above. The flames danced before them, crackling in what was otherwise silence. Lena leaned on Kars's shoulder, drowsiness weighing on her face. Kars had a distant look in the orange glow. Most of the others had retreated to the nearby tents.

Aurora beamed a thought to Silvia, *What now?*

Not here, Silvia responded. Aurora withdrew to her own thoughts.

The House that was not a house began to stir with the sounds of the woods at night. It felt so wonderfully familiar to Aurora. It reminded her of so many adventures with Kars and Lena, trips with her mother into the mountains. They would hunt and trap, collecting what they could catch.

She remembered a time where she and Kars had gotten lost for a winter night, huddled by a little fire beneath the overhang of a cliff face. It had been terribly cold, and they had woken up throughout the night to feed the fire and hold back the night. The night hurt on so many levels—hunger, cold, exhaustion, all eclipsed by a true fear that they could die.

But then she remembered one of her frigid awakenings. The last flames had retreated into the coals, but the darkness of the moonless night had not surrounded them. The details of the forest were bathed in a ghost glow. The sky danced with the cyan light of the northern aurora. She watched as her namesake washed across the stars, reds and blues dripped down from the whirls of green. Her fingers forgot the gnaw of cold as she took in the sight. The aurora danced through the stars and galaxies, a cosmic wind buffeting their delicate world. An icy gust of winter air rushed by her face.

She remembered she had wanted to share the moment with Kars. She had reached out to wake him, but before she touched him, he nodded. He was watching as well, awake and transfixed, impervious to the cold. They watched the lights sweep across the sky until the rose glow of winter dawn overtook the night.

She looked across the fire in the House of Coyote at her brother. He fitfully dozed sitting on the log, his head propped against the top of Lena's head. Aurora felt a sudden surge of love for the two of them.

"You have the look of someone who's been out there." Their companion by the fire spoke.

"I was raised in Prospector in the Cerra Mountains," Aurora responded.

The name registered with vague familiarity on the man's face. She had a moment of fear that he was searching the networks for her. Silvia had a distant gaze lost in the coals of the fire, her eyes gently slipping closed.

"That's east of here?" the man asked.

"I don't know," she said.

He seemed satisfied with the answer.

"Your friends?"

"Yes. They are from Prospector too."

"No machines?" he asked.

She shook her head. The fire popped.

"Have you been out of the city?" Aurora asked the man.

He nodded.

"I guess you liked being away from it?" Aurora asked.

He looked her in the eye.

"I came here with questions and Coyote sent me north. Did I like it? I think you already know the answer." His quiet response stoked up memories of cold nights in the mountains. She had dressed a nightlong conversation in a single flat question.

They settled back into silence until sleep arrived.

*   *   *   *   *

Aurora awoke in darkness, the warm remnants of the firepit nearby, the faint light of the city visible through the shaded skylights. Everyone was sleeping, and the camp was quiet.

She rolled over and started to settle back into sleep. Then she saw a lurking shape beyond the edge of the camp circle. She sat up and let her eyes focus in the dark.

The murky mass resolved into a furry figure. There was a wolf sitting there watching her. A moment of fear shot through her. She held totally still, perhaps if she did not move it would not see her. The wolf did not move.

You are dreaming, the wolf spoke to her mind.

Are you Coyote? Aurora asked, remembering Spiderfly's intrusions into her mind while she slept.

I am not Coyote, the wolf said. *But he is watching.*

Who are you? she asked.

I am a wolf. I don't have a name, the wolf responded. *Come with me.*

She rose from the fireside and followed the wolf into the woods. As they continued, the woods grew wilder and thicker. She fully crossed from the House of Coyote into the world of her dream.

She followed the wolf through the woods and onto a gravel road. The path opened slightly as it cut through a dense forest of cedar and fir trees. The two walked together until they came upon a stone castle. Torchlight flickered in the empty space, playing off of the rough-hewn granite blocks.

She and the wolf walked through the gate of the structure, entering the courtyard. The rectangular space was divided into several levels—the courtyard floor, a middle landing, and an upper level—connected by stairs on the outer edges. She could see the highest level had a large doorway wrought with iron hinges. Positioned in front of the door were two stately thrones.

Aurora and the wolf walked up the staircases to the top. She felt she needed to walk through the door, but when she tried to pull the doors, she discovered they were wedged in place by the empty thrones. Upon inspecting the thrones, she discovered two crowns, one in each throne. The castle was otherwise empty.

She lifted one of the crowns, seeing its ornate detail. The jewel in the center of the crown was a black diamond carved into the shape of a chess piece—the queen. The other crown matched with its own diamond carved into the shape of the king.

The wolf sniffed around the door, pawing at the ground. Aurora set down the crown and went over to the wolf. It had left hatched claw marks in the packed dirt of the platform. Aurora reached down and scooped away the loosened soil. She felt an object in the dirt. It was a large seed or perhaps a stone.

A bellowing roar burst over the castle. Aurora jumped, and the wolf crouched and pinned its ears back. There was a second thunderous roar, closer than the last. They could hear the sound of tree trunks cracking in half and branches falling. Rhythmic footfalls shook the area.

The Destroyer, we have to leave! *the wolf shouted.*

Destroyer? *she thought in a panic.* The crashing of trees grew louder. She ran.

Aurora and the wolf sprinted back to the forest, but the booming sound of the beast's stomping progress and the catastrophic cracks of tree trunks bursting did not abate. She dared not look but knew the beast must have been fifty feet tall, a mountain of horns and fur and metal. She pumped her legs and arms, running as hard has she could muster, cold terror washing through her. Yet her progress was unbelievably slow. The frustration and disbelief in her speed slowly sank beneath the surface of her terror, and she lost herself to fear.

Only because she had nothing left to do, she turned her head to see the charging monster behind her. The shadow was more than fifty feet, more of a weather event than a creature. Between her terror and the darkness, she could only discern a murky outline of spikes and animal skins and tattered leather. It seemed shrouded in a robe of smoke. The beast roared and reared up.

Her body was paralyzed in fear. She screamed—tried to scream—but no sound came forth. The beast had her.

44

The Alchemist

Aurora startled awake. Someone had rekindled the fire. There were no wolves or monsters. Silvia sat across from her, staring distantly into the flames. She barely registered Aurora. Her heart still thundering from the dream, Aurora sat up and tried to calm herself.

"A nightmare?" Silvia said quietly.

"Yes."

Silvia nodded as though she had expected this since they arrived at the House of Coyote.

"Spiderfly tests people in all sorts of ways. Octave and Beat learn from music," Aurora said. "So what is this place?"

"The House of Coyote," Silvia said. "The Curious that found people have the strange tendency to imagine worlds or even create them spontaneously."

"Dreams?"

"Yes," Silvia responded. "And other things."

"That's right, we search the wilderness of the human psyche to better understand what gives meaning." Aurora jumped as a third voice entered the conversation. Silvia still stared into the flames.

"I apologize for my late and unannounced arrival," he said, his voice deep and smooth. "My name is Jinan."

"Jinan the Alchemist," Silvia said. She looked up at him with a warm smile.

Aurora now saw the man from the darkness. He wore beige linen robes, tied at the waist. His dark beard was streaked with gray. He was lean and tall. The firelight made his dark eyes seem even darker.

"As some have called me," Jinan said. "Welcome back, Silvia Glass. I understand you came here under duress. I hope your troubles did not follow you into our House."

"Pretend as you may, Jinan, your House sits in the middle of one of the last great cities. You exist beneath layers of government and military rule."

"*Coexist*," Jinan corrected. "We coexist with Perpetual, Attila, and the other Houses. Only they do not see the role that we play in that balance."

"A static balance will eventually crumble under its weight and weather," Silvia responded.

"A point of agreement," Jinan said, "but our methods of invigorating the balance of life could not be more different. The Spider intervenes. We know there is no need to sow chaos, for entropy is the fundamental state of the cosmos. The universe will endure whatever happens on this mote of stardust floating in the void."

"I do not disagree with you," she said, "but you also know that the struggles of people, their choices, passions, and failures, are the story of this rock drifting through the universe."

"Yes," he responded. "The reason why you were allowed to pass through our door. Coyote does not open its doors freely as many of the other Curious do. Your duress was only one part of your safe harbor in House Coyote. For now, you should both come with me. Leave your companions to rest. We must speak in private."

Aurora and Silvia followed Jinan away from the fire pit. After a walk down a short path, they arrived at a small hill in the woods. Looming in the darkness, an arch of a cave opened in the side of the slope. Jinan led them inside and they descended into murkier darkness.

Finally, an orange glow seeped in from the tunnel ahead of them. They emerged into a small chamber in the rock. The room was comfortably furnished; bookshelves lined the wall, along with various glass beakers, bronze burners, and jars of colored powders. One of the walls in the cavern was made of brick, and pipes and conduits ran along it. Gaslights glowed in the space. Jinan waved his hand and a fire sprung up in the iron stove in the corner.

"Please have a seat," Jinan said, gesturing to two large armchairs. Aurora and Silvia sat.

Jinan spoke as he made tea for them.

"Few people seek out our House, even fewer stumble in on accident. And of all of them, only a handful have been here, inside of my workshop. I hope you are comfortable. I've left some of the city's infrastructure exposed as a reminder of my

436

corporeal duties in this place. As much as I would like to lose myself in Coyote's studies, someone must be the steward." He brought two cups of tea to Silvia and Aurora.

"And Coyote will not do it?" Silvia asked. Aurora, meanwhile, felt particularly quiet and reserved. The late-night arrival and her nightmare had left her feeling as though she might still be dreaming.

"Coyote cannot do it," Jinan said. "The Spiderfly kernel that gave sentience to Coyote continued to change based on experience. Coyote's mediations on the dreams and visions of people and the interplay between their conscious and unconscious created and informed Coyote. A sudden concern with the politics of the city would be a reversion. Coyote would cease to be Coyote."

Something about what he said struck Aurora. If a person stopped thinking their own thoughts, they still had a body as identity. Even then, if all of the thoughts and motivations vanished, would the person still remain?

"So you made the decision to give us safe harbor?" Silvia asked.

"No. Spiderfly and Coyote held council," Jinan said. Aurora was still adjusting to the knowledge that Spiderfly lurked in every corner of her new world. She was not sure whether she would ever feel at ease with what these the Curious meant for her. It seemed like she could not paint them in one shade or label them with a sufficient label to place them in a singular context. It was more like the nuance of a person, but with a strange incorporeal presence.

"Can we meet Coyote?" Aurora asked.

"Coyote will meet you when you are ready," Jinan said. "For now, be content with your safe haven. The details of that safe haven are why I brought you here."

Silvia had worried that their stay with Coyote came with terms attached.

"Are we part of an agreement? It would not be the first time."

"Not exactly," Jinan said. "As you know, many of the people who seek out Coyote must make an offering before they enter the House, the most frequent of which is the sojourn and renunciation of civilization.

"However," Jinan said after a lingering silence, "Coyote needs something else in place of the renunciation."

Silvia gave a solemn nod. There was some term. It was the way of the Curious.

"And what would that be?" Silvia said, unmoved. Aurora had no idea of the precariousness of their presence in this House.

"Her dream?" Jinan asked. "Coyote watched her dream. She dreamed of The Destroyer."

"How did you know?" Aurora asked, but she already knew. The wolf had told her that Coyote was watching.

"Don't be naïve, girl," Jinan said. "You knew Coyote was there and knew that it was a dream. The question is why did you dream of The Destroyer?"

"I don't know anything about it. It was a nightmare," Aurora said.

"Yes, but a nightmare of particular significance. You don't know anything about it? Can you communicate with it?" Jinan asked.

"No. I thought it was just a nightmare," Aurora said.

"First, there's no such thing as 'just a nightmare.' We run away from the things that are too big for our minds to understand. In this case, it was The Destroyer, which is somehow a construct in your unconscious mind," Jinan explained.

Silvia sprang to defend Aurora. "Who's to say it was The Destroyer? She's been through a lot recently. All sorts of material could be stirred up in her dreams."

"Her own mind called it The Destroyer, Silvia."

"Wait. Can someone please tell me, what is The Destroyer?" Aurora said.

"Now that we've established that you don't know why you dreamed of it, yes," Jinan said, glancing at Silvia for approval.

"Far to the north, past the limits of territories recognized as belonging to one group or another, deep in the wilderness, there is a robot; although, it could hardly be recognized as a robot after its time in the wilderness. The machine is the size of a building, fast and powerful as a giant animal. It mindlessly roams destroying anything and everything it comes across. Only a few people know of its existence as more than a fairytale."

Aurora remembered the creature from her nightmare. It was a terrible colossus, covered in hives. Perhaps it was like the Protek and their strange ritualistic markings.

"I really don't know, Jinan. There seem to be so many things I don't know anymore," Aurora admitted. "I feel like I have the memories of another, although I don't know why."

"Yes. Memories of another might offer some explanation. Spiderfly mentioned Alcarn," Jinan said, watching her response. "And by the look on your face, you are familiar with the name. It is a name we had not heard for many years."

Silvia shot Jinan a stern look, and he raised an eyebrow. Aurora watched as the two of them shared a series of expressions. Her frustration grew. What did they know? She resolved to find out, however she could.

"Who is Mirien Alcarn?" Aurora asked outright.

Jinan did not respond kindly to her intrusion. "Fool girl. You've paid no penance and we will pay the price on the danger that follows you. The answer to that question could cost us even after you leave," Jinan snapped, his deep voice delivered a thundering reproach. "Now leave my workshop. We will summon you if we need you."

Aurora opened her mouth to question, but Silvia cut her off.

"Go now, girl."

Aurora quickly left the chamber, before she could even process the command. She stormed back to the camp where morning's light was pouring in from the skylights above. The reptilian distrust welled up from the depths. She would protect herself.

Kars and Lena were both awake. Kars was telling a few strangers around the campfire about their village and the escape through the cave. His story telling captivated the crowd. Each cradled a tin mug full of thick coffee.

440

Kars stopped as Aurora approached.

"Morning, Ror? Where've ya been?" he asked.

"Can I talk to you and Lena for a moment?" Aurora asked.

"Sure." He immediately perceived the masked urgency of her tone. Lena got up with him, and they followed Aurora out of the camp.

"What's up?" Kars asked.

"I was just talking with Silvia and Jinan. They are keeping something important from us. I think that we need to leave." Her tone was hushed and urgent.

"We just got here, and aren't we being followed by all sorts of people?" Kars asked. He seemed critical of her plan.

"Kars, whatever they are keeping—it's important. I've asked Silvia about it and she refuses to tell me. I can't trust them," Aurora said.

"Where are we going to go if we leave?" Lena asked.

"I don't know yet. If we could get out of the city, maybe we could make our way back to the village. Anywhere. I just need to get away from them. Away from whatever Lannius is planning," Aurora said.

Kars paused, thinking on the situation. His brow furrowed.

"Do you think we can make it?" Kars asked.

"If I can use all the augmentations, I might be able to get us out, at least far enough that we could run. I was able to fight Jackal and the Pinkerton. I know I'm asking a lot of you both. Maybe I could at least get you far enough that you could find safety. We haven't had any plan except the one handed to us by Lannius."

"That's a big 'if.' Didn't Silvia block your access? How are you going to get rid of that block?" Lena asked.

"I'm going to ask to have it removed," Aurora said.

"There's no way Silvia is going to take the block down so you can run away," Kars said, shocked.

"I'm not going to ask Silvia," Aurora responded. "I think I can strike a bargain. I'm going to call Spiderfly."

"Why? Spiderfly has his own agenda," Kars said.

"Exactly," Aurora responded. "I've had it all wrong. We've just fit into their agendas. We didn't ask for anything in return. I don't think Spiderfly and Lannius have the same interests. Spiderfly wants things for itself."

Lena seemed hesitant. "I don't know if I would trust it. Maybe you don't know what you're bargaining?"

"I don't," Aurora admitted. "But I know that there's lots they aren't telling me, and I can't take the risk of what they might do with me."

"Do with you?" Lena asked.

"They treat me like some tool. I think it's something about the old memories. Maybe I'm just some memory storage container for some important person," Aurora said. "I don't think I can stay and see how that ends."

"No," Kars agreed. "I think we should go. We're with you. And you're not just a memory container."

Lena gave an emphatic nod.

Aurora closed her eyes and thought. She hoped that she could carry them, get them to safety. Whatever happened with her, she just hoped that this world would leave them alone after they escaped.

Spiderfly, Aurora thought, *I need you.*

*   *   *   *   *

Silvia and Jinan were left alone in his laboratory, but they still resorted to transmitting their thoughts. The subject matter was too sensitive for potential eavesdropping.

Drink? Jinan beamed the word and an image of an amber beverage in a tumbler.

Silvia could tell from the thought he shared that it was Brown Dog Single Malt. She nodded. Brown Dog was one of a handful of independent producers that had escaped Amurtan and the Consolidation. A sojourner must have acquired it during their travels and shared it with Jinan upon renunciation. Offering fine contraband was a peace offering to Silvia.

Jinan removed a hand-blown decanter from the shelves of various brass and glassware. He poured two glasses.

Sacrament. To our friendship. She raised the glass and took a sip with him. The liquid gleamed like crystal copper in the gas light lamps and tasted of butterscotch and maple smoke.

We've been placed in a terrible position, Silvia thought to Jinan.

Do you mean with tending to an amnesiac Mirien Alcarn or in denying the girl the information she desired? Jinan responded.

Denying the girl. The order feels like a betrayal, regardless of Lannius's reasons, Silvia thought. *No matter what he learned in his travels, there is still an innocent in our protection. And her name is Aurora.*

Jinan sensed her defiance through the message. *Is she? Or has she just forgotten who she is? And if she remembered, would she be forgetting Aurora? Silvia, you are too sentimental in your approach. The girl assumes that she is more important than she is.*

Silvia quickly responded, *I understand your point, Jinan, but I wonder if you are missing the bigger picture. Perhaps Aurora is the point. Maybe Mirien is just a memory.*

There was a pause between the two of them as Jinan played out the hypothesis. His mouth bent downward as he gave genuine interest to the implications of her proposition.

Regardless, I'm worried that we have gone too far. I was her age once. She had a vexed look that makes me fear she's going to do something rash, Silvia said.

Coyote will subdue her if she acts out in the House, Jinan responded.

I'm not so worried about what she could do in here. Is there any way that she could get out? Silvia asked.

No, Jinan responded, *not unless she has help.*

45

The Hall of Doorways

Aurora was not sure exactly how calling Spiderfly would work. Was it like calling a genie? Would he spontaneously appear when she called his name? She knew by this point that he was watching every moment, and that he had been gently shaping her path to this point. She was about to take his love of disrupting the system to a logical conclusion: disrupting his own plan.

Spiderfly, she repeated the thought, *if you can hear me, I need you.*

Could Spiderfly even reach her while she was in the House of Coyote? It seemed like these Houses had different levels of jamming and interference toward the different layers of the network. She waited with her thoughts, but there was no response.

Spiderfly. She would try one more time. It could be anything: whether he could hear her, whether he wanted to help here, whether he could help her. She might be shouting into a void.

Then he responded, *Yes?* His voice chimed in her head. It hung with syrupy satisfied menace. *You called.*

Aurora didn't know where to go from here. She had rehearsed calling out and a response but composed herself.

I need to leave the city. I need help escaping, she thought into the network. She was not sure what level she was communicating through, but it seemed to work.

Why do you want to access to such a perilous place? Spiderfly responded, toying with the question.

I am already in peril, Aurora answered.

You'll have to tell me what sort of peril before I grant you such a request, Spiderfly said.

People claim to look out for my interests. I do not trust them, Aurora explained.

And why not? Spiderfly continued his questioning.

They won't tell me about Mirien Alcarn.

Then why not ask me about Mirien Alcarn? Spiderfly asked.

Aurora paused, asking herself the question. That seemed a much more straightforward route to her intrigue.

Who is Mirien Alcarn? Aurora asked.

You won't get it that easy, Spiderfly answered.

The question smoldered in her mind. The other memories had drowned her and educated her. She had remembered Lannius before hearing his name. Mirien Alcarn's memories had given her information essential to her survival—let her battle Jackal, restarted her mind in the dream, helped them escape the Pinkerton—yet it still felt like scorpions filled her mind. Sometimes her mind was not her own.

What will it take? Aurora challenged.

The same terms as last time: yourself, Spiderfly said, menacingly. *I will tell you about Mirien Alcarn, but then you give me your mind. I could help all of you out of the city too. Safety for your friends.*

Aurora sensed the trick; it was a short deal. The realization felt somehow liberating.

No deal, Spiderfly, she responded.

Good, Spiderfly said.

Is there anything else you want? Aurora thought.

In exchange for the identity of Mirien Alcarn? No. There's nothing else that will satisfy the bargain short of yourself.

Aurora tried to think her way around the trick. *Fine. No deal,* she thought to Spiderfly. *Now back to my original request: I need help escaping, and I need access to the personal layer. What do you need in exchange?*

I like this new attitude! Down to business. Bold. The only issue is that you have so little to give, Spiderfly said.

Name your price.

There was a long pause. Aurora had never seen the Curious think for such a period. She was suddenly aware of her surroundings. Kars looked up as she refocused. Lena watched expectantly. The Spider's silence continued. She grew nervous for what was looming in her future. She was dealing with the Master of Bargains.

I've thought of my terms. Spiderfly returned. *In exchange for the block being lifted, someday, at time of my choosing, you must disobey someone.*

Who? Aurora responded.

Anyone. You will only know when I call my request, Spiderfly responded. *And you will answer.*

Aurora thought through the request. At first, it felt strangely ironic as she was asking for his help in order to betray Silvia. But the request felt dangerous in its indefiniteness. Anytime? Anyone? The term was very specific though—disobey. She looked at Kars and Lena, watching her and trusting her.

What about Kars and Lena? Are they part of this betrayal?

Yes, Spiderfly responded.

You can't ask me to betray them, Aurora responded. Kars had noticed his sister was watching him with concern.

Oh, I can and may—should you take the deal, Spiderfly menaced. *What is trust worth to you? Is your mistrust in the others greater than the cost of your loyalty?*

Aurora looked at her friends once more, seeing them for all their vulnerability. Without access, could she protect them? Her stomach twisted as she tried to measure a certain danger with an unknown threat.

Tell me, Spiderfly. Are you helping me?

More than you'll ever know, Spiderfly responded.

She continued to process his offer. The indefiniteness could mean that he never even called his payment. She thought about Silvia and Jinan still in their conversation in his cave. They could return any moment.

Please don't make me betray them, Aurora said.

Deal or no deal? Spiderfly responded.

Aurora bit her lip and glanced over her shoulder. Silvia could appear at any time to keep them from their escape. The mass of augmentations teemed in her mind, and the fear that she was just a living box full of another's memories surged through her.

Okay. I agree, Aurora sent in response.

The deal is done. Don't get yourself in any trouble. Try to use those tricks we taught you—stay hidden. You'll know when I'm ready for my payment.

And that was how she gained access to the personal layer.

"We're good," she said to Kars and Lena. She did not want to explain.

Squire teetered up. "Aurora, you are projecting on the personal layer. I must block the signals."

Aurora looked around to see what she was projecting. Just at the edge of the wooded area, the wolf from her dream sat watching them. She felt a wave of embarrassment displace her pride, and the wolf turned and disappeared in the woods.

"No, Squire. That will be fine. Spiderfly removed the block. We need to leave immediately. Can you find us a back door to this building?"

"Should we not wait for Ms. Glass?" Squire's tenor voice carried some concern.

"We need to leave now," Aurora repeated.

"I will query Coyote for an exit," Squire said.

"No!" Aurora demanded. "Lannius said we need to leave immediately without alerting anyone."

"I did not receive any messages," Squire said, sounding innocently perplexed.

Aurora continued to lie. "I got the message while I was sleeping."

"He must have been using the unconscious layer, although it's strange there was no transmitter. Perhaps there is a new technique," Squire surmised.

"Either way, we need to leave now," Aurora said.

Kars looked into the trees surrounding them in the arboreal forest of the House of Coyote. He bounced on his toes and sweat formed across his palms.

"According to the records, there is an access point to the utility conduit that runs beneath this structure. It seems that the building has some access points throughout. Follow me." Squire led them through the forest.

Aurora felt a charged sense of victory and doubt. She had duped the little robot and mortgaged some part of her future. Who knew what would happen out in the city if they even managed to escape?

They followed the robot down one of the footpaths in the House of Coyote. Aurora looked around for the glorious extravagance of the personal layer, longing to see imagination given form once more, but there were no grand illusions. Instead, she only saw shadowy beings just beyond the trees, shades of leaf and mottled fur hiding at the edge of her vision. The beings watched them as they made their way along the paths that carved through the glades of the House. Their eyes glowed red and gold and sapphire beyond the trees.

Squire led them through the woods to a small clearing. In its center there was a rather primitive looking hatch. Kars tried to spin the round handle, but it wouldn't move.

Squire said, "The hatch is protected by Coyote and basic security."

I'll throw Coyote off your trail, Spiderfly said to Aurora. *The rest is up to you.*

Aurora probed the plain lock and found an intricate process woven into its mechanism. She thought into the process, looking at the different glyphs and connections that her mind projected to represent the lock. It felt good to her to use the tools she had only recently discovered and then had been blocked from. She sensed some sort of turbulence in the aether. It must have been Spiderfly and Coyote interacting at their point of attack. Spiderfly was true to the deal, slowing Coyote from pursuit.

Sweat prickled across her brow as Aurora wrestled with the processes within the lock. She tried to shunt her fear, knowing distractions barred her from her goal. Her pinky drummed against her finger and she bit her tongue. Finally, the processes snapped into place and the lock clicked open.

At the bottom, the hatch opened onto a long ladder descending into a shaft. Squire climbed back into Aurora's bag with the other supplies and artifacts that she carried. Aurora started down the ladder, telling Kars and Lena that she was probably best equipped to descend first. They waited at the top.

The utility conduit was a clean concrete space with white bar lights running along the crown of the corners. The walls were lined with thick cables and pipes. It was a kind of pragmatic artery buried beneath the technological gem of a city that was East Bay. Aurora sensed tiny maintenance robots by points of their processes throughout the tunnel. They were arachnid in their design, like tiny mining machines.

Kars and Lena hopped off the ladder moments later, their weeks of physical training evident in the speed at which they climbed.

"Alright, I admit it, I never know what's going on any more," Kars said. "Which way?" He looked either way down the tunnel.

"We're going that way," Aurora said, repeating the instruction that Squire had beamed to her.

A short distance from the shaft, they came across two doors on either side of the hallway, one labeled *Emerald Glass*, the other labeled *Cerulean Glance*. The doors were thick metal with no windows. The neat labels were a departure from the utilitarian reserve of the rest of the conduit. The writing was lavish script engraved on an ornate bronze plate.

They continued walking and passed another set of doors. It had the same bronze labels with fine script: *Tangerine Mirror. Vermillion Crater. Rose Spire.* The cables and pipes diverted around the doors in neat elbows of conduits.

"Aurora, do you know what these are? Are we still in Coyote's House?" Lena asked.

"I'm not sure."

The conduit path opened into a central chamber. Several other paths led to the chamber like spokes on a hub. The cables and pipes crossed and interwove, running through each other and out of a point in the center of the ceiling.

A low voice startled them as they entered the room. It came from a small, bespectacled man sitting at a desk.

"Hello, may I help you?"

Aurora attempted to bury her anxiety. She had blundered into the second test of her control of the personal layer. She queried Squire in her pack for any information that he could provide, but he returned nothing.

"Um, yes. We were just looking for the exit," she said.

"The ground floor has a street level exit," he said. "Unless you were looking for an 'exit' through one of the Doorways," he said with a thin smile, crooking his fingers in the air into quotation marks.

"No, not exactly. I think we were just passing through," Aurora said.

"Well then allow me to lead you back upstairs. Bean will help you to the front door."

Aurora tensed, but Kars intervened.

"I'm sorry, friend, I didn't catch your name?" Kars said, pouring sudden charm.

"I'm Orvis. I am the Keeper of the Doorways."

"Well, Orvis," Kars said, rolling past the honorific. "Bean's actually a bit of our problem. I was just tagging along with my friend when she came to the House. I don't even have augmentations. I got in a bit of a card game with Bean, and he didn't exactly like the outcome. I may have said something about his name too. You know how these things go, and you've seen him, he could squash me like a bug."

Lena hid her smile as a rather confused look spread across Orvis's face.

"Actually, I'm not sure that I understand," Orvis said. "I don't get out much. But yes, Bean is a formidable opponent. I think that I could help. I could show you out through the Breakwater."

"Perfect!" Kars said, clapping his hand on the scrawny man's shoulder.

The confused look turned to a confused smile. "Just let me get my keys, and we'll be right on our way." Orvis produced a large ring of keys that looked identical to Lena's master key. He hooked it on his belt beneath his long robe.

"Thank you so much, Orv," Kars said. "You should've seen the look on the big guy's face. It was a mean Bean scene if you know what I mean." He elbowed Orvis. Aurora looked at him in disbelief.

"I'm beginning to understand Bean's perspective," Orvis said, in an almost resigned tone. "Right this way."

Orvis lead them down one of the spoke corridors. They continued to pass the curious labeled doorways. *Byzantium Shore. Sable Ink. Jade Hammer.* The strange names flowed by as they followed Orvis through the hallways.

"So you've no desire to pass through the Doorways?" Orvis asked as they walked.

"Actually, I'm guessing that I couldn't if I wanted to—no augmentations," Kars said.

"No augmentations?" Orvis asked incredulously.

"That's right—none." Kars saw Orvis inspecting him, so he offered his prepared excuse. "Came in as a refugee a few years ago, been working hard security."

"Oh, well. You should definitely consider getting some. The newest versions grow in just a few weeks and barely cause any side effects. Just a fever and a headache, some disorientation and discombobulation, and the dramatic need to sleep for long periods."

"That's all?" Kars said.

Orvis smiled a toothy smile at Kars. "That's all—kids these days have it easy."

"Must've been pretty rugged for you?"

"Rugged. Yes. You don't even want to know," Orvis responded.

"You're probably right," Kars said. "So, on a different note, what are all these doors?" He decided to steer the conversation away from the topic of augmentations, as it would inevitably lead to scrutiny of Aurora.

"These are the Doorways of Coyote," Orvis said. "These halls house the masterwork of human thought."

"That's all?" Kars asked, prodding old Orvis for another response.

The bespectacled man rolled his eyes. "Each leads to another world. Some people who sought Coyote dreamed of other worlds, found them through a drug, or just uncovered them within their own imagination. Coyote found a way to stabilize the others' worlds, creating a Doorway. They are totally different worlds, places with different laws of physics and different manifestations of time and space. We are cataloguing them like the elements. Each world is unique, like the colors of the spectrum."

The explanation seemed opaque to Kars. It terrified Aurora. Behind each of these doors there was a person held in a trance, their mind stabilized into a gateway to an imaginary alien world as robust and complete as their own. Her mind swam with the implications of the Doorways. They passed by two more, *Azure Wind* and *Onyx Smoke*.

"Nice names," Kars said.

"Yes, the host of the Doorway always attempts to capture the essence of their experience when they enter the catalogue."

"So these worlds, do they actually exist?" Kars asked.

"Does ours?" Orvis responded.

"Orv, if you unplug the Doorway from Coyote and someone else is using their augmentations, are they stuck on the other side?"

"Their body stays here the whole time, and they will just wake up," Orvis said. "So, no, these are virtual universes contained in the minds of individuals. But there's no complete evidence ours is any different."

"Still, pretty neat trick. You're making me really consider getting a set of augmentations," Kars lied.

"I think that you'd find it a satisfactory investment," Orvis said. "I think your friend agrees."

Aurora blushed as Orvis nodded to her. She had been trying so hard to mask that feeling. How could civilization run with no privacy? She had also started to hear Silvia trying to beam a message to her. Aurora ignored the calls.

"Don't worry about it," Orvis said. "I don't mean to pry. We're just about to the exit anyway."

The corridor terminated at a bulkhead door with another large round latch. They paused at the doors.

"I'll ask again, are you sure that you want to use this exit? The Breakwater can be a dangerous place. There are rarely patrols down here to keep the peace."

"We will be fine. Thank you taking us to the exit," Aurora responded–they were counting on the lack of patrols.

"I'll keep an eye out for Bean." Orvis winked at them. Then he gave the handle a great turn. The door swung open. The three of them stepped out of the House of Coyote and into the Breakwater.

46

The Breakwater

Surrounded by light surveillance equipment, Marcus Stormgard watched from a building across from the House of Coyote. The hulking doorman admitted a few lonesome and worn travelers carrying huge packs over the course of the evening, but none left. Marcus forced himself to stay awake through the night, documenting the comings and goings at the House.

Then, sometime after dawn, the door opened. A visibly upset Silvia Glass stepped out. Marcus watched as she and the doorman shared a rapid exchange before she stormed back into the building. Alone. Had they both missed them leaving the House?

Marcus played through a time-lapse of his surveillance. No one had left through the front door. But for Silvia to be so perturbed, they must also be outside of the House. Marcus raised an eyebrow and called up the logs for the infrastructure in the area, using the Securitor network to access the utilities.

Then he saw it. Someone had accessed the utility conduits this morning. He cursed himself for allowing such a hole in his net. No doubt they had help from the Spider. Whoever had picked the lock had been sloppy about it. Then later, there was unscheduled access of the conduits where they met the Breakwater.

"Gotcha," he said to himself. They were in the Breakwater.

He accessed one of the super-secure channels of the Securitor network, tracing access points to the Breakwater. After finding a large access tunnel, he summoned a hovercraft to meet him at the location. A driverless podcycle rolled up at his command and stopped in front of the building in which he was staying.

He packed up the equipment that he had brought, hurried downstairs and boarded the podcycle. He would find them in the Breakwater before they were back in Silvia's or Spiderfly's control. The podcycle lunged forward. After the embarrassment at the House of Octave and Beat, it was going to be a good day.

*   *   *   *   *

"No, Silvia, I'm sure that they didn't come this way," Bean said apologetically.

She frowned, panic setting in. If they hadn't come this way, then they must still be in the House, unless they had managed to find a separate way out of the structure.

It had been pleasant meeting with Jinan, sharing a drink and a conversation. So often they were lost in the business of their own Houses. Nonetheless, her meeting with Jinan had continued too long. Silvia cursed herself for allowing the luxury of a conversation. She should have left with Aurora. The girl had been through too much to be dismissed like that.

Jinan, are there other ways out of this House?

Yes. There are many Doorways to the House of Coyote.

Silvia would have smacked him if they had been in the same space. Their insistence on celebrating the magic of the House

Curious was wearing at times. Fortunately for her, Spiderfly inspired little of the sycophantic love.

Cut the crap, Jinan. How did the kids get out of the House? Silvia thought.

I do not know, Jinan responded, his serenity still holding through their messages.

Silvia felt a bolt of anger. Spiderfly.

Why didn't you tell me? When did you know? Silvia asked.

Only a moment ago, Jinan responded. *It appears that there was some interference in our security.*

"Spiderfly!" Silvia shouted.

Yes? the Curious responded with a slow drawl, appearing with a wicked smile in her mind.

Why? What did I do to deserve this? We are supposed to be protecting them, Silvia thought to Spiderfly.

Do not presume my prerogative or my methods.

Of course not, Silvia responded. *You and Lannius both— methods and motives are above the soldier's paygrade. Silvia always will follow.*

Why are you loyal, then?

Sometimes her frustration with the Spider crystallized into hate.

Maybe I'll change. She closed off her mind, feeling her own rage seething. Spiderfly no doubt enjoyed the dimensions of her own feeling and history she revealed in the moment. She would not feed him anymore—besides, she had to find the kids.

Beyond her anger with the Curious, Silvia was flabbergasted but impressed that the three youths had slipped her escort. It might bode well for their escape. They had made it out without alerting her. Maybe they stood a chance. She breathed a sigh of relief that they had not gone through any of the Doorways. That was one of the projects the Curious had undertaken since they spun out of the Spiderfly kernel that scared her most. Strange and terrible things lurked behind those elegant plaques. The House of Coyote delved further into the abyssal dark of the human mind than she thought was appropriate.

Thank you for your cooperation, Jinan, she beamed the thought to him and shared one of the many countermeasures they had developed during the Rebellion. *This might help with future intruders.*

Jinan did not respond, likely going to lick the wounds on his ego.

Silvia pulled up an infrastructure map of the area, assigning part of her consciousness to the task of walking her body to an access shaft. The map showed the bottom half of East Bay. During the early days of climate change, sea levels rose at an alarming rate, and the architects of the city had attempted to build sea walls to hold back the ocean. The fortifications inevitably failed as the waters continued to rise and the storms surged, leading to large sections of the city being inundated by the rising ocean. All but the poorest people and businesses relocated to higher ground, but the buildings and infrastructure remained, abandoned to the tides.

After the Consolidation War, after more extreme waves of climate change and the near collapse of the ocean food system, only a few or the major cities remained. The population of East Bay swelled with an unfathomable number of refugees. The space above the flooded forgotten neighborhoods was suddenly at a premium again. The next generation of city architects, however, would not make the mistake of trying build on fill while trying to hold back the ocean; they decided to build above it, turning the old inundated wards into an urban estuary. The new roads had been built with subtle translucent brick sections, fine mesh grates, and airshafts to allow the ecosystem to thrive. Building a sewer had not been the architect's purpose. It had been to create a living barrier island subject to tides and natural life that would regenerate and protect the city above from future super storms. In essence, the glittering new sections of East Bay were built on the bones of the old city. The marshland beneath had come to be called the Breakwater.

The map filled her focus, showing the interlocking utility conduits and the ragged canals of the Breakwater beneath the House of Coyote.

Spiderfly, Arc, she sent the message to her comrades.

Yes, Silvia? It was Arc.

Are you following my situation? Silvia asked.

As soon as you pulled up the map, I shared the facts of your situation, Arc updated her.

Can you reach them while I catch up with them in the Breakwater? she asked.

I have nothing. I don't know if we have any connections down there. I'm sorry I'm not more help.

I think that they are on their own, Spiderfly said. *They will be fine.*

Silvia didn't feel comforted. She remembered Jinan saying that they would not be able to leave without help.

Spider. You helped them escape? Silvia dared to ask.

We made a deal, Spiderfly responded.

Silvia reached out to her bag of tricks, even though she knew her attacks and countermeasures could not touch an artificial intelligence like Spiderfly. She wanted to scream. Working with Spiderfly was impossible. She hoped that the deal was worth it to both of them.

Enjoy your deals and tricks, Silvia sent to the AI, lacing the message with layers of her anger, frustration, and disappointment. She slid down the ladder into the utility conduit. *I'll keep cleaning up the mess.*

*   *   *   *   *

The door to the House of Coyote shut behind them and they stood at the edge of a small catwalk in the Breakwater. Shafts of sunlight lanced down through the intermittent frosted glass brick grids nearly fifty feet above. Shadows of people and cars crossed the sunbeams, heightening the sense of quiet in the Breakwater. Below them was still green water, alive with marsh plants and lily pads. Disintegrating automobiles loomed just beneath the surface.

Old brick building storefronts sat half submerged, while the tops of the buildings had been incorporated into the concrete and steel supports of the new city above. Cables arced above the water that filled the old streets between forgotten buildings. Large fish lazily coasted just beneath the surface. The still air smelled more of marsh than city. Birds called and darted between long ago shattered windows. Sand bars pushed up in the middle of intersections, dotted with dune grasses and stilt-legged birds.

The catwalk that Aurora, Kars, and Lena stood on doubled back on switchbacks until it reached a concrete embankment below. Whatever architects had envisioned this place had left a bank to the vast urban marsh. As they reached the edge, Aurora, Kars, and Lena paused to get their bearings and take in their surroundings. The shadows of the city commute above continued to pass across the sunbeams coming through the glass brick ceiling.

"What is this place?" Kars asked. He seemed in a daze from the sudden changes in surroundings.

"We are in the old Harbor ward, now known colloquially as the Breakwater," Squire said from Aurora's bag. "The area flooded several times after which reclamation efforts were abandoned. After the Consolidation War, a new set of planners and architects redesigned the space into a living flood plain and tidal surge shield. Essentially, we are standing beneath the pier on which the new city is built."

"This place opens to the bay?" Kars asked.

"Yes. Actually, it is more correct to say that it is part of the bay," Squire said.

Aurora noted the slick mud just above the waterline—low tide. It might be hard going, but they could take this waterway out of the city.

"Let's keep moving. Who knows if we've been followed," Aurora said.

They picked their way along the shoreline, maneuvering between soft mud patches, old vehicles wrapped in vegetation, and stands of cattails. They had to make several detours at points where the shoreline met deep water. Sometimes, they were able to access catwalks like the one they had used to enter the Breakwater. Other times, the catwalks would place them on the roofs of the abandoned city. The infrastructure from the city above reached down into the flooded ruin, storing large flow battery installations and redundant server blocks out of the sight of the citizens that needed it.

After some time of weaving through the catwalks, rooftops, and shorelines of the Breakwater, they emerged from an opening into the old city. Aurora crouched low, signaling to her friends to follow.

Peering down from the parapet of one of the rooftops, they saw what seemed to be a city plaza left to a century of nature. Unlike the rest of the Breakwater, however, this space was not abandoned. They looked down on a small village.

People walked on raised wooden paths running between ramshackle buildings on stilts and refurbished spaces in the old inundated buildings. A few people fished off the edges of the walkways, while others pulled up crab pots and dug for mussels in the tide-exposed mud. Metal fire pits held small smoky fires. The Breakwater had a city of its own.

"Who do you think lives down here?" Kars asked.

"I'm not sure," Aurora said. "But it's probably better to avoid them, right?"

"Can't hurt to steer clear," Lena agreed.

"Well, it depends. Where exactly are we trying to go, Aurora?" Kars asked.

"I think it's best to try to make it to the docks at the harbor. It'd be easiest for us to get out of the city by sea. Stowaway or something." As she said it, she realized how desperate and farfetched her plan had become.

"You're pretty hell-bent on getting away from here," Kars said.

"You don't know what it's like!" Aurora snapped. "It's like they know I'm not myself, like there's some other secret person living in my mind! They treat me like I'm some valuable, delicate prize. Or like some kind of dangerous demon. I wish I could just give them what they want so I could go on with my life!"

Kars looked at her with patient sympathy. It was unfair what she was going through. The past now pulled at her, and she fought the strings tying her to the masterminds.

"I'm sorry," Aurora said, composing herself. "I just don't know what to think. For all I know, I'm just living storage for someone else's memories. And no, I don't know where to go."

"We understand," Lena said. "And I think I have an idea. Silvia mentioned a city where Perpetual and the military AI refused to go. I think it was called Sol. While it didn't sound ideal, maybe we could go there? Get a chance to make a plan and start over."

"She called it the mad city," Kars said. "Lena and I might be fine with no augmentations, but what about you Aurora?"

"Mad city? I'm not sure it would be much worse than my life now. No one understands," Aurora said. "At the very least we could get you there, and maybe then I'll figure something out. Maybe it's a place where we could regroup to find the people from home."

Aurora thought about it for a moment. Sol, the Mad City. Could it really be their refuge?

"Is it right?" Aurora questioned herself aloud. "Do we leave?"

Lena and Kars were silent. They heard the distant rumble of the city above the gentle sounds of the village below them. Aurora felt a pang of sadness though, thinking about leaving this city so soon. The joy of dancing with her friends in the House of Octave and Beat was still fresh, and she longed to see more of the incredible spectacles she had seen just walking the streets. Her deal with Spiderfly would come with a heavy price if she never used the personal layer, but his price might never be redeemed if she ran away to Sol. If she got away from Lannius and Perpetual, there would be no one to betray. They would be free.

"I don't know. I just don't know. What if I'm wrong about all of this?"

"Aurora! You're the one that needed to run. You said we needed to get away from Lannius. Sol is probably as far away as we can get on the planet," Kars snapped. "You're asking Lena and I like *any* of these decisions have been ours to make."

"They have been. We left together. You said that we are all in this together," Aurora responded, hurt.

"We are. Lena and I are here with you—together," her brother responded. "But that doesn't mean we've made any decisions. We're hanging on just the same. At least you have some choice in the matter."

It didn't help Aurora feel any better. She thought for another moment. Was it Lannius that she was running away from? No. It wasn't Silvia or even the curious AIs they had met. It was not even the looming specter of Perpetual or the gathering thunderheads of the military AIs. She was running from Mirien Alcarn and whatever Mirien meant to her. She was running from the fear that whatever dormant memories or unconscious person lurked in her mind might return to claim her place.

"Kars. Lena. I'm sorry. I don't know if I have a choice either. There's this name they keep saying—Mirien Alcarn. They keep saying that I am Mirien Alcarn!"

"Aurora, I," Lena hesitated, "I've heard the name before."

Aurora looked at her. An awful weight seemed to set in Aurora's features, a wave of a new reality crashing on her face.

"Tell me." It was all she could muster.

"Aurora, it was something my father used to say when he had too much to drink and I'd leave. The times when I couldn't bear to see him," Lena said. "I'd leave for your house, and he'd say 'hide with Em and that Alcarn girl.'"

They knew too, Aurora thought. Her whole life was part of Lannius's plot. *Aurora Koren* was the plot. Mirien was the one who was trapped. Did Em know?

"They knew," Aurora said. Her face seemed to age and grow cold.

468

"Ror, maybe it was just a coincidence. Ben might have just been saying something without any idea," Kars said, wary.

"Did you know?" Her voice simmered low and hot.

"No! Of course not! Ror, I was just trying to say maybe there was something else!"

"Kars, don't try to placate me with speculation you know to be a lie!" Aurora's words crashed down upon him, frightening and unfamiliar.

"I was just—"

"You were just trying to make it disappear," Aurora snapped, "trying to make the ugly reality that everyone I know has lied to me my entire life disappear? Well, that's not—"

"Not everyone!" Lena snapped. "Aurora. It wasn't just you. We were lied to as well. They used *our* hearts and *our* lives to lie to you. He's still your brother. You should treat him that way."

The words struck like a hammer on hot irons. Kars watched with a kind of awe as these two fierce women collided in their argument. He had been battered by Aurora's sudden rage, rolled back into his role as a younger brother. But Lena, she stood tall against the challenge, said what he needed to say. The rooftop was quiet, and he had a sudden concern that the small village below would notice.

The two women were oblivious. Aurora glared at Lena, who returned the gaze knowing she had the moral high ground.

"Aurora, I know you must be hurt and confused, but you've got to know that we are too. We'll figure it out together," Lena said.

Aurora looked like her anger might melt, but the moment shattered as the whine of repulsors filled the air. Their pursuers had arrived.

47

Trapped

Lena and Aurora cocked their heads toward the sudden noise and ducked behind the edge of the roof. Kars threw himself down next to them. The people of the village scattered down the catwalks as they heard the whine.

"What is it? Did you see it?" Aurora hissed.

"I didn't see anything," Lena said.

Aurora pressed her back against the wall. How could she have been so simple? They should have kept moving!

"Ror! It's almost on us!" Kars said, dropping back behind the short wall.

Aurora did not respond. She held her head in her hands.

"Pull it together, Ror," Lena hissed.

Kars was on his feet, dragging his sister up by her sleeve. He checked the tabula to see if it was responding in any way.

The whine of the repulsors reached a crescendo. Lena peered over the side of the building. A snub-nose rectangular barge floated above the water next to the wooden walkways. A small squad of armored men and floating drones scrambled down the gangplanks.

"I can't go." Aurora rocked against the parapet. "I don't want to be someone else."

"Aurora. We need to go! Snap out of it," Lena said, forcing Aurora to look into her eyes. "If you don't want to be someone else, fight."

Aurora nodded and exhaled. She forced her mind to channel focus. She couldn't let her friends face this alone. They had come too far, and she had given up too much. Her pinky started to twitch, but she stopped herself. She would do this on her own.

"I'm here," Aurora said, forcing certainty into her voice. "And they are going to regret coming for us."

They ran for the rooftop doorway to the stairs, hurtling into the dark floors of the building. Aurora felt the drones as they swarmed the building, their processes glowing like lanterns behind the walls.

The strangeness of her augmentations awakened within her. While she had flexed these muscles training with Spiderfly, she had not truly let them rage since the battles in the wilderness. Now her strange skills roared, pulling at their leashes to be unchained. It felt intoxicating. She let her awareness expand, pulsing out through the delicate bubbles of the personal layer of each of the officers entering the building. What would they see in this building? She mulled her decision, her rage simmering. Aurora became the wolf, black smoke writhing down the stairs before them, tendrils clamoring beneath doorjambs and prying at windows. She could sense the men were trained, and their personal layers formed armored crystals in her perception. She smiled a snarl that was barely her own. Their defenses would not keep her out. She would still get through.

Kars and Lena sprinted down the stairs, unaware of the cyber warfare that had already begun. Beams of flashlights wildly arced through the air below them as the men stormed up the building. Kars threw a shoulder against one of the exit doors, nearly breaking the old door off its hinges. They plunged into a dank hallway, scattering dry leaves and other leftover debris from before the Breakwater. They ducked into a room.

"Aurora, what's going on? Can you tell us anything?" Kars whispered.

Aurora had a wild grin on her face. She took a moment before she responded. "Fools thought they could stop me with just a few countermeasures. They shouldn't have brought their drones," she said, distant, as though she was talking to herself.

"Yes. But how are we going to get out of here?" Kars asked.

"I'm taking care of it," Aurora said.

Shrieks and the chaotic pounding of boot steps sounded from outside.

If they could have seen beyond their room, they would have seen the drones turn on their companions. The angry swarm turned their stun prods on the squad. Some were knocked out by the first hit, while others recoiled and shrieked from the strong electrical sting. The men tried to run, but Aurora's drones were systematic in pushing them back from their hovercraft. After a few minutes, the drones outside circled around the floating craft.

"It's safe. I've got us our ride out of the city," Aurora said. "Walk out the front door. We're going to take their ship."

Kars looked at Aurora, wide eyed. Lena's expression wavered with doubt. Aurora faced them and crossed her arms, as though to make her point that they had no choice. Neither protested. Silent, they left the room and cautiously proceeded down the stairs.

The bottom floor was a mess of unconscious and moaning troopers. Their uniforms were adorned with an official looking emblem, but none made an effort to stop them as they picked their way toward the door. As they approached the open double doors, Kars saw the ring of drones spaced around the floating craft. It felt surreal that they were just going to walk out of the building and board this massive craft as though it was waiting for them.

They managed a few steps out of the door before the ooze struck.

There was a pop like a giant bubble bursting. The sudden warm wave of viscous liquid crash into Kars first. The force of the unnaturally heavy material nearly knocked him from his feet. He tried to move, but the ooze expanded into foam, trapping his legs and arms.

Lena tried to jump, but the liquid caught her. the foam hardening and holding her in place. The foam squeezed against her chest as she tried to squirm free.

Aurora tried to leap out of the way but the ooze gushed around her limbs in a slow wave. It was cold against her skin as it expanded, then nearly burned her as it cured into a crisp foam. She turned to the drones to help, but they fell out of the air if they responded to her thoughts at all. Rage boiled up inside her as the foam hardened on her limbs. Her instincts lashed out through the augmentations before a restraining block fell in place in her mind. She felt the torrent welling up behind the block, picking at symbolic points in the wall of the block, but she found no traction. Her mind was trapped.

The Chime? Would the Curious help? She tried to picture the spinning orbs, tried to call up the sound in her augmentations. The Chime of Spheres orbited in her imagination, accelerating as she focused. Relief washed over her as the tone began to ring through her mind.

Then the spheres in her mind started to wobble on their axis, off-balance and vibrating at an increasing rate. The sound turned to discord as the spheres cracked and blew away on an imaginary wind. The Curious could not help. She was alone.

After a few minutes of warmth trapped in the curing foam, the side door of the hovercraft slid open. A tall, muscular man emerged with a confident grin on his face. He strode up to them with his hands tucked behind his back.

"Marcus Stormgard, Chief of the East Bay Office of the Securitor. You are under arrest for destruction of property, unregistered augmentations, aiding a known terrorist, aiding a known rogue AI, and are wanted in conjunction with an act of criminal mischief. Not sure what kind of trouble you've gotten yourselves into, but I'm going to sort it out. You have the right to remain silent, you have the right to ..."

Aurora lost track of what he was saying as their rights continued. It had finally happened. Through their entire journey, something intervened, or luck spat them out somewhere safe, but not this time. She struggled against the foam, felt for Squire,

475

tried to tear out of her prison. There was no one to help. They had been captured.

48

Revolt

The sleeping giant within the townspeople roared to life. It began in a moment. A single unmarked trooper ran to the gate of the enclosure, unlocked the latch, and sprinted away. The fastest and fiercest poured out and split into separate groups.

Em led her own group into the camp. She snarled as she imagined smashing the skeleton crew at the armory before they could mount a defense. The still air seemed to hum with the energy of a gathering storm. She jogged with a cadre of trusted friends, moving at a determined pace.

Her raiding group continued through the dusty pathways of the camp, surprising the guards who thought they had an afternoon off from regular camp duties. One went for his rifle, but Em knocked him out without a sound and took the weapon. She tossed the rifle to a companion, opting for an axe hanging with the fire suppression equipment. Em appraised the weapon, passing it between her hands. It had decent balance and the head held its edge. She gestured her group forward with a flick of her two fingers, and they continued following the path to the armory.

Em had fought and killed people before but hoped that she would not have to call on that cruel aspect of herself. She didn't notice her palms were dry on the shaft of axe. Each step was a

477

silent moment between her and her senses, a potential decision ready to burst in a flash of violence.

They reached the armory when the storm broke. It was a low-profile, reinforced building near the empty aircraft landing pad. Two guards had set up a small table, and they were drinking beer in the shade of the awning. The first guard saw them and lost himself in a moment of confusion.

Em saw the realization crystallize in his mind. He flailed, failing to stand and draw his weapon, and his misplaced effort sent the table flying. His chair toppled backward as he sprang to his feet. He was fast, but a momentary fumble for his sidearm proved his undoing.

The savagery overwhelmed Em as he started to raise his pistol from his hip to her chest. In some peripheral awareness she felt her companions react, their shouts crashing through the silence. Fear filled the guard's eyes, and Em read his intent to kill her. She swung the axe downward.

The second guard screamed and fell backward out of his chair. He tried to scramble and run into the shelter of the armory. Two of Em's men leapt on his back before he could cross the threshold. He shouted, and they shouted back as they held his face against the ground.

"Set up here," Em ordered. "Tie him, gag him, until we've got everything else secure. We'll sort out whoever's left."

She felt as though her voice was coming from some distant command center in her mind. The body of the guard sagged against the wall of the building. Em felt the rise of bile in her throat that came whenever she killed someone. She quashed her response—they had started this battle, and her children might depend on her escaping this prison. She left the body and entered the armory.

Em tossed weapons and body armor to her retinue without ceremony, and they suited up for the next stage of the takeover. The townsfolk had seamlessly returned to their days of guerilla warfare, and they moved with the silken efficiency of a military unit.

Deliberate moves saved time in the long run, but Em knew they had to operate with some haste for the other part of the takeover. They would need to take over the communications to keep the remnant forces from calling for support. If Perpetual kept one camp in the desert, there might be others available to respond.

Em grabbed the remaining guard and jabbed her weapon in his gut.

"You're going to take us to the radios," Em said, "or I'll make you wish you were your buddy over there."

"Please! I didn't want to do this. They took me. They were going to kill my—"

"Shut up," Em grunted. "Just take us to the radios."

The communications building was a two-story structure, retrofitted on a relic pre-war building. Em left two of her retinue outside the door and nudged her captive through the door. Fortunately, it was another ghost building. The operator had fallen asleep in one of the chairs. The radio was silent.

Em gently poked the operator with her weapon, smiling as she captured the post.

"Alright," Em said. "Tie him up as well and hold this location. If anything comes across that radio, respond like nothing is happening. And you," she said to the operator, "you say the right thing like someone's holding a gun to your head."

Em hauled their first prisoner over, spinning her axe in her hands. The captured armory guard whimpered.

"Tell your friend that we're serious," Em menaced.

"They are serious," the man sputtered. "Just do what she says. Savage killed Gareth."

Em cracked a wicked smile.

Em's people blockaded the other doors to the communications building and set up near the front door. While the communications building would be a secure location, the armory was a better command post. Em's retinue looked to her for more instruction.

"Hold this point," she said. "Two with me. I've got to get out there to oversee the rest of the takeover. I'd like to do this without anyone else getting hurt if we can."

Em assigned one of Kars's school friends, to unlock the other enclosures, telling him to direct the prisoners to meet at the armory. He nodded with wide, harrowed eyes before trotting out of the building.

Em left with her remaining companions to return to the armory. They gathered more weapons from the armory, sorting through the stockpile. One of the men shouted with excitement as he found the plasma cannon Cutter called "Scarlett" on one of the racks. She wondered if Cutter was still with them.

"Let's see that our people are free and reunited, then make sure that these weapons are redistributed. For now, leave a crew here to secure the armory. Everyone else with me, we need to oversee the rest of the prison," Em said. There was no telling whether all of Perpetual's prisoners were dissidents and Em didn't want to risk unleashing some greater threat.

Em and her companions arrived at the enclosures to see much celebration as the townsfolk were reunited with missing people. Families had been separated with no way of exchanging messages. The townsfolk had subdued another hapless guard. Em's companions started distributing weapons.

Em climbed atop a nearby crate to address her people.

"Alright, everyone! We are taking over this camp. I saw our moment and we took it. If you hadn't put it together, we're in Amurtan, so our goal is *not* to hang around. The man that took us from our homes left on a raid. His ships are our only way out of here, so when he returns, it's going to be a fight. Only this time, the element of surprise is ours."

Familiar faces from their time in the Rebellion snapped to action, and their old hierarchy started to reassemble. Em supposed that the town had never left behind those old lines of command; they waited and steeped in their blood.

Kars's friend remained, waiting for a moment to speak with Em. She gestured for him to approach.

"Em." He sounded uncertain of how to talk to her. He had been too young to know the martial dynamics of the Rebellion. "I found other prisoners. I didn't recognize anyone, so I thought I should get you first."

"Good work," Em said. "Some of them helped us get out of our prison. This is more of a political prison than one for criminals. Let's go get them."

Em was eager to finally meet Ranjit. At the same time, she felt a certain fear. She remembered the Seventy-Seven from the Rebellion. While their purpose was noble, they had made sacrifices that pushed them toward the outer rim of human. They were wolves among livestock.

Em opened the gate.

Four haggard figures sat in the enclosure. Only one of them looked up.

He stood up in the back of the enclosure; a tall man with broad shoulders, a gray streaked beard and a faded blue turban. Ranjit. His gentle regal demeanor reminded her of Arthur Lannius. He approached her with a warm smile spreading across his face.

Ranjit drew Em into a hug.

"Thank you," he said.

"Thank you," Em responded.

His smile was warm, and tears welled in his dark eyes. It was the look of a man's spirit returning after a long winter.

"Enough delay. We have much to attend," Ranjit said. "My comrades, this is the one I have been talking to behind the wall— Emilia Koren."

The three other figures rose from the back of the cell. They barely grunted a greeting as they stalked out of their prison, grizzled and gray. It was that old wolf presence Em remembered.

If anything, they seemed impatient that their long imprisonment had kept them from the fight.

Em nodded to the Seventy-Seven. Stern expressions framed some silent conversation between them. Without a word, they left. Their hunt had resumed.

"It appears she ran with our opportunity and is taking over the camp. Jackal made the mistake of underestimating a village of Cerra mountainfolk," Ranjit said.

"It was just a few sleeping guards or tired soldiers drinking on the job," Em said.

"Nonetheless, we are in your debt," Ranjit said.

"We will settle up tabs later," Em said. "For now, my people are securing the camp and trying to do it without any casualties. We could use your help."

"Of course. We will free our own and join your people," Ranjit said. "And thank you again."

Em wondered what went on behind the noble face. As one of the Seventy-Seven, Ranjit was heavily augmented and no doubt dangerous. He turned to join the hunt scouring the camp.

Em left after a moment. Kars's friend stood slack-jawed at seeing Em interact with the strange old prisoners. They had once more crossed into a different world. The Seventy-Seven rode again.

*   *   *   *   *

In a different corner of the camp, a group of mountain folk accompanied one of the Seventy-Seven, an old battle formation from the Rebellion. They stormed through, clearing buildings as they passed. Despite two decades of imprisonment, Jahzara Thoreau still moved like a wraith in smoke.

A ping of complex processes drew Jahzara's attention to one of the bunkers. Unlike the other buildings, this one radiated different processes, which she saw as a swirl of glyphs through her augmentations. She cocked her long lean neck in curiosity and approached the building.

Jahzara probed one of the processes. It unfolded in her mind's eye with a vicious countermeasure that would have torn through her mind, absent of her own defenses. She smiled as her deeper interest grew. Whatever secret Perpetual had buried in this building was not meant for casual guests. She beamed an order to her companions before remembering they would not hear her. She cleared her throat and spoke for the first time in two decades.

"With me. Be careful," she said to the townsfolk following her, her voice crackled before finding its register. "There is something secret within these walls. Something dangerous."

The mountain folk drew close, raising their pillaged firearms. They descended into the darkness of the building.

*　　*　　*　　*　　*

Em watched as her people marched captured soldiers into the enclosures. Most looked resigned to their captors' will, others resisted through indignance. A few thrashed like animals—those bound up in the scripter's paranoia engines.

Thirty guard-prisoners, ten of whom were conscripts that claimed no allegiance to Jackal. Eighteen more loyal to the doctor. Twelve members of the Seventy-Seven, including Ranjit. Twenty freed prisoners claimed to be from all over different countries. Em felt a concern that she might have underestimated the reach of Perpetual's political schemes imprisoned in the gulag.

Once they had completed a full sweep of the camp, Em met with her old lieutenants, Ranjit and Doc Hayes. They had converted the armory into a war room. Each reported their findings in the summary of the takeover.

Em contemplated their next steps. As the de facto leader, she was now responsible for almost three hundred and fifty people. They controlled the camp, but safety was still like a distant speck on the horizon. She nursed her own quiet hope that one of their parties would return with her missing husband.

One of Ranjit's people entered the room, disrupting the discussion. The Seventy-Seven, Jahzara Thoreau, and her vanguard had found something strange. A prisoner.

Em muted her hope that it was Robert.

Thoreau led them into the darkness of the building and down several flights of stairs. They felt the coolness of the rock and the humidity collecting in the air. Their destination was a large room hewn in the rock; arched ceiling high enough to house a spacious glass dome room. A hulking man sat inside, calm in a comfortable armchair. The room itself was furnished with a plush rug and walls of bookshelves. Whiteboards lined the walls, covered in frantic equations scripted like delicate calligraphy. Arches carved in the rock revealed branching rooms leading away from the central chamber. Altogether, it was as civilized an arrangement as she imagined a subterranean gulag might provide.

Unlike the other prisoners, this massive man was well kept, well fed. His graying hair was cropped close to his skull and a robust beard framed his rugged jawline against his muscular neck. Calf-thick forearms rested on his armchair, angled musculature visible below the rolled sleeve of his starched shirt and vest. He did not acknowledge their approach, staring through his spectacles into some distant space beyond them.

"Any augmentations?" Em asked the Seventy-Seven.

"Yes, but he's completely unresponsive to anything we say or any attempts to contact him. We have not even been able to crack him," Jahzara reported.

Taking in the private washroom and other rooms, Em wondered if his room required more infrastructure than the rest of their prison combined. Was his shirt and tie tailored?

"Do you think this cell was the purpose of the camp?" Em asked.

"I do not recall any time since I've been here when they could have moved this much equipment or built this kind of infrastructure unnoticed," Jahzara said. "Still, it does not rule out that this facility was here since before the fall of Amurtan, but it does make me think that this entire camp was planned with this one prison cell in mind."

"The deepest darkest hole Perpetual could find," Em noted. "Any threat? Can we get him out?"

Jahzara took personal offense at the notion of a threat. "I would hope he would try."

"Get him out then. See if you can find any information on why he had the penthouse while the rest of us were in the yard. Make sure we've got a Seventy-Seven and a non-augmented person guarding him until we figure out what's going on here. Someone big. I'll be back at the armory," Em said.

She looked at the man in the dome. There was some deep sadness etched in his eyes. It was a despondent darkness. Looking at him made Em feel lonely.

Back at the armory, Em directed her townsfolk-turned-lieutenants as they secured the camp. There was an unforeseen bonding across the generations as the young came to see the old in a new light. Despite the uplifted mood, Em felt a greater burden. There was an army somewhere chasing her children, and that army would return to this camp.

Doc's people had assembled information from across the camp, briefing the leadership on Jackal and the raid.

"It's unclear who gave the order, but briefings all seemed to indicate it was an extraction mission on a hard target—the East Bay Securitor headquarters," a junior communications conscript named Shiloh reported. Her voice cut with edge of the Mastean accent. "The goal was to retrieve a young woman. Although not mentioned in the briefing, Jackal called her 'the Alcarn girl.'"

She curled her fists, felt the muscles across her shoulder contract. Perpetual had sent Jackal's raid to capture Aurora. Worse yet, the depths of Lannius's lie continued to unfold. Who was Alcarn?

"The mission briefing did not lay out a specific time for return, only estimates for travel, mission time, and return," Shiloh continued. "With only that knowledge and the most conservative estimate of times, we can only surmise a thirty-hour return trip."

"Minus four hours since they left," Ranjit noted. Shiloh nodded.

"Twenty-six hours," Em said. It could be a reckoning.

"At least," Doc said optimistically, "we have an element of surprise on their return as well. We may be able to hold them hostage as they land."

"Not the Protek. They won't surrender," Ranjit said.

"Let's call it a fair fight this time." Cutter had joined the briefing. He patted "Scarlett" as though he could cast a protective spell if he channeled enough bravado through his talisman.

Em knew there was no amount of bravado that would conquer the Protek. Fighting was more than politics to the Protek. It was written in their design. Maybe there could be a negotiation. She wondered how much the man in the dome was worth to Jackal and Perpetual.

"Let's take a walk," Em said. She needed to get Ranjit and Doc out of earshot of the rest of the camp.

They climbed a steel ladder to reach the top of the armored western wall; Em and Ranjit saw the true starkness of Amurtan for the first time. Doc seemed uncomfortable looking out on the blasted landscape.

It was barren sand with bleached root bulbs of ancient trees scattered to the horizon. Intermittent husks of old-style cars dotted the hills and jagged canyons. Craters pocked the sandy land, as enduring reminders of the cruelty of the Consolidation War. A scorched breeze howled.

"I hope you two know we can't fight our way out of here," Em said. The backdrop of the desert added an edge to her words.

The two men nodded in agreement.

"Trickery or negotiation," Ranjit said. "Fighting, if it comes to it."

"Yes. That man they found in the dome," Em said. "He may be our only hostage."

Em could see the visible disdain on Doc's face.

"I hope it doesn't come to that," Em added before Doc could voice his disapproval.

"All of it might be moot," Doc said. "We need to think of contingencies if they don't come back. We are on an island. Eventually, the desert will swallow us up. Mankind turned over these lands to the machines. If Jackal does not return, the machines of the desert will come for us."

It was a grim thought. Em looked out on the desert. It was a small victory to take the camp, but greater dangers lay just beyond the wall. The air shimmered above the horizon, melding the setting sun with the desert edge.

The three leaders remained on the bulwark as the sun dropped past the horizon. They would wait and prepare. Hours left until the desert would be their enemy.

49

The Securitor

Silvia arrived just as the repulsors spun up, their whine growing as the hovercraft gained speed. She shouted at nothing as the sound grew distant. It was too late.

Still, she continued to where the hovercraft had been, slinging her rifle to her back. She saw the leftover chunks of foamlock stuck to the building and the drones lying doomed in the shallow water. It looked like they had walked into a trap. Silvia reached into the dormant processes of one of the disabled drones. The scene played out in her mind. The kids had almost made it.

They were plucky but inexperienced and had not counted on a cunning foe setting a trap. She closed her right eye and scanned the area in a hyper spectral analysis, but she knew it would not tell her anything new. It was Stormgard.

It meant they were being held in the Office of the Securitor.

Silvia turned and consulted her map of the Breakwater, then set off toward the nearest city access shaft. She would return to the surface, consult with Spiderfly—make him help her if needed— then break them out of Securitor. The thought was a mix of daunting and exhilarating. It made her long for her old allies.

If only she could enlist Jack Mortanis or Kip Henringer or any of the Seventy-Seven. Launching a one-woman siege of the Securitor fortress was the stuff of songs.

Unfortunately, the only old men that had returned to the city were either locked up in the Securitor or were city-soft dandies like Maxmillian Ward. It would fall to her, maybe with an accompaniment of Spiderfly's acolytes and a display of its power or mischief—who knew? She felt a flash of weariness in dealing with the Spider, of feeling as though she clung to a board in storm seas, and of frustration with the curious AI's whimsy and disorder. Spiderfly had reached that true level of intelligence: the insufferable ability to do what he wanted for no good reason.

She popped open the round door and ascended an iron ladder. Opening the hatch on the other side, she was assaulted by the sensory overload of the city. Its layers of information filled her vision. She backgrounded the personal and public layers for a moment to bring up the map again, plotting a course for the House of the Spider.

The mixed feeling of despair and exhilaration continued to well up. Some acolytes might help, or maybe she could coax Arc into action. Either way, there was one person that she missed most as she approached the altercation. Where was Arthur Lannius?

*　　　*　　　*　　　*　　　*

Kars did not struggle against the shackles restraining him in the hold of the hovercraft. Stormgard handled his duty with an air of smug charisma that made Kars feel worse. After Aurora had dispatched all his troops, Stormgard had handily dispatched them with his trap—a motion sensitive charge filled with the quick-hardening pink goo. They walked into it like mice in the storehouse. Stormgard showed just enough satisfaction to make it feel personal but not enough to show any kind of respect. Kars could tell the defeat had devastated Aurora's pride and left her stranded with her troubled thoughts of Mirien Alcarn. The implication left him with stranded thoughts as well.

Kars preferred the simple answer, particularly when confronting multiple predicaments. The situation on the rooftop in the Breakwater had qualified as too many problems to fully process Aurora's Alcarn predicament. Everything spun, as though each problem tugged his attention with a gravity of its own.

They had just fled their only safety and thrown themselves into the precipice of a world unknown. Their failed plan hinged on finding some distant city full of augmented lunatics. Aurora had been wrestling with fear of capture, fear of manipulation, and a fear of vanishing from her own mind. Lingering behind her struggle was the legend of Lannius and time travel. The implications of that legend bent Kars's mind to its limit, and he was an observer. Aurora must have been lost in the maelstrom.

Kars couldn't handle all the events in series, but he did not fault himself for this weakness. It had been a moment where escape was all that mattered.

But now, trapped in a cell in the belly of a hovercraft, Kars found his thoughts surprisingly clear to focus on the issue. He saw the pained look on his sister's face. He wanted to intervene somehow, but so much of this felt out of his control and continued to spin further out of his reach. They had failed. Being in the clutches of consequences made their struggle less abstract, as though the swamps of fear had been drained to reveal the underlying hills and pits. He could navigate the issues without feeling over his head.

The revelations that Aurora had neural augmentations had taken effort to understand and store in his mind. But this new question, the question of Mirien Alcarn, smashed the foundation. Suddenly, they were no longer navigating a world of omitted facts, but instead found themselves in an intricate landscape of orchestrated lies. If Mirien Alcarn did exist, then who was Aurora? Did Aurora cease to exist? The complexity of the lie didn't even reach the depth of its cruelty.

Poor Aurora, he thought. He understood her sudden need to flee and resolved to help her whenever they had the chance. He also liked the idea of spoiling that arrogant Stormgard's day.

The guards had not been able to remove his tabula gauntlet—it shocked them when they tried—and Lena's necklace was still plastered to her chest by a chunk of foam. Stormgard and his team had taken Aurora's bag and Squire, but the tiny robot had remained furled in its inert disc configuration.

Outside the holding cell, the hovercraft glided over the stillness of the Breakwater. It navigated the old flooded avenues, carving turns to avoid sandbar islands that had formed since the days of the first sea level rise. Estuary animals scattered at the craft's approach, turtles scrambling to dive beneath the surface, herons taking off on slowly looping wing beats. The hovercraft passed, leaving little more than a ripple, and the Breakwater returned to its quiet rise and fall of the tides.

Finally, the hovercraft rounded a corner and arrived at a dock that reached down into the sunken city from the metropolis above. The plain white ceramic structure was noticeably sleek compared to the derelict brick buildings standing in the water, like it was crafted of the same bone ceramic as the bridges of the resource highway.

Winches and cargo arms snatched the hovercraft and held it above the water, locking it in place in the slip. The whine of the engines faded as they cycled down. Armed officers fanned out along the concrete dock, preparing for their new arrivals.

Kars stared straight ahead as they were escorted to the building. He wouldn't give Stormgard the satisfaction of breaking him. They passed beneath a large shield emblem as they moved into the heart of the headquarters.

The headquarters carried the same clean line motif of the docks, all high ceilings and stark-white ceramic panels. A few of the people in the headquarters stopped to stare at the retinue. Among the city and the officers of the Securitor, Stormgard had more of a mythos than a reputation. Most of the criminals stashed in the cell blocks of the Securitor had been caught and convicted by Stormgard. Whoever he brought in was usually the most notorious cryptowizards and technowraiths in East Bay.

The retinue passed through several sets of large double doors, losing members at each turn until the group was down to Stormgard, Aurora, Kars, Lena, and a few handlers to help keep them walking. They stopped and delivered the three of them to three separate holding cells, white and neat, and closed the doors.

*   *   *   *   *

Aurora felt defeated and alone in her cell. All her training and bargaining with Spiderfly had ended in a quiet room with no escape. She had no connection with the augmentations, the air was clear of the golden haze of the aether. They had taken her bag and Squire, leaving her trapped in the room with nothing to do but pick flakes of foam off of her clothes.

She paced back and forth, trying to avoid her own thoughts. Painful emotions lurked just beneath the surface and the cell left little room to hide. Its harsh white light seemed to penetrate her thoughts, leaving no shadow. She felt remorse for leaving Silvia, regret for her useless deal with Spiderfly, guilt for dragging her friends into this prison with her, and the ever-present anxiety that she would cease to exist whenever Mirien Alcarn came to claim her body. The cell felt claustrophobic.

She lay on the floor, channeling her breathing through her nose. She tried to return to the peace of the seaside castle to hear the reassuring words of the stranger with the rose. The white lights would have none of it, forcing her to stay with her loneliness and anguish. Lying on the floor, tears leaked out of the corners of her eyes and down the sides of her face.

*　　　*　　　*　　　*　　　*

After what felt like hours, the door to Aurora's cell slid open, and a guard retrieved her and brought her to another room. He seated her at a table and locked her anklet to the chair. The lights in this room seemed even brighter than those in her cell. She waited in silence.

A door at the far side of the room opened and Marcus Stormgard entered. He sat down across from her. The dark table was polished to the point it showed an upside-down shadow universe in its surface. Aurora tried to probe the table for processes but only felt the edge of her augmentations blunted and blind.

"Welcome to East Bay," he said, his voice deep and confident. "From what I can tell, you're not from around here."

Aurora looked at him flatly. Her eyes were still raw from her tears.

"Look, I'm not out to get you. It seems like you've gotten in pretty deep and I'm just trying to understand what's going on. We don't have any records of you or your friends, and your neural augmentations are unregistered and . . . unique. You tripped some high-security protocols and keep some interesting friends. That alone could end in trouble. Help me here," Stormgard said, leaning back in his chair.

Aurora thought about it for a moment, looking more weary than defiant. Then she spoke.

"My name is Aurora Koren. I came to the city after a man named Jackal attacked my town. I didn't know I had any augmentations until the morning before he attacked, when they just started doing things," Aurora explained.

"I'm sorry, did you say *Koren*?" Stormgard asked, raising an eyebrow. Aurora nodded, and he asked her to continue. Even without her augmentations, she knew that he was racing through the networks for some piece of information.

"My brother, Kars, my friend Lena, and I were lucky to make it out."

"So how did you get from your home to the resource freighter?" Stormgard asked. "That seems like a big task. Also, your brother has a pretty nifty piece of tech strapped on his arm. You managed a lot all by yourself."

He watched; she looked away.

"It's okay. There's a whole list of charges against you and your friends, but I really wonder if you've just been in the wrong place at the wrong time. Maybe that you're in over your head with some people—or something else. Did you get any help on the way into the city?"

496

Aurora paused, weighing her answer.

She said, "Yes. We had instructions left for us by a man. A man named Arth–"

A sleek computer at Stormgard's wrist chimed, and he was suddenly distracted. She could tell that he was immersed in a flurry of sublingual communications. Aurora desperately longed to listen in to the signals to get some understanding of her predicament.

"I'm sorry. We're going to need to pick this up in a little bit," Stormgard said.

A look of puzzled disbelief spread across Aurora's face. Stormgard left without saying another word.

Arthur Lannius had just turned himself in.

50

The Siege Begins

Aurora needs our help, Silvia shouted to the House of the Spider. *I cannot make you go as the risk is great. But if there were a time for sacrifice, it would be now.*

Her face appeared in the minds of all the acolytes in the House of the Spider. Her virtual expression radiated urgency. The acolytes stopped their chores, looking up from their tasks and training. She had their full attention as though she had rung a morning bell.

Silvia's sudden intrusion into the House drew the Spider down its web.

Silvia, you sound passionate, Spiderfly said. The acolytes watched.

That's right, she responded.

I've never known you to be passionate beyond your duties, Spiderfly said.

I've always been passionate, it just happened to align with my duties, Silvia said. *This time, the duties—my orders, your decisions, Lannius's plots—have put an innocent girl well into harm's way. Under that circumstance, my passion and duties are at odds.*

The acolytes seemed confused, witnessing Silvia's dissent as she approached open Rebellion of their patron. Silence lingered.

Will any join me? Silvia asked, refusing to wait for Spiderfly's response. The personal layer served Silvia a cloud of indecision, confusion, and fear. Her hopes started to fade.

I'll help. It was Spiderfly.

Silvia raise her brow.

What do you want in return?

Nothing.

Nothing?

For years I've watched and tricked and bargained with humans. I can say in that time I've learned only one overarching truth: just when I think I've learned everything, I can still be surprised by people, Spiderfly said. *Allow me to return the favor.*

Silvia's mind sprinted. Perhaps it was true and the Spider had changed. Or maybe it was Spiderfly seizing an opportunity to show the acolytes that sometimes favors existed.

She shrugged. *All right. That's how it will be then.* Silvia sensed the mass of acolytes shift toward confidence and fortitude. A subset even blustered with resolve to join her mission.

＊　　　＊　　　＊　　　＊　　　＊

After crossing the city, they reached the gleaming pyramid of the Securitor. Silvia ushered her small cadre toward the entrance. It was the only entrance to the building that did not have an automated "shoot on sight" defense network. If they stood a chance, they would have to enter the main hall and fight their way into the protected core.

Standing a block away from the main entrance, she sent the group into the massive pyramid in small waves to avoid detection. She thought they might be able to amass on the inside of the exterior doors without being noticed. Hopefully, the acolytes were just a backup plan, and she would be able to stealth past the layers of security and impersonate an actual officer.

She grinned as she delved into the memories of the tools she had learned during the Rebellion: phobia inducers and counterphobias, depressors, weaponized drowsiness, mythic skin, demotivators, point anxiety, attention depletors, quantum distractors, self-loathing generators—the bag of tricks was deep. Most of the tools developed by the Seventy-Seven would still be unknown to the amateurish officers of the Securitor.

After sending the last of the acolytes ahead, Silvia went straight through the doors of the Office of the Securitor. The receiving hall was a busy corridor with countless clerks at islanded counters and with bench space scattered throughout. She did her best to look the part of an older woman with graying hair waiting to report her stolen jewelry and watched the vintage clock face for the shift change.

*   *   *   *   *

Angelo, Whitestone's Node, watched from beneath his hood as Silvia Glass and her troops dispersed. He relayed their

500

movements to the swarm of slaveminds networked to him. He keyed his augmentations to blunt the effect of his excitement. Nodes—even elite Nodes like himself—never enjoyed the freedom he now touched. The feeling of trust that he could operate alone and unchecked felt vast. It might be true that Perpetual did not know he existed, and that only Whitestone monitored his life.

The slaveminds began playing out—living out—the permutations of the situation based on new facts all flowing through him like one braided stream of experience. He knew each of the minds was a person, but right now they were rented space, sleeping in some distant pod in a safe facility. His senses were their senses, and they experienced an accelerated reality based on what might happen to him.

The distant slaveminds quickly reported back. Silvia Glass was waiting for the shift change, planning on going in through the front. Some had played out scenarios where her group launched an all-out assault, a strategy which always ended in failure. She may have been Lannius's old muscle, but she was not invincible. Other minds explored what happened if she used guile that trailed beyond the edge of their reasonable predictions. And still other slaveminds played out the scenario with Angelo intervening in a variety of fashions to varying degrees of success and failure. Scenarios where he lost were rejected until the Node had pared down his choices to a narrow task flow. So long as he had the facts, he would win.

New facts streamed in from other sources. Lannius had turned himself in to the Securitor.

Angelo felt little more than intrigue behind his emotional suppression. Slaveminds sensed the change and tasked themselves with learning about Lannius. Angelo split off a thread of his interest to the Lannius research, curious if his new independence might come with privileged information.

Mirien Alcarn. His quarry had a name. A surveillance memory drew his attention. Arthur Lannius handing the baby to Whitestone who then gently held her in his arms. He bore a huge warm smile. Angelo's brow twitched as the new memories settled in place.

The permutations spun through his consciousness, changing how he would approach the intruders, how the defenses of the Office would likely deploy. Details as subtle as the time of response changed. He would pause three seconds at the third door instead of seven. Details of the entire constellation changed how he would respond. Somewhere in the distant hive, his slaveminds dreamed through the scenarios living and dying to report back their experience.

Angelo suppressed a smile. What the Securitor and Silvia Glass did not know was that they were trapped between a knife and a hammer. He knew the hammer—Jackal and his army—had just slammed into the city air space. A flash of network warnings heralded the coming response from Attila, but their trajectory would have them on the Office of the Securitor before the military drones could intercept.

Under the din and fire of hammer blows, Angelo would creep in as a blade in the dark. He consulted his slaveminds again and sunk back into the shadows.

51

Lannius

Marcus Stormgard entered a room identical to the interrogation room where he had just held Aurora Koren. Arthur Lannius sat serene in the opposing chair, his ankle chained.

"You're back," Stormgard said.

"Hello, Marcus," Lannius said, a slight smile spreading on his lips, his voice undimmed by his incarceration.

"Here? Now?" Stormgard asked. His voice was shaken.

"I am sorry. I should have sent a message to you sooner," Lannius said.

"Sooner?" Marcus asked. "It's been twenty years. You are a ghost, or worse, a lost wraith fighting shadows! All these years; Arthur, you've lost your way."

"I'm turning myself in, Marcus," Lannius responded, his eyes bright, brimming with sorrow at what Marcus had said.

"Yes. But why?"

"There was no other way. I ran out of time," Lannius said. "You have three young people in your cells. They are in grave danger."

"Danger? Arthur, this is the Office of the Securitor. I know I was just a kid when you last saw me, but I've built this place. I built it to stand for something."

"I know you have, Marcus," Lannius said. His voice was patient and tender.

"I have been a middle path between Clark's juggernaut, the sleeping tiger Attila, and the wild-type AIs springing up everywhere. I know some people—the Seventy-Seven—think the Securitor is a façade, but you have to know it's the last thing that stands for anything like a sovereign government. That means something. This"—Marcus rapped his knuckles on the table—"is the work of people believing in society over money and power."

Lannius gazed ponderously at the spot Marcus had pounded before turning his attention to the younger man.

"Marcus, I respect your work, but the middle path is about to end. Perpetual has sent a mercenary army under the command of a maniac named Jackal to capture the girl. You are about to be under siege. The strike force is a trained army, assisted by a squad of Protek. They will be here any moment."

Protek? Stormgard couldn't believe it. The Protek never strayed outside of the Amurtan wastelands, save for stories told to scare children. They wouldn't cooperate for a coordinated attack. Jackal? That was the name the girl had mentioned just moments before.

"Protek? Arthur, that's not possible. Please don't bring your wild conspiracies and plots into my house. You left me twenty years ago, and I had to live here in the shadow of your betrayal. I had to make it work. I have a family now."

"Marcus, you must listen to me. This moment is why I told you to stay in the city all those years ago. The girl is why I left you behind from my rebellion. Clark was lost. I could trust you. You had the talent and fortitude to make your own way. I needed you here at this moment to make this decision. I need you to listen to me now. We do not have much time."

The moment swam up in Marcus's mind from another age, but the hurt still remained. The mentor rebuked the star pupil, told him he was not wanted and that he did not belong. Then Lannius was gone to the wilderness.

Stormgard tried to keep up with the situation. All that angst had been a part of Arthur's plan. He had brought in three mysterious vagabonds connected to Spiderfly and some minor offenses, and he now found himself sitting across the table from the most wanted man in the entire world. Marcus felt dizzy thinking Lannius had planted the seed of his entire life for this one moment—to save this girl.

"Arthur, I was never one of your Seventy-Seven. I've got a family now. You can't expect me to throw that all away." His gaze locked with Lannius.

Marcus, please. Lannius channeled the thought through all of Marcus's defenses. The city swirled through Marcus's mind. He was suddenly the clouds between the buildings, glowing with the light of the city below. The airship hurtled toward them flanked by giant dull chrome mantises—enormous Protek. He felt the

505

omnipotence of Attila scrambling to fend off an intruding foreign body, the first spasm of the city's immune response. Marcus swirled through the air as a cloud of awareness, the ethereal presence of Arthur Lannius as the wind whipping him through canyons between buildings. Lannius forced Marcus to watch the attack in its final approach.

As the moment hung between them, a seismic vibration rippled through the building. The siege had begun. Alarms started to howl, and messages poured to Marcus in an avalanche. They snapped back into their bodies. Lannius looked at him with a pleading stare.

"You haven't left me much choice," Marcus said. "But that's been true from the beginning." He threaded part of his consciousness toward sending orders to his lieutenants, executing siege protocols he thought he would never issue.

"I will take the girl to safety." Lannius said. "That is who they are after and why I came. I need you to make sure the other two—her brother and friend are safe. Take the robot you confiscated as well—the disc in the girl's bag. We will not need it. Stay safe. Live your life, Marcus."

Marcus looked uncertain. Pain of the old rebuke welled up in him, meeting the raw heat of knowing so much of his life was a lie. There might not be room there for forgiveness, but he only saw one path to get beyond his regret. He pressed his brow with his hand, squeezing his temples as he decided. Marcus unshackled Arthur Lannius, and the two of them set out into the chaos of the siege.

*   *   *   *   *

Lena had just picked the last piece of foam off the master key when she felt the shockwave ripple through the building. She looked nervously around her tiny cell, but there was no indication of trouble beyond the sound.

"Time to get out of here," she said to herself, clutching the strange heavy key in her hand She approached the door, and touched the end of the key to what she assumed was a locking mechanism. The metal touched. Nothing.

Lena felt her heart in her chest and tapped the key to the door again. Both objects remained inert. Had Lannius left her with a broken key? She felt panic rise from her guts and felt the cell close in around her. She swore and mashed the key against the surface.

To her relief, the key took over, responding by deploying filament-like legs to hold itself in place. The impossibly detailed bitings on the key seemed to melt into the surface, working some arcane technological miracle, then the lock sprung free and the door slid back limply. Relief flooded through her, mingling with a sense of wonder as the key did its work.

She gently tugged on the key and hung it back around her neck. She let loose a long breath as the door swung on its hinge.

Outside of her cell, the hallway was empty and sterile white, save for a pulsing alarm at the far end. She cautiously peered around the corner but saw no one, so she started down the hallway. Another boom reverberated through the building.

Lena pounded her fists on the door next to hers, hoping that Kars was inside, but there was no answer. She tried the trick with the master key, but it did not activate. Where were her friends?

She dashed down the length of the hallway. There had to be some sort of control panel for all the cells, some way to find her friends. She would get them out of this prison.

Each door she came to in the hallway was unlocked. It seemed like whatever had triggered the alarms had drawn the guards to some emergency. She continued to search the floor until she came to the control room. The doors were held open by an unseen patron.

"Spiderfly?" Lena whispered. There was no response.

Once inside, she tried to ply the panels, but she couldn't make sense of the controls. The lights in the room seemed to defy her effort. Whenever she would reach for the panel, it would fall into darkness and the spotlight above would shift to another section. It would glow blinding bright until anything outside the point of light was complete darkness. She could never see what she was trying to operate.

Still, she could see screens with various cells on them containing all sorts of people. She saw one room with Aurora sitting in front of a table under bright lights. Further scanning of the cells showed Kars pacing the short length of his room. The pulsing alarms continued and the sounds of explosions became more frequent. She had to get her friends out. The spotlight danced across the console, frustrating her attempts to make sense of the foreign control panel.

She shouted at the light to stop. Oddly, it seemed to listen, setting on one point—a single keyhole like the ignition for some

508

massive machine. Could something be helping her? She took her master key from around her neck and held it above the socket. She drew in a breath and touched the key to the keyhole.

*　　　*　　　*　　　*　　　*

Aurora pulled against her restraints as the building shook. She was still shackled in the interrogation room, waiting for Marcus Stormgard to return. The shaking and the muted wail of alarms filled her with concern. Something had gone wrong. She tugged at the chain connecting her ankle to the chair.

The minutes stretched on until the door swung open. The moment seemed to expand and inflate, slowly to the point she felt her pulse in the air. Aurora couldn't think as the most unexpected figure stepped through. As he entered, he lifted his hood and flourished his long cloak in a deep bow.

The other memories surged and threatened to overtake Aurora. She had remembered his face, the bright eyes. The warm smile sitting over sorrow piled so high one wondered how he managed to bury it. Her own memories of concern, fear, and mistrust gave over to the other memories of him as a teacher, mentor, and friend.

"Greetings, Aurora." He hesitated over her name. His voice was deep and rich. "Unfortunately, we are out of time for a more formal introduction. We must leave this place." With a glance, her shackle fell limp to the floor. He tossed her the satchel he had recovered from the evidence room.

As they stared at one another, he wrestled the awkwardness of meeting her, Aurora, for the first time.

"But how?" A dizzied flush passed through her as her experience and the strange memories mingled, like the line between two rivers meeting.

"I'll explain my delays later. For now, this is how our journey begins." He turned back out the door.

When a round of gunfire sounded nearby, she complied.

The siege had moved much more quickly into the Securitor than the defensive siege protocols had expected. That much was clear. Alarms wailed and unmarked soldiers fought officers in the hallways. Smoke hung in the air. The invaders had breached the walls before the defenders could mount their resistance, and now they fought in the tight quarters of the building.

Lannius stormed through the maelstrom without hesitation, his scowl like stone. The soldiers from both sides paused when they felt him near and stopped fighting to lie on the ground. Others started dismantling their weapons before running away. Some pointed their guns at the ceiling and fired until the weapon went silent, yet they continued pulling the trigger.

Aurora was still blocked, but the chaos made it clear: the old man was an engine of diabolical processes and countermeasures. Grizzled mercenaries dropped to the floor and hid their faces. Machines burst in showers of sparks. Huge security doors parted to allow their passage. He pushed forward like the eye of a hurricane.

"What's going on!" she shouted.

The block lifted instantly.

Your old friend Jackal is here.

Jackal. The thought of the leering maniac scared Aurora.

He has come for you again. I do not intend to let that happen. We are going to the landing port. From there, I plan on taking one of the helipods to leave the city. We need to go north.

But what about Kars and Lena?

Marcus is going to get them. He will keep them safe. Jackal has no interest in your friends.

The realization that Lannius was taking her hit with sickening force. She might never see them again.

"No. Please. I can't do this without them!" Aurora cried out.

Lannius stopped, abruptly turning. The kindly eyes she knew from her memories were smoldering fire.

"You have no idea the sacrifices made for your life to this point. Everyone who has made those sacrifices has one thing in common: they believe in you. Now, we have reached a point where you must pick up the torch. You must believe in yourself, whoever you choose to be," Lannius bellowed with the force of a king.

"Whoever I choose to be?" Aurora said, her voice iced with a growing rage. The building rumbled with another explosion.

"Yes, whoever you choose to be." Lannius spoke as though he knew her rage was rushing forth like a tidal wave.

"Whoever I choose to be!" she screamed. "You've taken all of that away! All of you! My life, my memories—I don't know who I am anymore!"

Lannius remained stoic, a stone in the storm of her pain.

"My mind—your plans have torn it apart and left me hunted by madmen, and I don't even know why! Whoever I choose to be? Your cruelty knows no limit. I have been torn to pieces!" Aurora screamed amidst the smoke of the battle.

"Then turn away!" Lannius boomed. Fires glowed behind him. "Go to your friends, run to your home. Turn from our sacrifice."

Aurora squeezed back tears. She thought of Em and Silvia. She thought of all the plans Lannius had laid to keep her safe. Their motives might have been unknown to her, but their sacrifice was clear. She thought of Kars and Lena nodding to her to continue. She knew it was true.

"Or take the next step. I can help you put it back together," Lannius challenged.

The building rumbled. Aurora clenched her fists and stood up. She scrubbed a tear from the corner of her eye and drew a choked sniffle through her nose. Sparks showered from a shattered light fixture. She knew the broken parts would never fit. She straightened herself and faced the old man.

"There was only ever one way—forward."

52

Siege

Kars grew frantic as the building shook. He was trapped and desperate. All the training meant nothing behind the door. He pounded his fist against it until it hurt. He paced the narrow length of his cell and did it again. The heel of his hand stung from his hopeless hammering.

Then the cell door slid open. His fist fell through the open air. A man grabbed his wrist.

Kars threw himself at the man, tackling him into the hallway. They bounced across the corridor in brief scrum. Kars landed a blow against his opponent's ribs before the large man pinned him to the wall. It was Stormgard.

"Give it up! I'm here to get you out of here." Stormgard grunted through his teeth.

"What do you mean?" Kars responded, his cheek mashed against the wall.

"That merc that attacked your town, Jackal? He's here. An old friend of mine needs me to get you and your friend out of here." Stormgard's voice was strained, loaded with a frustration that

Kars couldn't discern. Kars relaxed before Stormgard released him. He shook off the last contact, dusting off his arms.

"Where's Lena? Where's my sister?" Kars asked, scowling.

The bigger man straightened his jacket. "Lena's in the next cell block. Your sister is with Arthur Lannius. We need to get to the upper landing port to connect with Lannius and get out of here."

The weight of Stormgard's words barely reached Kars when all of the doors on the cellblock slid open. Stormgard looked shocked, stunned for a moment at what was happening. The prisoners within the cells also seemed shocked that there were no guards in the hall. They peered out into the hallway before overcoming their doubt in their unexpected freedom.

Stormgard shoved Kars. "Go!"

The two of them hurtled through the awakening mass of prisoners, sprinting into the next hallway. Chaos erupted on all sides. These people had turned their augmentations into scams, weapons, tricks, and tools to harm the innocent. The Securitor prison spilled into the bowels of the building and the mercenary army crashed in from the top: the castle was lost.

"We need to find Lena!" Kars shouted over the din.

"This place is falling apart!"

"I can't leave her!" Kars responded.

"She's out of the cell, just like everybody else! I told Lannius I would keep you safe, that's what I'm going do!" Stormgard shouted back.

"Then keep me safe! I'm going to find her!" Kars shouted and headed off down a corridor into the frenzied combat that had overtaken in the headquarters.

"If you need to do this," Stormgard said, grabbing the younger man's sleeve, "at least go the right way."

As he said it, he pushed Kars down the hallway. The mass of criminals boiled out into the corridor. Kars and Stormgard dodged through the fray, rolling shoulders and shoving as they went. Stormgard tried to keep his head down as vengeful blows rained down. He wouldn't make it for long in the hall. They reached a bend in the hall where Stormgard shoved Kars onto an elevator and stepped in with him. The doors slid closed, sealing the other side. They panted in silence.

"If we go up, we can get to one of the control consoles. I might be able to find her and get her to safety. Wandering around in this firefight is *not* going to help your friend," Stormgard said.

Kars realized he was panting and trembling. Adrenaline surged through him from fighting through the crowds. The maelstrom had clouded his mind. Stormgard was right.

"I just need to help her," Kars said. "Thank you."

"Don't thank me yet," Stormgard said. "We've got a long way to go."

*   *   *   *   *

Lena watched from her screen as the elevator doors closed with Kars and Stormgard inside. From the arrow on the outside, she knew they were heading up. She sighed relief as the elevator carried them out of the melee. The master key had done its unpredictable work, releasing all of the prisoners in the entire hold of the Securitor.

Moments earlier, she had seen Lannius surrender himself and retrieve Aurora, then she had seen the two of them pass through the battlefield as though they were cloaked in some force that brought time to a stop. She couldn't believe as she watched—the man they had been chasing and hoping for was here. Now, he led Aurora away. Her path was vanishing with them.

Lena knew that she had to make her way up.

Looking at the screens, it was not going to be an easy path. She had little sense of where she was in the building and knew from the monitors that every floor had been overrun by some emergency. Nonetheless, she steeled herself for the crossing. If she was going to reunite with her friends, she would have to make her way to one of the elevators.

Lena took several deep breaths, bounced on her toes, and stretched her neck from side to side. All the training with Kars had come down to this moment. It was time to use it. The door to her control room refuge slid open. She looked either way, and one of the hallways went black. The lights in the other pulsed toward the end and then stayed on. Spiderfly must have been watching her, which felt like some relief—she was not alone. She started her sprint down the lit hallway.

She turned down several corridors, meeting no people or obstacles, continuing to follow the lighting. It guided her along the edges of the fray. Spiderfly was trying to keep her out of the way and use the smaller secondary lifts.

The outskirts of the building were not free of tumult. Occasional guards cowered, and prisoners ran amok. She came upon a wandering man, a wild-eyed maniac that looked to be one of the prisoners she had set free. He menaced and approached. When his violence became clear, she lunged into the forms of the gan'ko, falling to the left with a punch to the throat followed by a roundhouse to the stomach. He fell against the wall. Her fear surged into self-satisfaction. Em would have been proud. She continued at a jog through the corridors.

Lena picked her way through the skirmishes, keeping low to avoid conflict where possible. She rested when she reached the first elevator and rode it to the highest level that it would take her.

It opened onto another level of more intense fighting. Her shadowy protector still watched. Malfunctions changed her course—individual fire suppression systems would snap on, throwing combatants out of her path, doors would open and close to give her sole passage. The building fought for her. She weaved through different hallways and rooms, making slow, safe progress. Always in the back of her mind, she kept a thought of her friends, a vague countdown she raced against.

She reached one of the core lifts and boarded. The thought of losing them was worse than the fear of the battles, and it prodded her forward. She would find her friends.

*   *   *   *   *

The first explosion rocked the entry hall, sending a wave of shock and confusion through everyone present, including Silvia and her volunteer acolytes. She leapt to her feet, all array of autonomic processes springing to action in her neural augmentations.

Silvia. It was Spiderfly. *First, Lannius just turned himself in to Marcus. He's with Aurora now. Second, the Securitor is under attack by a group of mercenaries and an airborne Protek unit.*

Arthur! Her spirit surged. *Damn fine time to show up.*

The update spurred Silvia to action before the Securitor officers could respond. Alarms were coming to life, and there was a mass scramble of booted guards toward their armory. They were implementing their siege protocols, gearing up to fortify and garrison specific points. She would have to act fast.

She flipped up her hood and deployed multi-layer detection countermeasures. She pushed deep into her tricks, activating a process that would trigger an undefended augmentation to release a temporarily crippling amount of cortisol and dopamine—the "freakout." Tending the final details of her attack, Silvia booted up her favorite avatar, a four-armed goddess with a head of flaming hair and a cloak of smoke billowing out from her.

Of course, all of this only mattered to someone with augmentations. But in East Bay, that meant pretty much everyone.

When Silvia Glass emerged in her full power, the entry hall erupted in screams. The guards fled or cowered behind whatever they were near. Bystanders stood paralyzed. When she turned and looked at them, they saw the flaming four-armed goddess glare at them and shout in a discordant multi-octave roar: "Leave here!"

With a flick of her wrist she turned all the lights off in the room.

Silvia expanded her consciousness into the network of the building, bowling back the petty defenses the low-level Securitor systems threw in her path. Where were her kids?

Through the eyes of the building, she saw Aurora and Arthur in the landing port, and Kars and Stormgard fighting their way through a crowd. Lena was alone in a control room in the cellblocks.

Spider, Silvia thought, *it's time you and I had some fun. Can you keep an eye on Lena?*

Of course. I liked that one since the moment I met her.

Very well. Do what you must.

Through her expanded consciousness, she saw Lena leave the control room and start heading down various corridors. Silvia swept deep within the building after her, meeting a more satisfying level of resistance when she reached the mercenary incursion. They were coordinated and had some neural defenses—just enough to avoid collapsing into gurgling masses on her initial approach. She knew they still saw her fiery avatar in the personal layer. With another thought she assaulted their cochlear nerve interface, triggering a crippling bout of vertigo and a sudden deafening ring. She tightened the focus of the assault so they heard a roar of unnerving whispers and felt as though they were hanging upside-down. Then she turned off the lights in the room.

She saw the hapless fools in the aether. With the hyperspectral filter in her left eye she watched panic fan through their bodies like wildfire. The cochlear attack rendered them unable to fight beneath the assault of a terrible imagined noise. She walked, her avatar laughing in a horrifying polytone roar.

Her progress was surgical and automatic. Her old comrades would have loved this battle and the hopeless little resistance she encountered. The artificial intelligences during the Rebellion had few of these weaknesses and fought back with relentless purpose. These humans stood little chance against the full might of one of the Seventy-Seven.

Silvia continued her assault, reaching one of the elevators. She would rendezvous with Lannius and save the kids.

*   *   *   *   *

Aurora and Lannius stepped onto the landing port. The hangar opened onto the city, and the sky blazed with an aerial battle. Jackal's ship circled the Securitor pyramid, accompanied by two more agile crafts that looked like Protek. Swarms of drones dipped and darted around an extruder blimp bobbing on its mooring off on of the sides of the pyramid. Sirens howled from the city below.

Jackal's forces are being attacked by Attila and by the Securitor defenses. Hopefully, we can slip out unnoticed, Lannius sent to Aurora as they rounded the corner into the main hangar space. The lot was almost clear as many of the aircraft were engaged in the battle.

He stopped, holding her back. As they peered around the corner, three Protek worked to destroy the helipods. There was the rhythmic thump of their railguns spinning up before discharging. Organized destruction.

Stay back, Aurora. Keep out of sight.

She ducked behind some storage crates.

Lannius stepped out from behind the corner, holding his hands in the air. The Protek turned and spun on him, their single red eyes focused. They trained their weapons on him, but Lannius did not waver. An explosion rumbled in the distance as he stared down his machine progeny. The Protek all crossed their right arm across their thorax, then turned and pointed their railguns at Jackal's circling ship.

You can control Protek? Aurora asked.

The large flying Protek attacked the ship. Fire bloomed across the hull. The destruction was swift and thorough. The ship keeled forward, crashing onto the tarmac, and skidding in a mangled pile of debris. Lannius stood still as a statue as the build shook under the shockwaves of the exploding craft.

No, not control. We have a troubled relationship. Come now, Aurora. We need to go now.

She leapt out from behind the corner, following Lannius to the nearest helipod. He accessed the processes triggering the pod door to slide open; the engines were already spinning up as they climbed into the leather seats. As the pod door slid closed, the hulk of Jackal's ship turned its turrets towards the remaining pods.

Spiderfly, we could use some of your specific vision here, Lannius said to the AI.

Spiderfly intervened on cue, his mayhem playing out all over the building. The targeting systems of Jackal's ship and Attila's drones saw a thousand copies of the helipod take off into the air, a thousand Aurora's looking wide eyed out of the capsule. Spiderfly painted some drones as helipods, spurring a spontaneous civil war between Attila's commands.

Aurora and Lannius lifted off amidst the wild shooting. Lannius heeled the pod in a wide low arc from the fray, and they surveyed the battle. Drones filled the sky like a swatted beehive, while the remaining airborne Protek attacked Securitor drones like hornets in the cloud of smaller bees. As they circled, the airborne Protek seemed to realize their fate, and swooped down to the landing port to scoop up some of their smaller brethren and flee.

The pod felt invisible amidst the chaos, heightened by Spiderfly and Lannius focusing their combined efforts to mangle the digital landscape to ensure their escape. It was not the Lannius she had imagined. Her memories of him were of a kindly mentor, a wise old man, or some kind of beloved grandfather. The man in the pod was a spectacle of power, an invincible wizard to whom the Protek bowed.

She looked out the window as they took their last arc around the pyramid. One of the lifts opened. Two men stepped out. It was Stormgard and Kars. Tears filled her eyes seeing his tiny figure run for cover on the rooftop. She saw him look up in the sky. He saw their craft and waved his arms in the air. She cried out against the glass, clawing against the window as if it would keep him there for her. But the helipod kept moving off into the night, and they were gone.

*   *   *   *   *

"Aurora!" Kars screamed as he waved his arms at the pod. Did she see him? He kept waving and shouting for several seconds after the pod had passed out of sight. Stormgard grabbed him and dragged him back into cover.

"Get it together. We'll find her. Standing out there and waving is going to get you killed," he hissed. Beyond their cover, the battle-raged drones burst in the sky while the hulking mass of the ship burned on the landing strip.

Kars couldn't respond. He just nodded.

"Kars!" Stormgard shook him. "Come on, tough guy. We've got to get out of here!"

Across the tarmac, the hatch of the burning ship opened. A man hauled himself out of the wreckage, dropping to the scarred surface below. He tilted his mohawked head and cracked his neck. The sweat-sheen of his skin glowed with the reflection of the fires.

"Come out, come out! I know you're there!" the man yelled. Laser bolts lanced down next to him, but he was un-phased.

Kars recognized the shout. It was Jackal.

"Marcus, that's Jackal. The mercenary that did this, the same one that destroyed my home," Kars whispered.

"I know who he is. But he's taken out all the helipods. We've got no choice," Stormgard responded.

"He'll kill us."

The sound of the drones was growing louder. The entire area was swarmed with Attila's response to the incursion.

"Let's go, cowards! I'm getting bored here!" Jackal yelled.

The elevator lift across the tarmac lit up and the doors opened, releasing a blazing demon. It was Silvia Glass.

She leaped onto the tarmac in a terrific avatar, the person that Stormgard knew as the legend. The woman stole around his city with Spiderfly's riff raff like just another vagabond. Now he saw. She was still a terrible force to behold.

Jackal's face twisted in a violent sneer and he advanced.

"You're Jackal?" Silvia said. "That's what you're calling yourself now?"

"Tough talk. Drop the charade, hag."

"Careful what you wish for; the charade might be better than reality."

"Who the hell do you think you are?" Jackal sneered.

"You know. Silvia Glass." The night breeze caught her gray hair. Her gaze was unflinching. Then she cocked her head as though she had just noticed something pitiful about him. "What's that? Poor dear, they've addled your brain. Did you let them do that to you?"

The question drove the mohawk man over the edge. Jackal charged her and swung.

Silvia's feet moved in tiny precise footsteps as she flowed to the dance led by the maniac. His blows never hit.

Jackal launched a flurry of kicks that Silvia deflected before chopping her hand into the back of his knee. He stumbled forward, howling. Silvia's left eye reported Jackal's elevated pulse and blood pressure. The hyperspectral analysis revealed a change in his blood chemistry, a shift toward acidosis as he pushed himself toward fatigue. He spun and came straight back at her in his wild-eyed rage. She continued her dance, ducking to his side to drum him six times in the rib cage. He hacked hard, gasping for air.

Kars felt a wave of hope. Silvia outmatched Jackal. Her expression was a distant and casual.

"Jackal, are you ready yet? I'm going to undo what they did to you," Silvia said, posturing across from him.

He gasped for air. "You can't fix it. And I don't want to be fixed!" Spittle rattled from his lips as he shouted at her. He lunged forward again.

She parried the attack, watching his exhalation grow more acidic and his pulse run to frantic highs. Three more shots to the ribs and Jackal stumbled. He moaned as though he forgot he was in the landing port.

"It's time, child," Silvia said, and gestured for his next charge. Jackal threw himself at her.

Without stepping any direction, Silvia stopped the charging man with a foot square to the chest. He made a wet sound as he pulled for air. He collapsed to his knees, gasping.

Silvia strode around behind him, withdrawing something from her belt with casual ease that turned Kars's stomach. It resembled a sewing awl. His sick deepened as he realized what she was going to do with it.

With gentle precision, Silvia tilted Jackals head forward, inserting the point of the tiny instrument. He closed his eyes as though he expected relief.

"There, there. I'm going to fix it now." There was something soothing and maternal in Silvia's voice.

Jackal sucked air, but a wave of quiet passed his eyes. Silvia looked up at the two of them, distant. Somehow the awl in his neck seemed to bring relief.

The drones still waged a wild battle above, but seeing Silvia reprogram Jackal gave Kars the sense that the battle was finished. They were going to walk away. Kars started to stand when he noticed the elevator light blink on. The door opened and a pretty young man stood in the opening.

The next moment unfolded as frames snapped in the smoke. The Node dashed out of the elevator with perfect form, closing the gap with Silvia. In his last stride, she sensed his approach and yanked out the awl from Jackal's neck. She turned but was only fast enough to redirect the attack. His knife struck her in the side of her abdomen. She let out a cry and leapt to a defensive posture.

"Run, you fools!" Silvia yelled to Kars and Stormgard. "Marcus, get him out of here!"

Silvia and the man fought, but the dance was much different. The man seemed to know her every move. Kars watched in horror as he picked her apart with much the same ease that she had taken apart Jackal. A kind of trance appeared to set in on the Node as he fought.

"Kars, we've got to go!" Stormgard shouted.

"But Silvia! He's going to kill her!" Kars responded.

"It's one of Perpetual's experimentals, Kars. A Node. He'll kill all three of us now that he knows we're here. Silvia is giving us a chance to escape."

Kars continued to watch the fight. Silvia was a whirl of gray and crimson tangling with a leopard of a man. Jackal lay twitching on the ground nearby. Silvia spun out of the fight and looked Kars in the eye. She mouthed the word "Go."

"We have to find Lena," Kars said.

"No. We just have to hope that she got out safe."

Kars stared at the experimental man on the roof–he would dispatch them if they remained. Kars nodded.

But he would never forgive himself.

"What's the plan, Marcus?" Kars asked with urgency.

He gestured toward the extruder blimp. "The blimp. None of the drones would risk firing on that gas bag."

"That's tied up four stories down from here," Kars said.

"Well then don't miss," Marcus said.

They hurled themselves off the edge.

They slid down the sloped glass, spinning and clawing to direct their fall. Kars smashed into the blimps moorings, coughing and gasping before he scrambled onto the gondola. Drone fire followed them as they dove beneath the gondola cables. They scrambled for cover amidst the fury of the assault.

The screech of metal grew louder and louder until there was a tremendous pop as the first of the mooring broke. The gondola swayed, and Kars hugged a cable while his feet dangled above the city. Another supernatural rupture of metal pop rung through the air and the gondola heaved, free of its anchors, and started to rise. Kars and Stormgard stood on the roof of the gondola, silent as they realized what was happening. Resin gushed from the damaged supply tank, and the craft accelerated upward.

They crested the edge of the landing port. Silvia still waged a valiant battle, but the end was drawing near. She was bloodied and spent. Both Silvia and the experimental paused as the gondola floated into view. At that moment, a third combatant darted out from behind a crate.

A woman. And she started a furious assault on the Node.

The first blow—a roundhouse to the head—met its mark. Then the woman jumped on top of him, savagely hitting him in the face. Kars could see the braid, but he already knew.

It was Lena.

The Node rolled her off, but the tide had turned. Lena and bloody Silvia had caught him unprepared and did not yield in their assault. He was fast as a ghost, but that didn't matter. They had disrupted his defenses, and Spiderfly was blocking his network. The two women, old and young, were unrelenting in their attack. The Node stumbled backward from them, a disbelieving look on his face, and fell off the edge.

The extruder blimp was now accelerating upward as the resin gushed out of the tank. Lena and Silvia looked up at them, realizing the predicament. They couldn't stop their ascent.

"Kars!" Lena shouted.

"Lena!" Kars screamed.

She yelled back, but he couldn't hear her. He shouted again, collapsing as he forced the last air from his lungs. But it was hopeless; the drones turned on Silvia and Lena, forcing them to hobble to shelter. Lena had one of Silvia's arms draped over her shoulders as the older woman sagged to a limp.

"Lena!" Kars shouted one last time, but his words were ripped away by a gust. The blimp rushed upward and through the clouds, leaving just the shrouded glow of East Bay. A cold wind buffeted them, tilting the gondola. The battle grew distant and they were left standing silent in the cold as they disappeared into the night.

53

Copperdown

Arthur Lannius brought the helipod into a steep cleft valley after hours of flight. The pine-cloaked slopes rose from the valley floor to the abrupt tree line of bare rock and scattered patches of snow. Aurora could see a small cluster of metal roof buildings and a tiny clearing in the evergreens. A creek carved through the valley, a bone-white gash of whitewater tumbling between the stands of cedar and fir. The valley was dim in the moonlight, but Aurora felt a wave of homesickness seeing the wooded mountains again.

The helipod dipped between the mountainsides, following a steep descent toward the moonlit camp. The small craft handled the turns well as it was built for negotiating the cramped quarters of the megacity skyline.

They had travelled in silence. Much to Aurora's own surprise, she had nothing to say and instead used their flight as a time to organize the events of the past day. Retrospect revealed the awful fact that she had not said goodbye to Lena or to her brother. That realization was blooming into the possibility of a lifetime regret—something she had never contemplated as possible. Youth had a way of engendering the idea that one could and would live their life without regrets.

She thought about how she finally had Lannius, the mysterious man from those other Mirien memories. All the times Silvia had twisted away from her questions, all Squire's diverted answers, Spiderfly's puzzles, Jinan's mysteries—all of her questions ended with the man sitting in front of her. She watched as the white-haired man guided the helipod into the valley and onto the small landing pad. Both of them remained silent as the engines spun to a stop. The cockpit dome slid back, allowing a gush of cool night air to fill the pod. Then it was still.

"We should get into the cabin and send this craft on its way. Undoubtedly, it's within Attila's ability to track it despite my best efforts at stealth," Lannius said. His voice was changed from the kind and patient man. Urgency cut through like cold wind.

They climbed out of the pod, gathering the few belongings that they brought with them. Lannius turned and manipulated the glowing processes of the craft. In response, the cockpit slid closed and the craft lifted off, climbing into the night sky until they could no longer see it. The distant whir of the engines faded to nothing and they were alone in the night.

"This way," Lannius said. Aurora remained quiet, still corralling her thoughts about the escape and trying to bring order to the cacophony of questions that filled her mind since the day in the mining camp with Kars. He led her past two derelict buildings to a smaller cabin.

Inside, Lannius lit a hurricane lantern and adjusted the wick until it filled the room with a soft glow. A few faded oil paintings lined the walls. The floorboards had been worn smooth over years of use. A great armchair and an old sofa formed an elbow around a hardwood coffee table. A dusty chess set sat on the table, pieces frozen vigilant in time waiting for their first move. Aurora took in the room with a certain familiarity as Lannius busied himself with lighting the wood stove in the corner.

"There's a bunk in the next room. You should sleep. We have a long journey ahead." He was distant as he spoke, busying himself in the kitchen. "I call this place Copperdown. It's a place that you once knew. I built it as a place of respite."

Aurora remained standing in the center of the cabin. The hurricane lantern carved deep contrast in the corners of the room. It felt like a shadow of her home. It was quiet, free of the aether and processes. Lannius was drawing shutters across the windows and organizing supplies. It felt sudden and odd having Arthur Lannius, the figment of her memory, in the same room. Her heart dropped—had it been worth it?

"What about Kars and Lena?" Aurora asked, blurting the words into the silence of the cabin.

Lannius did not respond, instead removing a rifle from a cabinet and laying it on the table. He wiped it with a cloth and set it down again.

"Over so many years, I have grown close with struggle and loss. I have come to see that hope can be just a breath away from despair. We have to trust those with us to prevail against their own odds." He spoke with a tenderness fitting for a friend returned from a shipwreck. "I cannot tell you they will be fine, only to trust our people to sacrifice for them."

"Trust," Aurora said. She stared into the flame inside the glass, a static ribbon floating above the wick.

Lannius was silent. He knew she had more.

"Trust?" Aurora repeated, her voice trembling. "You gave me a lie to live as a life and now you tell me to trust?"

"What would you have had me do?" he responded, his voice growing. "Fight the entire army? Leave you? Tear down the walls on top of us and end this entire struggle?"

"Why?" Aurora retorted, un-phased by the kingly old man. "Why not them? Why me?"

"You have no idea of the sacrifice made for your life." His voice loomed at the edge of rage and sorrow.

"Then tell me. Show me," Aurora said. "I sacrificed them to be here. Trust me with my own life!"

The wrinkled canyons on his face trembled. She could hear him take several deep breaths through his nose. He said nothing.

"The Spider was right. I should never have believed any of you. I might just be alone in the end," Aurora said.

The words seemed to cut Lannius. Aurora thought she might see tears welling in the old man's eyes.

"Perhaps I have broken you. I hoped I might keep you from such pain," Lannius said. His voice drifted into the silence of the cabin. After a moment, he looked up straight into her eyes.

"Would you like to know?" he asked.

"Am I Mirien Alcarn?"

"Yes," Lannius said. "But to understand what that means, I need to give you my memory."

The memories of Arthur Lannius swam up around her.

54

Parallel

I was busy in those days, always attended by department heads, assistants, accountants, and managers fawning for promotions into the upper echelons of my prize: Perpetual, the first independent and publicly-owned corporation since the Consolidation War. For its sovereignty from the Great Companies, I had paid an exorbitant price. The Protek filled my dreams.

That particular day, I wore slacks, a plain brown sweater, and a neat driving cap, my favorite casual wear to hide with the common folk and sit among the oaks in the East Bay Park to watch the families. It reminded me that life went on and that someday, the world might forget what I had done. It reminded me of Margot and my son.

So when two of my employees shambled up to me during my secret off time, I was less than pleased to see them. They were a young couple, husband and wife. The woman was pretty and tall, red hair and gentle skin untouched by the rays of the sun. The man's curly dark hair was unkempt, his green eyes bright as he approached. They had also dressed in plain clothes, aware of the need for secrecy in their meeting.

"Professor Lannius," the man said.

"You humor me with that title," I said. "No one has called me for years."

"Doctor?" the woman said.

"Better, I suppose," I responded. "Now be quick in telling me why you're bothering me on my time off. If this is about a promotion, I assure you this approach will yield the opposite."

"It's not about a promotion," the man said, glancing at the woman. "We need our own corporation."

There was a pregnant pause in the air. I burst out laughing.

"Bold, son!" I exclaimed, clapping the younger man on the shoulder. "Bold! Do you know the price I paid for Perpetual's freedom? How many years Charles Agrion lobbied—No, I don't even have to lecture here! While I respect your bravado mister—"

"Doctor."

"Doctor—"

"Alcarn."

"Doctor Alcarn." I paused. "I think your request is a bit far-fetched."

"Come see what we've built and you'll reconsider," the woman said.

"Will I? And what have you built?" Their earnestness somehow endeared me to them, reminded me of myself before my terrible machine progeny destroyed half the world.

The man bit his lip, looking to his wife to help ward off his self-doubt, and she gave a nod. I did my best to appear impatient, but they were a welcome change from the groveling managers that mistook my private moments for an opportunity.

"A time machine," he responded.

I felt a smile curl across my face. I waited for a pregnant moment for him to give up his joke, but he stood firm.

My laughter broke through. The young man was serious!

"Thank you very much, Doctors. I come to this place when I need to secretly affirm the humanity of the world, and you have delivered that gift this morning. But now, I must be on with my day." I rose to leave, straightening my sweater and slacks.

The woman grabbed my sleeve.

"Please. We need you." Her eyes burned with a desperate fury. "We did our part for our daughter, now we need you. She is sick from the War."

The young woman's words struck a blow. The cruelties of the Consolidation War sat heavy on the ledgers of my soul.

"We can't change the past." My role in the War was my own burden.

"We know," she said. "We're just asking for your help and your blessing. She's wonderful, and we can't lose her again."

The sincerity in her voice made me listen.

"Again?" I asked.

537

"Yes, the future—a future. We raised her and lost her five times." The woman's voice trembled.

The pain. I remembered it. She spoke with the pain that I felt, the pain that I had come to the park bench to forget. Those who knew it could see that pain like a lighthouse.

Perhaps fate had given me another chance at redemption?

"Clear all my appointments and send my double in a private jet to the villa." I spoke into the slim wristwatch tucked past the edge of my sleeve.

"Alright, you have got my attention. I can stand a bit of intrigue. Excuse my manners, I fear power has gotten the better of me, and I did not get your names." I extended my hand.

"James," the man said, shaking hands.

"Anna Alcarn," the woman said, taking a turn shaking my hand.

"Excellent. You should call me Arthur, at least until this little venture is complete," I said. "Now, let's go see your time machine."

*   *   *   *   *

The Alcarn's lab was a nondescript space in a satellite building to the central Perpetual campus. I insisted on taking a public charter vehicle to help lose any potential followers from the media or the company. We entered the building and followed its bland hallways until we stopped at their door. Anna pressed her hand to a pad next to the door, and it unlocked. We stepped inside.

"Welcome to our humble abode. Not much to look at, but I promise you that we are on the verge of something great."

"I am here and at heart, I am a scientist, so I will judge as deliberately as I learn," I said. "So please begin: tell me what you are doing here and in turn, what I am doing here."

Anna began.

"We only recently brought our labs together, after we got the War syndrome–Wexler diagnosis. Prior to that, I was pursuing my work in artificial intelligence while James worked in neuroprosthetics."

"An odd starting point for time travel," I noted.

"Yes and no," Anna said. "It was the starting point of my research: I was always dissatisfied with the disconnect between consciousness and time in the discussion of artificial intelligence, specifically on the issue of *understanding* versus *processing* information. To me there had to be a nexus between understanding and being in the world. Time was the link."

"Time, the arrow of the cosmic archer," I said. Anna's scientific enthusiasm was charming me.

"Exactly. The immutable and unsatisfactory truth remains: time moves forward. Except, we have no fundamental theory that demands the arrow travel forward. Quantum theory, string theory, M-theory, all permit some reversibility of time and states. Just by living, we can't go back."

"Doctor Alcarn, are you chasing a unified theory?" I asked. There was something revitalizing to me in returning to the presence of scientists. Since the day I took the stage with the Protek, my mind had been offered precious little pure science. The boardroom represented a degree of freedom, but it rarely asked me to contemplate the nature of the cosmos.

"Inadvertently, yes," she said, her eyes were excited and bright. "I was trying to develop sensors that would help the AI kernel seat itself in the world, help it experience time and that human condition of 'understanding.'"

"And I presume I am sitting here because you caught the tiger by the tail?"

Anna smiled, collecting herself. I could see her pride and excitement in sharing their secret. James threw a loving smile her way.

Anna began again. "During my studies, I was deeply frustrated with the idea that the human mind was a computer—encode, store, recall. It all seemed too convenient to explain the mystery of consciousness. It missed the human being, the part that loves, dances, feels, the part that has meaning.

"It fit an age-old pattern. The earliest humans talked about mythic animals rising from the ocean, then classical antiquity talked about stealing fire, onto traditional monotheism describing creation in terms of clay and artisan gods. Even as secularism arose during the Enlightenment, the origin myth turned clocks and machines. Each age symbolized consciousness with the technology of the era. Now we think we are a computer—encode, store, recall."

I watched Anna as she slowed to a pause. James looked at me as though he was appraising my response. Anna moved her hands, as though she was conducting her thoughts to order.

"The theory of evolution gave us a framework to understand how we came to be, and a blueprint to the final daunting leap. We could seize the tools of the cosmos and make true consciousness in our image, but instead we seized the tools, but stopped asking the questions. Intelligence is data. We allowed our tools to explain our great mystery of being."

"Yes, Doctor Alcarn," I admitted, "except for the fact that people, specifically myself, tried to go further than data and breathe life into inanimate machines. The Protek were a spectacular failure and misuse of technology beyond the scale of thermonuclear weapons."

"I hate to make the Protek the counter-example," Anna said, "but it's inevitable. Giving computers even infinite processing power and memory fails to bridge the gap between programming and understanding. Being is not data. Evolution does not program."

"If not a program, then what?"

"Accidents of action systems and perceiving systems," Anna said, as though she had rehearsed her conversation with me. "The mind is not a computer. It is a perceiving system like your eyes. Except, instead of detecting light, the mind directly senses gravity—the brain 'sees' space and time. Sure, it could be reduced to zeros and ones, but that's not its first state. To perceive is to swim through an ocean of phenomenon and experience. We don't encode, store, and recall like computers; we sense the world around us, including the intricate mass within our own body, which allows us to experience ourselves—consciousness."

"Not bad." I tried to hide my enjoyment of her excitement. "And what you are about to tell me is that you somehow replicated this sense in an artificial intelligence."

"No, not yet, but we think we can. For now, we used an AI to collate data into a coherent format that we can use as a virtual world for our mind to perceive." She shot an apprehensive look to James, and they paused for a moment.

"Might as well finish. We've got him here," James said.

"We call our mind's eye the 'gravity clock.' The rudimentary AI we built is able to accelerate all other stimulus and feed it to us through the gravity clock in our minds. It's like watching a film in fast forward, except our perception of time is augmented to compensate," Anna said.

"Which allows you to experience more time in a given period," I concluded.

"Yes," Anna agreed.

"An interesting thesis, but how do you receive all the other stimuli through the gravity clock?" I asked.

"That's where James's work came in," Anna said.

"I was working on neuroprosthetics, specifically replacing or enhancing the sensation of touch. It's a neuro-augmentation, a computer that runs directly into the brain." James gathered himself and leaned forward, turning down his collar. Lannius saw a metal socket at the nape of his neck. He withdrew at the sight of the dull metal lodged in the flesh.

"You've made yourselves into an experiment!" I could not stand for this kind of recklessness. "In good faith, I can't allow this atrocity! I was willing to entertain your crackpot theories of space and time, but it appears that madness is the true root of your pursuit."

I began to stand up to leave.

"No!" James said to me, taking a stern stand that gambled the rest of their employment. "You are incorrect. It is not madness, but love. Arthur, our daughter will die. We saw it last night for the fifth time, but we loved her until the end. It feels real."

The pain was there again, the sorrow of loss. I recognized it from my own. I regretted my rebuff of the young couple's choice. The War had been my generation's sin on the world. The genetic weapon called Wexler and my nightmare of the Protek were decisions borne out of the shortsighted rage of war. I had played my role in their loss.

"I am sorry for your loss," Lannius said. "And I am sorry for my forwardness, but I am confused. Is your daughter living?"

"Yes," Anna said, touching her belly. "She has not been born yet. But our time to save her life is running short."

"We used the gravity clock each night last week to live a virtual life in which we could learn about our unborn daughter's disease. We let the AI operating system pull together information from the network—the laws of physics, weather data, and forecasts, political information, even our own history—to

543

create an approximation of our world. We let it build a world, then we lived a lifetime inside. We gave ourselves the time to become experts. Our daughter was born and died in the future simulation," James finished, with sincere sadness, but also looked confused. "Mirien. We love her."

I listened and thought about what these two young geniuses had embarked upon. The looks on their faces told of honesty, not madness, mingled with a doubt that they had embarked into uncharted territory. They had a grand vision, grander than any prior human vision, and had tasted its fruit.

"You lived a life. It felt real?" I asked.

"It felt real, but incomplete. The AI doesn't have enough power or data to create a perfect simulation. But we lived a life. We celebrated our fiftieth anniversary with our friends and their families. We learned about our daughter's disease. We learned more about the gravity clock itself. Each night, we built on what we learned by feeding the information back into the system."

"In essence, traveling to the future and bringing information back with you," I concluded.

"Yes," Anna agreed. "It's not reversing the arrow of time, just riding a faster arrow on a parallel path."

"In fact, that's what we call the AI operating system," James said with a smile. "Parallel."

55

The Child Who Was Mirien

The cabin seemed to reform around Aurora's awareness. Lannius's memory of meeting her parents settled into her mind.

"Your parents, James and Anna Alcarn, recruited me to help make their time traveling operating system, Parallel, better and more precise. Through Perpetual's fortunes, I helped them keep it secret from the world for a time. I later joined them on their nightly expeditions into time. Mirien Alcarn was their daughter, a product of miracle genetic science taken from the future. You and Mirien are the first survivor of Wexler syndrome," Lannius explained.

Aurora saw the tears billow at the edges of the old man's eyes. She felt a sudden compassion for him dislodge her mistrust. It wasn't Mirien's trust either. It was a trust all her own.

"What happened to them? Why did you take me away?" Aurora asked.

"We played with forces that human nature could not tolerate in the world. Aurora, they are both dead."

She fought a choking gasp.

"The military would not allow a band of civilians to use Parallel," Lannius said. "Your father died so that you could escape."

Aurora controlled the desire for tears; she nodded, grim. The truth was hard, but better.

"What about my mother?" she asked.

Lannius drew a long deep breath, as though he was confronting a long gestating struggle.

"Your mother died in childbirth. The solution to your disease that we had sought for so long was lethal to your mother," Lannius said. "But it was not that simple. Your father would not stand for the bitter irony of their quest. None of us would stand for it. With nearly seven months'—almost fourteen thousand years—worth of Anna's mind, behavior, and physiology, stored inside Parallel, we had enough to recreate her. Your father merged Parallel with Anna. Your mother became our guide in our travels, in your travels."

The weight of what Lannius said crashed into her, threatening to topple her sense of self from its foundation.

"I—Mirien—was raised by an AI?"

Lannius nodded. "Raised by an AI mother in a hyper-real simulation of your life. Every night we returned to Parallel and started anew, fresh with knowledge and data that we had uncovered the night before."

"Entire lifetimes in one night?" Aurora asked, the numbers ticked through her mind at a dizzying pace.

"It's okay. It is a lot to take in," Lannius said.

"A memory of a life? Or an entire life?"

"Entire lifetimes. Every day, down to its most mundane detail. From outside of Parallel it was time travel; within we lived forever over and over. Our minds accrued the experience, and the system retained the knowledge like a great library.

"Every morning we would share our new knowledge with the outside world. The next night, Parallel would factor in the changes we made into the iteration and play them forward into our new world. We sprinted into the future. Within the first week we solved the global energy crisis.

"I entered Parallel for the first time when I was seventy-five, and spent nearly six months prior to your birth, plus the six months after you were born, traveling. I would usually live about fifty to sixty years after entering the Parallel—I was old when I started. In total, I experienced roughly twenty-three-thousand years' worth of life through the lens of the gravity clock."

"Twenty-three-thousand years." Aurora spoke the number in amazement. The memory of Mirien playing chess with the old man swam up from the depths. "If Mirien was born into Parallel, that would mean she lived that long—which means, I lived that long."

"Longer actually. Mirien woke up from Parallel as a baby every morning, unable to speak or take care of herself, yet she would retain the memories of a lifetime and grow old again. Mirien was more of Parallel than this world. The math gets a little fuzzy when dealing in hundreds of lifetimes, but Mirien experienced nearly forty-eight-thousand years of life before our journey came

547

to an end." The bright-eyed, white-haired man paused then spoke. "And our journey began."

His warm smile and lantern light put her at ease despite learning just how inverted her world could be.

"I remember some of Mirien, but it's just pieces out of context, like shattered pottery. Why don't I remember more? Why don't I remember thousands of years' worth of life?" Aurora asked.

"When your parents sent you with me, they wanted me to make sure that you had a chance to lead a life on your own," Lannius said. "Your mother deleted the memories before she was destroyed."

Aurora turned away from him, staring into the window of the wood stove. She watched the fire glowing in its belly. The orange flames danced behind the dull screen of the glass. She felt deep sadness warm to rage.

"Why?" Tears welled in her eyes.

"Aurora," Lannius said, "you must know, your parents loved you to the end of the earth. Over and over they gave you the gift of life. As the one entrusted with your life, I know how much they loved you. And as one who has lived a hundred lives, I know that a blank slate is a gift of endless wonder."

She looked at him, still pinching back her tears. "I'm sure that's true when you've lived thousands of years, but it hurts knowing they decided I shouldn't remember them, that I should be an orphan left to wonder about my fate. I love Em, but there's a hole in my heart, one that blew open when the drone appeared. It's a hole that you knew would appear. You laid such careful plans for

548

me knowing that the past would find me. How can you say I had a blank slate?"

"It is true. I built an intricate scheme around the possibility that your past would find you. But do not lay that blame at your parents' feet. Their lives were a continuous sacrifice so you could live yours."

"Take me there," Aurora said. "Take me to the moment when the said goodbye. Give me the moment when I became Aurora."

Lannius drew another deep breath, drifting into the eons of his memories.

"Very well. I will remember for you. We must go to the fall of the Hourglass."

56

The Fall of the Hourglass

James and I stood on the seaward balcony. I remember the clouds rolling in with the evening, glowing like fire with the light of sunset. A wind had started to stir. I pulled my cloak against the chill.

"We're certain?" James asked.

"My loyalists report the same intelligence as Anna. It seems Clark and the military have thrown in together. They will come for us tonight," I said. "They will come for Parallel to make it their own."

"We have all witnessed the future of a militarized AI. Why is Clark doing this?" James asked.

"The Anomaly," I responded. It tore my heart to think that a champion like Clark could have succumbed. "Anna and I tracked it as it emerged in Clark in our last lifetime."

"We should have been more careful," James said.

"I agree, my friend," I responded. "But we are not in Parallel, and we must live with this consequence."

James scowled. It was a look I hated to see, so far from the man that had stalked me in the park to show me a time machine.

He spoke to me after some time.

"I need you to take Mirien," James said. "I can't leave Anna alone to this fate."

"James . . ." It was all I could muster.

"Arthur. I need you to do this for us."

I stared down at the tiny sapling we planted on the seaward balcony. Each lifetime in Parallel, it would grow in different ways, different branches would break and thrive in the wind as the tree grew old and gnarled over its lifetime, but its blossoms would always bathe the deck in color when the spring rains came. I had so many memories of Mirien playing beneath its branches—thousands of days beneath this tree, looking out on the ocean. Parallel was all Mirien knew. It was her world.

"She will be lost, James," I said.

"We know. Anna and I discussed . . ." James choked on his words. "Arthur, I think we were wrong. We never gave her the chance to be in the world. We made our own and trapped her inside."

"It is hardly a trap. We have put our lifetimes of effort to curing all the world's ills. Someday, this world may be the same. Over our travels, Parallel has become a perfect world in almost every way," I said.

"Except for consequence," James retorted. "Are we really human without consequence?"

The alarm systems of the Hourglass sliced through the awareness of augmentations. Something had breached the outer perimeter.

"The first wave. They are here," I said.

"We should get to the center of the Hourglass with Anna. Mirien is there, too. She told us once that it was where she liked to spend the days outside Parallel." James seemed resigned to the coming fate. It pained me to see the sorrow capture him.

The two of us left the seaward balcony and followed the halls of the Hourglass. It was only a year old in this world, just a memory of what I had seen in so many futures. I remembered it as a sparkling castle, a stern fortress, a lush terrace wrapped in gardens. Each time we had reimagined the Hourglass as something different—some reflection of the future we would craft.

Now the Hourglass felt like the future lost.

We arrived at the center. The thick conduits still wove their way across the floor, leading to various banks of servers and processors. Coolant lines spiraled around critical components. The other Travelers and I had started the long process of adorning the space with ferns. I remembered it from so many futures as being a lush altar, centered around the core that was both Anna and Parallel.

The core. Every time I saw it, it robbed me of my soul—the heart of Parallel.

The crystal seemed to float on its tress of filaments at the center of the room. We travelled through ten lifetimes before we perfected its design and manufacture, a processor we built atom by atom, then painted in a trillion quantum hues until it was capable of carrying our minds into the future. Soon all those memories would be purged from the system.

The building rumbled. One of my lieutenants, a stern woman named Sydney, scrambled into the chamber. She had started fastening lean plate armor to an exoskeletal frame.

"They just blew the third wall near the north gate. Kiran and his unit are engaged," Sydney reported. "James, your armor is ready. I'm moving my unit to the Rose Arch. We will hold there as long as we can." She hurried from the chamber.

She meant until the death.

"Again, we've crossed the point of no return," I whispered to myself. I had been a fool to return to a life of trying to change the world.

Arthur, you must take her for us. It was Anna's voice, piping through my augmentations. It was tender like a gentle forest breeze.

Anna, please. Don't make this choice, I responded. James pleaded to me with his eyes.

We already have made the choice. Now we must say our goodbyes, she said. *Please be our witness, so that someday our daughter may see us again.*

Tears spilled from my eyes. I looked into the ornate crib next to the heart of Parallel. I had made it for them after Mirien was born.

"I will be your witness, and I will take your child into the world," I said. I felt the weight of their choice settle into my chest. Another burden for my sins.

The room vanished into a wildflower meadow as Anna drew James and I into her world, Parallel, one last time. The crystal core was gone, and only Anna remained. She looked down into the crib. The ghost of the woman wore a crown of flowers in her hair, which flowed down past her shoulders over her diaphanous dress. James rushed to hold her.

I remained at the periphery as they said goodbye.

"Mirien," Anna said to the child in the crib. "Sweet Mirien. All of this for you."

"Our child," James said. "I'm so sorry for everything. We did it all out of love. We need you to go with Arthur, and"—he choked on the words—"we will not see you again."

"This world we've created, it wasn't fair. You deserve a chance to be your own person," Anna said. "Someday you will understand."

I watched as Anna and James each leaned into the crib to kiss the child. James stepped back, tears streaming down his face. Anna reached into the crib and touched the baby's head. The baby cried, and I felt the world around me tremble and warp as Anna deleted the memory of Mirien. James and Anna recoiled from what they had done and wept.

The meadow vanished and the light of the crystal core dimmed. James and I were alone in the chamber. Tears streamed down our faces.

"Please, Arthur. Take her into the world."

"I will, James." I took the sleeping child and tucked her swaddled body beneath my cloak. The building rumbled again. I wiped a tear from my face.

"I'm going to be with Anna, one last time," James said.

"Be well," I said, "and thank you for the hope you brought to my life. I will take yours into the world."

We embraced. My friend's eyes were raw. Their journey had reached its end. I turned and left the chamber.

The next moments erupted in chaos.

Once distant rumbles now shook plaster from the ceiling. Loyalists shouted over the staccato pop of gunfire. Whitestone's partners in the military were drawing close.

The east tunnel remains clear. It was Anna's voice in my mind. *I will seal the emergency routes behind you. We've saddled a horse for your escape. You should be invisible to their sensors.*

Thank you, Anna, I responded as a hidden panel slid back to reveal a secret elevator.

Thank you, Arthur, she responded. *I've been gone for a long time. You're holding my legacy. Thank you.*

It is not over, yet, I said, feeling the confusion I felt when she reflected on her own artificial nature.

Take care of her, Arthur. It was her only response.

The door to the elevator slid closed and I was alone in the dim light. My stomach pitched as the car descended. I pulled back my cloak to look at the warm bundle beneath.

She looked up at me—the child who was no longer Mirien. Her eyes were bright, her round cheeks formed a smile as though she was recognizing a face for the first time.

"It will be okay, little one. It will be okay," I told myself.

The elevator doors opened onto a long hallway, the secret east entrance. At the end of the hall, one of our loyalists waited, holding the reins of a horse. He handed the reins to me and grasped my hand, before turning down the tunnel. Another goodbye.

I looked out into the forest as the gray gloom of dusk settled on it. The sounds of the conflict drifted to me. The horse snorted as I settled into the saddle and checked the baby. I urged it forward and left the Hourglass. We rode into the night.

*   *   *   *   *

The light of the hurricane lantern guided Aurora back into her own awareness. Lannius's eyes were red, and he seemed weakened by the return to his past.

Emotion flooded through her. She stared into the tiny flame, feeling one need to sob and another to roar, but neither felt

556

adequate. The spitting of the fire was the only sound in the cabin.

"Thank you," she murmured.

Lannius bowed.

Her parents. He had given her back her parents, but it was full of the agony that they had taken themselves from her. The story resisted her understanding. Somehow, she would need to make room for the knowledge that she was both Mirien and Aurora tangled in thousands of years of memories.

"Thank you for giving this to me, but this is going to take some time." Her heart ached in her chest, but she felt a deep rage quenched.

"As you need."

The confusion threatened to drown her in her thoughts. The tiny cabin spun around the flame. Maybe time was all she needed? Aurora turned to leave, wanting solitude to place all she had lost and gained, but stopped. One detail would not fit, jagged in her mind.

"I have one more question," Aurora asked.

Lannius nodded for her to continue.

"My mother deleted Mirien?" Aurora asked.

"Yes, a mercy to give you your life," Lannius said.

"Then why do I remember?" Aurora responded.

"A question I've asked myself," Lannius said, "and to which, I have no answer. It is a mystery that's leading us to our next destination."

"Where are we going?" Aurora asked.

"I mentioned that there were others who traveled with your parents and me. We are going to visit some of them. They will be glad to see you again and they may be able to help you find a place for this pain."

"How will they help?" Aurora asked.

"I cannot answer exactly, except that they built something incredible." Lannius hesitated, and a mischievous spark lit his eye.

"They built a second Parallel."

About the Author

John Bowie lives in Pacifica, California, with his wife and two dogs. He was First Prize winner in the 2017 Writer's Digest Popular Fiction Awards' Horror Category for the baffling apocalyptic short story, *The Hole*. John has a background in environmental law and policy, along with degrees in both biochemistry and Jungian psychology. When not writing, John surfs, skis, and bikes, and in general, tries to enjoy as much of the outdoors as possible.

Special thanks to the crowdfunders

Your willingness to join this adventure made a dream possible.

Alexis Asselin

Lauren Baron

Carol Berzonsky

Arthur Bond

Dre "Viking Brother" Cerbin

Ben Corrigan

Lisa Covert & Jason Rashkow

Patrick Crane

Preston Cunningham

Willi Farrales

Angie Foster

Lhotse Foster

Justin Fung

James Galloway

Jordan Gerow

Michael Jarvis

Ferseni Jimenez

Gabe Krenza

Lee Anderegg

Rob & Aurora Menter Cleaver

Nick Monzy Martin

Eric Mishkin

Mom & Dad

Rod Napier

Madeline O'Donoghue

Erik Roth

Taryn Rucinski

Ericka Sohlberg

Tom Taft

Luke Taylor

Jacqueline Terry

Radina Valova

Daniel Walker

And many more...

Thank you.

19552517R00346

Made in the USA
San Bernardino, CA
23 December 2018